Return to

Kirk's Landing

By

Mike Young

Deux Voiliers Publishing

Aylmer, Quebec

This book is a work of fiction. Names, characters, businesses, organizations, places, events, and incidents are either the product of the author's imagination or are used fictitiously. Any resemblance to actual persons, living or dead, events, or locales is entirely coincidental.

First Edition

Copyright © 2016 by Mike Young

Published in Canada by

Deux Voiliers Publishing, Aylmer, Quebec.

www.deuxvoilierspublishing.com

Library and Archives Canada Cataloguing in Publication

Young, Mike, 1946-, author

    Return to Kirk's Landing / Mike Young.

Sequel to: Kirk's Landing.

ISBN 978-1-928049-47-0 (softcover)

    I. Title.

PS8647.O74R47 2016   C813'.6   C2016-907660-1

Cover Design – Gerry Fostaty and Ian Thomas Shaw

To my grandfather, Onesime Beauchesne, for being my mentor and friend as I grew up in the northern town of Kirkland Lake. He took me snaring rabbits, hunting deer, and fishing for whatever would bite. And passed on to me some of his sense of humour.

Chapter 1

*S*lowly, stealthily, it drifted through the trees, a wandering wisp of morning fog, pausing as it caught on the tips of the lanky pines of the Canadian Shield, then tearing free. But it was more than just a bit of fog. It had a purpose, and a direction, and a craving for flesh. It had memories too: of power, of pursuit, of possession and control, of feeding, of draining the spirit from its weak and soft hosts. There were many of these memories, from many winters, stretching back to the time of the Creator, but the latest one was the best. This winter it had found a strong spirit, a delicious spirit, burning like a flame. It had feasted eagerly, but then had been driven out from its prey too soon, tricked by the elders, Guardians of the People. It was a creature of the winter months, so now, with the snows melted, it would be safer to rest and just wait. But this time the drive was too strong. The taste of its latest victim was still out there, and the promise of new ones too, their own evil leaving chinks in their spirits that it could creep through.

There was a rumble in the spring air, rolling through the quiet like thunder from a distant storm. Dave was quite familiar with the throaty voice of a Harley, so was not surprised when ten choppers emerged from the morning mist.

He smiled, aimed his gun carefully at the lead bike, and pulled the trigger. "Gotcha," he murmured.

The deafening noise faded slightly as the bikes all throttled back. They knew they'd been busted. Dave glanced down and noted that he'd clocked one at 122 kilometres, in an 80 zone. Technically, he could seize the vehicle, but he wouldn't bother. Aside from all the paperwork, it wasn't as if he could just toss one of these into the back of his police 4x4. Too bad, as it would be a good speeding stat for the day. He lowered the gun, ready to wave the bikes over to Constable Reese, patiently waiting to intercept, just past the turnoff into town.

Dave took a step forward, then froze as a chill swept over him. He peered closely at the approaching bikes, and swore under his breath. Sure enough, the first one and at least two others were familiar.

"What are you guys doing way up here?" he muttered

He'd lived for months with these bikes, and their riders, back in Toronto. Six months ago, he'd been working undercover down there, helped by his unique ability to actually disappear, to become invisible. He'd managed to infiltrate the local chapter of the Hell's Angels, run by the lead biker in this pack, a bearded giant of a man appropriately named Sasquatch. It was at one of Sasquatch's meetings that Dave's biker cover was almost blown. For his own protection, the RCMP had staged a fake arrest and quickly reassigned him to the detachment in a small quiet town in southern Manitoba. He wasn't exactly in hiding, but very few people would make the connection between the bearded, tattooed, cold-eyed native biker he used to look like, and the clean-faced RCMP corporal with mirrored sunglasses, ironed uniform and polished shoes. Even his tattoos were covered by his long-sleeved uniform shirts, with only the tip of a Raven's wing poking above his shirt collar. Now he just wanted to blend in and enjoy his new peaceful career as a competent, normal cop, chief of police for Kirk's Landing. He'd even started to make some friends up here, a big change for him after years on his own in undercover. He was done with his past and with using his special ability as a crutch, especially since it had turned on him, showing its evil side.

He'd set up with Reese on the highway an hour earlier. This was a great place to catch people taking the scenic route to Winnipeg, as it wound past the lakes and forests of the provincial park. It was a beautiful warm June morning in the quiet little town of Kirk's Landing —or had been until now.

His radio squawked. "Boss, Reese here. I saw these guys fly in, want me to pull them over when they reach me?"

"No," he said, "just let them roll through. I'll explain later." With that many bikers, he'd have to assist Reese with the stop, and he couldn't take that risk. As much as he knew that this group warranted police attention, the last thing he wanted was for Sasquatch to recognize him. He actually started to fade away, to hide, then remembered he didn't want to depend on that power anymore, so stopped it. Instead, he turned away slightly and lifted the mike to shield his face, trying to make it appear casual. There was that chill again, as they rode by, and a tickle of the hairs on the back of his neck. Maybe a storm was coming in. He waited for a moment, then let out his breath as the rumble built again and the pack of bikes accelerated down the two lane highway. They didn't look back. Hopefully they hadn't made him.

He shook his head, and keyed his mike. "Reese, let's pack up for now. Come and get me and we'll head back to the detachment office."

Badger wasn't pleased when Sasquatch signalled a pull over just a mile past the speed trap. He would have preferred to keep going, as he'd sensed something as they rode through, something familiar, something that probed at him.

He was about to speak up when Spider beat him to it. "Damn it Sas. Why are we stopping here? They didn't make us, but they still might change their mind."

Sasquatch turned angrily toward Spider. "We're stopping because I said we're stopping. I don't give a shit about some jerk-water cops and I don't need you thinking you can tell me what to do. Got a problem with that?"

By the time he finished, the two bikers were chest to chest, their faces inches apart, and even Badger could see Sas's eyes glint dangerously black. Where had that come from? Badger stepped forward. "Whoa, Sas. Chill out, he don't mean no harm. A break is fine. I know I could do with a piss in the ditch and stretch my legs a bit."

It had been a long and tiring ride up from Toronto. These hard-tail bikes took a toll on the body, especially on older highways like this one. They wore their colours of course, so even though they obeyed all the traffic rules they'd been stopped dozens of times by the cops. They were all tired, but he was still surprised at the violence of their leader's outburst. Badger had heard some pretty impressive stories about Sasquatch's rise to power, how he'd easily managed to out-fight or out-think his opponents, but up to now he'd been acting like someone ready to retire, just mellowing out in his old age. His last stint in jail, for just a minor drug bust, had really aged him. This was supposed to be one easy last run, just to get the Winnipeg chapter properly set up to manage the local drug trade. Now here was their leader acting ready to bust some heads again.

Sasquatch stepped back a bit, but still glowered at Spider. "Yeah, whatever. Just a quick break. I'll be looking for some cold beer once we hit Winnipeg tonight." He rubbed his neck. "I don't know what got into me. I just got hit with a bitch of a headache as we passed by that last town. Felt like a damn knife through my skull."

Badger just nodded. He liked road trips because they gave him a chance to think, to be part of the group yet alone, away from their annoying voices. Now all his thoughts were about that last town. He knew every inch of Kirk's Landing and the land around it. He'd been born there, and grew up there. He frowned at the fence of sombre pine trees on either side of the highway. He hated this country. He especially hated the feeling that something was always watching him from the trees.

"We were lucky to get through there," he said. "Speed limit dropped just as we came around the corner."

"I forgot about this little shit-hole until it was too late," said Sasquatch, "but the cop just acted like we were doing the limit. Didn't even look at us. If anything, I thought he was turning away on purpose."

"You know, he looked a bit familiar," said Badger. "And I could feel something not right as we rode by. It reminded me of the weird vibe that I got from that guy we caught in Toronto."

Even as a kid, Badger had a knack for sensing something extra in people. Others just thought it was intuition, but it went deeper than that. His skill had helped him get into this gang, and made him a key member, with Sasquatch relying on what they called his hunches.

"What guy? You mean Bear?" said Spider. "Shit, what a loser. He was just a spy from another gang. When we made him he managed to stumble right into the arms of the cops. Heard he's locked up somewhere in Quebec."

"He was a pretty good spy, though," said Badger. "We didn't even notice at first that he was at the meeting. I'm not saying that it is him, just saying it felt the same." He stared back at the dark trees. "I used to live here."

The others stared at him in astonishment.

"Not California?" said Sasquatch.

"Way out here in the middle of nowhere?" added Spider.

Badger shrugged. "When I was a teenager. There's not much here. Just a smelly paper mill, stupid tourists in the summer, and a long boring winter. It's a small place, with maybe 1000 people counting our reserve."

"You're from a reservation?" said Spider.

Badger was already regretting even mentioning this place. He sneered at Spider, then gave him a shove. "Reserve, dumb-ass, not a reservation. We are of the Anishinaabe, what you people call the Ojibway. Or worse. My uncle was a band chief."

"No way!" said Spider. "Did you live in tee-pees and wear face paint?" He started to do a little dance.

Badger briefly considered slashing Spider's throat with a screwdriver. So easy. Spider was slow, and soft. Then at least one voice would be gone. He smiled and let the thought pass. Spider was useful to them; he could usually calm Sasquatch down when their leader got in one of his moods. Badger sighed and moved back to his bike. "Nope, just like regular kids in regular houses, but with less money and more drugs. Grownups were always with the rules, pushing us to go to school and be nice to all the whities. I had some friends that thought different—we were always getting grief from the elders."

"Elders?" said Spider. "Like old folks?"

"Yeah, usually old," said Badger. "But special ones, that thought they knew it all, and tried to run the place. I just ignored the old farts, and did my thing. It seemed the more bad things I got into, the better I felt. It gave me sort of a rush, you know? They tried to make me give it all up. I could have, but just didn't want to. Finally they had this big ceremony and kicked me out. On my own, with just the shirt on my back."

"Your own family? That sucks," said Spider.

Sasquatch nodded. "Big time. So, I'm guessing you don't want to go back there and check it out, right?"

Badger hadn't liked what he'd felt back there. Maybe it was time to move on. He grunted, then shook his head. "No, I can't be bothered with them anymore. I need to catch up with some of my native friends in Winnipeg, and set up some deals for us. After that, I'll be heading back into the States. Nothing personal, but I miss all my buddies in California. If you guys do decide to stop in on the way back, well, it's not that exciting."

"No, we'll just fly back to Toronto and ship the bikes back," said Sasquatch. "It's a pretty long ride. But that little town is just like the ones we want to expand to back in Ontario's cottage country. Sleepy places, lazy small town cops, a chance to catch summer tourists wishing they'd brought some drugs with them. I might get the guys from Winnipeg to drive down and check out the possibilities."

Sasquatch swung back onto his bike and waved at the others to mount up too. "Let's go. Only a couple more hours to Winnipeg. I'm looking forward to slapping some sense into those idiots up there."

Dave stared out the window as Reese drove back to the turnoff, past the gas station and motel, then headed down the road to the lake and town. Dave drummed his fingers on the dash, then shifted in his seat.

Finally Reese spoke up. "What was that all about back there?"

Dave paused. He supposed he owed his young constable some answers. As Dave kept telling his staff, they were a team. "Remember, when I came up in January, I mentioned problems with gangs in Toronto?"

"Have they found you already?" said Reese.

"No, I don't think so, at least not on purpose," said Dave. "Not way up here."

When Dave had left Toronto his old boss had spread several false rumours about his sudden disappearance. As it turned out, although the bikers were pissed off and wanted to track him down, they had more pressing local issues to deal with. Business was business. Apparently a missing striker with a Bear tattoo was not as significant as losing the drug markets to the younger Somalian, Asian, and Chinese gangs.

"It's probably just a coincidence," said Dave. "Lots of bikers like this route. I recognized some of those bikes and their riders, though. First one belonged to their leader, Sasquatch. Another one might have been Badger."

"Did they make you?"

"I doubt it," said Dave, "I look a lot different from the last time they saw me. And they have no reason to suspect I'm up here. Still, I had a bad feeling when they went by."

Dave had never mentioned to Reese or the other police officers his mysterious ability to fade from people's awareness. He was only part Anishinaabe, but suspected he owed this talent to that side of the family. His grandmother had tried to explain his gift to him, when he was young.

"Most people and animals see what they expect to see, little bear," she said as he bent over, trying to knot a snare with small six year old fingers. "Just think of the light bending around you and their thoughts will follow with it. Be very still and they will forget you are there."

Unfortunately his grandmother had died the year later, taking with her his only link to his native culture. But he continued to develop his new power, his fade, as he called it. He used it mainly for sneaking up on rabbits and deer, and hiding from a sometimes abusive father. As a single parent, in the military, his father resented having to drag his son around from posting to posting, so Dave learned early on how to stay out of the way. He was careful to keep his ability secret as he grew up, and did use it very effectively in the drug squad, early in his RCMP career. Unfortunately, a slip in maintaining that shield was how he'd gotten in trouble with the bike gangs in January. Once up here, though, for some reason his power had grown and changed. It showed that it had a dark side too, that almost took him over. Luckily, with the help of the local aboriginal elders, he was able to get rid of what had crept into him, just leaving things as before, with just his original ability. His gift had helped him to solve some major crimes up here, by eavesdropping unseen on the crooks, and impressing his co-workers with what he maintained were just lucky guesses blended with deductive reasoning. But he really didn't need his ability now, in this quiet little town, and felt uncomfortable using it on all his new friends. Most importantly, the memory of being out of control was fresh in his mind, and frightened him. He was determined to prove once and for all that he could be a good cop on his own, without using his power.

"Just call it one of my hunches," he said, "but I think we should keep our eyes open around town just in case."

They drove slowly down the town's main street, lined not with the tidy boutique trees of a big city, but lofty pines from the last century. A gentle breeze sighed through the tall trees, as locals and visitors wandered back and forth across the street. At the far end, just by the mill turnoff, squatted the Grande Hotel, framed by the sun sparkling off the lake. He was really getting to like the peace and quiet up here, as opposed to the noise and pollution of downtown Toronto. To think that only a few months earlier he'd been counting the days until he could get transferred back to a drug squad down south.

"Collar too tight?" said Reese.

Dave realized he'd been scratching at his Raven tattoo, a sure sign that something was bothering him. He sighed. "No, just worried. I've a feeling my past is about to catch up with me and disturb my quiet life."

Reese laughed. "Quiet? Since January we uncovered a massive case of fraud and corruption at the local pulp and paper mill, cleaned up a drug problem, solved a murder, sent a handful of locals to jail, and persuaded the Feds to set up a Centre of Excellence here to study pollution. I just graduated a year ago, and they never said this was what quiet meant."

"Alright," said Dave. "Maybe not that quiet, but everyone assures me that was just a fluke, that it really is different up here. There certainly is none of the gangs and violence I'm used to. Here the problems are mostly local, and solving them has a direct impact on the people we live with. And care about."

Reese smiled. "I've noticed some changes in you since you came here."

Dave glanced at him quizzically. "Such as?"

"Well," said Reese, "when you first arrived your conversation maximum was one sentence. Now you sometimes get up to three sentences!"

Dave smiled. He'd been a loner most of his life, and when he joined the Force he'd enjoyed the independence of undercover work. This latest job, and the town, had eventually drawn him out.

"Sometimes I get carried away," he said. "It's hard to avoid in this chatty town."

"Or with JB as a girlfriend," said Reese. "She's a real bundle of energy. I'm not sure how you slowed her down enough to snag her."

"I'm not sure if I really snagged JB," said Dave. He glanced over to find Reese trying to stare at him and drive at the same time.

"What?"

"Nothing," said Reese, as he swerved back onto the road.

"Well she's not here, is she?" said Dave. "Just took off and moved to Ottawa. That's not much of a snagging. Whatever. Let's just drop it, okay?

He'd rather not discuss his love life with Reese, or the rest of his staff for that matter. Norris was the other constable at the RCMP detachment and she was reasonably discrete in questions about Dave's girlfriend, but still, he was her boss. As for Sheila, the detachment clerk, she felt that her role as administrative commander of the office and unofficial mother figure gave her licence to probe and give unsolicited advice.

"No problem," said Reese. "Topic closed."

In fact, Dave wasn't sure where he stood with JB. A few months ago they were getting along well. Very well. Dave smiled as he remembered a trip to a hunting cabin where they'd snuggled all night. That was definitely not a one night stand, like most of his relationships in Toronto had been. Most? More like all. He felt connected to JB, at ease when they were together. In addition, despite the initial misgivings of JB's grandfather and other elders on the reserve, they were now starting to approve of him as boyfriend material. Then, right when everything seemed to be fitting into place, JB had announced that she was going back to university, leaving Kirk's Landing and leaving him.

It wasn't as if they'd had a big fight. He'd told her that he was no longer ready to rush back down south, but had decided he wanted to stay in Kirk's Landing. And apparently she'd decided she wanted to leave, and was ready to head back to Ottawa. She said he'd inspired her to want to do more with her life by helping her people, so this time, instead of just a general arts degree, she'd signed up for some specific courses. She had a plan. They had talked a couple of times on the phone after she left, but it wasn't the same as before. Maybe he'd done something wrong or she was trying to distance herself so she could let him down easy. It didn't help that JB was the only person he'd ever been comfortable talking to about things like feelings. Or about his concerns over his power. He was baffled.

Dave rubbed the back of his neck. "Damn. I've got a headache coming on. I thought they were gone for good. It started off as such a nice day too, until trouble rode out of the mist." He pointed out the window. "Drop me off here at Rosie's, would you? I think it's time for another chat with him over a coffee."

He wanted to talk with the elders too, and soon. It was their sweat lodge ceremony that had helped him regain his original powers, by driving out that destructive spirit, the one they called Wendigo. He wanted the elders' reassurance that the evil was gone for good, from him and the town. This latest sensation when the bike gang rode by bothered him. Maybe the evil was still out there, just waiting for him to rely on his power again.

Chapter 2

JB aimed carefully at the bikers. "Gotcha," she said. She handed the camera back to their leader, Ron. He'd been in a few times to chat, usually after pedalling around the countryside. He was friendly, and easy to talk to. Like Dave had been, until she'd announced her plans to leave. And he'd announced he was staying. They both had thought they'd figured out where they were going in life, but she'd assumed it would be together.

Ron smiled back at her. "Thanks. We had a hard ride today." He rubbed at his calf, and frowned. "Ouch. We've been out all day, mostly on the Quebec side. We came back over at Island Park when the rain started, though. Some of those hills are pretty brutal, so we're definitely in need of some fluids. I decided to bring my friends to enjoy my favourite little pub and my favourite little bartender."

"Already?" she said. She laughed. "Hell, I've only been here a few weeks. I'm glad I've made such a good impression. What can I get you?"

"A couple of pitchers of Keith's, please," said Ron. "And some water—there's six of us today. Two are in the can still trying to peel off sweaty spandex bike shorts."

"Ewww, TMI," she said. "Beer and water coming up, for the cyclists."

Ron smiled as JB headed back behind the bar, chattering to all as she went. As always, there was a mix of people in here, old and young, walk-ins off the street and regulars. He sat back in his chair, soaking up the beer and the atmosphere and enjoying the ache of a long day's ride. This was certainly different from his years on a Harley, wearing a gang patch. His old buddies would still give him a wave as they thundered by, and he'd join them for a ride on occasion, but he'd managed so far to stay less involved, out of their rides, their conflicts with other gangs, their drug business. And so far, they respected that. He liked this little place, with its mix of customers, old and young, walk-ins off the street and regulars. And with JB. He loved the way her dark eyes sparkled.

His friend Jim elbowed him. "Hello? Ron? Lost in space? She certainly is cute. I can see why you like to come here. What's the JB stand for?"

"Her name's Jackie Bourbeau, but she prefers just JB. She's First Nations from up in Manitoba. She reminds me of a little bird as she flits around here, chattering to us all. And it sort of fits, as apparently her native spirit or whatever is supposed to be a Whisky-Jack."

"As in Jay Bird?" asked Jim. "Like those black and white ones we saw at our biking break?"

"Yes, I guess you're right. Didn't make the connection."

"Probably too busy making goofy eyes at her," said Jim. "So have you asked her out yet?"

"I sort of mentioned it," said Ron. "But she was non-committal, talking about her heavy course load here at Ottawa U and a possible boyfriend back home."

"Possible boyfriend?"

"Not sure how serious it is right now. She sort of clammed up about it."

"Well, don't give up yet," said Jim.

It was busy today in the little pub, but JB liked that, as it made the shift go faster. She needed the distraction from worrying about her decision to come back here. She really did want to make this work, this new field of studies, but she also missed home, and her friends and family, and Dave. This time around she'd managed to avoid most of the clubs, and also fit in some part-time work somehow. Her job was near her apartment, and buses, in a recently gentrified area. The hookers and most of the drug dealers had moved on, except for a few customers. She'd probably seen more drugs back home, before Dave's big cleanup there. She liked the mixed bag of friends down here in Ottawa, friends from her job and school and the clubs. Writers, musicians, lawyers, welders, dancers, some people local, some diplomats and exchange students. And cyclists. She glanced across the room at Ron, joking with his friends. He was bigger than his other friends, but very charming, and quickly becoming a favoured customer. She could picture him better on a big motorcycle than a fifteen-speed touring bike, though. He'd suggested a couple of times that they meet up but so far she'd used the busy busy line. She still felt committed to Dave back in Kirk's Landing, but she just wasn't sure how committed Dave was to her.

At the thought of Dave an empty spot opened in her chest. They still talked on the phone, but it seemed different. What had gone wrong? She'd thought they had a really good thing going. In fact, she was hoping there might be a future with him. But for now, it was important for her to do something to help her own people, rather than just keep drifting. Heading back to university for the summer term was a last minute decision but this time it felt right for her. It would have been nice to have a few more months getting to know Dave better. She wished she knew what he was thinking, but he rarely opened up about any of that. His main focus was still his work, and to avoid using his unique ability to help him in it. Did he have another girlfriend? JB was baffled. Maybe a break was best for both of them. She smiled over at Ron and his buddies as she filled a tray with their drinks. Sharing a coffee wouldn't hurt, but she'd wait for him to ask again.

Chapter 3

Dave had paused for a moment in front of Rosie's, appreciating the tranquillity of his town's Main Street, when suddenly a small tornado exploded out of the alley. As he scooped up the ball of squirming rags the distinctive odour of solvent gave him a clue about what was going on.

"Hold on, buddy," he said. "You're not going anywhere." He was not surprised when JB's brother Junior came loping around the corner of the building, spray can in hand. Junior stopped with a grin when he saw Dave.

"Hi, Junior," said Dave. "I assume your artist mentorship program is going well?"

Junior ran a youth drop-in centre in the back of Rosie's restaurant. At eighteen, he was older than most of the youth, but had been through enough, including a year on the streets of Winnipeg, that he could relate to a lot of their issues. His big passion was graffiti art, so the side and back walls of Rosie's were a constant evolution of images, and Junior's apprentices happily but respectfully added new material whenever they felt inspired. The only rule was that it had to be art and not just casual tagging.

"The program is quite successful," said Junior. "Even so, we seem to be going through paint supplies very fast." He peered closely at Dave's bundle.

"'s not me racking yur stuff," said a defiant voice.

Dave changed his assessment from an eight-year-old boy to a small skinny 12-year-old girl, who looked like she cut her hair with a switch blade and was using mud to prevent mosquito bites. He put her down, keeping a hand wrapped in the shoulder of her hoodie.

"Any charges here?" he asked.

"I brung my own paint," she said belligerently, showing two well-used cans to Junior.

Dave looked enquiringly at Junior. This kid was new to him, but he needed to make sure even the young ones knew the limits.

Junior inspected the cans and shrugged. "She's right, they aren't our supplies. Nothing wrong. Maybe we're okay here." He crouched down and peered into her face. "So why were you doing a runner? You do know this is a free wall, right? As in legal?"

"Really?" She looked up at Dave, who just nodded. "Cool. Didn't know places had those. I was just improving yur stuff. That lame happy face garbage that just went up was just too cutesy. It made me want to hurl, so I was gunna do a dope throw-up." She squinted her eyes challengingly "You'll see, my stuff is good."

She and Junior stared at each other for a full five seconds.

Junior paused. "Fine then. From what I saw you do seem to have a good hand style. Got a black book?"

She pulled a tattered sketch book out of a pocket. "Yup. Here."

Junior flipped through the images. "Nice work. I like the characters —sort of other-world looking." He handed her book back to her. "You're welcome to stay and work on your art. Talk to the other kids, put something up on the wall."

She looked skeptical.

"And we have free paint of course. Monsanto."

Skepticism changed to guarded interest—and a little flash of raw desire.

"We can go there right now if you want."

Guarded face again. "I don't go with strangers." Dave cleared his throat. Looked like Junior had this one under control. "I can assure you that the youth centre is a municipally approved facility that meets the oversight requirements of your parents. Be glad to talk to them."

"What do you mean?" she said. "Oh, them." Her face darkened again. "Those losers don't care. I look after myself." She looked at Junior, then at Dave, then appeared to make up her mind. "Well, I can come in for a minute and see what you've got going on, but I'll only share my art if—."

A loud scream broke the air like a siren. A heavy woman, feet crammed into a pair of red stiletto heels, rushed out of Rosie's, then charged at Dave, wielding her plastic purse like a weapon.

"You damn cop, get your mitts off my kid. I see you pawing away and I'm going to sue the pants off you for sexual assault. Melissa, you get away from that Indian boy before you get bugs off him."

Melissa froze, then glanced up at Dave.

The kid probably could use a break. "Okay, you're good to go," he said. "And I won't need to talk to your parents, not this time. Just you mind what Junior says."

Melissa gave him a quick smile. "Thanks, copper. Sorry about my stepmother. We're here all summer though, so I can be back tomorrow." She then turned to the large woman. "Don't bust a strap, Tammy. I was just asking directions to the library. Let's get back to the trailer before your Wheel of Fortune starts."

Junior patted Dave on the shoulder. "Thanks for cutting her some slack—you're a good cop. Don't worry, I'll keep an eye on her. Her art does remind me of some of my friend Janie's work though. Good stuff but there are some darker elements too."

Dave frowned. "Not sure I like the sound of that." He outlined his encounter with bikers from his past, and the sense of evil he'd felt.

"Is that feeling still with you?" said Junior. The young man was one of the few who knew of Dave's fading power and his struggle against the Wendigo.

Dave paused. "No, it was just there when I started to use my fade. It's gone now."

"Did you recognize anyone besides Sasquatch?" asked Junior.

"Such as your cousin, Badger?" said Dave. "No, I couldn't tell. It's likely he was somewhere in the pack, though. He still rides with the Toronto chapter."

Junior shook his head. "Now, that guy is just plain bad. We tried to help him before, but the only thing to do in the end was to cut him out like a cancer and banish him. The darkness had already crept in. We suspect that was what helped him sense you back in Toronto. Maybe that's what you felt again, that link."

Dave frowned. "Do you think using my power somehow has called that spirit back to me?"

"I don't think so," said Junior. He put his hands on Dave's shoulders and stared deeply into his eyes. "You look fine to me. Your spirit is still clean. Remember, you're the one that took back control and cast the spirit out. Myself and the elders just helped you do it. But the evil still does exist in the spirit world all around us."

"And it still could enter into other people?" said Dave.

"Not usually," said Junior. "In most of us our own spirit is strong enough to keep this evil away."

"Not usually?" said Dave. That was not reassuring.

"Let me talk to Grandfather and the others," said Junior. "They will know more about any risks. Go ahead into Rosie's—I'll get back to you later."

Dave wanted to believe Junior, but still had his doubts. His fading ability was nice to have, and was a good resource in his job, but maybe it wasn't worth the risk.

Dave paused in the doorway and breathed in the aroma of fresh coffee. Rosie's cafe was hot, humid, and noisy now, a big change from the quiet winter months. More people, more business, and more challenges for the small police force, unfortunately. Dave peered through the espresso machine steam, and waved a hand at the cafe owner, "Hey Rosie, another busy day?"

"Never stops, Dave," said the older man. "Just your regular or maybe change up with something foamy and flavourful?"

"No, thanks. Black, one sugar."

Rosie smiled. "The usual, coming right up. Good luck finding a place to sit, though. We're packed."

He wasn't kidding. Every booth and table was taken, as were the counter stools. It was as crowded as a Toronto cafe, but without the suits. Most of the new summer visitors were now in designer summer wear, showing off a lot of pasty white skin. They were a law-abiding group, so far, but his team was staying alert. He didn't want a return of the drug problems of last winter. The quiet corner at the back, usually filled by the knitting club, was full of teenagers—sprawled on the comfy chairs, chattering at each other, and listening to their ubiquitous earphones.

"What's with all the kids in here? Are you planning a rave?"

Rosie laughed. "In quiet little Kirk's Landing? Nope. Some are college kids, up here now that exams are done, looking to party at the cottage. Most in here are younger locals, though. They don't spend a lot, but they pay their tab and keep it fairly quiet. That's my nephew Kurt over there—the one with the Mohawk and piercings." He shook his head. "Under all that disguise he's not a bad kid, but he started to run a little wild in Toronto. My sister finally got tired of trying to rein him in, so she sent him up here for the summer. He was just starting up a t-shirt business down there with a friend of his, girlfriend I guess, with her art. Good work, but he just couldn't seem to focus on it. Now that he's up here, he's trying to grow some business, with her back in

Toronto as his supplier. Must be doing well too, as he always has cash to buy music from bands I've never even heard of. And of course for his main addiction, video games."

"Does he help you out with the cafe too?" asked Dave.

"When he finally gets up," said Rosie. "And when he's in the mood. I'm sure it puts off some customers, having to be served by someone that so obviously wants to be elsewhere." He handed Dave a mug. "Here you go. Me, I'm a morning person from all those years my late wife and I ran our Toronto cafe, and he's more of a night owl. He looks after things here some evenings, plays online till all hours, then when he can't sleep he roams our streets—all four of them. He's checked out the beach a few times, though, so maybe that will widen his horizons a bit."

"Should I keep an eye on him?" asked Dave.

"Not specifically," said Rosie. "I think he's pretty clean now, so I wouldn't want him to feel he was still being singled out. Now, I do sometimes smell a whiff of dope out back, but it's likely one of the newer kids from the drop-in centre. They are all trying to be straight, with Junior's help, but some find it more of a challenge."

Dave wasn't so sure Kurt was completely clean. He'd seen a lot of young kids suddenly come into extra cash, with their parents unaware of where it came from. He'd definitively add Kurt to his list of kids to watch, and mention it to Junior. Best to catch these things before the kids got too involved. "I just saw Junior outside," he said. "He seems to be doing okay with the centre."

"Yes, JB's brother is a big help with the kids," said Rosie. "He's good with them because he knows exactly what it feels like to be a bit lost. It's a good thing his big sister came back home a few years back, and got him back on track. It's a mixed blessing, having your grandfather as band chief, as that means higher expectations too. This centre he's running is a big draw now for the local kids, though, both from the town and the reserve. I'm hoping my nephew will check it out eventually. Speaking of JB—how is she?"

Dave shrugged. "Fine, I guess." He knew the real question was how were he and JB getting on. He wished he knew himself. They did call each other every few days, but nothing serious was discussed. Such as her announcing she'd changed her mind and was heading back. "I'd like to get together with you, maybe Friday after supper. I have some issues in town I'd like to run by you. Meanwhile, I need to go have a chat with our buddy Mike."

As Dave worked his way through the cafe, he nodded to the many townspeople he had met in the past four months.

"Mayor Belanger," he said, squatting down next to Mike's chair. "How's life as the big cheese?"

Mike nodded. "Corporal Browne. I'm doing well, thanks. Things keeping you busy?"

"Just a bit," said Dave. "We both have a better understanding now of the curse, 'May you live in interesting times'. Here I was planning on a quiet year in a little town, you on an easy life as database manager at the mill and part time councillor. Who knew that we'd end up working together to bust things wide open."

"So true," said Mike. "And now we start the busy summer. It's a good thing Sheila stayed on as your clerk."

"She's better at it now," said Dave. "More focused. She just needed some encouragement to be herself rather than just be known as 'the ex-mayor's wife'. She's been busy coordinating the summer uniforms—"

"There's rules for that?" said Mike.

"Of course," said Dave. "On May 1st, Headquarters sent out a memo, what we call 'Summer Order of Dress'. Long or Short sleeves, no tie, SBA—that's soft body armour. Memo goes to all detachments, whether it's warm out or not. She also swapped the ski-doo for the patrol boat, made sure we got in mosquito repellent—all those little details. She loves it. In addition, we've got approval to hire an extra constable for the summer, before we get even busier."

Dave was pretty sure Mike knew exactly how busy the constables were, since there was a rumour the interim mayor and Constable Norris were seeing a lot of each other. She was a single mother, with a young son, so, according to Sheila, had been cautious at first. "Norris will continue as senior constable, but she'll now have a retired Staff Sergeant reporting to her. It should be interesting."

That was an understatement. Bringing new personalities into a small group was always a challenge. The new guy might be too set in his ways, or try to resume his old Staff Sergeant attitudes. Dave trusted Norris to handle this new relationship diplomatically, but in a police station there was often little time to sort out pecking order.

Mike smiled. "Violet is really looking forward to having more free time, but how did you manage to get a senior NCO to come to Kirk's Landing?"

Dave had noticed a few 'police lingo' terms were sneaking into Mike's conversation, thanks no doubt to Dave's enthusiastic constable. NCO meant non-commissioned officer, but was generally used as a term for all supervisors over the rank of constable.

"It was Staff Sergeant Scully, up in the District Office, who arranged it. The RCMP has a Reserve Program where we can hire retired members part time in certain circumstances, and Kirk's Landing qualifies, so Staff gave it his blessing. And funding. We found a former member living in the area who wanted to have a little part-time work to fill his day, so we hired him on at Constable rank. In fact, he'll be starting this week. I'm sure his experience will be a big help."

"I gather your boss is pleased with your work so far?"

At this Dave gave a quick laugh, then shook his head. "It's not that easy to tell when Staff is pleased. He is not generally in favour of thinking outside the box. I think he may be softening a bit. The success of our big bust, plus good feedback on it from the press and from the Inspector really helped. Staff is happy when his boss is happy."

"I was glad we were able to get the town back on an even keel," said Mike. "Also, I got to know Violet better as part of it. This just proves that computer skills do sometimes attract the ladies. I really like her, but we're taking it slowly for now. How about you, any news from JB?"

Dave smiled. There was no escaping these questions. It was nice though, to know that they all cared. He glanced around and lowered his voice. "Yes, we talk, once in a while. She had to head down south early to give herself time to find an apartment and a part-time job at some pub. She's keen on some summer courses at Ottawa U. It's a new mix of aboriginal studies and sociology and art she's put together. I'm not sure what kind of degree she ends up with, though. She talked about staying on in the fall, but I'm hoping she'll tire of life down there and come back up here with me."

"Ah, Dave," said Mike, "you've still got a lot to learn about relationships. Stop pushing her to move back. Just pay attention to what she says as well as to what she doesn't say."

"I do try," said Dave. "but I can't help thinking that there are lots of good-looking guys down there, both in her classes and at her pub. Maybe she'll hook up with one of them. Or maybe she's hoping I'll meet someone new here, in the midst of all these summer gals up from the big city."

"Calm down," said Mike. "I don't think either of you is moving on. She's a bit of a flirt and social butterfly, but it's all on the surface. Deep down she's made a choice. As have you, if you'd just listen to your heart. And to her."

Mike clapped Dave on the shoulder. "Listen, you and I should get together soon. Could we do your place again, or maybe meet at the Grande? I know the Raven's Roost pub isn't the same since JB left as bartender, but Sid is managing it not too badly, and it still has great cold pints and hot wings. We can grab a table and chat about the challenges of the coming summer. Drugs for a start—like every year."

"Yes, on my mind too," said Dave. "Good idea, it's been a while since I've been to the pub. Let's do it." As chief of police he definitely couldn't be a regular at the pub, but did try to drop in occasionally. It did give him a way to network and keep a finger on the pulse of the town. And it would let the new residents know he was out there. "I already mentioned it to Rosie. We were thinking Friday, say eight? Just no more talking about relationships!" He stood up and winced, grabbing his leg.

"Getting old?" asked Mike.

Dave bent over close to Mike. "Nope, just some setting up. The detachment has a team in next week's baseball tournament, but Rosie's is one of the best I hear. I need to fake a bum leg to help the odds against him. We may have a few sleepers on board the team with us, again. I'm hoping we can pull another scam, like we did for the curling bonspiel last winter. Keep it mum, all right?"

Chapter 4

Sasquatch rang the bell again, then banged on the door with his fist. Finally the loud music stopped. He glared at the camera again. "Open the goddamn door, I'm tired and dying for a piss."

With a rattle of bolts and chains, the door swung open to reveal a scrawny little blonde in a miniskirt, torn stockings, and a leather bra.

"Who are you?" she asked, looking up at him.

"I'm Sasquatch, and Louie has five seconds to get his ass out here before I come in and break some heads."

She was suddenly pushed aside by a biker, as short and skinny as her, arms covered in tattoos and ears full of piercings. "Sasquatch! We didn't know you was coming, come on in, good to see you. Bonnie, this is my best buddy Sasquatch."

"Not best buddies, Louie. Don't push it. I decided it was time to come up from Toronto, both for the ride and to straighten out some things up here. The rest of the guys are at a motel along with the crash car; we can all meet up later at the bar."

Sasquatch handed his duffel bag to the blonde, and pushed past her. He wrinkled his nose at the smell of sweat and pot. "Christ, could you open a window?"

"Louie says it has to stay closed," said Bonnie. "The neighbours kept like complaining about the music."

"We figured it was simpler to just close it all up," said Louie.

"Damn it," said Sasquatch. "Bonnie, open a goddamn window. Shit, if you strikers want to be able to form a chapter, you can't be giving in just because it's easier. Let the locals know you're in charge, or next they'll want you to stop riding your bikes on the weekends. It's not as if Scotia Street is that fancy—what do they expect?" Sasquatch lifted his leg and cleared all the bottles off the coffee table with one swipe of his foot. "And clean this place up—not only that crap on the front lawn but inside here. Get some of these women off their backs and behind a broom."

"I will, I will," said Louie. "It's been a long cold winter here in Winnipeg. Jesus, as soon as it warmed up we just wanted to get out and hit the road. Anyway, the pisser's just down that hall. And it's clean." He glared at Bonnie, who just nodded. "Here's a cold beer to go with it."

While Sasquatch was gone, Louie got everyone hustling to clean up, and started calls going out to the rest of the members. Hopefully this surprise visit was to be good news.

Sasquatch walked back in, wiping his face with a towel. "That feels a bit better," he said. "Got some dirt off, but I still want a shower once we're done." He looked around and nodded. It looked a little better. He hadn't used to be such a clean freak, but a few stints in a crowded prison cell had changed his habits. "Not quite as disgusting, keep at it."

"How was the ride?" said Louie.

"Scenic," said Sasquatch. "And good weather, with not too many cops." He'd enjoyed the open road, cruising with his friends. Right up to when they passed by Badger's old haunts. He'd been mellowing out, looking forward to a semi-retirement, letting the young guys carry on. As long as he got a good cut of the action, of course. And then that place just put him in a bad mood somehow. He just wanted to hit someone—or something. "Right now, I want to find out why you guys have been sitting around on your asses instead of getting out there to make money."

"Hey man, it's been a cold winter," said Louie. "Things were slow. We'll do better this summer, I know. Here, grab another beer. A few of the gang are here already, and I've sent word out to the rest. Want to wait for them?"

"No, let's get going," said Sasquatch. "Any of your guys that are late get on my list for some special attention." He paused and lit a cigarette. "So, first off, it's good to see you've finally started using the tracking system we set you up with."

"Well, it was a challenge for some of the guys," said Louie. "Not used to using a computer for other than porn. I convinced them it wasn't a choice, you needed it to track everything. Some I just had to convince a little harder than others. Is it true you got the system from some guy in jail?"

"Yeah," said Sasquatch. "He was a banker in there for fraud, and a real computer whiz. When he heard I was working on my MBA in there he offered to team up and develop this system." The banker hadn't really been given any choice. He was a scrawny little guy, an easy target, desperate for some protection. Sasquatch was hoping this system would make things run more efficiently, which would mean less running around for him.

"But is it safe?" said Louie "What if the cops hack into it? I heard they do that now."

Sasquatch glared at him. Louie was always looking for excuses. "Stop worrying. He added security too, so no one can read what you send me. Or even read the hard drive—if you happen to screw up and let the cops get their hands on it. The only other person with access is me. And it has been showing me that you've been doing a crappy job up here. You need to get out there and bash some heads! Get your street cred back, start pushing the local gangs more. Let them know you've got some quality product. In town and outside in the country too." He sighed. There was hope for this crew, but probably not with Louie leading it. Louie was fast with a knife but he was still a runt, and was getting lazy. Maybe he just needed a new challenge, away from here. Sasquatch was sure he could convince Badger to help out with things here in Winnipeg, at least for a few weeks. There seemed to be a lot of his kind of people in Winnipeg, so would be easy for him to improve their contacts. Sasquatch sipped on his beer and nodded. "You've been selling to a place called Kirk's Landing, right?"

"Sounds familiar," said Louie. "That's that small town by the park, right? Lots of tourists and rich summer residents."

"That's the one," said Sasquatch. "It used to be pretty good for a small town, with all the money from the mill lining people's pockets. But sales look bad for the last month or so. What happened? The system here says your contact is some Risso guy. The low returns got flagged all right, but I don't see no follow-up by anyone here. Just more laziness?" He stared at Louie with his cold black eyes and raised a fist.

"No, no," said Louie. "Now I remember. There was a big bust there a month or so ago. I think Risso almost got caught in it, so he's laying low for a while. He said the mill managers and some townspeople were skimming off a lot of cash meant for improvements. Spending it on big houses, and cars, and of course dope. Then their new cop busted it all up."

"New cop?" asked Sasquatch. This was interesting. "Did he say from where?"

"He wasn't sure," said Louie. "Some people had said from down south, some from out west. He just showed up suddenly last January to take things over. A big guy, quiet, with a scary look."

Sasquatch drummed his fingers on the table. He'd been ready to dismiss this little town and its little people, but maybe Badger had something after all. Could he afford to ignore it? It had been suspicious the way the cop had not only let them go but had even turned away. He needed to find out more about this. Should he send Badger to check it out? Maybe not, what with the native's bad history there, and obvious fear of the place, like it was haunted or something. Sasquatch leaned forward. He'd have to use what he had. "Louie, I think that place needs some personal attention from you. I want you to drive down and check it out, see why Risso can't get business up again. And check out that cop too. Where's he from, what's he up to. If he's just there temporary like or do they think he's settling in."

"Why don't you just look for him on the way back?" said Louie.

"We'll be flying back," said Sasquatch. "And ship the bikes with a friend." He felt a surge of irritation and gave Louie a shove—hard enough to push the half-pint off his chair. "Anyways, what's it to you? That's the last time I hear insolent questions coming out of your yap hole or there will be blood. Understand? Just follow orders. Bring Bonnie down with you too, rent a family car and just pretend to be tourists. Find out what's happening there, scope it out, meet up with Risso and give him a kick in the ass. I might pay it a visit too later on." This was starting to look like more than just a coincidence. He would have to be careful though, until he knew what was there, and found out what had spooked Badger like that.

"How about up here, though?" said Louie nervously. "I just mean, with Bonnie and me gone, you know."

Sasquatch glared at him. "Don't worry about it. I'll get Badger to stay for a bit and make some new contacts for you with his own people. Pick someone to take over for and bump them up. Always good to change things up."

Louie didn't look happy with that, but he just nodded. "You're the boss."

"Damn right I am," said Sasquatch. "Listen, I want the traffic in that town back to where it was, and then up some. We're going to start pushing in these areas to the summer crowd, all up from the big city without their normal suppliers, those goddamn Asian gangs. No competition up here, and just dumb local cops."

There was a thump at the door.

"Must be the rest of the guys," said Louie. "Hopefully they brought more beer. I'll get the Tequila. Bonnie—drop the broom and grab the door."

Sasquatch was in pain. He could still drink as well as he could when younger, he just couldn't recover the same. There'd been shooters at the bar, and some arm-wrestling, and possibly wheelies up and down the street. He wasn't sure.

He stretched and realized that there was a warm body next to him. As he rolled over he hoped the hell it wasn't Louie.

"Hey there, babe," she said. "What a party that was. Can you stay a few days?"

"Hey yourself—Bonnie is it?" He nudged her. "Nope, have to head back. Get me a coffee, and then come back to bed and warm me up. Tell Louie he needs to crank the heat up, I'm freezing here."

By the time he got downstairs Louie was busy in the kitchen, frying up eggs and bacon and hash-browns, wearing nothing but an apron and faded boxer shorts, for a table full of hungover bikers.

"Jeez, cover up will you?" He threw a pair of jeans at Louie. "Your breakfast buns are gross!"

After breakfast he took his coffee out onto the back porch, and sat in the sun to try to chase the chills away. Coming up here had been a good idea, though. Always good first hand to see what was happening locally, or not happening. That little town, Kirk's Landing, and its cop, was an intriguing puzzle too. His first reaction had been to wait and find out more before heading down there, get Louie to do the scouting for him. But he never used to be cautious—the old Sasquatch would have ridden with a dozen bikes and busted up the town. And then done some jail time. He shook his head. So maybe some caution, but he still needed to find out who this cop was for himself, rather than trust it to that idiot Louie. Beside, that strange feeling, just as they passed the town, intrigued him. There'd been a flash of anger, but also a burst of invigorating energy.

Yes, he would go down. He'd have the others fly back as planned and still get Louie and Bonnie to get down, but he needed to check out this little town himself, see who the cop really was, and give this Risso a kick. He sipped his hot coffee then shivered. Maybe he was coming down with something.

The closer Sasquatch got to Kirk's Landing, the worse the weather and his mood became. By the time he turned and got to the turnoff, marked by a restaurant and a gas station, it was drizzling and he was pissed off. He slowly rode down the hill into the town, exhaust echoing off the walls of the small rock cut. Like Badger had said, Kirk's Landing was a typical small town: one main street leading right down to the lake, with shops on both sides, a couple of small side streets and an old hotel on the lake shore. Halfway down he passed the cop shop, so blipped his throttle just to get their attention. There were a few slow-moving locals, wandering across the street even in the rain, but they rushed to the sidewalk once they spotted him, or rather heard him.

He'd called ahead, so by the time he walked into the hotel bar, slapping the water from his leathers, he expected their local contact, Risso, to be there, waiting.

It was a small place, just one big room, with dark panelled walls, several big flat screen TV's, and a scattering of small tables and wooden chairs. It smelled like a tavern too, a blend of spilled beer, mildew, and fried food. Sasquatch smiled. He'd got drunk in, and been thrown out of, places just like this. There were a couple of old guys sitting at the bar along the back wall, playing cards, and four Indians nursing their beers by the open patio door. Back in the corner sat a tall but skinny guy, sporting a mullet, eyes darting nervously back and forth. Had to be Risso.

As Sasquatch approached, his contact stood quickly, almost knocking over his chair, and extended his hand. "You must be Sasquatch. Just as Louie described. Maybe even bigger." He paused. "Not that big is bad, I didn't mean fat, I just meant…" He stopped, then realized he was still grasping Sas's hand and dropped it.

Sasquatch shook his head. This was their contact? "Yes, that's me." He lowered himself carefully into a fragile looking chair. "And you are obviously Risso. Next time we meet, or for that matter when any of my guys come here, be a little quieter with names, ass-hole."

Risso nodded quickly. "Sure, I got it. Have a seat—can I get you a beer, some shots, maybe a burger or something?"

"Just get a jug, Ex if they have it. I'm going for a piss."

When he got back Risso had grabbed some snacks from the machine in the corner and poured the beer. It felt good to relax after the wet ride, cold beer in hand, and plot out his next steps. Risso had the expected excuses about falling drug sales, but Sasquatch cut him off.

"I don't care, really, maggot. Summer is starting, hopefully with lots of new customers, so we'll be moving lots of supplies in for you to sell. I've got someone coming down from Winnipeg, name's Louie, to help set things up. He'll be coming down with this broad, Bonnie, keeping low-key in a family sedan. So don't stand on your chair and wave when they come in! Now, I think I need to tour the town a bit."

"Great, I'd be glad to show you around," said Risso.

"No, don't bother," said Sasquatch. "I don't need you showing me off to everyone like I'm your best buddy. I just want to get a quick feel for the place. Oh, and check out your local chief."

"Charlie, the band chief? He's a tough nut, at least with the other natives. No more drugs and alcohol like the old days, big into their culture—"

"No, you idiot, the police chief. He looked familiar when we rode through on our way to Winnipeg. What can you tell me about him?"

"Well, his name is Browne, with an 'e'," said Risso. "Dave

Browne. He's a big guy," said Risso, "not like you, but tall, and has some muscle. Clean shaven, brown hair—just looks like a standard ass-hole cop. He does have a scary way of staring at you though, like he's looking right through you."

Sasquatch wasn't sure. Might be the same guy. "Any tattoos?"

"No," said Risso, "he doesn't have—wait, there is part of one that shows above his collar. Looks like a bird's wing. I've never seen him without a shirt—he might have more, I guess."

"Yes," said Sasquatch. "That's my guy. When does he usually do his patrols? Maybe I'll see him drive by."

"He seems to like foot patrols," said Risso, "so you can often catch him somewhere along the main street. Or in Rosie's Cafe, across from the lock-up. He used to come in here too, when his girlfriend ran the place."

"Thanks," said Sas. He looked around and then passed Risso a package under the table. "Here. A little something to get your customers going. It's strong, top grade, but don't cut it or I'll have your balls. Let people know you'll have lots more soon." He drained the rest of his glass and pushed his chair back. "I'll head out now. Looking forward to meeting this guy face to face; we have some history to discuss."

But he didn't see the cop, even though he made several passes up and down the main drag, collar up against the cool wind, and even stopped into some places and casually asked about him. The cop had to have known someone was asking after him, as this was a small town. People probably were calling him as soon as Sasquatch was out of sight. He'd acted pretty tough as Bear in Toronto, but maybe he'd turned chicken after they busted him. That would make Sasquatch's takeover even easier. At any rate, everyone praised their chief, but none had many details from his past. Some said he was from down south, some said from out west, some said he was assigned here as punishment after screwing up his last job, some said it was to be near his family. There was no shortage of rumours.

Sasquatch wasn't about to march right into the police station, and he did want to head out before dark, so he decided to give up. For now. This did sound like the same snitch they'd almost caught, so he was definitely coming back up here later on to check on his drug business personally, and take care of this cop. He felt a little surge of energy as he made that decision—he was looking forward to coming back to deal with this Dave Browne with an 'e'.

Dave peered out between the slats of the blinds—yup, it sure looked like Sasquatch. He'd already fielded several phone calls from concerned citizens, warning him that some big biker was walking around looking for him. They all assured Dave that they had either been deliberately vague, or had used a good cover story. He had no doubt every story was different.

"Still raining out there?" said Sheila.

"Yes, still," he said. "Started out so nice too. I think I'll stay in."

"Good idea," she said. "I've a stack of reports that need signing. Let me get them for you."

When she returned she nodded to the phone. "Junior's on line one. Maybe he's calling to drag you out for a wet walk."

"Nope, won't be tempted," he said.

"Hello, Junior. Everything all right?"

"Sure Dave, I just wanted to add to what I'm sure are many calls already—"

"That there's some big guy out there, looking for information about the police chief?"

"Exactly," said Junior. "Sounds like it's that Sasquatch guy you'd mentioned. Have you seen him yet?"

"Yes, I just caught a glimpse of him through the blinds," said Dave.

"Are you going to run him out of town?"

"Can't really," said Dave. "He might be scary looking, but that's not illegal. He's told some people he's just passing through, and decided to take a break, so I'm sure he'll move on soon. I'll just stay out of his way."

Dave had briefly considered using his fade to spy on Sasquatch, but he was still worried about attracting the evil spirit and corrupting his power again.

"Up to you," said Junior. He paused. "Want me to see where this guy goes for you?"

"Sure, if you don't mind," said Dave. He didn't like having to let Junior do his work for him, but at least he'd be safe in here.

Chapter 5

Dave was glad to see Friday roll around. Sasquatch had left, as expected, and a week later the local gossip had moved on to something else. However, every day his detachment got a little busier, with a few more incidents on the log, and new decisions for him to make. He'd hoped for a leisurely ten minute stroll down Main Street to the Grande Hotel, but tonight it was far from quiet. The weather had turned cold again, with grey clouds rolling in, but the sidewalks in front of the stores were jammed with tables and racks, all piled high with what looked like their complete inventory. Music blared from cheap sound systems, and almost every tourist in town was out shopping.

He finally met up with Mike by the post office. "What's with all the shoppers? Are the stores having a late spring cleaning?"

"You need to get out of that office more," said Mike. "This has been on since yesterday. It's our annual Summer Daze sale. That's Daze spelled—"

"Yes, I get it. Bargains for the tourist?"

"Mostly old stock," said Mike. "But it's surprising how many people can't resist a chance to pick up junk—sorry, bargains—to take back to the big city. And then put it in their own garage sales."

"Not for me," said Dave. "The only bargain I need is a cold glass of draft. It's been a busy day in the office—again." Police work involved far more paperwork than most people realized from just watching it on TV. Dave had finally finished all the reports for the fraud and murder charges from their big bust, but Staff seemed an insatiable pit when it came to reporting. Fortunately Sheila took at least half the load. She'd assured Dave that all she was seeing was just their typical summer complaints: lost keys and lost kids, a fender bender here and there, a few too many beers at a loud party. Not the excitement that Dave was used to, but he still missed being able to talk face to face to JB about it.

Mike paused as they entered the bar. "Whoa, busy night here!"

It definitely was crowded, and noisy. Dave glanced at his watch. The night was still young, as was the crowd. The wall TV's all featured some talking heads doing a sports commentary, thankfully muted. 80's music filled the air from the satellite feed, filling in while a local band set up on the stage. The wide patio doors at the other end were open, letting some of the fresh night air in, along with a whiff of smoke. He'd have to remind Sid to tell the smokers to keep a bit of distance. A crowd of kids, looking barely legal, crowded one end of the bar, doing shots with Sid and slamming their glasses down with a yell. Sam was doing her best to make her way through the crowd with a tray filled with quarts and glasses, while back in a corner he saw that Rosie had managed to save them some seats. He nudged Mike, "Go sit with Rosie, I'll be over after I talk to Sid. I assume we'll start with a pitcher."

Mike nodded and moved off, glad-handing along the way. He was a popular mayor, and likely to be around for a while.

Dave walked over to the quieter end of the bar, and motioned Sid over. "I just dropped by for a beer or two. Looks like you and Sam have things pretty well under control. Norris is on tonight. The number is forwarded to dispatch, but hopefully you won't need her. Except for maybe that crowd at the end of the bar. They're all legal, right?"

"Yes, I checked," said Sid, "They're in town for some cottage parties this weekend. Forecast is for showers, again, so we might see them in here more too, even if to just pick up beer. We've been doing some shots, but I'll slow them down a bit, and talk them into some appetizers."

"Sounds good," said Dave. JB had run the bar with a good combination of diplomacy and firmness but Sid was still learning how to balance being a buddy with customers with being a watchdog over them. Dave handed him a twenty. "I'm just over there with Rosie and Mike. I'll take a pitcher of Two Rivers over with me and save Sam the trip."

He threaded his way carefully back to the table, nodding to the regulars he knew from the town, as well as some of the tourists he'd met. He smiled when some did a double take at seeing him dressed casually. "Thanks for saving us a spot, Rosie. You can stop nursing that one beer, now. Here's a fresh supply. Me first though, I need one."

"Much appreciated," said Rosie, as he poured a round. "Been a long week, Dave?"

"Yeah, I heard tell you had a problem at a speed trap the other week," said Mike.

Dave sighed. Well, that didn't stay quiet for very long. He leaned forward. "I did, but keep it down, okay?"

"What, did you catch the mayor's wife again?" asked Rosie.

Dave chuckled. "No, not her. Sheila doesn't have to do any more high speed runs for hubby for a forgotten briefcase." He dropped his voice a bit. "Something more serious, from my past."

"From Toronto?" said Rosie.

"Right, from that undercover work I did on gangs. I don't want this spread around, but the guys that busted me passed through here."

He went on to tell them about seeing the bikers earlier that month, leaving out the part about getting strange vibes from the group.

"Are they still hunting for you?" asked Mike. "Oh wait—that biker that was snooping around the other week, he's one of them, right?"

"Yes, he is," said Dave. "But just one of many. And I think he was just being nosy. My contacts down south tell me that the gang hasn't forgotten me, but I'm not a high priority for them. They won't be back." He really didn't need his friends worrying about these bikers. And as for the evil feeling he'd had, well, that was just between him and his First Nations friends. "Don't worry guys, there'll be no more people snooping around for me."

"Other than that Minister's aide, Emily?" asked Rosie, with a grin.

Dave groaned. "Ah, yes. She'll certainly be back soon to check on the project here, and on me. Maybe Sheila can fend her off." Emily had tried very hard to get friendly with Dave last time she was up. She was young, pretty, fashionable, and driven to succeed. She worked hard, but partied hard when off, in many of the Toronto clubs where Dave had worked undercover. She hadn't recognized him from back then, but certainly had wanted to start up something. And she seemed used to getting what she wanted.

"We'll watch for her," said Mike. "Don't want JB getting jealous again. How are you two doing now?"

"We're taking a break, I guess," said Dave. He wasn't sure that was what they were doing, but he did know he missed her. "She's pretty busy with her summer courses, plus she has a part time job in a pub near her place, downtown somewhere."

"So who's turn is it?" said Mike.

Dave looked confused. "What do you mean?"

"Well, in my experience with these 'taking a break' things, someone does or says something to trigger it, and the other person reacts, then both get offended and pull back and wait for the other person to make the first move. Maybe you two aren't sure of how you feel yet. And you're both afraid to be the first one to blink, to let down their guard."

"Wow, pretty deep," said Dave. "Enough about me and JB. You should run a call-in advice show on the local radio station. If we had a local radio station, that is. But is it really that complicated? Is that what you and your wife did?"

"We did have a few buttons we'd push, but we were solid enough to know when to be firm, when to compromise, when to give a few hours space and when to move in and give a hug. You'll get there."

"I suppose I could call her," Dave said. "Later. Anyways, there are lots of local issues to keep me distracted. We're seeing an increase in drug related crime lately. Not just from specific busts, but finding them as part of searches for other crimes. Like DUI or kids at parties. Wilder parties too. Not just soft drugs either, we've run into meth and crack too. No Fentanyl yet, but I'm sure that's next."

"Maybe it's our summer rush bringing supplies up with them," said Rosie. "How about here in the Roost?"

"Nothing major," said Dave. "Sid doesn't have the same touch JB had with people, but he's learning. He's getting pretty good at spotting underage drinkers. I don't see kids sneak out the back door anymore as I come in the front."

"Actually, I heard they've set up a sort of early warning network," said Mike. "When you're spotted a text goes out to their friends. If any are here, well, they're out the door."

"That's just great," said Dave. "We really need to get into more social media. I'll ask about it when I'm up for training next month."

"You have to head off in the summer?" asked Rosie.

"Yes, but just for some basic things, mostly refreshers and firearms qualification. It's every year, up in Winnipeg. And of course when there's an opening you have to go or Staff Scully makes your manly parts into bookends. Only about five days worth of training, with a weekend in between. But, enough work talk, let's talk baseball. I'm looking forward to the big tournament."

"It's ours already," said Rosie. "I've seen your team. You might have been good at the curling bonspiel, but in baseball—even slow-pitch—you've got nothing."

That was what Dave was hoping to hear. "I disagree. I'm confident that our perseverance and teamwork will more than compensate for that. Shall we make some side bets?"

Dave pushed back from his desk and glared at the pile of forms. Here it was, still June, and already things were getting a lot busier, what with the summer crowd moving into their cottages and park visitors coming in for camping supplies. Some also came in to have a few too many drinks at the highway restaurant or the hotel bar. At least the party crowd was not as wild as when he worked at downtown bars in Toronto. Or maybe it was some of the same people, but just mellowed out with summer. He looked up as Reese walked by the door. "Reese! Heading out on patrol? Wait up."

As Dave climbed into the SUV he patted the dash. "You're managing to keep this fairly new looking."

Reese smiled. "Except for my embarrassing slide on an ice patch last winter, I'm doing well. It hurt my pride more than the fender. You'd think that growing up in Kenora I would have learned to drive better in winter."

"Don't be too hard on yourself, you're good. I hardly noticed it next to the dent I did."

"So, is this a ride along to check my driving?" said Reese.

"No, I just wanted to get your viewpoint on something. Last month it had looked like we cleaned the whole drug scene up, but now I'm not sure. You're from a small northern town like this, with a lot of summer traffic coming in, a nearby reserve, and many similar issues. How do you read the atmosphere in Kirk's Landing? We're getting more calls every day—mostly minor issues but still very much on the rise. Is this a normal summer buildup?" He thought he knew part of the answer, but it wouldn't hurt to get his rookie thinking about it.

"Actually, it's more activity than I would have expected," said Reese. "We did discover quite a drug trade going on as part of those problems at the mill, but I'm pretty sure most of that is busted up now. Maybe that crew were working behind the scenes back then to keep things quiet. Maybe they wanted the town to run smoothly to avoid drawing attention to themselves."

Dave nodded. "So they acted like their own police force, and this is the rebound back to normal. That was my thought." He didn't think that was all the answer, though. He still had those occasional twinges to his senses, a feeling of being watched, a hint of something evil in the town. Maybe this bad vibe was affecting others, without them being aware of it. "But do people just seem somehow different to you? Less of the laid-back small town atmosphere?"

"I think so," said Reese. "We've had more drug related calls, too. Not a lot of people mellowing out from whatever they're taking; it seems to be bringing out the bad side of some people, especially the summer visitors."

"I saw you interrogating one of those visitors the other night on the dance floor, a pretty little redhead."

Reese grinned. "Oh, Sara. Just chatting her up, she's just up for a month. She was sitting with Darlene, from the post office. Back to drugs though, Darlene had mentioned them to me the other day."

"What, as in she's selling?" asked Dave.

"Ha. No, nothing like that," said Reese. "She just mentioned there seemed to be more slightly spacey-looking kids around this year, both local and tourist. She's from Winnipeg, and said she'd seen her fair share of them there at a drop-in centre she helped out at."

"Well, glad you see the same trend in drugs here I do, but so far it's staying quiet. I've my eye on a few people, like Risso. And Kurt."

"Rosie's nephew?" Reese tilted his head. "Well, maybe. Has a bit of a record down south."

"And lots of extra cash lately," said Dave. "But him and Risso can't be the only ones pushing things up. I suspect more supplies are coming in, from a new player. But it's hard to track. Nothing to justify getting a drug dog down from Winnipeg." And definitely not enough for him to risk using his fade for intelligence gathering. "Thanks for your feedback. If we keep an eye on this we shouldn't have any problems." Dave pointed down the street. "I'll do a quick look at the beach area today, then walk back. Drop me off will you?"

Dave walked along the park, near the edge of the town beach edge. It was usually fairly quiet, but it didn't hurt to have one of them patrol it periodically. The water was supervised all summer by the lifeguards, local kids, but they didn't really watch the park. Everything looked okay, but that sense of being observed was back again. He glanced at the change house as he walked by, and saw a dark shape rush past the door of the men's side, and then around the side of the building.

"Hey," he yelled.

Dave had thought it might have been Risso, but by the time he got there he was nowhere to be seen. He'd been a minor player in the big scandal last winter, and undoubtedly he was involved in something illegal, yet again.

He put a call in to Reese, "Are you still downtown?"

"Nope, just out by the curling club. I was checking that it's still closed up for the summer. Do you have a problem?"

"I think I saw Risso skulking around here," said Dave, "but he just disappeared on me. Vanished into thin air."

"Maybe he ran off into those woods at the end," said Reese. "There's some cottages through that way. Supposedly empty."

"That's true," said Dave. "We should check them out. But right now, Risso's not worth chasing. I'm sure he'll be back. I thought he was fairly clean now, but you never know. We'd thought there was more drugs in town, maybe he found another supplier."

Dave took one more look around the park. Whoever was there, was gone now. As was that feeling of being watched. No matter.

Chapter 6

Norris drove carefully through the downtown traffic and managed to find a spot right in front of the cafe. Why didn't all these tourists just stay at their cottages or walk? It's not as if it was a huge town. Maybe they just missed having a suburban mall to drive to. She grabbed Kurt's parcel from the seat and headed in.

"Good to see you," said Rosie. "I heard you found a new summer guy to help out, someone you managed to entice out of retirement."

"Just for the summer," she said. "He retired from Vancouver last October and moved here. Nice guy. His name is Angus MacGregor. Angus for short."

"Not Mac?" said Rosie.

"No, he said that was fine when he was a Staff Sergeant, but now he's just a lowly constable again, so Angus is fine."

Rosie smiled. "How's he like being bossed by a sweet thing like you?"

Norris felt herself blush. "Hey, what's not to like! I'm a paragon of inspiration! But seriously, there's been no problem at all. He's an okay guy and we both know when to follow Sheila's orders. He's used to being in charge of a bigger detachment with lots of paperwork and rules, so he's fine with all these forms. He's just part time for now, but I would guess that will change."

"I'll look him up," said Rosie, "and give him an official welcome." He pointed to her hand, "What's in the parcel?"

"Oh, it's for your nephew, Kurt. I was up at the junction when the bus came in from the east. This was on it." She walked over to the group of teenagers in the corner. "Hi guys," she said. Some ignored her, some nodded back, but Rosie's nephew just glared. Bit of an attitude there.

"We're not doing anything wrong," Kurt said.

"Just saying hi," she said. "And dropping off your package. Looks like there was a problem with it." She pointed to a tear along one end, obviously re-taped.

Kurt looked at her, pale, wide-eyed. He glanced at the side door next to him, then back at her, then slowly walked forward.

"M-m-m-y parcel?" he stammered.

"Yes, from your supplier in Toronto—your girlfriend is it?"

He nodded.

"Looks like it was torn in shipping. It might be damaged, but if you want to check it out I can confirm it was like this when I picked it up. They're pretty good about claims here."

"No, I'm sure its fine," he said, clutching it to his chest.

"Well as long as there's nothing illegal in there," she said, "I'd hate to see you smuggling in Tim Horton's coffee for the southern customers to get their fix. Rosie already makes good premium selling it to city people who don't prefer his fresh roasted blends."

Kurt just nodded, then shoved the package under a table.

She glanced down at the pile of t-shirts on the table, then picked one up. "Good you have more stock coming. Rosie had told us you were selling these."

Kurt scowled. "Trust my uncle to snitch. Won't even let me make some money. What laws have I broken now?"

"Actually, I don't think there will be any problems with this," she said. "I do like this one. It has an interesting design, with some strong colours. The others look good too. These should sell well with the tourists."

Kurt looked surprised, then gave a little smile. "Actually, this design is one of my girlfriend's. She's the artist. So I'm okay?"

She nodded her head. "Yup, I've no problem, unless someone complains. I assume Rosie is all right with it, and it's not as if there's another place in town carrying these styles. You know, Junior is helping set up a pow-wow here for the end of August. Just a small one but maybe you can sell stuff there too. Just don't start up a head shop back in here and start selling pipes and incense."

Kurt gave a little nervous laugh. "No, we're clean."

She laughed. "Just teasing. Take care, guys." She noticed that a few more nodded back. Tiny steps. She turned back to the lunch counter. "Rosie—just a decaf please."

Rosie slid over a mug and poured. "Kurt looked to be a little jumpy with you, but maybe he just had a little too much caffeine to wake him up. But speaking of getting a fix, rumours are we still have a drug problem here in town."

"The summer crowd this year does seem to be a noisier crowd," she said, "especially when they all pack into a cottage. We've had to close a few parties down. They don't realize, or maybe don't care, how far noise can carry across the water late at night. And we don't always shut them down that graciously either. One warning visit then that's it. We're still a small staff, even with Angus on board, so there always seem to be extra shifts. The overtime is nice but if I'm planning a quiet evening at home I get grumpy if called out. But anything specific, Rosie?"

"No, it's nothing definite. The town seems grumpier, if that's something a town can be. Maybe it's the weather—hasn't been a great season so far. But, nobody's too extreme, other than that scary looking biker last week, snooping around."

"I heard," she said. "Dave didn't seem very concerned about him though. I'm sure he found our little town completely boring."

"Boring is fine with me," said Rosie. "Anyway, I don't see anybody trying to deal here in my cafe, but I hear talk. Junior has some concerns too. Just more from what the kids tell him than any real evidence. He does have strict rules about drugs for all the kids he's trying to help. He's caught the occasional one with a joint, but nothing more serious. However, they do tell him there's more coming into town this summer, more than last year, and not just weed."

"And he's sure that none of the kids in the drop-in are involved?"

"He's pretty sure," said Rosie. "He's been through all this himself, so once he gets to know a kid a bit he can read the signs and tell if he's hiding something. He's good at it too. And says he's sensing more negative vibes—however he does that."

Norris had noticed that Junior, as well as the native elders, seemed unusually skilled at reading people. They claimed it was just from watching carefully, but Norris wondered if there might be more involved than that.

"How about Kurt?" she said. "Do you think he's okay? Is his new business keeping him out of trouble?" Dave had asked her to keep an eye on Rosie's nephew.

"Oh yeah, he's a good kid. He wasn't that keen on coming up, but it was sort of an ultimatum. The deal was sweetened by a new gaming system—an X-Box I think. He's on it all hours of the night. Must be lonely but at least it keeps him off the Internet."

"Actually if he's playing games, he's still on the Internet. And a lot of games now are multi-player, with voice chat added, so he's not really alone. Didn't you notice your data usage going up?"

"To tell the truth, I don't really monitor it that much," said Rosie. "I have a box upstairs for myself. But I set up some free wi-fi so people could come in and check their email and maybe read news sites on-line. That's what I use it for."

"You should check," said Norris, "Your customers can likely access anything they want if everything just has the initial set-up. And these game consoles also have email and chat and web browsers, so they can do a lot more, even download movies. Legally or illegally. The games aren't cheap to buy either, at sixty or seventy bucks each. His t-shirt business must be doing quite well. If you want I can tell my friend Mike to drop by and lend some of his computer savvy. He can make sure your free wi-fi has limits on it."

"That would help," said Rosie. "Shit, I feel old. Where did you learn all this stuff?"

Norris laughed, "From being a single mother with an eight-year-old. Amazing how many questions they ask, and how fast they learn."

Chapter 7

JB slouched at a table in the university library, surrounded by her friends and their books. Most of the others were just picking up the odd course over the summer, so were from a variety of programs, with different interests and backgrounds. Life in Kirk's Landing was fine, but she'd missed this kind of interaction with so many different kinds of people. None of the others around her were in the Integrated Studies program, like she was, since it was still fairly new. She sipped on her luke-warm can of ginger ale, then leaned forward. She was busy trying to explain to a new student what she was hoping to learn in the program.

"It's pretty neat, Mary. I think you'd like it. You can mix around pretty well anything when you put it together, as long as you can convince your adviser that it isn't just four years of easy courses. They need to see that there really is enough hard work and focus in it to justify a degree."

"Still sounds like it could be a bit of a scam to me," said Mary.

"No, they are pretty strict," said JB. "If anything, you have to work harder than the regular program, and if your average slips at all you can be kicked out."

"So, what's your mix?" said Mary.

"Well, I want to find a way to help my people more. I'm Anishinaabe—Ojibway—from a small reserve in Manitoba, and I really want to focus on our youth. I had a lot of problems growing up there, in spite of my grandfather being band chief, so I want to help the younger ones to learn to avoid some of the worst pitfalls, and take pride in themselves."

"So you want to be a teacher?"

"No, not up there. It's too small a place for a high school—everyone buses out. And the public school in town is pretty small, so it would be hard to get into. Something a bit more general, I think. Maybe supported by the band council, as a way to apply some of the funding we get into more of a cultural program. My plan is to take some sociology, First Nations history, criminology, art, anthropology, conflict resolution, and business."

"And they'll let you mix all that?"

"Hopefully," said JB. "First I have to get good grades in my summer courses, to show that I'm serious this time. It won't be easy, and I'll still be a bit of a loner on campus. Even now, I have a few courses with you guys but most classes I don't know a soul."

Yvon looked up from his book. "And she's working too. Quite a busy little thing."

"Yeah, I'm doing some shifts at a pub near where I live. It's a nice little place, and fun to work in. I'm just west of downtown actually. Can be a little sketchy but that adds to the character. Back home I ran my own pub, so it's nice to be just another server. This way I can still get out and see people without as much late night bar-hopping that brought me down last time." In truth, her resolve to avoid all the parties had lasted only a couple of weeks.

"It sounds like a full load," said Mary. "I couldn't handle all that. Have you met any cute guys in your spare time? Other than our Yvon here of course?"

JB laughed. "I have no spare time. Besides, I've sort of got a guy back home."

"Sort of a guy?" said Yvon.

"No, Dave is definitely a guy. RCMP."

"Wow, with that sexy red uniform and everything?" asked Mary.

"That's for dress occasions. His day to day stuff is plainer, but, yes, sexy."

"Still cool," said Sue. "Does he have a gun?"

"Yes, but so do most of us in the town," said JB. "Even me. No big deal, it's for hunting, to fill the freezer. Partridge, moose, deer."

"Ewww," said Sue. "I'm quite happy to get my freezer stuff from Loblaws. But back to this hot guy back home. Why did you come down here so early? Somebody get too serious too fast?"

"No, not that," said JB. "My Criminology prof offered me some work interviewing local First Nations people and their issues. Right up my alley." Truth was, as far as Dave went, she still wasn't sure what had happened. "This guy—my guy—he really changed over a few months. For the better, though. I mean he started off as a real loner. He'd been assigned up there temporarily, so he was just waiting to finish his time and go back to the big city after a few months. But something happened to him. He opened up, took an interest in our town and our issues, and ended up doing a great job. Really cleaned the place up." She left out all the evil spirit details as being a little too much to try to explain.

Mary gestured for her to go on. "So all the more reason to stay?"

"Well, I was impressed," said JB. "A guy that knows where he's going and what he wants is kind of sexy. Myself, I'd been sort of drifting along for a while, with no real plans. I'd been down here a couple of years ago, but I wasn't sure why at the time. Back then I took some general courses, partied, learned how to do graffiti—"

"What, like tagging?" said Mary.

"No, mural type stuff," said JB. "It was fun. I met some great kids, helped a few with their ideas, mastered a new art form, but none of that was part of the course. I ended up dropping out. Anyway, seeing the changes Dave made in himself motivated me to decide to do the same. He was planning on moving back down south anyway, so I figured I could go back to school, he'd be moving down here too, and we'd be together. But when I told him my plans, he blind-sided me. Said he liked it up there and had decided to stay. And he assumed that therefore I would stay too."

"Typical male," said Mary.

"Hey," said Yvon.

"Well, I tried to explain why I wanted to come here," said JB, "but he wasn't listening, really. He just heard that I wasn't staying. Then he acted like it was no big deal if we were apart."

"Jeez, dump the guy," said Mary. "You're cute, there's lots of available guys down here."

"There are, but I think this guy is the one," said JB. "We really clicked, and have a good match on things."

"And the sex?" said Sue. "Is that one of the good match things?"

Yvon laughed. "Yes, tell us more."

JB blushed. "It's just fine. Let's leave it at that, okay?" She checked her watch. "Shit, I have to head back to my place. It's near the Transitway, only a short walk from the Tunney's stop, but still can be a little sketchy late at night. See you guys tomorrow."

JB thought about Dave as she walked to the bus stop. She'd got an email, all chatty about the town, but it wasn't the same. Neither were the calls. She wished they could just talk about what was wrong between them.

Chapter 8

Rosie looked up, as the cafe door opened, and frowned. "Risso, I didn't think I'd see you in here again. Not that you were ever much of a customer."

"Hey, I paid my fine and took my punishment. I got rights. Gimme a Timmie's coffee to go."

Rosie poured his coffee, and pushed it across the counter. "I saw you driving around today with some friends in a flashy car. Have some new buddies here?"

"They're some business acquaintances from Winnipeg," said Risso. "Just here on a vacation, so I'm showing them around. They heard all about the big bust here, and my frame-up."

"Frame-up is debatable," said Rosie, "and you did manage to get off pretty easily, so far. I'm thinking more might come out once all the investigators start digging deeper."

"No worries," said Risso, "I'm clean now. Said that to the judge. All that's in the past, done with. I told him I just needed to get back to work to help support my girlfriend's kid. We all make mistakes, right?" He added four packets of sugar and three creams, tossing the garbage carelessly on the counter. "No, I've a new idea now. I'm looking to get into some tourist business here—maybe manage some cottages. My associates are going to bankroll me on some things, that's why they are touring here. They were saying they heard even up in Winnipeg our local police chief was a hero. I told them Browne was a new guy, from down south, right?"

"Yes, I was glad we were able to clean up the town," said Rosie. He certainly didn't want to share any more details about Dave than he had to with slimy Risso. "Things have changed now, you know. You'll find people are a lot more aware of what's going on. It's like the whole place is on neighbourhood watch now. If your new associates are looking to cause problems here, you might want to tell them to try another town."

"Hey, my friends are just here on business. And it's a free country, they can go wherever they want. I don't like this poking into my affairs."

"Just saying," said Rosie. "I'm not prying, but I do wonder at some of your connections. There was apparently a lot of drugs floating around here last year, and talk of bikers in town from Winnipeg. Is that where your new friends are from?"

"Oh, here and there," said Risso. "Look, I'd better get going. Thanks for the coffee."

As Rosie cleaned up the counter he watched Risso swagger across the street to his friend's SUV, and climb in. The driver glared at Rosie, who in turn smiled and scratched his cheek with his middle finger. The driver scowled and roared away as Rosie turned back to start clearing some tables. He'd only done a couple when Dave walked in.

"Speak of the devil," said Rosie. "Your friend was just in here asking about you."

"Risso? Yes, I saw him leaving. He looked very guilty when he saw me, so I was wondering what scheme he's up to now."

"Something about cottage rentals," said Rosie. "Maybe it might keep him from being such a pest."

"Don't hold your breath," said Dave. "It's only a matter of time before he gets bold enough again to start complaining about all the wrong things everyone else is doing. What did he want this time?"

"He kept poking around trying to find out where you were from and what you'd done before."

"What did you tell him?" asked Dave.

"I evaded his questions, but I'm sure he'll keep asking around town and find out eventually. I'm betting it's not on his own initiative, though. He's probably asking on behalf of his new 'business associates'."

"The ones in that big black SUV?" said Dave. "I saw them cruising around earlier. Very much a gangster look, but I think they're more comfortable riding on a chopper."

"They seem to be trying to stay low-key, like regular tourists," said Rosie, "but they look more like trouble. Pretty rough around the edges. I wonder if their visit is related to that big hairy biker that blew through here?"

"Oh, I don't think so," said Dave. "But I've already added them to my list of people to keep an eye on." Privately, he had his suspicions that those two were linked to Sasquatch, but he didn't want to alarm others. It would have been so easy to just fade and eavesdrop on Risso and his friends, but he remained firm in his resolve to not use his power. He had no desire to let that evil force get near him again.

Dave had just left Rosie's when his cell phone rang. "Corporal Browne here."

"Hello Corporal, it's Emily." There was a pause. "Emily Boucher? Aide to Harriet Gottman, the Minister of Northern Economic Development."

"Yes, sorry, I remember you now," said Dave. "Hi, how are you?"

"I'm well, thank you. How about you, busy?"

"I usually am," he said, "but it's a rare quiet day today, so far. I'm just heading back into the office."

"Are you still up for that lunch we promised each other last time I was up?"

"Sure," he said, carefully. He didn't remember a lunch promise but Emily reconstructed the past better than any salesman or political aide he'd known. "It's on my to-do list."

"Well, to-do is today," she said. "The Minister sent me up here to check on the Centre of Excellence she's helping set up. I've a couple of meetings, but I'm free for lunch. My treat—I've bought some picnic things already. I can drop by and take you to that park by the lake. It's such a beautiful day, it would be a shame to waste it. When can you sneak away? Dave? Still there?"

Dave scratched at his neck. He was at a loss for words, a common thing with Emily it seemed. He was never sure how to fend her off. "Ah, yes, I'm here. Sure, okay, drop by at 12."

He was busy working on yet another report for Staff, when there was a call from the front counter.

"Boss, someone one here for you, says she's your lunch date," said Sheila.

He rushed out. "Not a date, just a meeting."

Sheila just smiled, with a raised eyebrow.

"Hi there," said Emily, as she gave him a big hug. "So glad to see you again, I swear you look nicer every time."

She handed him some bags. "Goodies in here. It's so nice out—why don't we walk down to the park?"

It seemed to Dave that everyone in town happened to be out for a walk just as he and Emily decided to head down Main Street. He wondered briefly if Sheila had initiated the emergency phone tree call-out, just to keep him under surveillance. When Dave had arrived her main function had seemed to be to spy for her husband the mayor. Now she was a loyal member of Dave's team, keeping their work confidential, for the most part. However, she still did love her gossip. All the locals, and some of the summer people, knew he'd been serious about JB, and that now things were not as serious. As he walked down the street, a few people recognized Emily, her hand on his arm as they stepped off the sidewalk. She was chattering away, fashionably dressed, carefully made up, and with the most interesting perfume. All were likely speculating like mad behind his back. He carefully disengaged Emily's arm from his, just as Reese drove by and blipped the siren.

"Sorry, I'm on duty," Dave said. He just hoped news of this lunch didn't get back to Staff, and was glad to reach the relative peace of the park. "How about that table over there?"

"Oh no, here is good, right in the middle. I brought a blanket," she said, spreading it out beneath a tree. "It's not huge, but we can squeeze together."

Dave settled down carefully in one corner, as she unpacked dishes, cups, cutlery, napkins, and a myriad of containers and baggies of food. "Wow, you sure are organized."

She smiled, "I hope you meant that as a compliment." Emily carefully set out their lunch, while still talking. She was always politically focused, saying the right thing, speaking in sound bites, likely filing away his every comment. Politics, hitting the fancy clubs in Toronto, and hitting on him seemed her only interests. But he had to play this game if he wanted to know what she was planning. Emily always had a game plan. He was suddenly homesick for JB and how he always felt relaxed and comfortable with her.

"Dave, hello. Earth to Dave." Emily was leaning forward looking into his eyes. Leaning very forward.

"Sorry," he said, quickly grabbing some food and sitting back. He tried to ignore the way her skirt was creeping up her leg as she sat next to him. "Just thinking."

"Hopefully about me," said Emily.

"Well, sort of," he said. "I was thinking of the program your Minister is setting up. Tell me, did the meetings go well so far?"

Emily sat back with a disappointed look.

"Yes, all went quite well. We were working out the details of startup funding, and who could be on a sort of oversight committee for the centre. The band chief had some good suggestions. Of course, we're arranging some suitable signage to remind people how their government is using its money for this program for them."

"Their money," said Dave.

"Sorry, what do you mean?"

"It's actually their money that they gave to you and now you're giving some of it back."

The air seemed to have chilled.

"That's what I meant," said Emily. "Pickle?"

They continued to chat about Kirk's Landing and its people, with Emily even asking about 'his little native friend'. He was non-committal, as he wasn't sure where he and JB stood. He noticed Emily looking at him speculatively, as she held up a tetra pack of wine.

"Care to loosen up a bit?"

"No, thanks," said Dave. "On duty. And illegal here in public."

"Spoilsport," she said, and brushed carefully at the front of her blouse. "Oops, bread crumbs. Tell me, is it quieter here after the big mill scandal?"

"Sort of," he said. "We've lots of summer residents in town now. It's just the normal list of minor complaints and infractions, but it still keeps us busy."

"Good," she said. "We of course would rather not have any more news of scandals or hard drugs or corruption. Or murders. Word is that you impressed a lot of people, though, when you cleaned it all up. I'm sure we can use that to help you move out of here and back down south. And a couple of steps up also."

Dave paused. Little pieces of the Emily agenda were peeking out.

And just like her to assume she could get her boss to ensure Dave was back down closer to her. "To be truthful," he said, "I'm starting to like the quiet country life. Weird eh?"

"It's all right for a change, I'm sure," she said. "But I think you're a better fit for the social life in Toronto. Mind you, some of the places down there are getting a little too wild now. Lots of drug busts to ruin the evening. How about up here in Quietsville, more drugs?"

"We're seeing some with the summer traffic, a bit more than expected, though," he said. "Why do you ask?"

"Oh, nothing official," she said. "I heard some talk at meetings, that drug problems seem to be on the rise in smaller towns, more so than the usual summer rise."

"Isn't 'Tough on Crime' supposed to solve all that?"

"Supposedly," she said. "Not everyone shares the same enthusiasm for that approach, though. Unofficially of course. And besides, you have to catch them first. I'd be glad to pass back any suggestions you might have for ways to approach this—again unofficially. And with credit of course. You can't stay up here forever, and my Minister does have some influence. Think about it."

He liked the idea but was spared trying to balance that with his official chain of command, when his radio squawked. It was Reese, saying he needed him back at the station.

"Sorry, gotta run," he said. "But thanks for the nice lunch, and a visit."

Emily leaned in for a hug but he'd already scrambled to his feet. She sat back, then smiled brightly as she adjusted her skirt. "My pleasure, Dave. I'll keep in touch. And not just for those future club dates."

Chapter 9

Sasquatch put his feet up on his desk and opened another beer. It felt good to be back in Toronto. Not that the trip to Winnipeg hadn't been a good idea, though. Aside from getting out to show the colours, he'd been able to see what was really going on, and slap some people around a bit. They were getting soft up there. If they didn't hurry up and figure out what it took to intimidate their competition, their whole supply chain would get run over by the new gangs of immigrants. Same problem everywhere, really. This was an operation that he had taken years to build up and he had no intention of giving it away. He rubbed his shoulder and frowned. He'd been back a few days but still had some aches and pains—he wasn't as young as he used to be. In addition, looked like they were losing their monopoly here in Toronto, in spite of his best efforts. He was looking forward to setting up new markets in some small towns and then just sitting back and skimming off the profits. The trip had been worthwhile, but the weather in Manitoba had been miserable, with just one rainstorm after another. Same with the return trip. He'd been glad to load his bike on his friend's truck in Thunder Bay and board the flight to Toronto. His detour into that little town had been a good idea, though. He never did meet that cop face to face, but he'd pretty well confirmed it was the same narc that they'd busted in Toronto. He rubbed his eyes. Damned headache. He took another sip of beer then held the bottle to his forehead. Next on his list was to follow up with that idiot up north, Risso.

He grabbed his cell and dialed.

"Risso? Hey, it's Sasquatch. I've been checking the Winnipeg reports again, and it looks like business used to be good, but you've managed to pretty well kill it all by yourself."

He listened for a while. "Blah, blah, blah—whatever. So it was a big bust, I get it. And now it's over. Most of your customers are still there, right? Plus now the summer crowd. They still have needs, and it's up to you to supply them before they find another source. I think you're either getting lazy or you're trying to screw me over." He paused. "Whatever. Look, you had a good operation going before, all you had to do was get to work and put things back together. Louie and Bonnie are down there to make sure that happens. But I can't afford to babysit you, either, so this is your last chance. Once they're satisfied, they're taking off, so stop your whining. I'll be back too in person, later on, so you'd better have a busy summer. Now, is there anything else I should know about?"

He cradled the phone while lighting a cigarette.

"Wait a sec. Are you saying your biggest competitor is a scrawny loser kid from Toronto? Come on Risso, grow a pair! Don't you even know how to deal with a mail order drug trafficking scheme! Geez, were you born last night?"

Sasquatch sighed heavily and rubbed his forehead. "What's his name? Kurt Wilson? I'll check him out. How about the cops?" He listened, then frowned. "I know about that new guy. Don't worry, the cops won't be a problem. I'll be up later on to deal with them." He frowned as Risso continued, then slammed his fist down on the table. "Christ, you are so pathetic. That's it. I'm not waiting until August.

When I get up there I'm kicking your ass all the way up and down their main street." He banged the phone down, then sat back, shaking his head. What a loser.

"Another trip?" asked Spider.

"Yeah, looks like it. Kirk's Landing, back in Manitoba. That Risso sounds like such a screw-up, I don't think Louie will be enough to fix things. I need to check this one out in person, and soon. After the July weekend, once I clean up things here."

"That's a long ride to do again, though."

"Which is why I'm flying. I'll use all those points we scammed last year. Plus, this lets me be a little more subtle."

"You're a little big to ever be subtle," said Spider. "Is that the same place you ran the speed trap?"

"Yes, and I'm pretty sure the cop I saw was our old buddy Bear from down here. Maybe he wasn't just snooping from another gang, maybe he was working undercover."

"Pretty good cover if it was," said Spider. "I think you're wrong, 'cause I heard he was still causing trouble up in Chicoutimi." Spider saw the look of rage building on Sasquatch's face and immediately back-pedalled. "But maybe not. Good idea. So if it's him, will you take care of him permanently?"

Sasquatch sat back into his chair. He'd been ready to pound Spider out for a minute there. "Yeah, I'd like to do that." He smiled at the thought.

"Sure you don't want me up there to add some muscle?"

"No, you stay here. The other cops all sound like losers, sent there just to get rid of them. There's some young kid, an old guy out of retirement, and a woman. We'll be able to move in and start things rolling right under their noses, once I decide what to do with this snitch. Plus a couple of my Winnipeg people are there already, Louie and Bonnie. He's tough, and she's sneaky, a real charmer."

"Is Badger looking after Winnipeg for you?" said Spider.

"No, he decided to take off after all, back out West. He said something about too many Indian ghosts and relatives around there. No loss, really. He was starting to drive me nuts, acting all jumpy, always staring above my head, like there was somebody standing behind me."

"Maybe he sniffed too much glue in prison," said Spider.

"Or not enough," said Sasquatch. "They'll manage okay up there." He let out a belch and added his empty bottle to the pile on the table. "See you tomorrow. I'm off to the mall. I need to get a haircut and buy a suit. Funny, I always said the only person that would get me into a suit would be an undertaker. Guess I was wrong."

Spider dropped a case of empties by the meeting room door. "So, when's your big trip? It's been a week—not that I'm pushing."

"Shut up, you ass," said Sasquatch as he peered at his monitor. "I'll go when I'm ready. That Risso maggot said the cop was going out of town in early July. Not that I have to explain anything to a useless dipstick like you." He looked around the clubhouse. "Shit, clean this place up, will ya? It looks like that dump those losers in Winnipeg live in. Go on! I've some email to check."

Sasquatch sat for a while, scrolling through messages, while Spider collected empty bottles and full ashtrays.

"Aha," said Sasquatch. "Finally something useful from Risso. He found a local article about that bust they had, that has a photo of their new chief cop. Come here—look familiar?"

Spider peered at the screen. "Yup, that could be Bear. Hair is trimmed, and no beard, but same build, and there's those spooky eyes that could look right into you."

Sasquatch laughed and slapped Spider on the back. "I knew it. We need to teach him a lesson. Speaking of which, what about that kid up there. The one what was sneaking in drugs. Kurt, I think. Any more news around here about him?"

"Yeah, I asked around," said Spider. "Street talk was that he was a little punk around the neighbourhood last year, almost got busted a few times. Mostly running a bit of dope, some little scams. I think he's from a rich family in Rosedale, and just comes downtown for some excitement. He and his girlfriend were starting up some sort of business selling these dumb t-shirts she makes, and then suddenly he takes off. To Kirk's Landing it turns out."

"Did he dump the girlfriend?"

"No," said Spider. "They still look to be in business at least, she does all these designs here, then sends packages of t-shirts to him."

"Yeah, yeah—get to it—what's the point?"

"Point is she's been buying a lot more lately—mostly hash. But not passing it on locally."

"Aha," said Sasquatch, "So care packages to the boyfriend. That fits in with what Risso was saying, for a change."

"I can't see them hurting our business that much up there though," said Spider. "Maybe we just forget about it."

Sasquatch wheeled around, anger building in him, and gave Spider a shove into the wall. "Are you crazy? Jeez, don't go soft on me here. We need to teach these two kids not to mess around with us, remind them who's in charge. Same goes for that cop up there. Have someone pay the girlfriend a visit, rough her up a bit."

"I'll get to it, boss," said Spider. "Don't get upset. My guys can handle that. No broken bones, but they'll trash her apartment. They'll convince her to see the error of her ways."

Sasquatch turned back to the desk. "Good. I need Risso to find me a place up there to work from too, starting after the July weekend. I've already arranged for a new supply of drugs to get to him from Winnipeg."

"So he's still going to be our main contact there for things?" asked Spider.

"So far," said Sasquatch. "But it depends what I find up there. If this slump is because of his screw ups, he's finished. I want to see first hand what the place is like, who some potential customers are, if he has any Indian contacts we can use, who he uses in his network. And this damn cop. Then I'll make some decisions."

"This whole business of supplying drugs to the small towns is a pretty big change for us," said Spider. "Some of the guys have been talking, saying they don't like it."

Sasquatch slammed his fist down. "Too damn bad. If they don't like it they can get out. Are you bailing on me?"

Spider just shook his head.

"Good. If we stop thinking up new angles those chink gangs will screw us. Small towns have lots of tourists and that means sweet little spoilt rich kids with daddy's charge cards and no daddy to see what they spend it on. All day parties, big boats, hot cars and back woods cops who wouldn't know a hit of acid if it fell on them. And if we play it right we can get the Indians to market it and then it's harder to trace back to us. You got to start thinking big picture Spider or you'll be left in the dust. My dust."

So what about the cop," said Spider. "Is there any way you can get at him?"

Sasquatch paused for a moment. "You know, there might be something. Risso had mentioned this cop had a girlfriend down here too. Maybe at university."

"Here in Toronto?" said Spider.

"He wasn't sure, but thought maybe Ottawa. An Indian girl, he said. Shouldn't be that hard to find one that's at a university. Look around, see what you can find. I'll see if Risso can get a name. Now go get some beer, I'm dying here."

Chapter 10

JB checked her fan. Yes, it was on high. It was sweltering in her little apartment, up on the third floor of the old house. She wondered if another fan would really cool her or would just move the hot air around. She supposed she could head over to nearby Westboro beach for the afternoon, but she did have a paper to work on and needed to focus. She missed the fresh air of home. Granted she was near the river here but it was still in the middle of the city—noisy, dirty, and crowded.

She didn't just miss the fresh air, she also missed her friends, her family, the town, her bar, and Dave. The new school friends here were fun to talk to, all full of their studies and dreams, and her job was good, and she managed to spend the occasional evening downtown in the Market's pubs. Last night had been a late one though, again. She was tired now and the heat didn't help. She really did miss Dave. She wanted to call him and have a talk, but didn't want to push. Maybe she could just call her little brother and chat. She'd try her new toy, a tablet with video calling on it. Junior had set it up for his artsy sister so she could keep in touch.

"Hi Junior," she said, "it's me."

"Yes, I can see that," he said. "Long time no hear from you. So, sis, how are you?"

"Lonely."

"I thought you said you'd be too busy to miss us?"

"Well I was wrong, wasn't I. Sorry, it's hotter in here than the kitchen at the Roost and I'm grumpy." She decided to leave out the hangover. "It certainly has been busy, though. Work is good, and my courses are great. The one on First Nations history is fascinating, in spite of the few militants taking it that seem always ready to lead a march. Much of it I know already from talking to grandfather and the others, but this adds material from across Canada. I like finding out more about our roots."

"You'll have to give a little seminar when you get back. Are you coming up during your reading week?"

"It's not really a week," she said. "The summer is already a tight schedule, so we get basically a long weekend. I may just stay here."

"I thought you were lonely," he said.

"Yes, but I can always call you, right? I really do have a lot of work to do in my courses too. If I'm here then I can do some extra shifts at the pub. The long weekend is really busy so it's great for tips. The forecast is for sun so the patio will be packed."

"How is that pub, as good as our Roost?" asked Junior.

"It's fun. A tiny place though, much smaller. It gets pretty packed with the musicians and their audience, plus the regulars."

"Are the customers as nice as ours?" he asked.

"As nice, and as peculiar. There's quite a mix. Some are kind and gentle, some are rough and ready, from bikers to businessmen."

"Bikers as in motorcycles?"

"Yes," she said, "some on those, in leather. Or on racing bikes, in spandex."

"Hey, any catch your eye?"

She laughed. "There is one that's interesting, just as a friend, though. Dave and I aren't out playing the field, we're just trying to sort things out. I do miss him though."

There was a long pause. "You guys seem such a great match, sis. I don't understand what's going on. However, I do think you should check the ground rules with your guy again, sis, just in case he has a different set of them."

"What do you mean? Is he seeing other women?"

"Just one, but it's that Minister's aide that was here earlier, the one from Toronto."

It was her turn to pause. She'd disliked that woman from first sight.

"JB? Still there?"

"Yes, I'm here Junior, just took me back a bit. Guess I've been assuming too much."

"Well, to give him credit, she is very pushy and insistent. She showed up with a picnic basket and wouldn't take no for an answer."

"They went for a picnic?"

"Yup. They walked down to the park by the lake, spread a blanket, and were there for about 40 minutes."

"You were watching?"

"Didn't have to, JB, most of the town found an excuse to wander past the park."

"Oh, she is clever." Maybe it was less like a date and more of an ambush. And unfortunately, Dave could be a little naive at times.

"She left right after their lunch, anyway," said Junior. "Off to do more political stuff."

JB sighed. Maybe it was all okay. "Thanks for the update. I will have a talk with him. But anything else new? Another scandal? Floods? Locusts?"

Junior chuckled. "Nothing that exciting. We do seem to have a drug problem again, though."

"We as in our people?"

"No," said Junior. "We as in the town, and mostly the summer folks. And we've been seeing more strangers in town, not just part of the summer crew this year, but strange strangers. Tougher people, that seem pretty edgy to just be on vacation. Dave told me a weird story too, about a speed trap he'd set up." Junior filled her in on the peculiar feeling that had come over Dave. A feeling that had reminded him of when the evil had taken him over last winter.

"That's serious," she said. "Did you tell grandfather?"

"Yes, but he looked carefully at Dave's spirit, and didn't see anything wrong. Dave's power still works too—he just doesn't want to use it anymore. I think it scares him a bit, but his excuse is that he doesn't like to spy on his friends, that he's just a regular cop now."

"That won't last," she said. "He likes a challenge. And it's a gift he's been given and should use to help him deal with all these new people. Can you reassure him again that he's safe to use this power now?"

"I'm pretty sure it's safe, but not positive. We're looking into it."

"Good. How about your new youth centre? Having fun?"

"It's a challenge at times, but good to have it," he said. "It was nice of Rosie to give us that whole space in the back. That's where I am now, actually, just cleaning up. We've got some tables and chairs, and a small pool table that was donated to us by that business reporter last spring. Kids drop by after school for a bit, or after supper, just for a place to hang with friends. There's this interesting new kid showed up too, a summer kid, possibly even more hyper than you, and with an attitude sky high." He filled in JB about Melissa being captured by Dave and then described the obnoxious step-mother in detail. By the time he finished JB was lying on her back, hooting with laughter.

"Hello? Are you there?" he said. "Looks like I'm talking to your ceiling now."

"Stop," she said. "I can't take it." She paused and wiped her eyes. "Sorry, I had to put the tablet down. I can always count on my little brother to cheer me up. But it does sound like that girl needs your group. Good luck."

"Thanks," said Junior. "She's really quite the artist though. Good stuff, but some of it a little dark. There's not a lot of sunshine in her pictures. Sort of reminds me of those monsters that my friend Janie draws, that she says she sees around town."

"I thought she just did things, like fairies and castles and stuff," she said.

"She used to, but it's changed. She's been sketching her fantasy world since we were in kindergarten, I think. She's always maintained, at least to me, that she sees another world around her, sort of like a layer over this one. Then a few years ago they changed her meds, to control her flare-ups better. A side effect from that was more creatures. Sort of reminds me of the spirit world we talk about, but in her case I'm assuming she means in her imagination. Like writers saying they hear voices in their head. But maybe not, maybe she's seeing what's there. Her meds have changed her awareness somehow."

JB had heard stories of Janie's step-father hassling her too. He didn't ever seem to have a real job, just lay around watching TV and demanding he be waited on. "It's a good thing she has you for a friend, but she does need to get out more. As do all the kids up there, likely."

"I'm working on that already," said her brother. "I've been having issues with a few of the kids. Nothing big, just fights, stealing, and a shitty attitude. I'm hoping it's just normal teenage stuff but I don't want it to get even worse, so I'm encouraging them to get off their butts and do something. Some wanted to play soccer so I bought some balls and then told them to go ahead and organize it. I want them to figure out some of this on their own, not just sit around and wait for me, then complain they don't like it. I took them out on some hikes too. Summer kids, locals, natives all of us together on a hike. It was surprising how much about nature some of the summer kids know, and how little about it some of our people know."

"It is a worrisome loss," she said. "I'd be glad to drop by when I get back and talk about some things from here, about our culture and history. But you're managing to keep your centre drug-free?"

"As far as I know. And I can tell when they're being honest with me, at least the native kids. I use my power to see their true nature, to see what their spirit is telling me."

She laughed. "Do you tell them that?"

"Hell no, I want to keep it mysterious."

"How's grandfather doing?" she said.

"He's cool. He's enjoying the summer, always off fishing somewhere."

"Isn't he supposed to be planning the pow-wow for the end of August?"

"I thought so, but he's more like the ideas guy this year. I'm the one that does the magic."

Magic?" she said. "As in—"

"No, not our magic. Just all the logistics that make it happen. But the others on our committee are a big help. It's kinda fun juggling all these things. People are getting excited too, making costumes and practising dance moves. But grandfather did ask about you and Dave when I last saw him. I just said it was complicated."

"Oh, and what did he say to that?" she asked.

"He said it always seems that way, to just be patient. I did manage to grab him while he was there for a story session in the centre. Most of them liked it once they realized it wasn't a five-minute TV sound bite, but would be a long process to actually tell the story. Grandfather has quite a style."

"And the Roost? I assume Sid is managing, as I haven't had any panic calls."

"Yes, he's doing okay. Hasn't burned it down, no angry creditors at the door, Liquor Commission hasn't lifted the licence."

"Well that's encouraging," she said. "Anyway, thanks for talking, little brother. I'd better get back to my research paper now. Say hi to Dave if you see him, will you?"

"I just saw him come in the front. He's with Rosie now. Want me to get him? You can ask him yourself about his surprise lunch."

"No, that's okay," she said. "I'll catch him later. Gotta run. Love you." She hung up and shook her head. She'd chickened out.

JB leaned over toward one of her regulars, Matt, as he sat in the corner of the bar making notes.

"Matt, I know you're a writer, but there's a couple of serious bikers in the corner—don't look—who think different. The older one in particular is convinced you must be a cop taking notes on him and is talking of following you when you leave to find out for sure. I know the other one, and am trying to convince them otherwise. Just letting you know."

Matt sipped his beer and casually glanced over. "Serious and large bikers, I see. They're almost done their pints, could you bring them a couple more from me?"

When she did so, they paused in their conversation, and looked over at Matt. The younger one nodded, and they started talking again. A few minutes later she noticed Matt walking past them on the way to the toilet. More nods were exchanged, so she relaxed a bit. When Matt came out, the younger one invited him to sit. Next time she went by they were calling for shots, and he and the older biker were sharing what looked like baby photos—grandchildren, she assumed.

An hour later when the table settled up, Matt and the older biker left, amiably it seemed. She watched as Matt walked off, and the biker rode off in the opposite direction.

She stopped by the table. "Ron, everything seemed to work out?"

"Sure," said Ron. "His ID convinced us he was older than he looked, and he looked a little too soft and pudgy to be a cop. Twister and he seemed to hit it off once they got onto parenting and grandchildren. Not BFF's, but friendly."

"Twister? Let me guess, he's good at twisting people's arms."

"No, in his younger and thinner days he was quite a dancer."

"Really?" she said. "But I'm used to seeing you with another kind of biker. Is this a new friend?"

Ron paused. "No, an old one. We go way back. I used to ride with them, but then had some serious family issues and needed a break. He dropped a few interesting hints tonight, after I mentioned that you were a friend, and where you were from." Ron glanced around. "Best I tell you about that, but not in here."

"I was heading out for a smoke," she said. "Join me?"

"In the rain?"

"We'll stand just under the awning in front," she said. She waved to the other bartender that she was heading out, and grabbed her jacket.

She turned her collar up as they huddled against the window. "So?"

"This is because you said you're heading back home for a bit," said Ron "I'm worried what might happen to you up there."

"It's a pretty quiet little place," she said.

"Well, that may change. Twister is part of the Outlaws motorcycle gang here in Ottawa, and so am I. I mean I was, but still am, I guess. Anyway, the big gang in Toronto is the Hell's Angels, and the Outlaws hate them. Twister has heard the Toronto people are looking to make up for lost business in the big cities by tackling some smaller towns, especially those with lots of rich summer residents."

"Even Kirk's Landing?" This would explain the new people Junior had mentioned.

"Even Kirk's Landing. It's one of their first ventures. Some kind of partnership with a Winnipeg chapter. They've already started shipping some stuff, with locals as their distributors. Supposedly one of their top guys is heading up there to make sure it goes as planned, even if he has to break a few bones to make it happen. He used to be a pretty tough number. He's also going to be looking for someone up there he thinks ratted him out in Toronto. It could get ugly, so you need to be really careful."

"Thanks, I appreciate the warning," she said, "I've friends and family up there that I need to tell." Especially Dave. He could be the snitch they were looking for, and could be in real danger.

"Whoa, don't go blabbing it all over up there. Then it will get back to me and my friends here that I tipped people off."

JB was quiet. She didn't want to put Ron at risk, but she really did need to talk to Dave and pass this on.

"I'll keep it under control," she said. "I know a cop up there."

"A cop?" said Ron.

"And a friend," she said. "He's pretty smart about these things, and he's very discreet, from working undercover —"

"In Toronto?" asked Ron.

JB remembered Dave did not advertise where he worked before.

"He's worked out west," she said, "Anyway, I know he'll keep it quiet. But he really needs to hear about this. Trust me."

"I do" he said. "And watch out for yourself, just in case word gets around you're from there too. Now, what about that coffee?"

She nodded. "Alright, just a coffee." What the heck, why not?

Chapter 11

Rosie looked up as Dave walked in and shook his head. "Jeez Dave, you look like hell."

"Thanks Rosie, I always appreciate the support." He was feeling run down lately. Too much stress, too little sleep.

"Sorry, but I'm not sure if I should offer you a coffee or a sleeping pill. What's up?"

Dave shrugged. "Just another busy day." It felt like everything was piling up at once. Using his power might have helped a few times, but he was determined to do this as a regular cop, a normal one.

"Too many late nights doing paperwork?"

"No, Sheila and the rest have that under control," said Dave. "I just don't sleep well." The dreams were back again, like last winter's nightmares. Being chased all the time, by something dark and cold.

"I'm just closing up," said Rosie. "Let me finish here and switch the lights off. Go ahead into the back room. Junior has just closed up the youth centre for the night so we can relax there."

Dave walked into the back room, shrugged off his jacket, and sank gratefully into one of the chairs. The room was nicely set up, with some old but comfy looking furniture, a pop machine, pegs for coats, stacks of magazines, a book case, and a small pool table. He put his feet up, and focused on relaxing. He was about to drift off when his phone buzzed with a text from Reese. Although he was the newest and youngest member Reese was also the biggest techie of them, and had always been on Twitter and Facebook before he joined up. Hopefully he'd be able to help Dave work out some sort of social media policy. There was potential to use it for more than just lurking and trying to sneak into some groups—hopefully they could be more positive.

"More trouble?" said Rosie.

"Nope, a note about an early shift change. They're switching over to Constable MacGregor for the night shift. Others are on call, including me, in case something big comes up."

"What, is anything big expected?"

"Oh no," said Dave. "Likely will be just the usual house parties that get going a little too much. Even in the middle of the week the summer crowd still likes to party. Surely you remember from your younger days."

"I may have had friends that had that happen to them, but I never had my parents go away to Detroit one weekend and forget to tell Aunt Bertha to check in on me."

Dave laughed. "Thanks for that, Rosie."

"Glad to help. So, and I'm making a random guess, not based on any experience, if the parties don't close down you're back at them in a few hours?"

"Yes, they get only one warning before we get serious. Besides some noise tickets we might manage a few underage drinkers. Used to be the occasional soft drugs too, but we're seeing some hard stuff now too."

"You'd mentioned that," said Rosie, "but is it still mostly summer people?"

"Yes, I think so. Most of them have the cash, and the boredom. It looks like it's more than just people with a stash they brought up with them, though, as new supplies are coming into town for them too. I'm just not sure how. We can handle it, but I'd prefer to shut all that down sooner than later, especially with more people rolling in. More drugs means wilder parties, more petty crime, and this year, more fights too. Plus I keep waiting for those bikers to show up. I don't know if they made me or not, but if Risso keeps nosing around he may find something." He sighed. "How is Junior doing with his youth centre?"

"It's growing, slowly," said Rosie. "There's some new art going up on the free wall out back that's pretty good too. I think it's by a new summer kid."

Dave laughed. "I think I know who. Just a warning, stay clear of her mother!"

"I've heard," said Rosie. "You know, I really sympathize with the kids up here. That's why I'm helping to get this drop-in centre going. I remember seeing some of the same depressed looks on Toronto kids that I started seeing last year up here on some of our local kids. I wanted to do something to help them out. It was just good timing that Junior was looking for a way to get involved too."

"He's good with them," said Dave, "He has a nice firmness but doesn't handhold them either."

"He does some wilderness stuff too. Nothing fancy but seems to be helping some to slow down and smell the flowers, so to speak."

"How about Kurt, your nephew," said Dave. "Does he ever show up?"

"He's dropped by and talked to Junior a couple of times, but he's also pretty busy with that t-shirt business. Right now he's upstairs. He was on-line but I think he's talking to his mom now."

There was a sudden yell and crash above their heads. Rosie headed for the stairway, but was almost knocked over as Kurt rushed down. "What's the matter?"

"They got her, those bastards," cried Kurt. "Out of my way, I need out." He pushed past them, and out, slamming the door.

Rosie picked up the phone extension. "Hello? ... Sis? Still there?" He covered the mouthpiece. "It's his mom, sounds upset ... give me a minute."

Dave grabbed a ginger ale from the machine then sat back down. Whatever it was it seemed serious, with Rosie asking lots of questions. Dave wondered if he should chase after Kurt, then decided to wait and leave it to Rosie.

Rosie hung up and shook his head. "Not good," he said. "It's Kurt's girlfriend, Crystal, back in Toronto. Someone busted into her place, roughed her and it up pretty badly."

"Where is she now?" said Dave.

"She's at a friend's place. My sister's heading over, but she said no bones broken, just some bruises."

"Did she call 911?"

"My sister says no. From the description, sounds like some bikers. She thinks Crystal is caught up in some drug thing."

Dave raised an eyebrow. "Using or selling?"

"Selling, she thinks."

"And Kurt?"

"She has her suspicions. I'll talk to him when he calms down and comes back. He can't go far, but he'll be gone for a bit."

"I suspect he's more into it than you think," said Dave. But I'll leave that to you for now. He really doesn't trust me, but may have no choice."

"I'll try but he really doesn't talk to me a lot either," said Rosie.

"Well, keep me in the loop," said Dave. "You did say he seemed to have a lot of cash lately. I'll make some enquiries with my Toronto contacts." He felt better already, this was something more definite he could deal with. "What's her last name?"

"Castles."

Dave chuckled. "No, really?"

Rosie shrugged. "Some parents don't really think. But I'll let you know. Back to you though, other than party bust-ups, is there anything new? How's JB?"

Dave sipped his pop then sighed. "Yes, I guess that's bothering me the most. I do miss her."

"The Minister's aide didn't distract you?"

"No," said Dave, "if anything she made me think more about JB."

"So go home and call her," said Rosie. "JB, I mean."

"I think I will," said Dave. "Thanks, buddy."

He finished his drink and headed back home. It was a short and quiet walk up the block, with the streets unusually empty. The clouds were back, deepening the shadows along the street. He had a bad feeling. The gangs had made a connection between Crystal and her boyfriend up here. What if they connected him and JB? Once inside his place he grabbed a beer, and his phone, and called JB's number in Ottawa.

He got her voice mail, cheerful and giggling, saying she was either at school or working or out with her friends, so just leave a message.

"Hi JB, it's Dave. Uh, I guess you're out, I mean you're not there. Hope you're having a good time somewhere or doing something. I miss you, babe. Ah, and stay safe."

He hung up. That was lame. He hated message machines. He turned out the lights and headed to bed, not really looking forward to another day.

Chapter 12

Dave could still hear the phone, even with a pillow over his head. It was supposed to be his morning to sleep in. His staff all knew that.

He grabbed at the receiver and growled into it. "What!"

There was a pause, then a hesitant voice. "Dave?"

He sat up and smiled. "Oh, JB. Sorry, I was fast asleep and not expecting any calls."

"Well, I got your message last night—"

"Oh, that lame message?" He groaned. "I hate those machines. There's no way to back up and try again."

"That's okay, it was still nice to hear your slightly awkward voice. So, what's up?"

"I just wondered how things were going down there with you. You know, school and stuff."

"School is good," she said. "It's a hard mix of courses but I finally feel I've found my groove, and I'm looking forward to being able to apply this back home. The job at the pub is a good break too."

Dave settled back under the covers as JB described her courses and the bar where she worked. The sound of her voice was warm and comforting, just like old times. He was drifting along when a question brought him up short.

"I hear you had a hot date recently?" she asked.

He'd been afraid of that. "Oh, I didn't mean to," he said. "And it wasn't really a date. That Minister's aide appeared on a visit and practically abducted me for a picnic."

"Abducted? Big burly Dave? Hero of Kirk's Landing?"

He chuckled. "Well, she can be very persuasive. But it wasn't much of a date—not that I wanted one. She walked me down the main street and onto a blanket in the park. I think we had half the town watching as chaperones."

JB laughed. "I know, I've seen her in action, that's why she's good at her job. Very convincing, a good marketer."

"It was more stressful than enjoyable," he said. "She was pumping me for information on drugs in town, trying to pass it off as rumours she heard in Ottawa. I deflected pretty good and pretended I didn't notice, but I'm not sure what she was after. Other than me of course! Maybe she and her Minister are just afraid our town will stop being quiet again. Fortunately, I'd prearranged an exit strategy with Reese before I had to get rude with her."

"Exit strategy?" JB asked.

"Exactly, just like what people use on blind dates. I told Reese to give me 45 minutes and then radio me with some office emergency so I could get out of there in one piece!"

JB chuckled. "Good one. I'll have to watch out for that. How's work?"

Dave sighed. "Challenging. We've been seeing more drugs lately coming into town, from several sources we think, but we can't seem to track it down. Maybe some bad sources too, as we're seeing more bad reactions. And I think some bikers that passed through one of my speed traps were the same that I ran from in Toronto."

"Junior had mentioned that. Did they recognize you?" she asked.

"Maybe. We didn't stop them, just let them ride through. I'm hoping they're not planning a return." He decided to not mention the shiver he had felt, in case she started worrying about his special power again. She'd probably try to talk him into using it. And Sasquatch was another worry he'd keep to himself, at least until he had more to go on. "In addition, our local pest, Risso, is suddenly asking a lot of questions around town about my past."

"Why would he care now?" she said.

"Probably related to his new friends. There's a couple who are visiting from Winnipeg and pretending to be respectable tourists. Not doing a good job of it, though, as his tattoos and her fishnet stockings sort of point to their roots."

"Charming," she said. "What else?"

"Rosie's nephew, Kurt is staying up here now. He was having some problems back in Toronto so his mom decided he needed to get away for a bit. But we just learned that his girlfriend down there, Crystal, was beat up, maybe because of her involvement in some drug thing. Actually, we suspect Kurt was part of it too, and still is."

"Jeez," she said. "You do have a lot to worry about—how are you sleeping lately?"

"Not that well actually, but I'm hoping things calm down soon." He wouldn't mention the return of his nightmares.

"Well, I'm pretty sure your biker problem is just going to go away. I heard something from a guy I know that hangs out in my bar. He's a biker, as in pedals around the local back roads with his friends. But he has a motorcycle too, and said that he used to be in the Outlaws."

"Nobody 'used to be' in the Outlaws".

"Well, anyways, he appears to be a nice enough guy now, and I think a reliable source."

"How nice?" said Dave.

"Look Dave, do you want this information or not? This guy's just a friend, okay?"

He heard her pause and take a breath. "Sorry, go ahead," he said. She had been pretty understanding about Emily.

"So, I was outside the pub having a smoke with this friend, and he mentioned that he'd heard the Toronto Hell's Angels were thinking of expanding to other places."

"Did he say who he'd heard it from?" asked Dave.

"He said it was from one of his former Outlaw friends. Apparently the two clubs don't like each other, so he didn't feel any loyalty to the Toronto crew."

She went on to tell Dave about the drug expansion, the selection of Kirk's Landing as one of the places they were starting in, and that they seemed to be trying to hunt down someone that had ratted them out from Toronto.

"Oh, all not good," said Dave. "What else? Would he have any more details on people or dates?"

"No," she said, "and please don't try to track him down to question him further. He told me this in strict confidence and is still worried the Outlaws have their eye on him. Just saying that your problems may get worse."

"Alright," he said. "Thanks. Glad you called. I mean, it's great to just chat again with you, but this news will be a big help. First off, it confirms my suspicions, that they're likely supplying Risso. More importantly, it sounds like they do suspect I'm here and will be looking for me. They'll make the cop connection pretty quickly. This doesn't make things much better but it takes some of the worry and guesswork out of it, so is good news I guess." He tapped his finger thoughtfully. Better the devil you know, as they said. Bad news that this was a specific focus on his town, but at least he had some more definite things to go on, and maybe wouldn't have to lean on his special ability after all.

"I'm wondering if what happened to Kurt's girlfriend is connected to all this too," she said.

"Might be," he said. "Or maybe Kurt and Crystal just had the bad luck to pick Kirk's Landing as the place to run their little importing business. I had a friend checking up, discreetly, to see who was after her in Toronto. He did confirm it was bikers, and he suspects they may visit her again. He assumes the crowd she's with will just get her into another drug deal, if they haven't already. Too bad, as I hear she's a great artist and has an eye for the next clothing trend the kids will be into. When I finally got to talk with Kurt about her, he said she had started in fashion school then just got distracted. And now she seems stuck."

"I know the feeling," she said. "Does he think she has potential?"

"Well, I'm just going on what I heard from him and Rosie, but apparently so. She just needs to get out of the rut she's in."

"So tell her to come here." said JB.

"What, to Ottawa?"

"Sure, there's a fashion school just opened near me. I can help her find a place to crash too."

"Thanks, that would be great," he said. "I mean, I don't know her or how messed up she is, but hopefully it will work. If we could get her out of there it just might make a difference in her life. That would make her, and Kurt, and Rosie very happy."

Dave closed his eyes and relaxed, as they kept on talking about her school, his work, the fishing derby, her new second hand bike. Dave's stress was melting away, for the first time in a while. He suppressed a yawn.

"Sorry," he said. "All this lack of sleep is catching up, now that I feel a little more relaxed. I miss our chats."

"I miss you too, Dave," she said.

Dave paused. Might as well get it over with. Damn, he'd faced down armed criminals with less worry. "So, are we good?"

"What do you mean?" she said.

"I don't know," he said. "It just feels different. Weird."

He heard a sigh.

"Yeah, I know what you mean." It was her turn to pause.

"JB?" he said.

"Yes, still here. Not sure how to say this so I just will."

Shit, here it comes. The brush-off. "Please, tell me," he said.

"Well, I've come down here because I needed to do that in my life. It's where I need to be right now. I have some things to learn about myself, and my people, and I need to pick up some new skills to help them. Because, as much as I do enjoy my friends here, the pubs, and the parties, this is short term, just a means to an end. Long term, I want to be back home, and hopefully with you."

He let out his breath. "So we're good? You're still my girl?"

She chuckled. "Of course, and you're still my guy."

Alright! "So do you think you might be coming up for your reading break?"

"I would love to, but between work and my heavy course load, I may be one of the few that actually uses it as a reading break. But we can still phone, or email, or Skype."

"Skype?"

She laughed. "Ask Mike, he's a techie. And come the fall, I have a lighter schedule, so hopefully can get home more. Look, I have to run and catch a bus for school. Glad we talked, I mean really talked. Love you."

"Me too," he said.

After they hung up, he curled back up under the blankets. Her news took some of the guesswork out of the issues he was facing—including their relationship. He fell back asleep listening to the birds chirping outside his window.

Dave sipped his morning coffee and stared at the email from his old boss. This was a surprise. Inspector Williams had managed to talk him into hiding out up here for the standard two-year posting, and now it seemed he was trying to talk him out of it. There was an opening back in Toronto, working on the Integrated Task Force with border security at the airport. It would include a promotion to Sergeant, and a chance to write promotional exams for Inspector rank. It wouldn't be until January, but Williams thought it would be a good career move. As for the heat around Dave from the gangs, his old boss was sure that had died down already.

Dave certainly didn't agree with that, not with all the recent attention he'd been attracting, plus JB's warning. It was a tempting offer, and a few months ago he might have taken it, but he liked his little town now. And he liked running the detachment. And he really liked JB. Granted, it looked like for the most part their romance would be mostly long distance, but at least it was a romance again. His only reservation was whether he could deal with these drug threats, and the associated bikers, without relying on his ability to disappear and putting himself at risk. Maybe Junior finally had some answers. It was time to call and check.

"Junior," he said. "Dave here. . . . Doing fine, thanks. Quick question—did you ever hear back from the elders about my power, whether I was safe against whatever evil is roaming around town? . . . Really? Are they sure? . . . Okay, thanks for checking buddy, I just wanted to find out one way or the other."

Dave sat back and stared out the window. So, no worries, they had said. That was a relief. As much as he wanted to prove to himself he could be a regular cop, he appreciated the help his power gave him, enhancing his abilities, acting as a tool he could use. Junior had settled the last of Dave's concerns—he would stay. Now he just had to write a careful refusal back to the Inspector, emphasizing the people skills he was developing and his First Nations connections. Maybe even hint at extending his tour. He'd leave out JB, though, and while he'd mention the challenge of new drug sources coming into town, he'd definitely not mention that they were likely headed up by Sasquatch. This was a problem that Dave wanted to deal with on his own.

Chapter 13

Dave sat at his desk going through the Monday morning pile of emails. They seemed to accumulate like mosquitoes, an analogy he would never have considered before moving to this province. Fortunately Sheila had already sorted them for him, into urgent, routine and interesting. He noticed with a smile that she had already replied to some urgent ones from Staff Scully requesting status updates and crime statistics. He'd already shared with his staff that he was not bailing on them at the end of the year. They had all been relieved to hear of his decision, including Sheila, who immediately started developing some long term reports.

Dave could hear her at her own desk, just outside his office, humming away as she double checked all the complaint files that the constables had entered on the computer over the weekend. He had tried to tell her months ago that she didn't have to do that since the system was supposed to be automatic, at which she had rolled her eyes and challenged him to find even one file without an error.

"You members just give me the raw data, and I will mold it into a masterpiece of accuracy and uniformity," she had said.

Dave was not going to argue with a gift like that, and it had reaped many rewards. Now he could pull up statistics to show when their busiest times were, relative crime rates, and exactly where they were in their budget. Plus, on her own, Sheila could easily answer requests for status updates from Staff Scully, who apparently had not yet figured out how to access the data from his own terminal. She had come a long way from being the former mayor's mousy little wife, there only to spy on the detachment for her husband. She'd just needed some encouragement, and the realization that her husband was just using her. She'd certainly come into her element.

Dave called out to the main office. "Sheila, thanks again for sorting the e-mails and even answering some of them. I don't know how I would get along without you."

"Don't think I'm going to do this all the time," she said. "I was in early anyway. But seeing as you're sticking around, I don't mind keeping this under control."

Dave smiled to himself. So far, even though she said she wasn't going to, Sheila had in fact looked after his e-mails every day. At first he thought it was just because she was still being nosey, but recently he suspected that she was really enjoying her work. But he wouldn't accuse her of that and ruin her game.

Sheila poked her head in the door. "From the incident log it looks like it was a relatively quiet weekend. I guess now that the weather has finally cleared up, all those teenagers can get outdoors and blow off some steam. And there weren't even any complaints from Risso for a change. Should we check if he's okay?"

Dave laughed. "No, we'll let him be. He's been quieter since we got him on a violation of that protection order. A lot less calls from him now complaining about how rotten all kids are, or that people are rolling through stop signs, or there's too much noise from the bar."

"People were surprised he got off so easy," she said, "with just a big fine. A fine that didn't seem to bother him much, either. I didn't think he had a huge salary as a quality supervisor."

"Well, he was involved somehow in that whole quality cover-up," said Dave, "so we think he picked up some extra cash that way. Nothing we could prove, and he did spill a lot of dirt on Barbaro, the head of security. Turned out Risso was pretty pissed off they had tried to set him up as the fall guy. So that information cut him a bit of a deal. He'd already lost his truck and of course his guns, from that issue with his ex, but once again he managed to avoid jail. Personally, I would have preferred to skip the leads he had and keep him locked up and out of our hair."

"He's still the same sleaze, too," she said. "Gives me the creeps, the way he looks at me."

"I know, Norris says the same." Dave was pretty sure Risso was involved in some of the drug dealings that were still going on, slipping back into his old life of petty crime. "Don't worry, we're just giving him some rope and leaving him free to dig himself into another hole. Or whatever, you know what I mean. He's a bad enough crook, it will only be a matter of time. Rest assured, he's on our radar."

"Don't mention radar," she said. "I still get teased about that speeding ticket I got last year. Rushing around for that silly husband of mine." She paused, then continued. "I'd like to thank you for not going on about my husband like most everybody else in town. I know he was weak, but we're trying to put that behind us. I get a bit tired of everybody always asking for all sorts of details, like we were some stupid reality TV show. I think being a mayor just went to his head too much and he lost his path. He's a good man even though he doesn't think things through sometimes."

Dave nodded. "That's okay. No need for me to pry." The irony was not lost on him that Sheila, although she meant well, was his biggest inquisitor when it came to his relationship with JB.

Sheila continued. "Anyway, I'm over it now. He's started building furniture again, like he used to before he got elected."

"And the Highway Restaurant?" said Dave.

"He would like to sell it, I think. That whole affair was a close call for him, but he's in a better frame of mind now. As for me, I'm just happy to get out of the house and keep this all running smoothly." She waved a hand at Dave. "Get out of here now and enjoy the sunshine of this lovely day. It's time for your constitutional walk down Main Street. By the way, if you're by the post office, drop by and see Darlene. She told me after our last knitting meeting at Rosie's that she has something she wants to talk over with you."

"Will do," said Dave. He grabbed his hat from the rack, snugged up his belt and holster, and headed outside.

Sheila was right, it was a nice day to get out and walk, especially after a weekend of rain. On the way to the post office Dave met Chief Bourbeau, and gave him a respectful nod.

"Morning, sir," he said.

"Morning, Corporal," said the chief. "Charlie will do for a casual hello. Beautiful day in our quiet little town."

"It certainly is," said Dave, "but looks are deceiving. We can't let the hot suns of spring distract us from the growing cracks in the ice." Dave was a little smug that he could pull out a cryptic native style saying but he tried hard not to show it. Or maybe it was something his grandmother used to say. "At any rate, right now we are trying to find the source of all the drugs that seem to be coming into town."

Charlie looked at him with a faint smile, then nodded. "My band police tell me the same thing," he said. "More drugs around, but we're not sure from where or how. We should talk soon. Has your power been a help in getting some information?"

"Actually, I haven't been using it," said Dave. "I was uneasy about spying on friends, and more than a little gun-shy after the way it turned on me before. But Junior tells me you've all decided that I'm fine to use it, it's safe."

Charlie patted Dave on the shoulder. "Exactly. Your power is a part of you, of what makes you a policeman." He paused. "What about that 'power of the hand' thing you did last winter? Where you just 'pushed' at us all?"

"Oh that," said Dave. "No, I think that's gone. Why?"

"I think that was from the Wendigo. It's good that it's no longer there. Dave, I think you know deep inside yourself that the evil is gone from you, and cannot return. You'll recognize it now for what it is, and deny it any space to get in."

"You're sure it's all right?" said Dave.

"Absolutely," said Charlie. "Here, let me walk with you while you try it out. I'll let you know if I see anything to worry about."

Dave trusted the chief more than anybody he knew. And he certainly could use whatever help he could get to dig into these latest problems. As they continued down the street, he carefully tried his fade. He paused to listen to the chatter from a group of tourists, but heard nothing very revealing, other than talk of dinners planned and work projects waiting for them back home down south. It did feel okay as he used it, and it was nice to know that he still had that ability, if needed, especially with the guarantee that it was no longer an evil spirit that consumed him. He paused outside the post office and looked at the chief.

"Looks good to me, Dave. Stop worrying and trust your instincts. You're a good guy and a good cop. We're glad you've decided to not rush off at the end of the year."

"You heard?" said Dave. "I just told my staff this morning. Did Sheila . . . ?"

"No, not this time," said Charlie. "It was Reese. All happy you were staying, sharing the news. I think he assumed it was okay. What did my granddaughter say?"

"I was going to call her tonight," Dave said. "Please, not a word. If she finds out from someone else, I'm dead."

"Mum's the word," said Charlie. "I won't send a psychic message." He paused. "I'm joking Dave. We don't do that. Carry on. I'm sure I'll see you later."

Chapter 14

The post office was busy, like the rest of the town, with both locals and summer visitors. Several people were checking their mailboxes along the wall, and there was a long lineup at the wicket.

Finally it was Dave's turn at the counter. "Hi Darlene, I hear you're running out of post office boxes."

"Yup, looks like the busiest summer yet." She looked around, then leaned forward and lowered her voice. "Our new Mayor had passed the word to the business owners to be on the lookout for unusual things in our quiet little town. Well, I've been noticing that more people than usual want post boxes for all their mail from down south. Usually they don't bother while they're up here, just use general delivery for some odds and ends. And a lot of them are getting small parcels—more than I remember from last year. Not from online shopping either, but private mail. Might be nothing, you know, but I thought I'd pass it on."

"Thanks," he said. "While I'm here, I need some stamps for some snail mail, maybe ten. Have you got any new designs?"

"I have some nice summer flower ones here, maybe not you. Here's a First Nations series—selling fast."

Dave bought his stamps and turned to go, almost bumping into the woman behind him. Just as he excused himself he caught the eye of one of the summer residents, reaching into her mailbox. It was a young woman he'd seen almost every time he dropped by the Raven's Roost, but she looked startled at seeing him there and quickly yanked her small parcel out of the box. The wrapper caught on the latch, there was a tearing sound, and two small baggies of white powder fell on the floor. Everyone froze, except the woman. As Dave yelled to her to stop she just bolted out the door.

No problem, he knew where she lived. He motioned toward the door. "Sorry folks. Could I ask you to leave for now?" Looked like he might have just solved the mystery of where the extra drugs were coming from. Maybe there was more. "Please don't open any more boxes, I need to secure the area. Darlene?"

"You can come back later for your mail folks," she said, "We're locking up now."

While she herded everyone out and locked up, Dave contacted Norris to send Sheila down with a roll of crime scene tape and some evidence kits, and to go herself to the suspect's cottage to see if she'd run back there.

"Good call Darlene," he said. "I guess your suspicions were well founded. I'm going to call up to Winnipeg to see if they can get a dog down here today to sniff around."

It was late afternoon before the dog handler from Winnipeg called to say he was at the turnoff, looking for directions to the post office.

Dave met him at the door. "Hi Fred, thanks for coming down so fast. I was hoping we could do this today, as people are antsy to get their mail—well except for those that heard we busted someone earlier. They may never be back. I think you'll find something in some of the boxes, and maybe in today's batch of mail."

"So what's our grounds for search?" asked Fred.

"A resident dropped those two bags of powder on the ground as she emptied her mail box. I suspect the bags are drugs but I'm not sure. Although she fled, we think there may be more." replied Dave.

"And what are our grounds should Shadow indicate other targets," asked Fred.

"It's a grey area so I phoned Staff on this one to get his take on it. Case law varies. We could use the two bags as grounds for a search warrant for the whole mail area but we aren't going to be able to prove possession. I suggested to Staff we are more interested in tracking down the sources than laying charges. He agreed."

The two men stared at each other as they mentally sifted through the murky nuances of Canadian common law.

Fred made up his mind "Okay, let's get to it. The unsorted mail we can just spread out on the table."

"I know you like to let your dog work the scene on his own," said Dave, "so I'll stay out of your way. Go ahead in through the wicket door when you're ready. I closed the connecting door to the store next door, so you don't get distracted by other things."

"Shadow is pretty good at focusing," said Fred. "We had to do a search once in an auto repair shop. They refused to stop working but we just kept at it. We found drugs all over. I guess they figured all the smells would confuse him."

Dave stood quietly while Fred and his dog quickly worked the lobby, finding nothing except the spot on the floor where the woman had dropped her package. They then went through the wicket and started checking the individual boxes methodically, one row at a time. After that, they spread out the day's mail and checked it all. When they were done Fred called Dave in behind the counter.

"Good call. Shadow indicated on packages in six of the boxes, and gave me a maybe on one empty box. There may have been something in it before, can't be sure. I used a bit of chalk to mark them for you one x on maybe's, two on a definite. And we found two on the incoming mail pile. I set them aside."

"Thanks a lot," said Dave. "You two do a great job. I would have expected even more, though, given how much I suspect is in town, but at least I've found one source."

"Now what?" said Fred "Do you want some help tracking these people down? I'm sure Shadow would find more in their houses."

"No, I think I'll back off a bit," said Dave. "I know which people to keep an eye on now. Maybe they'll help expose some local suppliers. If you'll give me a hand I'll take a sample out of each marked package for testing. I'll stick them back here in the safe and leave a card for people to call at the wicket for them."

"Would they do that?" said Fred.

"You never know," said Dave. He paused. "I'm guessing that you'll likely want to head back today, but can I buy you coffee and a piece of pie at the cafe? It's very good. And your dog will be welcome too, as a member of the Force."

"Sure," said Fred. "I'd like that. Shadow might settle for just some water and a biscuit though."

Dave gave Darlene an update, then they took all the marked parcels out and replaced them with cards. They'd found five suspicious customers in all. One was a local, the rest summer visitors. He stripped off the crime scene tape, then headed up the street with Fred and the dog.

Chapter 15

Dave held the door and ushered his guests into Rosie's. "Rosie, this is Constable Grey, and his dog Shadow. Fred, this is Rosie, chef and owner."

Fred smiled and shook hands, while Shadow just sniffed the air eagerly.

"Lots of coffee smells here for him," said Rosie.

"Oh, he notices those," said Fred, "but I think he's picking up more." He looked at Dave, raising an eyebrow.

"Should be fine here. Rosie is cool, let him explore," said Dave.

"Lots of gossip about the post office today," said Rosie. "Any luck? Or is it just 'no comment'."

"We did find some good leads," said Dave. "But for now, if anyone asks, tell them it's an ongoing investigation. Keep people guessing for a bit, and I'll see what happens."

They followed as Shadow led Fred past the counter and booths, the dog casually sniffing here and there. Once he got to the back couches, he headed for a pile of t-shirts in the corner, under a box, and suddenly was more interested. Fred spread the pile out, then pointed Shadow back at it. He sniffed again, then sat back.

Fred flipped through the pile. "Nothing here, but there was.."

"Thanks," said Dave. "I think I've found another of the sources for drugs this summer."

"That damn girlfriend of his," said Rosie. "I bet she was sending him stuff up here. No wonder he had lots of cash." He glanced at Fred, then Dave. "Now what, guys?"

"It's Rosie's nephew," said Dave. He looked at Rosie and shrugged. "I'll just start off with a talk with him. He might just be new at this. Bring him in to the station tomorrow."

"Thanks," said Rosie. "Say, can we check the youth centre in the back too?"

"Dave, do you suspect anything in there?" asked Fred.

"No," said Dave, "it should be okay. But it would give my friend here some piece of mind, if you don't mind taking a quick look. It's empty now, as they're all off somewhere exploring in the woods with Junior."

Fred and Shadow headed into the back room, and found that it was clean except for a long sniff the dog took at a jacket on a hook. Dave reached in a pocket, rooted around a bit, then opened a small inside zipper. He took out a joint, sniffed it, then put it back in.

"Not worth busting somebody over," said Dave. "For now."

"I think I know that kid, he's new here," said Rosie. "I'll let Junior handle it."

"Is he good at that?" asked Dave.

"He's amazing, can read the kids like a book, freaks them right out. New ones try to snow him with some story, he just narrows his brows and gives them a hard, quiet look. Kids that know him just sit there with a grin, waiting for the boom to fall. He's the same with adults too, I know I can't put anything over on him. Not that I'd want to, mind you, it's just that he can seem downright spooky."

"I'd like to meet this kid," said Fred. "Maybe he could team up with my dog. Shadow could point out the crooks, and this kid could sweat out their confessions with his evil eye."

Dave smiled. They didn't realize the edge Junior had, at actually seeing the spirit side of other natives. One of the benefits of that was that he could 'see' good or evil, truth or a lie. Dave wished his own power extended to that—it would be a big help. "He's not that weird," he said. "Well, maybe a bit. Now, how about some coffee and pie for us hard working defenders of justice?"

"Sure," said Rosie. "And I can get some water and a snack for Fred's partner."

Dave and Norris were going over some duty rosters at the front counter when Rosie and Kurt walked in.

Dave nodded to his friend. "Hi Rosie, Kurt, thanks for coming over."

"Didn't have any choice," mumbled Kurt.

Dave smiled. "I know you'll only roll your eyes if I say this is for your own good, see, there you go!"

Kurt gave a little smile. "I always hear that line," he said.

"Why don't we go into my office," said Dave. "I have some good news and some bad news, and hardly any lectures at all. Norris, could you join us?"

"Will we all fit?" asked Rosie.

"It's a little better now," said Norris. "We persuaded him to knock out a wall into our storage room, which gave him another five feet of space. Now he doesn't have the excuse that it's too small to do his paperwork in."

They all crowded in around Dave's new desk, slightly larger now, and remarkably clear. One wall was filled with shelves of clear plastic storage boxes, all neatly labelled.

"Nice," said Rosie, looking around.

"Angus's work. He likes organizing things, and seems to have a magic touch," said Dave.

"You sure he didn't used to be an interior decorator?" asked Rosie.

Norris laughed. "You've seen Angus MacGregor, right? Looks more like he used to be a wild Scottish chieftain."

"Well, first some good news," said Dave. "Kurt, I heard about your girlfriend's problems, and made some calls. I got my last answer this morning. She'll be fine. She'll call you tonight."

Kurt glared at Dave. "What do you mean, she'll be okay? She was beat up. And what are you doing snooping around her now?"

Dave leaned forward. "Listen again, I said 'she'll be okay'. Let me explain why."

"Come on Kurt," said Rosie. "You're in enough trouble as it is. Don't be so damned ungrateful."

As Kurt started to get up, Dave held up his hand. "Whoa now, both of you. Let me finish."

Kurt slumped back in his chair, arms folded.

Dave took a breath. "Kurt, my contacts found out that it was bikers from a major Toronto gang that beat up Crystal. It wasn't just some casual punks upset over a deal gone bad. They seem to have targeted her specifically because of her connection to you, and they have also spread the word they might come after her again."

Kurt jumped to his feet. "What the hell are you talking about? Now I'm the reason she got beat up? That's a load of crap. I'm clean, and you know it. You're just making all this up to set me up! You cops are all the same. And Crystal is clean too. This is all bullshit."

Kurt stopped yelling and looked back at the three of them, still watching him patiently. His shoulders dropped.

"What? Why are you staring at me?" he said. "I'm upset, okay? Crystal is in danger. Uncle Rosie, I have to get down to Toronto and get her out of there." He shook his head. "Shit, but then where would we go? Hell, those guys are everywhere!"

Dave could see that Kurt was trying hard not to cry, but it looked like tears were not far off.

Rosie reached over and pulled at his sleeve gently. "Kurt, sit down," he said.

Kurt suddenly lost all his bluster and sagged back into the chair. He stared at the floor and finally murmured, "So what can we do?"

"I think she should just leave Toronto," said Dave. "It looks like she's somehow managed to get caught up in the wrong sort of crowd, and now she's too far in to get back out."

Kurt shook his head. "What did we ever do to them?"

"Sure there's nothing you want to tell us about?" asked Rosie.

Kurt paused a bit, then shook his head. He stared at Dave. "I'm not a rat, I'm taking the 5th Amendment."

Norris leaned forward. "This is not an interrogation, we're just trying to help you and your girlfriend. And you've watched too much American TV, we don't have a 5th up here. Why don't we lay out what we have, Boss?"

"Thanks, Constable," said Dave. "Kurt, when we had that big drug bust in the post office, I had a drug dog brought in. After we finished, I took the handler and the dog into Rosie's for a bite to eat. But while in there, the dog started sniffing around, and found something that caught his attention—guess where?"

Kurt paused, then seemed to make up his mind. "My t-shirts?"

"Yes," said Norris. "Those same t-shirts, I might add, that you were so nervous about earlier. Remember, when I brought that ripped package of them from the bus terminal?"

"Kurt, I think I know what was going on," said Dave, "and I think you know I know, but won't admit it. Hopefully you've seen this is not all just for a few laughs, like trying to rack some cans or skipping on a lunch bill. These bikers mean business. This is grownup crime, with possibly deadly consequences. Now, someone you care about has been hurt, and you could be next. And instead of all this you should still be having fun being a teenager."

"Well, he won't be having any on-line fun," said Rosie. "That system is off-limits."

"Thanks a lot," said Kurt.

He looked in shock, like the world was moving too fast. Dave was sympathetic. It was a lot of new information to process, and according to Rosie, Kurt didn't have a history of great coping skills. Sure enough, Kurt focused on the small part of the conversation he understood.

"Can't I at least have a few hours on it?" said Kurt.

"No," said Rosie. "I don't like all that time on-line, doing nothing. If you need to do email or whatever, you can use my PC, it will work just fine for that."

"This sucks," said Kurt.

"Well, it could be worse," said Norris. "Come on, focus on the big issue. We do have a way to help your girlfriend too."

"What, jail?" asked Kurt.

Dave sighed. "No, I've been talking with your mom and a friend of mine in Ottawa. We're going to get Crystal on a bus to Ottawa, find her a place to stay, and see what she needs to do to get into one of the fashion schools there. She's all for it, and is going to call you as soon as she can. But our first priority is to move her out quickly but quietly, before she gets another visit. She may be there already."

"How does that sound?" asked Rosie.

"You talked to my mom?" Kurt shouted, ready to resume his tirade, but then suddenly stopped as the rest of the words sunk in.

"It sounds okay, I guess. She did want to try a fashion course," said Kurt. He paused, then muttered, "thanks."

Rosie gave Dave a little smile.

"Kurt, I'd like you to talk a bit more to Junior," Rosie said. "He's been through a lot up here, had a rough life. Some of the kids that hang out there are really into gaming—"

"Not me anymore," said Kurt.

"Let me finish," said Rosie. "He's also got a couple of nice computers in there that they are using for various programs he's running. Design work, programming, all sorts of stuff."

"Open-source or commercial tools?"

"I have no idea what that even means," said Dave, "but, please, at least give him a chance. Consider it a part of your probation."

Kurt looked at Norris and Dave. "What about that other stuff? Look, I'm out of it now, we both are. I promise."

"Kurt, your actions are more important to me than empty promises," said Dave. "I am giving you a chance, but I assure you that I know exactly what you were doing. There are a number of charges I could make against you already. For now, I'll wait. This is a small town, though, so if you start up again, I will know immediately and there will be no second chances. A lot depends now on what choices you pick in the future. Okay?"

Kurt just nodded.

Dave stood up. "Now get out of here, all of you, I have some paperwork I'm just dying to get back to."

Dave peered into his fridge, then grabbed some leftovers and a beer. It had been a long day, and he just wanted to relax. He did use Rosie's place more than his own kitchen but he didn't even feel like chatting. Well, except to JB. He definitely needed to share his new plans with her, before someone else mentioned it. Maybe she'd reconsider her courses down there. He checked the clock. It was just after seven, but hopefully she'd be in. To his relief, she answered on the first ring.

"Hi Sweetie," he said. "Sitting on the phone?"

"I was just about to call," she said. "Know the schedule I sent shows me off work tonight but I plan to head downtown to hear a new band."

"More partying? I thought you had a paper due." He cringed. "Sorry, I don't mean to nag."

"No, that's okay," she said. "The paper went much better than I thought—everything just clicked. I love it when that happens. It isn't really a party thing, just some friends that have formed a group. They have a nice style, definitely more of a mellow band than metal. We have good groups into the Roost but I do sometimes miss these loud and crazy bands down here, with dancing until the place closes."

"I do at times too," he said. But now I think that while Toronto is a nice place to visit, I wouldn't want to live there. I do appreciate this small town life more."

"Didn't you already decide that?" she said.

He paused. She was right. "Yes, I did. But then you said you were going to stay down south—"

"Not forever," she said. "Sorry. Go on."

"And it looked like the normal upswing in drugs was going to be even more this year. Especially with those bikers moving in."

"But you can just sneak up on them, right?"

"Yes, theoretically," he said. "But I was afraid to use my power, in case I let that evil back in." He hurried on. "I know, over analyzing. The elders all looked into it—almost zero risk there."

"Anything else?"

"Then I got a tempting email from my boss, saying it looked like all was clear and he could set up something for me back down south. With a raise."

"Interesting," she said. "What brought that on?"

"Well, Emily had said she would be nudging her boss, the Minister—"

"That bitch!" said JB.

"No," said Dave. "I mean, yes, she is. But in this case I'm pretty sure that Minister Gottman would prefer me up here to help keep an eye on her new Centre of Excellence."

"True," said JB. "Pollution studies are big now, especially where my people are involved. So what's your new plan?"

"Well," he said. "I know when I first arrived I was hoping to escape here in a year. No longer. Short term I want to use my powers to help me deal with these bikers, especially Sasquatch."

"Who?" she said. "That biker from Toronto? You didn't tell me he was there too."

Oops. Dave apologized, and explained the whole Sasquatch connection with Risso and the Winnipeg gang. JB still sounded pretty upset.

"Damn it Dave, don't keep things like this from me, or I'll come up there and kick your ass."

"Sorry again. But I would like to see you up here."

"I know," she said. "Me too. I'm maxed out until term end, but I'll have a couple of weeks off at the end, before the Fall term starts."

"So you're still doing that?" he said.

"Of course I am, Dave. This is important to me, it's something I have to do. But the course load will be lighter, and I think I'll drop the job at the pub. So I should be able to get up there for a visit every few weeks, plus holidays. It's at least a three year program for me to get all the credits, but there's a big thesis component later on that I can work on from anywhere. And you're welcome to come down here to visit too, you know."

"Sorry, yes, you're right," he said.

"So we're good?" she said.

"Yes, very good. So, what's up for the rest of the week?"

"Well, I have to present this excellent paper," she said. "And a couple of tests, and a workshop, but nothing big. And this band tonight. You?"

"Well, keep an eye on Risso and the bikers. Get Sheila to churn out some more reports for Staff. And try to fit in another practice for the ball tournament, without the other teams realizing we can actually play."

"Oh, you are devious," she said. "Look, I should get running to that band, my friends just rang my bell. Miss you sweetie. Big hugs and kisses. Love you."

"You too," he said. He hung up and sipped his beer. That went pretty well after all, even with Sasquatch thrown in.

Chapter 16

Junior looked up as Rosie stepped into the youth centre. "Hey Rosie, quiet out front?"

"Mid-afternoon pause," he said. "How's it going back here?"

"More kids showing up lately, as the word is spreading. I'm making some progress with them. Maybe they're starting to trust me more."

Junior didn't dwell on his background when talking with the other kids, but he got some respect once they realized he'd been through a lot of things, including time on the streets of Winnipeg and all the racism and risks that entailed.

"You're good at this," said Rosie. "I'm glad I donated the space. It gives the kids—local and summer folk—somewhere to hang and opens up some other options. Speaking of which, did you settle who had that joint we found the other day?"

"Yes, I did. Kid was surprised when I mentioned it, as it was hidden in an inside pocket. Just adds to my mystique. I just give them a look and most don't even bother to try to trick me."

"How's that new kid doing, Melissa?"

"She's fitting in okay. She has mad skills with markers and cans, and is already a mentor to some of the younger kids. Who knew?"

"How about Kurt?" said Rosie.

"He did drop by one time for a few minutes, then an hour the next day. Oh, did you mean what did I think of him?"

"Yes. Is he maybe trying to fool us?" asked Rosie.

"No, I think he's changing," said Junior. "I get a better feeling from him now than I used to." His own ability only worked on other native kids, so for the others he just relied on his street-smarts. "I heard what Dave did for him and his girlfriend. Very nice."

"He seemed to clean up his act pretty fast after his girlfriend got roughed up by those bikers," said Rosie. "Hopefully their attention doesn't now focus on him. It was good for Dave to cut him some slack. He's a good kid, and has potential. Did Kurt find anyone in your group that was into programming video games?"

"Not really. I think he knows more about it than most of the kids here," said Junior. "I know he's on his X-Box a lot. There are a few ways he could use it for programming, but it's not cheap to upgrade. And you still need a good graphics package."

"Can you do any of that stuff with your computers here?"

"Sure, both are top of the line Mac's. We're starting a training program with them too. First just basic computer setup and networking, then we add training on some of the applications. The kids learn fast from each other."

Rosie looked around appreciatively. He wished he'd had a place like this when he was growing up. He was thinking of doing some renovations next year, maybe this could be spruced up. Or even moved to a bigger place—he'd have to mention it next town council meeting.

Junior looked up from where he was sorting out game controllers. "Truth is, I'm not an expert at this stuff, and I could use a hand around here in the game area. Somebody who knows the stuff, if you get my drift. As in Kurt. My wilderness training hikes are getting really popular, and I'd like to spend a bit more time on them."

"What hikes?" said Rosie. "Are they like when you took Dave out last winter to find himself?"

Junior nodded. "Something like that, only I don't leave them stranded for a couple of hours. And I talk more about nature and our relationship to it. It's mostly summer cottage kids, but also some from the reserve that have missed out on culture being passed down in their families. I enjoy that a lot." He paused and then continued. "So getting back to Kurt, do you think he'd be up for helping out around here? It would be volunteer, but we get free snacks from time to time from the softie that runs the place."

Rosie laughed. "You're welcome! But that's just what I was thinking too. I think he'd be interested, and working here would be good for Kurt. Long term he might even be able to help me out front, once his attitude improves. Why don't you start him off with a bit of responsibility in your group and see where it goes. Just keep an eye on him to make sure he's taking this seriously."

"Sure, be glad to try him out," said Junior. "But he's got to give up not just trafficking drugs but even using them. Otherwise we can't use him here. It infects the whole program."

"I agree completely," said Rosie. "And I think he has. Look, he was good at running that t-shirt program in Toronto, as well as up here. Maybe he has some business skills you could target too."

"Well, some of the local kids were admiring the shirts he had," said Junior, "and they were wishing they could do their own designs on them. With this graphics software and a printer they could do their own shirts."

"Keep that in mind," said Rosie. "Then introduce it slowly, so he and the others think it up on their own. As long as it doesn't keep them all inside too much."

"Slowly is good," said Junior. "That's the way my people teach. We make the knowledge available, and wait until you are ready for it."

"Well, it seems to be working with these kids," said Rosie.

"It does," said Junior, "Look, I hate to break this short, but I have to get going. I'm meeting this lady teacher from Sainte-Anne. She wants to talk about my wilderness training course, and maybe doing field trips out here with her class. Maybe you should meet her. She's kind of cute in an older way. And single!"

Chapter 17

Sheila was in a frenzy. Staff Sergeant Scully had phoned yesterday from District Headquarters and said he had some papers for Constable MacGregor to sign, and was planning to drop in and do it in person. Dave thought that sounded reasonable but Sheila looked at him with a withering look of pity.

"Senior managers never drop in because it's convenient. Don't you know that? Remember when you first arrived? Staff and the Superintendent both showed up. And you'll recall that wasn't just for a chat."

Dave remembered it well. The Superintendent had been congenial but Staff had ripped up one side of Dave and down the other, making sure that Dave knew there was to be no 'prima donna drug squad antics and thinking outside of the box'. Dave had promised to behave, but unfortunately the various crimes he'd uncovered had needed a few unorthodox methods to solve them. Luckily the resolution had shone a favourable light on both the RCMP in general as well as Staff's group, so all was forgiven. At least he hoped so. Dave wondered if Angus would get the same lecture or if it would change, out of respect for his previous police experience. Angus was on the books as a Constable, but he had retired at the same rank as Staff Sergeant Scully, with an equally impressive career. This would be interesting.

Dave had just returned to his task of straightening up the papers on his desk when Sheila raced in holding a stack of files and a dust cloth. She scrutinized Dave's ironed uniform shirt with the intensity of a drill instructor and nodded curtly.

"Good, you're presentable. Here are files he might ask about. I'll put them in your basket so you can make sure you've got them fresh in your mind. Angus is making sure the prisoner log book is complete, and Norris is bringing over cookies in 30 minutes. Right, then." She turned and rushed out.

Staff's arrival was almost anticlimactic after Sheila's pre-visit inspection. He gave a quick but penetrating look around the room and then focused his attention on Angus, who was standing casually at attention. His shirt was starchy and boots polished and Dave knew Sheila had nothing to do with it.

"Constable MacGregor," Staff started, with a very slight emphasis on the Constable. "It will take me a bit to get used to saying that."

"Aye, and for me too," replied Angus, "but it's easier to manage than plain Mr. MacGregor."

The two men looked at each other for a few moments. Dave was unaccountably reminded of two old dogs doing a stare down before they either attacked or sniffed behinds. Not a pleasant image.

"We appreciate you volunteering to help out here," said Staff. "It's a very busy detachment in the summer."

Angus just nodded.

"I served out on the West Coast too," said Staff. He continued with naming some members he knew in Burnaby, and Angus knew all of them, approved of some and said nothing about a few others. Apparently this was the correct response because Staff nodded and even smiled once, to Dave's astonishment.

As Staff wound down Angus noticed a pause and cleared his throat. "Staff, I assure you that I am delighted in my role as Constable. I've done more than enough supervision in my former life and I would prefer to leave all that headache to the fine staff here. If I can help out here and there, cover shifts when needed and still have time to fish and do a bit of woodworking, I'll be very happy."

Staff smiled yet again. "Excellent. Now, to the paperwork."

Dave handed over the folders, glad that Sheila had arranged them all for him, complete with colourful little 'sign here' tabs. Staff furrowed his brow when he saw those, but they soon had everything signed and whisked away by Sheila.

"Good report on Constable Norris too," Staff said. "She's progressing well. Good management, Corporal Browne. And I don't have to remind you once more—keep things quiet here. None of your theatrics. Now I'll just have a quick look around the office and then go for lunch at Rosie's."

Dave stared dumbfounded at Sheila who smiled serenely back, as if to say 'See, that's how its done'.

Dave sat comfortably in an Adirondack chair on the deck of Angus's cottage home, his face warm in the evening sun. Staff's meeting had been less stressful than he'd thought it would be. After a few hints Angus had suggested they unwind over dinner at his place. Dave was hoping it would also give him a chance to get to know Angus better and try to ease the tension between him and Norris. Not that there were any disagreements—quite the opposite in fact. At the office they were both acting insufferably polite to each other and it was time to get past that. Norris had made a valiant effort and accepted a glass of single malt scotch from Angus, only wincing a bit at the first swallow.

"Aye lassie, the first sip's always a grand assault, to sanitize your mouth for the rest of the glass!" Angus had advised sagely. Dave sipped at his glass of scotch reflectively. He wasn't a fan of hard liquor but he could see how it could get to become an acquired taste.

It was a perfect end to a perfect evening. Dave had to admire Angus for finding this little bit of heaven for his semi-retirement. According to Angus the realtor had explained that after some scandals in the town a few people had to get rid of their homes in a hurry—and this was one. "She quickly went on to reassure me everything was calm and quiet now. I didn't mention that since I was ex-RCMP I doubted any town was really that quiet and peaceful."

"And it's even less quiet than last year," said Dave.

Norris nodded. "We're seeing more drugs than there should be. We've stopped the postal route I think, but there must be new dealers moving in. Our regulars don't have that much initiative. Or the contacts."

"I noticed a few of my neighbours turned a little cool when they realized I was ex-RCMP," said Angus. "But others wanted me over for dinner to tell them juicy stories."

Over dinner Angus had told them about his early career, his short marriage and years of being transferred from one posting to another. Dave thought the story sounded very close to that of his own youth, when his father's military career kept them moving from base to base. Dave suspected Angus was not as heavy handed with the belt as his own father had been, though.

Angus had said he'd decided to move to Manitoba to be closer to his son and seven-year-old grandson, in Winnipeg. Angus and Norris were now in the kitchen cleaning up and Dave could hear Norris giving him some ideas for birthday presents a young boy might like.

Dave settled back in his chair, squinted into the setting sun, and imagined having JB sitting beside him. He'd thought at one point he'd miss the excitement of the big city, and of a career in undercover. But now he was seeing the possibilities up here. Especially if JB could pop up for visits. Or he down there, for some night life. Dave took another sip and smiled to himself. And, as Angus had said, quiet could be deceptive. Dave had only been in Kirk's Landing six months and there had been enough excitement to satisfy even the most demanding of appetites!

Norris and Angus came out carrying dessert, laughing about a story from when Angus had coached a junior baseball team.

"It will be a handy skill for our upcoming tournament," she said. "Dave, you look comfortable out here."

"Aye, it's a magical time of the day," said Angus, "when the world starts to go to sleep. And what would be filling your head with solemn thoughts on such a lovely evening, boss?" He handed over a dish of rhubarb crumble and ice cream.

"Thanks," said Dave. "I'm still adjusting to the idea of happily living in such a peaceful area."

Angus smiled. "I know what you're asking lad, as I've had the same pondering myself. There's two parts to that I think. Firstly, when you retire or move to another posting, the job misses you about as much as a bucket of water misses your fist when you pull it out of the water. Not to say they don't appreciate all you did, but the new NCO wants to do it themselves, and certainly doesn't want you around giving advice. However, we're all police officers and it's our nature to help people. So wherever you live, go find another bucket of water and stick your hand in. It doesn't matter where you are; it's who you are with, what you're doing, and how you support each other on the team that's important."

Angus smiled as he took a bite of dessert and looked at both of them. "The second part is more personal, and I expect applies to both of you. Rumour has it you're both in romantic relationships and you're wondering if a partner would be happy just sitting on a deck like this watching the sunset with you."

Dave looked up sharply. Was it possible Angus had some weird Scottish second sight and knew his thoughts? He glanced at Norris, who was nodding thoughtfully.

"Always some hard choices in this job," she said.

"Ach, that there are," said Angus. "But at the end of your life I'm betting you won't be lying there in bed and wishing you'd spent more time at work. You'll wonder what might have happened if you'd invested more time in relationships, spent more time with your family when you had the chance, or worked harder to keep people you love. I've spent most of my life alone and maybe I've lost the skills to share a home with somebody. But I sure wish there was somebody here with whom I could share these sunsets." He shook his head. "Ach! Blether! The whisky has addled my brains and I've forgotten the vital part of the evening."

Norris and Dave were startled out of their thoughts.

"We forgot the traditional Scottish toast!" he said. "'Tis nay an event without a proper toast to celebrate life, humanity and God's gift of scotch whisky to us lowly creatures. Now fill up you two and get ready."

They all rose and held glasses high to the setting sun as Angus recited.

May the best you've ever seen
Be the worst you'll ever see,

May a mouse never leave your kitchen
With a teardrop in his eye,

May you all keep hale and hearty
Till you're old enough to die,

May you all be just as happy
As I wish you all to be.

Chapter 18

Norris settled her hand into her glove. She could already feel the sun hot on her back. Summer had finally settled in, just in time for the Canada Day long weekend. It was a good day for a ball game, and a good day to surprise some people. They'd been teased about their team, a mash-up of everyone from the detachment, including Sheila, and Angus, as well as a couple of Natural Resource Officers, Darlene from the post office, and Mike the Mayor. The Detachment team had done quite well in the curling bonspiel earlier that year, partially due to their 'ringer', Reese. They'd managed to keep his active high school career—including a Provincial curling championship—quiet long enough to get some great odds on the games, which they parlayed into a full course meal catered by the losers, Rosie's team. A meal that included cooking, serving, and cleanup. They planned to win again.

"Ready to be beat?" asked Rosie. "I've watched you practise, you try hard but you've no stars this time. I checked on Reese, definitely sucked at baseball in high school. Want to repeat our last bet?"

"I don't know," said Norris. "We really could do with a couple of more practices." She tried her best to look worried.

"Chicken?"

"No, I think we're good. Okay, you're on, although my team may kill me when they find out. Loser cooks dinner at Dave's, just like last time, but now they also supply all the beer."

"Whatever," said Rosie, with a wave of his hand. "You're not going to win, we will." He waved and ran back to his team.

Dave walked up. "Don't you feel the least bit guilty this time?"

"Hell no," she said. "He's been teasing me all along about our team. Too bad he never thought to check under my maiden name back home. He doesn't know I'm the one with the solid high school sports background this time. And the two guys from Natural Resources both played a lot at their other postings. Plus Angus coached his kid's teams for years. No, our only challenge has been to sneak in a mix of public and poor practices between the real ones. We'll smear them." Or at least she hoped they would. Rosie's team included some of the kids from the back room youth group, including Mal and Junior. Mal didn't look like much of a player, but seemed to be bringing considerable enthusiasm to it.

As Norris had hoped, they did well. It was not too hot a day, and the rules had been modified to 'no sliding', which reduced the photo ops for the local reporter, but also reduced the wear and tear on the players. Angus had them hold back a bit for the first few innings, taking it easy, then swapped a few positions and told them to open up. Suddenly the fumbles and short throws disappeared, and they started picking off players on every base.

Norris found herself thinking back to what Angus had said about working at a relationship. Life was pretty dull if you were always trying to avoid taking risks, always playing it safe. She realized she was using the excuse of some hypothetical future transfer to avoid jumping in the pool and swimming.

She used to take risks, heck she was a police officer! Risk was inherent in the job. But she was an expert at not risking her heart, at not stepping out of the safe shadows. Maybe it was because Bobby's father had broken her heart. Or maybe it was just what most people did, avoiding things that might make them stretch out of their comfort zone.

She watched Mike as he played ball. He was making no secret of the fact that he liked her, along with Bobby. It was her that was holding back, saying she was not comfortable with showing affection in public. Maybe it was too much of a commitment. He was a really nice guy. And not a bad ball player. He looked pretty good in his ball pants too, swaggering around as he aimed a bit of trash talk at the other team.

He was up next at bat, with Sheila, Dave and Reese all on base. Mike wiggled his feet into the dirt, brought the bat up, stuck that butt out a little, and swung! Wow, that one was heading far into right field. Mal started running back for it, legs pumping like she was running from a bust. She leaped up and grabbed as she reached the fence, but just missed it.

Home run! Norris pumped her fist. "Yes! Nice one Mike!" She called out into the field. "Mal! Awesome try, great running." Mal grinned and waved back, as her team all gave her a cheer.

She took a big breath. No time like the present. Before she lost her nerve she strode over to the plate, and grabbed Mike as soon as he jogged over home plate. Right there, in front of the whole crowd and all their friends, she planted a massive lip lock on his face. A kiss that turned into an embrace that went on for a bit too long for crowd comfort.

When they finally broke apart, Mike kept a tight arm around her and grinned widely. "Wow, I'd have hit a homer the first inning if I'd known about this."

Norris managed to focus somehow on the rest of the game. Rosie's team played hard, but to no avail, finally losing by four runs.

After confirming the dinner Rosie owed them, Norris sat back in the dugout, tired, dusty. Reese sat down next to her and gave her a little elbow. "Well, it's about time," he said. "The whole town has been wondering when you'd make your move."

"I decided I was tired of being cautious," she said, "and didn't want to let this one slip away." She looked around. "I think Mike's gone off to get a few more beers, but do you have any left?"

"Sure, here's one," said Reese. "Oh, wait, I think actually you owe me. Several."

"What are you talking about?" she said. "Oh yeah, for your little cleanup job. Sorry I had to pull seniority on that."

The day before Reese had spent an eventful morning with the septic truck, watching as they pumped out a cottage tank. The cottage belonged to the woman who had bolted from the post office the week before, taking her bags of suspicious white powder with her. The truck then emptied the contents on to a sewer grate covered with screens, revealing several good sized bags of powder, still intact. It had been Angus's idea, learned from his previous years in rural areas.

"It was a good catch," said Reese. "She'd assumed she could just flush the evidence away. I did try to pass the job on to Angus but he just laughed at me. Claimed seniority."

"He's learned over the years," she said. "But we got some good leads from her too, once she started talking. Too bad nobody was dumb enough to pick up their drugs from the post office. It looks like the suppliers aren't mailing anymore either."

"We're still seeing drugs around, though," he said. "Especially after we tracked down the return addresses they had dutifully put on the packages. Nothing for the cute police dog to find on his return." He elbowed her again. "Or the cute handler."

She smiled. "He was, but I'm fine with the guy I already have. Fred did seem to like the chance to visit here again though. I guess we're a nice change from the normal places he looks for drugs. And he certainly likes Rosie's pies, even calling ahead to pre-order a whole lemon meringue to take back home."

"Does Rosie do all that baking on his own?" asked Reese.

"Actually, he now has a local woman come in to help with that, Mary Tyler. She picked up his recipes fast—I think actually improved some of them. She has a flair for desserts. Here, give me your empty, time we headed back—I've the late shift tonight."

Chapter 19

Dave was staring out his office window, watching some early morning joggers and wondering if he should join them some time. June had turned out to be surprisingly peaceful. The bikers had not shown up, at least so far, and they'd made a good drug bust. He was hoping July continued the trend. It certainly had started well with a great day yesterday for the ball tournament—which his team had won, and then fireworks on the town beach. Paid for by the mill of course, eager to improve their image.

"Corporal," called Sheila. "Janie's mother is on line two. She sounds upset."

"Mrs. Tyler, how are you?" said Dave.

"Oh, it's not good," she said, "Janie's off her meds again, and just took off now, all fired up. This time she's all pissed off because her father made her miss the latest episode of Ice Road Truckers."

"Great, which way is she headed?" asked Dave.

"Toward the beach. She also has a hate-on for seagulls today. Says she's going to take some of them out."

"Does she have a gun?" he said.

"Yes, Janie's got a gun," she said. "A pistol, from her step-father Egbert."

"Okay, we're on it," he said.

"Corporal, she's just a little confused and angry. Please don't be too hard on her."

"We won't, Mrs. T, don't worry." He rushed into the office and gestured to Norris. "Let's go. It's Janie, angry and armed. Sheila, if anyone calls, we're aware of the problem and are on our way. Tell them to stay away from the beach, to leave it to us." He ran out to the police truck with Norris close behind, fastening up their vests and adjusting equipment along the way. Although it was policy to call in a special team for weapons complaints, he didn't want to escalate this situation if he could avoid it. He supposed he could always use his secret power and sneak up on her, but that would be a last resort.

From what he knew of the family, Mrs. Tyler was a quiet timid person, trying hard to be a good mother. However, the step-father was a bully and a mean drunk, and often hung around with Risso. Likely for the drugs, as well as the company of a kindred spirit. In addition, Dave had no proof but suspected that he was a tyrant at home—as in abusive. Dave knew first hand what that could be like, having had a father who was big on discipline. Dave didn't know the girl very well; she was quiet and tried to stay in the background most of the time, similar to what Dave did when he was that age. Norris filled him in on some of Janie's history as they drove. Her meds were fairly mild, but necessary, and her previous lapses had just resulted in bouts of crying and depression.

He glanced over at Norris, working the terminal in the 4X4. "Anything else?"

"A few complaints of domestic disputes," she said. "No charges. I was at some of them, both of the women usually back right down from the little twerp. This is not like Janie though." They passed a few locals who waved them on toward the beach. Norris peered around intently and then pointed to a small figure sitting at a bench near the beach.

"I think she doesn't trust men very much, so let me go first and you stay by the truck. I'm pretty sure I can talk her down. I know her a bit from a baking circle we did last Christmas."

"You have time to bake?" he said. "Okay, go ahead. Do good and I'll bake some cookies for you."

"Thanks, but you can skip that," she said.

Norris walked slowly toward Janie, calling her name and staying slightly behind a tree, just in case. Janie looked up, then gave a small wave. Norris talked in a low voice for what seemed like ages to Dave, then gave him a thumbs up behind her back. Janie waved her closer. Janie lifted the gun—Dave tensed—then she handed it to Norris, who checked it quickly then stuck it in her belt.

Norris sat down next to Janie, and the two continued a conversation. After a few minutes Dave cleared his throat loudly. Janie jumped a little, so Norris put a hand on her arm and called out.

"It's alright. Come on over. Corporal, I'd like you to meet my friend, Janie. Janie, this is Corporal Browne."

"Hi Janie," he said. He saw a quiet-looking girl, pretty, with long dark hair. She'd obviously been crying and had a nasty cut over her eyebrow. "I've seen you around, often coming out of the library. I hear you like to read a lot."

Janie nodded sullenly. "Yes, fantasy and stuff. I've read most of the ones in the library, so now I have to wait for new ones to take back home."

"You live over on Pine Street, don't you?" he asked.

"Yes, we have a trailer there. Me and my mom. And my loser of a step-father. I just can't take it anymore with him there."

Norris quickly changed the subject and pointed to a brightly covered book Janie was clutching. "What's that? It looks very special."

"That's my journal, Constable," said Janie.

"Like a diary?"

"I like to write down things I see around town, even do some sketches, of people and things that are sort of different. I guess I'm so quiet people forget I'm there."

Norris put her hand on Janie's arm. "But sweetie, today you definitely reminded them."

Janie gave a little smile. "Yes, sorry. If I forget to take my pills I go a little crazy. It seemed a lot worse this time. I just grabbed the gun and ran. Then when I got here I didn't know what to do."

"Tell us more about this journal", said Norris. "Sounds like fun. I like to read, but can't write at all."

"It's nothing much. It's just things I see and hear around me, but then I blend it with fantasy creatures, the heroes and monsters and animals from books I've read. So I have stories of normal town scenes and people, but unknown to them they live in the midst of another world."

"That's different," said Dave. "Trolls and tourists. Sort of a Sunshine Sketches of a Scary Town."

"Wow," said Norris, "you're not as illiterate as I thought."

"Thanks," said Dave. He could see that Janie was still scared, but significantly less angry. "Do you skip your meds often?"

"No, I'm usually good," said Janie. "Sorry again about all this. Things have been getting more stressful around home. We end up arguing more. And all the fantasy creatures I see around here are getting scarier."

Dave paused, then nodded. "You're not alone in this, a lot of people seem to be getting jumpier around town. Maybe it's all this rainy weather. Come on, let's get back to the detachment. I'll radio ahead to have your mom meet us, if she's not already there."

As they drove back to the station, Norris handed him Janie's gun, a 9mm.

"Here," she said. "When I got closer I saw there was no clip in it. And it wasn't cocked."

"And the chamber?" asked Dave.

"I checked, it was empty."

"Thanks," he said. "Good work there, you have a nice touch. You handled that well."

"It wasn't that hard," she said. "She just needed to talk to someone. She's got a pretty shitty home life you know. I think she wants out, but feels she has to stay for her mother. She needs some counselling to help her deal with all this."

"We'll still need to see her step-father," said Dave, "and talk to him about leaving this gun accessible. And probably not registered, either."

Janie's mom jumped up as they walked into the detachment. She ran to her daughter, gave her a big hug, then held her by the shoulders.

"Why do you keep doing this?" she asked. She handed her a pill bottle. "Here. Take one now, damn you." She hugged Janie again. "Oh Violet—what should I do?"

Norris handed Janie a glass of water. "Here, sweetie, wash that down and then let's all sit and figure this out. Corporal, can we use your office for a bit?"

"Sure," he said. "No problem. Sheila, can you hold calls for a few minutes? If anyone calls about Janie, let them know it's all under control."

As they sat around his desk, Janie slumped against her mother.

"First the legal stuff," said Dave. "Janie, even though you are a minor, you cannot break the law with no consequences. We have to protect you and all the other people in the town that were scared silly when they saw you stomping around with a gun in your hand. Not to mention terrifying your mother.

"But I wasn't going to shoot anybody—" Janie started.

Dave continued "You knew that, and we know that now, but all those people didn't know that. One of them might have done something drastic to stop you, thinking they were protecting themselves. If things had gone differently we might have been faced with the decision to shoot you to prevent you from hurting other people. Misuse of a gun is a very very serious offence and we cannot ignore it. Constable Norris and I will discuss this with Child Family Services tomorrow—we have to—and we'll let your mom know what action we'll take."

Janie's mom gasped.

"However, from what I know of your family, and your issues," said Dave, "my report will be favourable, okay?" He suspected that whatever was affecting most of the townspeople had hit Janie especially hard. "Now I know being a teenager is stressful at the best of times, and you've got some tough circumstances at home. But, you still have to deal with these things, in a safe way. We have got to be sure you can control your behaviour. If you have medication you cannot just skip it, because look what happens. That's what being mature is all about, making decisions and being sure you can control your behaviour."

Janie looked defeated but still defiant. "Okay, but how come I have to do all this to be mature when that ass-hole who married my mother is such a childish moron?" She glanced at her mother. "Sorry mom."

Norris spoke up. "Janie, just worry about controlling yourself. I suggest you pick a different person than him as an example of who you could be like. Got that?"

She nodded, as did her mom, holding her daughter's hand.

"Mrs. Tyler, I assume the gun is your husband's?" said Dave.

"Yes, he just got it. Said he needed it to protect us from all the undesirables in town, but I think he bought it from Risso. I keep telling him to lock it up, he tells me to shut up and stop worrying."

"Well, we'll be charging him, as this is a restricted firearm and needs to be properly secured."

"Do you have to?" asked Janie. "He's always angry with me, I don't want to set him off again."

Norris looked carefully at her. "What does he do when he gets angry?"

"He yells and stuff."

"Stuff? Does he do more? What happened to your eyebrow?" Norris asked.

Janie looked at her mom, who was biting her lip. "I fell," said

Jamie. "I'm sometimes clumsy."

Norris frowned. "Does he do other things to you too?"

Janie looked puzzled for a moment, then angry. "Oh, that? He wouldn't dare."

Dave pointed to Janie's book. "Your daughter was showing us her journal."

"Yes, it's become quite a thing for her," said her mom. "She's let me see a couple of the stories."

"And?"

"They're good. Some people from here, and some from those books she reads. Very descriptive, even if some is a little scary."

Dave leaned forward. "Janie, you know that drop-in centre Junior runs behind Rosie's? He said he was looking for someone to help him do a newsletter. Want me to recommend you to him? No commitment, just drop by and see him."

"I guess," said Janie cautiously.

"And I'd heard he was an Ice Road Truckers fan too. He tapes them all and runs them at the centre. Might even lend you some."

"I'd like that," said Janie, with a shy smile.

Janie and her mother were just leaving Dave's office when a small but angry man pushed through the front door.

"Where is that little brat?"

Janie shrank back into the office, but not before he saw her.

"There you are. How dare you embarrass me like this. And stealing my gun too? I want her charged!" He moved to go behind the counter, but Dave stepped up to him. Right up to him.

"Just hold it, right there. I think I've sorted out things for now with Janie and her mother. They were just heading home, but I'd be glad to listen to your concerns. Norris, could you take Mr. Tyler to the side room please? Then drop Janie and her mom off."

The angry father tried to bluster a bit, and push past Norris, but she gently took his arm and led him aside. Dave knew her 'gentle' grips were often a disguise for an extensive knowledge of nerve endings. He was willing to bet she'd never had any problems with over-attentive men when training at Depot.

Janie's dad refused to sit, but paced back and forth in front of Dave's desk, chest puffed out like a Bantam rooster. Dave calmly pointed out that he was facing a weapons charge, and that they would keep the pistol, pending decision of the charges. As well as verifying that it was a legitimate purchase. In addition, they were concerned over his lack of anger management, so would be keeping an eye on his behaviour. Dave made it clear that they could and would take further steps if necessary. Like all bullies, Janie's dad backed down quickly, and switched to being obnoxiously ingratiating, which did not fool Dave for a minute. Egbert left after assuring Dave that there were no more weapons in the house and they were welcome to check. Providing they had a warrant of course.

"I can't see that man ever changing," said Sheila.

"I agree," said Dave. "I've seen the type. At least he knows now that we're watching him closely." Dave was still worried that he might go home and take it out on his wife or Janie. But there was not much they could do about that. Without evidence of violence, the law was pretty clear that a man's house was his castle. At least they might be able to get the step-daughter away from the home more often, over to the drop-in centre.

Dave finally sat down at his desk and breathed a long sigh. It had been a very eventful day. Who was it that was concerned this was a sleepy little town that would not be able to compete with the bright lights and action of Toronto? He was glad he had a good team to work with. He remembered Angus's advice about nurturing relationships and got out a performance form to write a good assessment on Norris about the day's events. She continued to amaze him with her abilities. And to think only six months ago Staff had labelled her a weak performer!

Chapter 20

Norris swerved and jammed on her brakes. The family just looked at her, then continued their slow amble down the road. She resisted the urge to give them a blast on her siren to hurry them up, but figured that there was no point in antagonizing them. They turned to the side, and when the last one—the youngest—finally reached the shoulder of the road, it twitched its butt at her, and joined the rest of them in the woods. It was nice to see some bears wandering about, in spite of the increased poaching, but she wished they'd stay off the highway. She continued into town, pulled up in front of Rosie's, and went in.

"You wouldn't know there was a bear shortage here," she said. "I almost ran into a family on the main highway."

"Natural Resources says their numbers indicate otherwise," said Rosie. "Why don't you ask your date?" He nodded at one of the booths.

"He's not a date," she said. "Brian and I talked a few times at the base-ball tournament, and now he's here to discuss some joint operations."

Rosie smiled, "Just teasing. After you attacked Mike at home plate we all got the message. I'll leave you two alone. Coffee?"

"No, a strawberry shake I think," she said. "Two actually, to go." She walked down to the end booth. "Hey Brian. Sorry I'm late. I was already a little behind and then had to wait up on the highway for a mother bear and her three cubs to cross the road. Are there really less of them?"

"Less in some areas," he said, "but the local population is higher. They're a hazard on the roads, especially with all the lumber trucks speeding through here. Not to mention hungry bears prowling around the campsites. But bears weren't part of your proposal, were they?"

"No, I want to talk to you about doing a blitz out on the lake in a few weeks," she said. Since it was divided down the middle by the Park boundary, Natural Resources split the monitoring with them too. "There's the big Bass Challenge on the August long weekend, so there will be a lot of extra boats out on the water for the derby. We should work to coordinate a big push to check them out."

They worked out a checklist of things to look for. Besides the usual, like drinking, proper licences, and life-jackets, Dave had asked them to try to do more on-board inspections. He had a feeling they'd be finding more drugs this summer. Not necessarily from the fishermen, but from the cottagers who would be out too.

"We'll have our boat out as much as we can," she said, "but it's getting pretty busy for our team just covering in town."

"Same for us," said Brian. "We'll have a lot of campers to look after that weekend. Bookings are way up, but we'll try to patrol our side the best we can. Maybe we can do some of the same shifts."

"We'll see," she said. "You mentioned a lot more campers this summer. Any increase in crime?"

"Yes, but normal for this time of year. Well, maybe a bit more, but it's still just drinking, noise, fishing and boating infractions. Some drugs."

"More drugs?" she asked.

"Well, yes, especially in the camp sites closest to the town. Do you have more here also?"

"Yes," she said. "Maybe there's a link. We have a few people we are keeping an eye on—why don't we compare notes after?"

"Can do," he said. "The other thing is those local bears. I think it's the dump, with more tourists heading out after supper to feed the animals. Their knowledge of nature is from whatever they've seen on TV. Some think it's Yogi Bear and Boo-Boo they're watching. Unfortunately, as you know, the bears seem tame right up until one of them takes a swipe at somebody. Not that they have, so far, but we did have a family get chased back into their car."

"I know Junior is doing some outdoor education program," she said, "with the kids in his youth centre here. He talks about respecting the animals, and their place in the ecology. Good stuff for the kids but doesn't really get to the parents."

"We do programs like that sometimes for the campers," said Brian. "Maybe he'd like to assist us."

"You can certainly ask," she said, "but I'm pretty sure he prefers the independence he has now, developing his own program."

"I'd still like to link up with him," said Brian. "I'll give him a call." He pointed to the counter. "There's your shakes. Two?"

She smiled. "I'm meeting Mike at the mill. He still does a bit of database work. Those managers that were turfed out last spring really messed things up, so he's been making sure all the pollution controls are working now. That and working on being the new mayor."

Brian smiled ruefully. "He is a great guy and I'm happy for you. You're a good catch."

"Thanks," she said. She started to get up then paused. "Do me a favour, would you? Could you check on your crime stats for any patterns? Are all the numbers larger in one area? And how much has it changed from last year?"

"What are you looking for?" he said.

"I'm not sure," she said.

Dave had spent the last two hours trying to leave the office.

"Guys, I really need to hit the road, I don't want to get caught in Winnipeg rush hour traffic, such as it is. It looks like it will be a good two hours drive too, with this mist." The day had started off cool, with a persistent fog that now seemed about to turn into a drizzle.

"Okay," said Norris. "So just go. You keep fussing around like a mother leaving her kids for the first time with a babysitter. We'll be fine. Next you'll be putting up little sticky notes all over reminding us to wash our hands and turn off the lights and order more coffee."

Dave started to open a desk drawer.

"No, I was joking," she said, "we don't need more notes, okay."

"You're right," said Dave. "It's only a few days. With a weekend in the middle."

"Exactly," said Norris. "You're only a few hours away. Sheila and I have been here several years, Angus has decades of experience. You're just afraid we'll all do just fine and not miss you at all."

Dave grabbed his bag. "Okay, you convinced me, I'm out of here. You're right, I need to trust you, it will be just life as usual in Kirk's Landing."

Some of the courses looked interesting, but he was not going to try to fade and sneak out of the boring ones. As he was about to get into his car, Mike waved to him from down the street.

"Hey, Dave, got a minute? Just a couple of things."

Dave sighed. He was a popular guy, respected in town, but he really needed people to trust that Norris would take care of things just fine.

"I wanted to catch you before you left," said Mike. "I saw Janie again today, she was wearing sunglasses, on a cloudy day, I think her step-father is at her again."

"Go ahead and let Norris know," said Dave. "She's up to speed on all our current issues and I've complete confidence in her."

"It's just that I thought he needed a big guy like you to put some fear into him."

"Doesn't usually work," said Dave. "You can slap a bully around, but once you're gone he just takes it out on someone weaker. I have seen him hanging around Risso more lately too. His wife is pretty sure he's using again."

Mike nodded. "Exactly. So arrest him and get him out of the way."

"Well, we have to catch him at it. But, still, it's not that effective. Short term it works since he's in jail, but I suspect he's not into drugs enough to have to spend any significant time away. We can put him away, for sure, but once he gets out, he'll go right back to it. We need to do more. The best thing for his wife and daughter is for them to testify against him for assault causing bodily harm, get him put away, divorce him, and get a restraining order so he has to stay away." Dave had his reservations about those orders, but in a small place like this, it would likely mean him having to leave town completely. So it just might work.

"Thing is," said Mike, "I hear some people saying that all he needs is some tough back alley justice."

Dave turned and looked right at Mike. "No, that's not going to happen in my town. As much as anyone thinks that might help—it won't. Make sure you tell that to anyone thinking they can fix this—or other problems. We don't need a pack of vigilantes out of a corny Western."

"Sorry Dave, I totally agree, not my idea. I've already given those that proposed it a blast."

"Anything else?" asked Dave.

"I do have some questions about schedules and coverage. There are more summer folks in town, and I've been seeing more sketchy people in among them lately. But I'll go in and ask Norris about it. You go ahead and get to your vacation."

"Training course," said Dave. "We've a full schedule all day."

"And the evenings?"

"Networking," said Dave, "possibly with liquids involved."

As Mike headed into the detachment office, Dave jumped quickly into his car, before anyone else stopped him. He headed up the road, wipers on. As he turned out on the highway he swerved to avoid a car that cut the corner a little too tight. Probably some business man on holiday, looking for a break. He felt a shiver down his back as he glanced behind in the mirror at his town.

Chapter 21

Sasquatch slowed as he neared the turn into Kirk's Landing, narrowly missing a car at the corner. He resisted the temptation to lay on the horn and give the idiot the finger, as he was supposed to be laying low for a while, as a respectable businessman. He looked up and realized that the day had turned dark suddenly, with heavy clouds hanging over the town, and a mist gathering in the trees. So much for a sunny vacation getaway. He drove slowly down the hill into town, and was pleased to see it was a little more lively than his last visit. Not all locals either, as there were a lot rushing about in garish vacation outfits, umbrellas overhead. Southerners—his customers.

He headed down the main street to the lake and parked under some trees, out of the way. He felt restless after the trip, and just wanted to get out and kick something. Or someone. He'd felt a bit off ever since the bike trip—maybe he'd picked something up. He'd been looking forward to the challenge of getting Risso and his dealers into shape, but the weather had spoiled his mood. And now he seemed to be getting another one of his headaches again, right between his eyes. He checked his phone list and dialled.

"Risso, it's Sasquatch. I just got in. I'm down by the lake. I assume your chief cop has gone?"

"Hey Sas, yup, you just missed him. It was supposed to be this morning, but he left only a few minutes ago."

"Good. I'll be seeing him soon enough, but in the meantime we've got work to do. I assume you found me a place?"

"Yes, I did," said Risso. "A small cottage just up the lake. Still within walking distance but a bit out of the way so no one should bother you. Louie and Bonnie are next door. I'm there now, come on up. I'll wait out by the road."

It looked more like a cabin than a cottage, but it did have a small garage about twenty feet behind it and was at the end of a row of three cabins. The place next door had a big black Lincoln SUV parked next to it, looking very much out of place. He drove in behind the garage and carried his bags inside. The place was small, but clean. It would do.

"Nice suit," said Risso. "I got us some food and some beer in, and Louie and Bonnie are just next door."

"That big SUV is Louie's idea of low profile? Idiot."

"Want me to get them now?" asked Risso.

"Give me an hour to clean up. I could use a shower and beer and a bite to eat."

It was mid-afternoon by the time they all got together.

"Hey, good to see you," said Bonnie, giving him a hug. Louie just nodded.

"Yeah, good to see you guys too," Sasquatch said. "First chance, Louie, take that flashy truck back and come back with something boring, like the one I got. And Bonnie, tone that look down. More homemaker, less hooker."

They brought Sasquatch up to speed on what they'd found out so far about the local drugs market, especially the latest bust.

"You were right," said Louie. "Big potential here. There was a lot of drugs moving through here to summer folk too, especially through the post office."

"Big bust," said Risso, "but we were lucky, didn't get hit at all."

"I heard about it," said Sasquatch. "But what about now? What's wrong with you, Risso? Why didn't you get us that market, rather than sit around being glad you weren't busted? What the hell have you been doing?" No initiative at all. He reached over and gave the shrimp a punch in the shoulder.

"Ow! Hey, I've been trying, honest," whined Risso. "When there was all that problem at the mill most of my network either got busted or scared."

"So, you build a new network. Which we now have to do for you. Where's the stuff you've been bringing in from Winnipeg?

"Got a secret spot in the garage," said Risso.

"Has it been moving?"

"Now it is," said Louie. "Bonnie and me, we've been working hard to get things started up again here." Risso glared at them, but Bonnie just smiled back sweetly.

"Keep talking, ass-hole, without me to back you no one would have been talking with you," said Risso.

"Whatever," said Sasquatch, "calm down you two. So what's the story on that post office mess? Anything point to us?"

Risso reassured him that it was just some small isolated deals people had made with friends down south.

"Don't worry, I can turn this around," said Risso. "I cleared away some of the brush around here, too. Just be careful, I haven't trimmed down all those little stumps yet, it can be a bitch to walk through."

"No, leave it," said Sasquatch, "It might keep people from wandering too close. Now, you guys get out of here. I've got to check my email to see what other screw-ups have happened lately."

"Tell you what," said Louie. "Why don't Bonnie and I get some supper together for us all—she's a good cook—then we can all drop down at the local bar. It's a nice place."

"Yes to the dinner, but no to everyone at the bar," said Sasquatch.

"Damn it, keep this low key, remember? The less we are all seen together in public the better. No, I'll just go there with Risso. He can point out some of the rich marks for me."

"And my contacts?" asked Risso. "Want to meet them?"

"No, not your contacts. Jesus, why don't you give them all a big sign, saying Drug Dealer? He glared at Risso. As far as he was concerned one more slip and the loser was out. Bonnie, get me another beer and then get started on that supper."

After supper, Sasquatch and Risso headed down the narrow road to town and the bar. Sasquatch had dressed down, but he still looked like a business man on holiday, he hoped. It was a cool night, and it sounded like a big storm was rolling in, quickly. He could hear the roll of thunder in the distance. He swatted angrily at his neck

"Damn it, can't they spray the town or something? And why are they only attacking me? They're really pissing me off."

"Sorry," said Risso, "I'll give you some bug spray when we get back, I forgot. Never seen them this focused on one person before, though. They can be even worse in the bush, driving a deer or moose crazy they say."

Sasquatch glared at him and kept swatting. "I'm close to losing it right here. Hurry up."

The whole drug business up here was a mess he would need to clean up. Plus Risso hadn't found anything useful on this chief of police. Dinner had been plain, Louie and Risso annoying, Bonnie sullen. Sasquatch was tired, thirsty, and in a foul mood. He'd felt annoyance and anger at things ever since he'd arrived. He was swatting at yet another insect when a small dog came yapping from a cottage yard.

"Jeez, piss off!" He whirled, kicked, and connected, sending the small animal soaring into a bush. It righted itself after a moment and ran off, still yapping. He smiled and pumped a fist in the air. "Alright!" He felt a real rush for a moment, less tension inside.

"Wow, what was that all about?" asked Risso.

"Stupid mutt," said Sasquatch. "Served it right. I just felt I had to hit someone—or something. Be glad it wasn't you."

"Well, you looked weird there for a moment," said Risso. "Your eyes were really scary looking." He hesitated. "And you seemed even bigger than you are. Not that I mean you're fat."

"Shut up, you idiot. You're probably just seeing all these stupid bugs swarming around me," said Sasquatch.

"Probably," said Risso. "They're mostly here in the woods, anyway. Look, there's the bar just ahead."

"You know, I think I'll take a walk around town first," said Sasquatch. "Check it out. You go ahead to the bar and I'll meet you there later."

"Want me to show you around town?" said Risso.

"No, I'd rather we start off with me just a random visitor. You go ahead and get a seat. And listen, shit for brains, when I get there please don't stand up and wave."

He walked slowly up the street, peering in windows, nodding to passersby. Typical small town, like dozens of places he'd ridden through over the years. He noticed a small cafe, probably the one that Risso had mentioned. It might be a good place to pick up some gossip and get a feel of the locals.

He sat in a booth by the window, enjoying his coffee, watching people walk by, listening to the buzz around him, soaking up the flavour of the town. He felt some of his irritation fading, being replaced by a bit of eagerness. He'd been slowing down too much lately, getting soft. It felt good to be back into action. It might not be that hard to get things rolling here, as long as Risso took some initiative, and didn't screw up. He turned at the sounds of a scuffle, but it was just some kids goofing around at the end of the cafe. Looked like some clean-cut college types—potential customers—as well as a few scruffy-looking locals. Maybe they were part of Risso's dealer chain. There was an Indian kid too, who kept looking his way.

He wondered if one of the kids was that guy Kurt, who'd been trying to push drugs. Sasquatch smiled. Those Toronto strikers certainly put the scare into that kid's girlfriend. They'd wanted to go after her once more, but she'd disappeared. No matter, they'd eventually track her down. Nobody could stay lost forever from Hell's Angels. And they'd track down that Indian girlfriend JB as well. He smiled with anticipation of what they'd do to her.

Enough day-dreaming. He got up and headed to the cash. "Nice coffee," he said.

The cashier jumped at the sound of his voice. "Oh, thanks, I'm Rosie. Sorry, you startled me. I'd forgotten you were here. Glad you liked it. New in town, I'm guessing."

"Yup. Just here to relax for a bit. This looks a nice peaceful place, with not a lot of crime, I'd guess. Big police force?"

"We had a few problems this spring, but cleaned them up pretty fast. Our new chief of police did a good job. It's busier now, though. What with all these new people here for the summer, it's all I can do to just keep the coffee flowing."

"New police chief, eh? From around here?" asked Sasquatch.

"He used to work out west. Hope you enjoy your stay. What was your name again?"

"Just Sam." Sasquatch nodded at Rosie and headed back outside. Nice guy but must be half blind to not see him sitting there in the booth.

Sasquatch kept one eye on the sky as he walked back to the bar. Masses of dark clouds were piling up, and there was a definite chill in the air. He paused inside the door, scanning the crowd, then spotted Risso across the crowded room. He was pleased to see that the numbskull didn't even nod to him. Sasquatch carefully made his way over to the bar. The bartender looked young and a little overwhelmed by the crowd but seemed to know everyone. It was a small town, likely with a lot of regulars in the bar, so they would notice anything out of the ordinary. He walked over to the bar, managed to finally get the attention of the young bartender, and ordered a draft from him. He paused and took a sip, casually looking over the room, then walked over to Risso.

"Mind if I sit here?" he asked.

"No problem, buddy. Hi, I'm Risso."

"Good to meet you. I'm Sam." He held out his hand, hoping Risso would take the cue.

"Welcome to Kirk's Landing, Sam."

As they sat talking, Risso carefully pointed out the various contacts he had already, and a few customers. Some seemed a little too friendly back at them, so he told Risso to talk to them later to dial it back a little, that a good network shouldn't be too obvious to outsiders. "That bartender looks like he hasn't a clue, but with all these locals in here you never know who might be watching."

Sasquatch pointed to a few Indians sitting in one corner, listening to an older one at their table. "How about those natives, any market there?"

"Not really," said Risso. "They're all pretty clean. The old guy is their chief, he's pretty tight with the chief of police and mayor. They have their own band police too. I tried to get at them but not much luck."

"Maybe you just didn't try hard enough," said Sasquatch. "Everyone has a price. I'll add them to my list."

As Risso chattered on, Sasquatch thought again about that feeling he'd had before in the cafe, like he was looking at things differently. As he did so, it came back again, and it seemed he was seeing and hearing things around him a little better. Then, after only a minute, the feeling suddenly disappeared.

Risso had been looking over at the bar, he turned back and jumped a bit.

"Wow, you snuck back on me, thought you'd gone to the can."

"No," said Sasquatch. "I was here all along."

Risso looked at him for a moment, then shrugged and continued his running commentary on life in Kirk's Landing.

Sasquatch pondered on what had just happened. This was weird. Twice now that someone didn't see him. He tried again to do whatever he'd just done in front of Risso, but all it did was make him a bit light-headed. He finished his beer and stood up. "I'm heading back, I have some work to do. Stay a while, but don't party all night. And be quiet when you come in, don't disturb me and Bonnie."

Risso smiled and gave him a thumbs up. "See you Sam."

Sasquatch paused again outside the bar. The storm had passed through already, leaving what looked like hail. In July. He leaned against the wall, relaxed, and tried to regain that feeling he'd had before. It seemed to be working, as the few people that walked by didn't even give him a glance. He staggered as a sudden pain lanced through his head, and one of the passersby reached out and grabbed his arm.

"Whoa, you okay buddy? Bit too many beer?"

"Piss off." Sasquatch angrily shook him off, then headed slowly back to the cottage. What was happening to him? Was this the same sort of thing that Toronto guy had used to hide from them? Whatever it was, it seemed just to flicker off and on. And that pain, it had cut him like a knife. However, he was still intrigued by this new sensation. He'd try again.

Chapter 22

Norris clutched a bundle of files as she pushed through the detachment door.

"Morning boss," said Sheila. "Homework?"

"Morning Sheila," said Norris. "Just some reports I wanted to get at." She hadn't realized how much paperwork there was in running a detachment—even with Sheila helping. "It's been two days since Dave left, with no real problems, so I guess we're doing okay. Other than having one less person to share the schedules with."

"I know" said Sheila. "It's been very smooth so far."

"Surprised?" asked Norris.

"No, no, it's a good thing. Coffee?"

"Thanks Sheila, I'll need it to go through the rest of these reports. Hopefully I can leave most of this stuff for Dave when he gets back in a week."

Norris had been at her chore for an hour when there was a knock on the door, and Angus poked his head in.

"Hey boss, got a minute?" he asked.

"Not you too. What's with the 'boss' stuff?"

"Just teasing," he said. "I've filled in enough over the years to know what a mixed blessing it is. More work, for the same pay. However, you're bound to get a good mark on your file. As long as all goes well here, that is. You're not planning any big crime take downs are you?"

He'd already heard all about the one she'd done on Risso last winter. Norris smiled. "No, I think we'll avoid those for now. We do need some better leads on the drug issues though."

"I was going to suggest some surveillance on likely suspects," said Angus, "then I remembered this is a small detachment, with no one to spare."

"You got it," said Norris. "It's a big list of suspects for a small town. We've a lot from that post office thing, and some left over from the mill scandal, and now some sketchy-looking new people wandering around town asking about Dave. Including some that look like bikers in suits, trying not to look as uncomfortable as I'm sure they feel. I got some numbers from my contact over in Natural Resources too, their numbers are up this year for infractions. Not a lot, but enough to bother him. He's added more patrols in the park. As for us here in town, we have lots of choices."

"Any one person that might be likely to make some mistakes?" he asked. "Someone to focus on?"

"Good point," she said. "Those biker types might be trouble, but I'm not sure what they are up to yet. Maybe our best bet for now is to take a closer look at Risso. I think we can count on him to mess up; he's dependable in that way. And I'm pretty sure he's linked up with these newcomers. Some people still think he should have been sent away for a while, but he can likely help us more from the street than a jail cell. He's cockier too, lately, with a smug look on his face. Let's keep an eye on him. I'll tell the band police too, as they come into town sometimes and he's not that familiar with them. Thanks."

Angus paused at the doorway. "No problem. And thank you for the birthday present suggestions for my little grandson. I got him that book of paper airplane designs. He and his dad are working on them together."

"Glad to help," said Norris. She gathered up the rest of the papers into a pile and pushed back from her desk. "I need a quick break. I'll drop by Rosie's then do a loop down the street." She didn't know how Dave stood it; she hated forms. She pulled on her raincoat and turned up the collar. She'd assumed the weather would be miserable for Dave in Winnipeg too, but he'd claimed that as soon as he got twenty minutes out of town it turned beautiful, and held that way all the way to the city.

As she'd hoped, Norris met Junior right outside Rosie's. "Junior, how's your newsletter going?"

"Not really started yet," he said. "I'm still waiting for Janie to come in and talk to me."

"I think you'll need to track her down. She's still kind of shy about her latest incident, you know. And don't act so reluctant about it either, Rosie tells me you fancy her."

"We're just friends," he said, but she could see a blush, even under his dark skin.

"Oh, another thing," she said. "While you're wandering about, could you keep a casual eye on Risso? Not for anything in particular, I just have a feeling he's up to no good again."

"Sure, want me to tell the kids in the centre also?"

"Thanks, but I need to keep this under control a bit. Just you. If we end up with most of the town keeping an eye on Risso without really looking at him it will be so obvious even he will notice it."

"I think there's someone else we should be watching," he said. "I was hanging out at Rosie's the other day with the guys, down at the end, on those nice soft chairs. And this big guy was there—like really big. Blond hair, and kinda weird-looking. Same one that was here before, asking about your boss, that Sasquatch. He was sitting on his own in a booth, just watching the people in there and out on the street."

"Okay," said Norris. "And the weird part was . . . "

"Well, he had a cold expressionless face, with a tiny little smile stuck on it. But the weird part was the vibe I got from him, a feeling that reminded me of what I used to see in Dave when he had that problem last winter."

"All the more reason to keep an eye on him," she said.

"Will you tell Dave about him?" said Junior.

"No, I'll let him enjoy his break. Thanks for the tip, but stay on Risso for now. I'll ask Rosie about this new biker. Now you go find your secret girlfriend."

Rosie had her coffee waiting on the counter as she walked in, shaking off her raincoat.

"Am I that predictable?" she said. "Actually, I was thinking of switching to tea, but I guess I'll have to retrain everyone first. But thanks. I'll take it here by the cash, as I need to talk when you've a minute."

Rosie cleared some dishes from the counter, whisked an order from the kitchen pass-through over to one of the booths, and came back to the front.

"All right," he said. "Shoot."

"I was talking to Junior a few minutes ago, and he mentioned when he was here the other day there was a peculiar guy here. Very large, cold hard face, blond hair. I know you get a lot in here everyday, but does that ring a bell?"

"I think I know who he means," said Rosie. "Big guy, with a scary look. He was in a while ago too. He tried to play the casual tourist, like before, but I felt he was sizing me up like some sort of predator. He asked a few questions about crime and policing here, and seemed particularly interested in who the detachment chief was and where he was from. I was non-committal, of course."

"What did he say about himself?" she asked.

"Nothing much, he was pretty evasive and took off. Oh, he calls himself Sam."

"Thanks," she said. "He's on our list. But for now, I was going to ask you to join some of us in a sort of Risso watch. Waiting for him to mess up."

"As he will," said Rosie.

"Of course," she said. "But looks like we need to keep an eye on this Sam character too. Thanks for the coffee."

Norris carried on down the street, following the regular beat. Part of being on foot was as a deterrent, to show people they were out and about, part was networking, and part was just social. In addition, the town council liked it. Her last stop before heading back would be the Raven's Roost. Although it was early, there might be an afternoon crowd, especially with this constant drizzle. Maybe Mike would be there too.

She stepped into the bar, then paused to let her eyes get used to the relative gloom. It was darker with the doors at the end closed against the rain, and was surprisingly quiet. Maybe the nasty weather was keeping people holed up. She saw Risso's two 'business associates' sitting in a corner, heads bent in conversation over a pitcher of beer. They glanced quickly at her then looked down. Not very good at looking innocent. Sid was standing, bored, behind the bar, so she walked over. He was trying—and failing—to spin a tray on his finger.

"See that in a movie?" she asked.

Startled, he dropped the tray again, with a crash.

"Hey," said the two guys at the bar, "keep it down, we're trying to watch Oprah."

"What's up," said Sid. "Want a coffee?"

"No, I just had one at Rosie's. I'd rather not make my patrols a series of bathroom breaks. Just popping in to show my face. How was last night?"

"Oh, that girl's birthday party did start to get a little wild. It was certainly good for business though. Just some kids having fun—sorry, young adults. We did check IDs carefully."

"Anything else?"

"Risso and his new buddies were here too. Pretty quiet, drinking, talking, sneaking out back for a joint."

At the mention of Risso's name, Norris glanced over toward the corner, but his friends had left, beer unfinished.

"Looks like I've scared them off," she said.

"I've seen another guy with them too," said Sid. "Big guy, blond, looks like trouble but keeps it low key. All of them trying to be casual, but I suspect Risso—with their help—is trying to start up some serious drug dealing again. More than the occasional bag of weed he sells out back."

"That's likely," she said. "I don't trust Risso at all."

"Nobody does," said Sid, "even his customers. I try to keep an eye on him." He wiped down the counter. "It's nice to have it quiet in here for a change. Now that JB's gone I realize what a big job it is to run this place. It helps having some extra summer staff, but it's surprising all the details that you have to catch, and all the questions you get, when you're in charge."

"Tell me about it," said Norris. "I'll add the back of your place to the occasional check on our patrols. I gotta run, but I might drop by later for a drink with Mike."

Chapter 23

Rosie turned from the cash as Junior whistled at him. "Wow, Rosie, looking pretty fly. Is that a new shirt?"

"Might be. Nothing that unusual. Sometimes I just like to dress up."

"What a coincidence," said Junior, "because today's the day that cute outdoor-ed teacher is coming." He laughed and walked back into the youth centre.

"Smart-ass," said Rosie. He started setting up for lunch, carefully, so as to keep his new shirt clean. He was looking under the counter for more menus when he heard a woman's voice.

"Hello? Is anybody here?"

He straightened up quickly, wiped his hand on his apron, and held it out.

"Hi, I'm Rosie. You must be Ms. Goodall." Junior was right, she was cute.

"Ah, hi," she said. "Rosie?"

"It's a bit of a story," he said. "I can explain it later over coffee, if you've time. But you'll be looking for Junior, right? He's out back in our youth centre. This way."

After he showed her back to the centre, he returned to his lunch prep, with the occasional glance toward the back room. Just as he was finishing up lunch service, the two of them came back out. Rosie smiled and set a couple of coffees out for them.

"Can I tempt you with a bit of dessert, Ms. Goodall?" he said.

"I haven't had lunch yet," she said. "Junior raved about your food so much I was about to faint from hunger, I think."

"I have some Leek and Potato soup left. I can do you a salad too."

"I'm sold," she said. "And call me Sharon, please."

"You got it. And Junior will be taking a piece of pie, I'm sure."

"No, I'll just take my coffee with me in back," said Junior. "You can pump her all about her proposal." He picked up his coffee and gave Rosie a smile and thumbs up behind the teacher's back.

Sharon sipped her soup and watched Rosie as he quickly put together the rest of her lunch.

"This is good," she said. "I like the added nutmeg. Obviously homemade." She reached out and touched his arm. "So, tell me the story behind Rosie."

Rosie filled her in on his saga—the early marriage, successful business in Toronto, loving relationship, unexpected death of his wife and partner, and his new home and friends in the north.

She shook her head. "Wow, such highs and lows. But you're happy now up here?"

"Very much so," he said. "So, what about Junior's plan? Does it look doable? He's really quite an accomplished young man."

"Yes he is," she said. "He told me of some of his earlier problems growing up as First Nations in a small town, and the strong influence from his grandfather. And his lifetime love of nature, and the bond he feels with it. I think he's well qualified to relate to the youth, be they troubled or not, and use his outdoor program to do it."

"He's just starting to realize his own capabilities," said Rosie. "It's good to see him grow."

"It's a good proposal," she said. "I'll try this in the fall as a pilot program. We've got a fair number of First Nations kids in our board area, so we are all looking for a way to turn them on to education. And to some of their culture."

"So when do you have to get back?" said Rosie.

"Not right away," said Sharon. "Junior suggested a tour of the town, then suddenly remembered he was too busy to do it, but that you often took a break after lunch."

"I think he's plotting something here," said Rosie.

"I think so too," said Sharon, "but I would like a town tour."

"I'll get Junior to watch things for a while, and we can go," said Rosie.

He enjoyed the tour, especially since the sun actually came out for a while. Sharon had an infectious laugh and a genuine interest in life in a small town. By the time they finished they were swapping stories of Toronto life, and how different it was from life up here, and she even grabbed his arm for a bit as they rushed across the street in a sudden rain shower.

Junior was at the counter when they rushed in, laughing and brushing the rain off their sleeves.

"Glad someone had fun while I was slaving away here behind the counter," he said.

"Looks like you managed to sooth your sorrows with a piece of pie," said Sharon. "I've got to run. Junior, excellent ideas, I'll be looking forward to that revised business plan. Rosie, great meeting you, thanks for the tour. See you both soon."

With a hug to both of them she was out the door, leaving Rosie and Junior smiling at each other.

Chapter 24

Angus looked up in surprise as Dave walked into the detachment. "Oh, hi Corporal. I didn't expect you back here in the office already. Did you get kicked out of school?"

"No, just back for the weekend. Friday is just a half day since they leave the afternoon for firearms remedial for people who don't pass the first time. My courses are going well, as it's mostly refresher stuff."

"I remember all those courses," said Angus. "Mostly because it seemed every time I'd get a good schedule going with my staff, someone would head off for some training."

Dave nodded to Reese. "Hi Reese, what are you up to today?"

"We're doing patrols on the lake. There's a big fishing derby, so should be lots of traffic. We're doing mostly spot checks for safety equipment and alcohol. Brian Gleason from Natural Resources is partnering with us. I think he was hoping Norris would be on again, but he'll have to make do with me. Other than that, just more summer people arriving. Nothing unusual, well, except one guy."

As Reese described the mysterious new-comer, Dave felt a chill. It did sound a lot like Sasquatch—a cleaned up version—but the same

Toronto biker. But up here?

Reese motioned Dave over to his computer. "Here's a picture I got from Rosie's security camera—I thought you might be interested."

Dave peered at the screen. Damn! Definitely was his old enemy. He didn't just happen to be up here either, not with the questions that were being asked around town. This was not just a random visit.

"Talk to him yourself," said Reese, "and see what we mean by how weird he is."

"I don't need to," said Dave. "Same guy as was here earlier, poking around, my old friend, Sasquatch."

"Friend?" said Angus.

Dave explained his connection to the biker and his concerns over seeing him back here. "He was just passing through before, but sounds like he's here for a while. I'm only back for the weekend, so I'll keep an eye out for him, but for now, should just watch and wait." He'd definitely be using his fade ability too, to try to sneak up on his old enemy. "I don't know if he's figured out yet who I am, but he will. But I don't think he'll be bold or stupid enough to make a move on me. I think he's up here mainly to try to get Risso back into the drug business."

"Well, just in case he gets any ideas," said Angus, "we've got your back."

Sasquatch was quietly lying in his cabin, trying to turn on his strange power again. Maybe he had it this time, as he could feel his senses sharpening. He'd been practising the last few days turning on his power, and then sneaking up on people. First his friends—who definitely didn't like it, and then people around town. At first it seemed to flicker off and on like a loose light bulb, and he'd suddenly find people looking his way, with a puzzled look. Especially that big Indian kid. It was kind of fun when it worked, because you could tell they were looking for something that wasn't there, as if they'd glimpsed it out of the corner of their eye.

Risso cautiously poked his head around the door, looked around the room—right past Sasquatch—and then walked over to the fridge and grabbed two cans of beer out of it.

The nerve—the squirt was ripping off his beer. Sasquatch felt a rage building in him as he growled and leaped out of bed.

Risso jumped back. "Holy shit, I didn't see you. I thought you'd be out on the prowl. I was going to repay you, honest!"

Sasquatch reached out and grabbed the little creep by the neck. Anger rose in him like a flame and he was delighted with its strength. He slapped the side of Risso's head then threw him clear across the room—slamming him into the wall. The only thing that stopped him from beating the little worm into a pulp was knowing he needed Risso for a few more weeks. That and the realization that he actually had the ability to become invisible. What a rush!

"What are you doing inside, Risso?" he said. "Why aren't you out working your contacts?"

"I was, boss, honest." He popped the can of beer and took a sip. "Guess who I ran into?"

"A wall?" said Sasquatch. He leaned toward Risso. "I don't know, just tell me. Now."

"Sure, no problem, Sas. It was your buddy from down south, our new chief of police. He's been away on a course but is back for the weekend. Good news, right?"

"Yes, very good news," said Sasquatch. "Thanks. I think I'll do a bit of undercover work myself now, and see if I can spy on him."

He was so far able to maintain what he called his fog for only a few minutes, but was assuming he'd soon be up to an hour. The lingering headaches after each session were a downside, but the upside was a great rush every time he turned his secret power on. He loved it! He'd already used it around town, eavesdropping on people in the post office, the stores, the cafe, even just gossiping at a corner.

He paused by the hotel, just before heading up the main street, focused, and felt his fog switch on again. Easily. He was just passing the cafe when he saw what looked like that cop inside. Sasquatch stepped back out of the way to wait for him to leave. He'd learned that people wouldn't bump into him even when invisible, but would somehow just go around. A minute later his quarry stepped out onto the street. Yes! Definitely was that bastard from their meeting in Toronto, the one they thought was just from another gang. He'd recognize the neck tattoo anywhere. Sasquatch was so startled he almost broke his concentration and became visible. This was a bonus. First a town ready for his drugs, then a strange power that let him work unseen, and now this cop. He'd have to think up a suitable revenge. Maybe his snooping would track down where the cop's girlfriend was. He loved his new power.

He glanced around to see if maybe that dumb Indian kid was around too, but when he looked back the cop was gone. In an instant. He must be using that power of his too, to try to hide. Trouble was, the cop probably had to stay visible most of the time, while he was on duty. Sasquatch had no such limitation. This was going to be a fun summer of hide and seek.

JB found a quiet corner of the library and took out her cell phone. She'd been studying all morning—on a Saturday yet—and needed a break. She and Dave had been just leaving brief voice mails back and forth lately, but he was supposedly back for the weekend. She sipped her tea, dialled, and listened to it ring and ring. She was already thinking of a message for his machine—casual yet friendly—when he surprised her by answering.

"Oh hi, Dave, it's JB. I wasn't sure if I'd catch you at home."

"I'm back for the weekend," he said. "Have the day off, sort of. It's so good to hear your voice. You're not working today?"

"No, I've a study group for my Criminology course this afternoon, so was getting in some studying," she said. "They're such keeners, meeting on a Saturday afternoon. I'm glad I caught you."

"Well, I just had to come home to do some laundry and relax."

"And you missed our little town, didn't you? The one you couldn't wait to leave back in January."

"Well, yes," he said. "Funny how our attitudes can change. Thanks for those tips about bikers and drugs coming up here. It feels better at least knowing what to look for. We're already noticing new people poking around too, people that are trying to look like summer tourists, but failing."

"Are you keeping Grandfather in the loop on this too?"

"Actually, he's one of the people I'd like to talk to this weekend, if I can find him."

"He's often off fishing somewhere," she said. "Or just takes off to visit someone on another reserve. I think there's one up the other side of the park he goes to—maybe Yellow River. We suspect he's got his eye on one of the women up there. Why'd you need him? Anything I can help with?"

"I'm afraid the biker problem is worse than I thought," said Dave. "I may need his help tracking down an old enemy, Sasquatch."

"What? He's up there? Be careful!"

"I will, sweetie. But I'm not 100% sure if he's here or not—that's the problem." He explained how he'd been talking to Kurt and felt he was being watched, but when he'd gone outside, there was nobody there. Yet that feeling had persisted, until he'd used his fade.

"But I can't use that all the time," he said. "People will think I've left town."

"Hmm. You got me," she said. "Guess you do need Grandfather. Ask Junior, he'll know where he is."

"Thanks, I'll do that. So, how is life in the big city?" he said.

"Still very busy between school and work and trying to have a life in-between. Not as much partying as last time, more just hangin' with friends." This time she had a real goal to head for, so it was a little easier to focus..

"Thanks for taking care of Crystal, too," he said.

"She's a great kid; I don't mind. I convinced her she should just dump all her connections and start fresh. She got rid of her old cellphone, email address, Twitter, Facebook. She realizes that the less she has to do with her old friends the better."

"And how's she doing for money?" he said.

"She'd saved a bit while in Toronto, but a lot went into art supplies. She brought that stuff here though, and might start painting again. In the meantime, a friend got her a job at a restaurant."

"She's not there at Danny's with you?"

"No, I wanted to keep her at arms length in case people come looking for her. Just in case. She's doing okay, sort of one step at a time, so that means people like me and her mother are starting to believe she really wants to make a change."

"Did she contact her mother?"

"Yes, but she made sure to not tell where she was. That beating made her really paranoid. She just said she was out of Toronto and out of the gang. Her mother wants to believe her this time, even sent her some cash via email transfer. Not a lot, but it helped."

They continued to talk, about the little things that had happened in their day, about their challenges and problems, mutual friends, dismal weather in Kirk's Landing, city versus country life—all the sort of rambling that she missed.

"This is nice," he said. "I like talking with you, even over little things."

"Me too," she said. "Sorry again I couldn't get back for a break, but I did get a lot of work done down here. Looks like I may even ace a couple of courses. It's different from the last time I was here, now that I've found something more specific. I'm really glad I decided to come back to this stuff, even if it did mean leaving home. And you."

"Well, I do miss you, but sounds like this is something that's really important to you," he said. "So of course you'll do better—you can focus when you need to. You're a smart cookie—not just a pretty face."

"Thanks," said JB. "Jeez, I miss talking to you too, and your hugs. I'm looking forward to my return."

"Me too! I think we need to talk face to face."

"What? A guy wants to talk? Wow! I'm in. Look Hon, I have to run, but glad I caught you. I'll give you a shout later in the week."

Chapter 25

After their call finally ended, Dave threw a load of laundry in and then started on his weights. While on course he missed his daily routines as well as the walking he normally did. He certainly never would be a desk jockey. After his workout, he grabbed a quick shower and headed downtown. For a change the sun was out, drying up the puddles. Hopefully, it would last. He was enjoying the sun when he bumped into Junior and his Grandfather.

"Hi Junior. Good afternoon sir—sorry, Charlie."

The elder laughed, "What are you doing back? Are you playing hooky from school?"

"No, just a break. Laundry and paperwork."

"Junior was telling me of something that happened in Rosie's while you were away," said Charlie.

They then recounted the strange feeling Junior had about the person in Rosie's, like there was something evil there reminiscent of Dave's spirit before. In addition, they had both felt it again around town a few times.

"Was this same guy around every time?" asked Dave.

"He was the first few times," said Junior. "That Sasquatch. Actually, I haven't seen him around for the last day or two. After that, all I saw was just regular people. But we still need to track down the source of this evil."

"Should I be worried?" said Dave.

"Not yet," said Charlie.

"Great," said Dave. "How about those business associates of Risso's?"

"Oh, they're still around," said Junior. "But less with Risso. Almost as if they had a falling-out."

"I'm not sure," said Charlie. "Looks to me from their body language that they are still good friends, but pretending to be just acquaintances. Watch them next time—carefully—it's kind of funny to see."

"Once I'm back from my course, I'll use my power and sneak up on them," said Dave. "I'll find out what they are up to. Right now I'm off to Rosie's, for dinner."

Junior laughed. "Before you go in, have a look at our new band practising out back!" That's all he would say but he was grinning widely.

As Dave approached Rosie's he could tell from a block away there was something going on outside the youth centre. The sound of native drums blended with what sounded like sticks and brooms beating against garbage cans, a guitar, and a couple of harmonicas. When he rounded the corner, he saw that his ear was accurate; a small crowd of young teenagers were doing a lively beat while their friends applied swirling images of mostly black and grey to the wall. He recognized Melissa immediately by the homeless style she was wearing. As she glanced up and saw him she froze and then raced toward him waving her aerosol cans like weapons.

"Whoa, whoa, whoa, copper!! No views before the piece is done"

As she got closer she continued in a low murmur. "Lissen up. I go by Mal now, that's my tag. Short for Malicious. That dumb Tammy started calling me that. It's a long story but it's good cred so I'm keeping it. And my gang thinks I'm a dude and I want to keep it that way."

She peered at him suspiciously. "Junior says yer solid, so I'll deal. If you stick with my cover I'll owe you one for laters."

Dave looked at her in amazement and nodded, and she continued in a loud voice. "Well copper, since you're the man, I guess you can go anywhere you want. So come on in. But don't interrupt my boys here. I talked them into starting up a band. I might even sing with them, but right now the tunes give me 'artistic respiration'."

As she headed back to the wall, the boys looked furtively at Dave but took their cue and started up the beats again. He nodded at them, then admired the new mural in progress. It was surprisingly good, despite the lack of bright colours. The mix of dark and light shapes almost looked like a battle of creatures on the wall. Once it was done he'd have to ask Melissa—Mal—what it all meant.

When Dave walked into the cafe he was pleased to see Kurt behind the counter, smiling, wiping it down with a cloth.

"Afternoon, sir," said Kurt.

"Hi Kurt. Moving up in the world, I see."

"Yup. My uncle has me filling in sometimes for him, just for break."

"Looks like a quiet afternoon in here for you, though," said Dave. He leaned closer. "What happened to your face? Run into a wall?"

Kurt shook his head. "No, a fight."

Dave just nodded and waited.

"It was about the drugs, sort of," said Kurt. "I'd told my friends—my former friends—that I was out of the drug business. They were worried a bit I'd squeal on them, but I convinced them no."

Dave already had a good idea which ones were dealing, as it was a small town and they weren't that good at it. Risso and his group were his main worry. "Did they come after you?"

"No, I came at them," said Kurt. "I caught then in back trying to do a deal with some young kids, like 12-year-olds. Pissed me right off. Young kids, and right here in Rosie's. So we had a discussion and I ran them off. Junior knows too."

Dave clapped him on the shoulder. "Good for you, Kurt. I appreciate your help, am glad to see you've changed for the better." He nodded toward the back room. "I noticed as I passed by that you now have patio entertainment out back."

Kurt grinned "Yup, that new kid is some little organizer. She talked Rosie into sponsoring happy hour every Friday at 4 in exchange for music. Cheap pop and free nachos usually. Their music ain't half bad either."

Dave nodded. "Is Rosie in?"

"No, he's off this afternoon with some friend from Toronto."

"A lady friend?" said Dave.

Kurt shook his head. "No, not this time. He said he was going to do some fishing, and to try not to burn the place down."

"Guess he trusts you," said Dave, "Wait a sec, you said 'not this time'."

Kurt smiled. "Well, Junior knows this teacher from his old high school that wants to work with him on some outdoor ed program. She's been down already, and met Rosie of course. Junior thinks they're a great match." He shrugged. "I don't know what he's thinking. Rosie's too old to have a girlfriend. I mean what's the point when you're that old. You can't really do anything interesting."

Dave just raised an eyebrow.

"No, no way," said Kurt. I don't even want to think about it." He paused. "Anyways, thanks again for helping out with Crystal. I've been talking with her. She's a lot happier in Ottawa with your girlfriend JB. Glad to be out of that mess in Toronto. I'm looking forward to visiting her soon."

"Just keep her location quiet," said Dave. "We don't want any eavesdroppers." He turned quickly—he'd thought he saw someone out of the corner of his eye, but there was no-one there. He shivered as he turned back.

"Cool day," said Kurt.

"It's not that," said Dave. "I had a funny feeling come over me, not a good feeling." He reached for the door. "Tell Rosie I'll be back for some of his home-style cooking."

"Or my Wonder Soup," said Kurt. "Rosie named it, as he said you wonder if it's soup. I sometimes get a little carried away with the barley. I'd recommend a small serving."

Dave used his fade as he walked down the main street. He would have preferred not to, as it meant he couldn't chat with people like he usually would. However, he did find Risso down by the beach—selling drugs as usual—but left him alone. Of Sasquatch, there was not a sign. It seemed as if he'd disappeared for good, but Dave had a feeling they wouldn't be so lucky. He was around somewhere, just making himself scarce, letting Risso and the other dealers do his work.

Chapter 26

Angus pointed over his cottage railing. "Careful of the edge, little guy. It's a big drop," he said.

Bobby looked up at him, solemnly. "I'm not little, I'm eight."

Norris laughed. How quickly he'd grown up. "Yes, you're a big boy. But you still need some sunscreen. Get over here. Mike, could you throw me his hat please?"

It was nice to relax and forget about work. Dave was back on course in Winnipeg, Reese on duty, and the town relatively quiet. She finished with Bobby and handed him his box of toys. "Why don't you set up your cars and soldiers over there?"

She looked at Angus and shrugged. "I started out thinking no guns, no G.I. Joes, no commercial TV. But it's not easy to hang tough on your own, and not start making some compromises."

"Looks like it worked out okay to me," said Mike.

"Is it alright if I get us all some drinks, with young Bobby here?" asked Angus.

"Sure," said Norris. "He knows adults like to have a drink once in a while. We just won't do shooters, okay?"

"Scotch for you again?" asked Angus.

"Thanks, no," she said. "Just a beer this time."

She noticed that Angus was watching her son play quietly in the corner. She suspected he was thinking of his own little grandson. Just then a bird swooped down and perched on the railing next to Angus. It chirped and cocked its head at him.

"Hey, little guy," said Angus. "Hungry?"

He reached under his chair, pulled out a plastic container, and emptied some seeds into his palm.

"Here you go, help yourself."

Bobby watched wide-eyed as the bird hopped onto the outstretched hand and pecked at the seeds before returning to the rail.

"Is that your bird?" he asked.

"No, I don't own him," said Angus. "He's just a friend that likes to drop by and visit. He's a Whisky-jack, I'm told. Would you like to try?"

Bobby looked at his mom.

"Sure, go ahead," she said. "Just be quiet and move slowly."

Bobby held out his hand for some seeds, then turned slowly toward the rail. He waited.

"Make some little 'pss, pss, pss' sounds," said Mike.

"Pss, pss, pss," said Bobby. "Here he comes—oh, it tickles!"

He jerked his hand and then watched sadly as the bird flew away.

"He'll be back later," said Angus. "He's just a little shy around new people."

Bobby peered through the railing and made a few 'pss pss' sounds before returning to his cars in the corner.

"Feedback at the council meeting was positive," said Mike. "The post office bust was a surprise to most, but they were relieved it was mostly summer people. But they have noticed, either on their own or from friends, that our crime rate is creeping up. We want to try to grow beyond being just a mill and summer holiday town; we want to be a place people choose for retirement too. That means they need to see it as safe and calm and quiet."

"The challenge is to do that without being boring," said Angus.

"We're working on a better balance here," said Mike. "We've linked up with the Manitoba Arts Network, for help to get tours through here—travelling art shows or performances. It would be nice to see something like the Canadian Brass here in February, or maybe some plays. Something different from ski-doo trips and ice fishing."

"Wait a bit, those last two sound like fun to me too," said Angus. "But I know what you mean. Where would you put these on? The community centre is pretty small."

"I'd like to use the curling club more. Rent out the bar and kitchen for banquets and parties. Maybe do a real community centre in a few years. Art is big here too, with some good local artists and a few semi-professional summer visitors. Maybe we could do a summer school or something."

Norris smiled. "He's a man with ideas, my Mike. But short term, we need to clean this town up a bit. We've made some positive strides already, but there still are rumblings and rumours. More drugs popping up now, with talk of new routes for supplies. It used to be just various forms of marijuana, but now we're seeing coke, meth, and ecstasy."

"Not a nice change for our town," said Mike. "More and more people, especially the younger ones, see this place as a resort they can use to just party all summer, trash the place, and leave. Not good for the town at all."

"Amen to that," said Angus. "I'm retired to here, I want it to stay nice."

He checked his watch, then got up. "I'd better fire up the BBQ for some burgers and hot dogs. I assume Bobby likes hot-dogs?"

"Very definitely," said Violet. "He'd live on them if I let him. I'll limit him to two, though."

Norris was just heading out on patrol when her cell rang. It was Dave.

"Hi Dave, thanks for calling back. Something's come up— nothing critical but I'd appreciate your input. It's about Risso."

"What's he done now?" he said.

"Well, I worked out a rotation to try to track Risso better," she said, "and we got lucky. We spotted him doing some drug sales down by the beach, in behind the change house, by the bushes. Looks like he keeps some stock under the sand, so people just walk by to chat, then he casually hands some over. Pretty regular at it now that we've watched the site for a bit. You'd think he would have been worried about his pasty skin standing out in the midst of all those tans."

"Well, he never was that swift. So, did you nab him?"

"Not yet," she said, "since we think he's one of the major conduits. I passed on Risso's info to my contact at Natural Resources, and he confirmed he's a frequent visitor to the park beaches. So he's pretty active, but I figure we really need to try and get his supplier."

"Good thinking," said Dave. "Any leads on that so far? Is it someone local?"

"We think we have it narrowed down," she said. "There's a small cottage just up the lake from his that was rented out a few weeks ago to someone. Actually, Risso picked up the lease when the initial occupant got caught up in our post office caper and left town. We do see him going in there late almost every night."

"Who's in the cottage?" said Dave.

"We thought it might be a new guy that was spotted in town just after you left. That big hairy biker in the fancy suit—your Sasquatch. But I don't think there have been any sightings of him lately, so I'm not sure he's still in town. I think he's skipped. Maybe Risso just stores his drugs in there now. Risso's new business associates, the ones with fishnets and a muscle car, are right next door."

"So, what's your recommendation, how would you handle this?" said Dave.

"Okay, so I think we've probable cause for a warrant to Risso's place," she said, "but not next door. I'd like to follow him back to there some evening and see what, and who, is in there. Maybe

Thursday night, before the weekend. I'm hoping they'll have lots of product on hand, ready to sell."

"Makes sense," said Dave. "Go for it. We could certainly justify some extra support from Headquarters for you."

"That would help, I'll look after that as well as the warrant request," said Norris.

"This is your operation, but would you like me there too, for some backup?" he asked.

"Well, might be nice, but you've your course. I could wait," she said.

"No, we should move on this. Thursday is the last day here, and the afternoon is a short seminar on identifying drugs. I got enough of that undercover in Toronto. I can skip out a bit early and be back late afternoon, with some backup. We'll need to make sure that we all filter into town quietly, though."

"Why don't we all stage up the highway at Natural Resources?" she said. "I can spread a rumour that there's something going down related to bear poaching up the road if you want."

"That should work," said Dave. "I'll see you Thursday afternoon, unless I hear otherwise."

Chapter 27

It was early evening, just starting to get dark, when Sasquatch headed down to the beach. Risso met a lot of his contacts there, as people were often coming and going, carrying beach bags and coolers, meeting up with friends. Sometimes the best place for secrets was in a crowd. Risso had claimed he had a system worked out so nobody was any the wiser. To lessen the risk, he did the initial contacts elsewhere, so whomever he met up with was already an established customer.

Sasquatch could see Risso up ahead, talking to a young customer—no more than a teenager. He turned on his fog, so he could sneak up and listen. He could enable it so easily that it was second nature to him now. In fact, he needed to remember to make an effort to turn it off. That rush, that feeling of dominance over lesser people, was getting to be better than any drug. But, turning it off felt good in a way too, as a break from that pressure in his head.

"Hey man, glad you could come by," said Risso. "Sorry, the price is still up, but it's way better shit. Cost you $120 now."

"Hell man, that's a jump."

"It's a better supplier, you'll like it. Got the cash?"

"Not much choice, I guess. Here."

Risso handed over a package and pocketed the cash, "Later, dude."

He scuffed over the sand covering where he kept his current stash and straightened his hat. Sasquatch moved right in front of him, composed his face in an angry scowl, then un-fogged.

Risso gave a yelp and stepped back. "Holy shit, I hate it when you do that!"

"So suddenly the price went up?" said Sasquatch. "Let me guess. You're skimming something for yourself. Idiot." He grabbed Risso by the shirt front and lifted him up onto his toes.

"Hey man, take it easy," said Risso. "I was going to pass on the extra cash, honest. And the new supplier and better stuff is just a line I give people, it's a load of shit."

"Bullshit! You said sales were down, so stop jacking up the prices. Leave it at $100 for now. You want any for yourself, you pay for it. This ain't no charity. As for a new supplier, there's nothing wrong with what we have now. Watch your step, buddy. I'm heading over to the bar, but I've got my eye on all you guys, so don't even think about jerking me around."

When he arrived at the bar, Sasquatch paused for a moment just inside the door, standing to one side. He'd gone invisible, almost automatically, but didn't want to block the door. That could get awkward. The place was only half full, but he recognized the faces of some regulars. That same young guy was behind the bar, doing some shooters with two guys. Drinking the profits.

Sasquatch spotted Louie and Bonnie sitting all by themselves, over in the corner. He sat down at their table, then turned off his power.

Bonnie jumped, and gave a little squeak. "Damn," said Louie, "that's spooky. Have you been sitting there all the time listening to us?"

"No, not this time," said Sasquatch. He took a sip from Bonnie's glass. "I just had a talk with Risso. The creep thought he could up his prices and not tell me. When did you guys start doing that too?"

Louie and Bonnie started to protest, then stopped as he stared back at them with cold black eyes. He spoke in a low conversational tone that belied the menace in his voice. "No more secrets, no more excuses. We have a chance to make a lot of money here. However, if I find out you guys are stiffing me, I will kill both of you and drop your sorry corpses in the lake. Is that very clear?" He paused as they nodded. "Now, let's have a pitcher of draft and some shots. Bonnie, get your skinny little ass over to the bar and order."

Chapter 28

Junior paused at the door of the drop-in centre. "I'm heading out for a bit. Kurt, can you keep an eye on things and make sure these guys don't get into too much trouble?" Junior was pleased to see some changes in Kurt, even after a few weeks. He'd found a new interest in graphics work, and was starting to be more responsible.

"Sure," said Kurt. "I'll be here for a while anyway, we're working on some different designs, trying out a new idea I had."

"What's that?" asked Junior.

"Some of the kids are using their cell phones to grab some images around town, then load into our computers here to play with them a bit before making a printable image for t-shirts and things. We think we can do a selection of all sorts of souvenirs for tourists here. We're having a lot of fun—no time for trouble. Go ahead. We're good here."

Junior needed to find out from Janie why she hadn't shown up. Dave said he'd talked to her about dropping in to help at the youth centre with the newsletter, and that she'd seemed keen at the time. She hadn't followed up, though. Maybe she was just being her normal shy self, but Dave had persuaded Junior to see what the issue was. Didn't take much persuading anyway, since he quite liked her. First stop was the library, which was part of the town hall and community centre. She'd already been in, checked out two new fantasy books, and left an hour ago.

He walked over to Janie's place, hoping to find her outside. If just her mom was there with her, there was a good chance he'd get a piece of her excellent strawberry pie, but if her stepfather dad was there all he'd get would be a piece of his mind. Egbert was a little guy that always tried to appear bigger, mostly by being belligerent, loud, and a bully. Trouble was, he almost always was home, so hard to avoid. He was supposedly on some kind of disability, so his wife had some part time jobs to try to support the family. To back up his claim, he often made a show of wincing and holding his back when downtown, but Junior had seen him playing ball at the beach and bouncing around on a snowmobile, so he was pretty sure it was a scam.

Junior walked up to the screen door of the trailer. He could hear a baseball game blaring inside on the TV. He braced himself, then rang the bell.

"Whatever you're selling, I don't want it," came the yell from inside.

He rang again.

"Goddamn it, I'm trying to watch the game here."

He heard a crash inside, then saw Janie's step-father Egbert walking toward him.

"Who the hell is it? Oh it's you. Don't you people have your own place? Do you have to keep pestering us hard working Canadians?"

"Is Janie here?" said Junior.

"No, she's not here. And if you find her, tell her to get her skinny ass home, she's got chores."

Junior saw Janie's mother come quietly up behind Egbert. She looked at him and mouthed some words at him. It was either 'son of a bitch' or 'gone to the beach'. Her husband whirled on her and raised his hand.

"Get back to the dishes before I slap you again."

She cringed and Junior reached automatically for the door handle.

Egbert reached up and latched it. "Stay away, you meddling punk, or I'll get my gun."

His wife shook her head, lips clenched, and motioned Junior to go. As he reached the sidewalk, Egbert opened the door and stepped onto the porch.

"And stay away," he yelled.

When Junior turned to look, he quickly scuttled back inside and locked the door.

As Junior headed for the beach, he met Mike Belanger, walking with a couple of councillors.

"Hey Junior, great work your guys are doing on that video," Mike said.

"What video?" said Junior.

"Oops. Maybe it's a surprise. Kurt and a couple of kids came to me with a proposal to do a video of the town. Something to promote this as a nice place to retire to. They even put together a business plan for me."

"Nope, I haven't heard," said Junior, "but it wouldn't surprise me. They have lots of great ideas. Did they say where they were getting a video camera?"

"Cell phones," said Mike, "They do anything now, right?"

"I'm looking forward to it," said Junior. He'd have to remind them to keep him in the loop on these projects. "Have you seen Janie?"

"We saw her heading to the beach," said Mike. "She didn't look too happy."

Junior found his friend on her favourite bench, down by the end of the park. It was shaded by some nearby trees, and had a nice view of the beach. A trail led off next to it into the woods, where she often disappeared with a book. He sat down next to her.

"Hey, Janie."

"Hey, Junior."

"What's up?" he said.

"Nothing."

He noticed she still had her wrap-around sunglasses on, even though it was shady.

"Trouble at home again?"

"Yes," she said.

He gently reached over and lifted her t-shirt short sleeve. There were some fresh cuts.

"Serious trouble," he said.

"Yup."

He sat quietly for a few moments, then put his arm around her. She didn't say anything, just settled a bit into him. He looked down and noticed a tear trickling down her cheek, but he stayed quiet for a few minutes. She liked it that way.

"Kurt is doing some neat things with those new computers," he said. "They're blending cell phone images and iPad art into some fantastic graphics. Looks like nature and First Nations images with an edge. He wants to do them for t-shirts and posters and stuff. He figures they could sell it locally, as well as online."

"I thought he was just Rosie's trouble-making nephew," she said.

"Well, he was," said Junior, "but he's changed. He's good at this, at being both an artist and a businessman. Unfortunately, when it comes to writing some words to describe it for a brochure or web site—not so good. If only we knew a local kid who could write."

She nudged him with her elbow. "Shut up. You're really not subtle at all."

"I was heading back there now," he said. "Want to come back for a sec? I'll buy the coffee."

"Rosie gives you all free coffee," she said. "Make it a milkshake and we've got a deal. Maybe I can get them to use some fantasy ones with my monster sketches, blended in with the town photos."

"I'm not sure if that would sell on a t-shirt," he said, "but I would still like to see it. Let's go."

Chapter 29

Dave pulled into the Natural Resources lot, followed by a black SUV with his backup constables. He'd delayed their arrival until late afternoon, as Norris had determined Risso liked to stop off at the Raven's Roost around supper time before heading over to meet his supplier. They thought he'd been getting sloppy lately, probably assuming his success was due to his own cleverness. It was sometimes difficult for them to look the other way, letting their bait dangle out there to see what would take it.

They joined Norris and Reese, who were already inside the office, and Dave introduced the team. The two from Winnipeg were calm and serious, ready for business, but Dave could see the excitement just under the surface for Reese and Norris.

"Where's Angus?" he said. Their newest member had the experience that would calm these two down a bit.

"He just finished a double," said Norris, "so I sent him home. We're good here."

"Why don't you outline the plan once more," he said. "What's the status?"

"Still quiet in town," said Norris. "Angus saw Risso down by the beach earlier. Not a lot of sales to people, just arguing, so it's obviously time for him to stock up his stash again. This crappy weather isn't helping him either."

She'd brought a map, as well as some photos Angus had taken of the area around the cottage. It looked like she'd planned this well, as she had for the big mill bust last winter. It did look pretty straight forward. Once Risso was at the bar, they'd deploy carefully around the cottages, and wait for him to arrive. When he'd go in, it would be a simple matter of grabbing him and the drugs, and whoever was staying there. Luckily someone had cleared around the place, so they wouldn't have to stumble through bushes in the dusk. Now all they had to do was wait. In the meantime, Dave checked for emails from JB with his smartphone. Nothing today. Phoning, Skyping, texting, emailing, they had a lot of ways to stay connected, but none of it was the same as seeing her face to face. Talking to her about his concerns when she was right there always went better—it was as if she could read his mind at times. No matter, as in a few hours this latest issue, Risso's little drug empire, would be done with and it would be back to normal again.

Risso walked carefully through town, keeping to the shadows. He kept glancing over his shoulder as he clutched his coat closed. The sky had darkened suddenly, and the wind was getting stronger, while thunder rumbled overhead. He was sure he wasn't being followed as he walked along, but he still continued to feel jumpy.

He'd had a feeling of being watched lately, yet there was never anyone there. He wasn't sure it was always Sasquatch either, as sometimes the timing was wrong for that. Between those suspicions and this weather his nerves were shattered. Nothing a good fix wouldn't cure, but first he needed to meet up with Sasquatch again, turn over his cash and get some more drugs—weed, E, coke, meth, maybe even some oxy and heroin—whatever had come in this time from the Winnipeg guys.

Business was booming, as the local cops seemed clueless as to what was going on. Sasquatch was running rings around them. In addition, that smart-ass police chief was out of town, leaving that stupid woman in charge. His fist clenched as he remembered how she'd humiliated him at work, coming in to arrest him for just trying to set his ex-girlfriend straight, grabbing him with some kind of trick judo hold right in front of everyone. He enjoyed pulling off this drug business right under her snooty little nose. He was almost at the Roost when there was a crack of lightning right overhead. "Jesus," he yelled. He pulled his hat down against a gust of wind and started to jog. Working with Sasquatch was getting on his nerves, as the guy kept sneaking up on him. Hopefully his boss would soon realize how much he was worth and give him the cut he deserved. Louie and Bonnie had it easier. In fact, they seemed to be buddies with Sasquatch.

Risso hurried up the steps of the Roost. He had time for a boost of courage before his meeting. Louie and Bonnie sat in a corner, backs to the wall, and Sam was working the bar, hot-looking as usual. He checked out her cleavage as he walked up, with a big smile.

She glared at him. "What?"

"Hey babe, be nice now. Give me an Ex and a shot of Jack. Take a shot for yourself too."

"No, thanks," she said.

Bitch. He threw down a ten, downed the shot, and took his beer over to sit with his friends. No need to rush, Sasquatch could wait a bit.

One beer turned into two, but finally Risso headed out. He kept checking behind him as he neared the little cottage. It was hard to tell in the shadows but everything looked okay, no followers. There was a light on in the garage, so he headed there instead of to the cottage, walking carefully across the open yard.

He knocked on the garage door, "Hey, it's me, Risso."

There was the clank of sliding bolts, then the door creaked open.

Sasquatch pulled him in and locked the door again. "What are you doing here again, didn't you say you were worried the cops were onto you?"

"Hey, I need new supplies for the weekend," said Risso. "Besides, I was careful, took a few turns, I lost those dummies and that stupid woman leading them."

"Lost them where?" asked Sasquatch. "In the rush hour traffic? Maybe in between the high-rises? This is not downtown Toronto, you idiot."

Risso stared at Sasquatch. His eyes were black pools of coal and he kept pacing back and forth, nervously slapping his fist into his hand. If he didn't know better, he'd have thought the guy was just finishing a week long bender. His skin was gaunt and grey looking and he kept peering around in a predatory way. In fact, he reminded Risso of a huge wolf, a crazy mean one that was ready for business. Risso sidled away nervously, suddenly reminded that Louie and Bonnie were off at the bar, and there were lots of empty houses between him and the next closest human being.

"I know these local dumb cops," said Risso. "They'll be inside, with their coffee and doughnuts." He peered out the window. "Nobody there, so stop worrying. You're safe in my town." Just as he turned away there was a flash of lightning and he saw some returning glints in the trees. "Oh shit."

Sasquatch immediately was beside Risso, staring out as the lightning flickered again. How did he move so fast?

"Dammit," said Sasquatch, "you simple bastard, you led them right here."

Risso backed up against the workbench as Sasquatch lunged toward him, grabbed him and tossed him against the far wall as if he was a child. As Risso hit the shelves, tools, nails and glass fell and broke with a deafening crash. Sas was coming toward him again, with those crazy black eyes and a snarl on his mouth that was complete evil contempt. Risso quickly got up and screamed for help as he frantically pulled a gun from under his shirt.

Sasquatch felt like he could explode. He grabbed a shovel and swung it with superhuman strength at his enemy, just as the gun went off. The sharp blade cut deeply into Risso's neck, slicing through it like butter. Sasquatch dropped the shovel just as the little creep's head slowly slipped off his neck and fell to the floor, rolling under the workbench. The rest of the body slowly toppled to the floor, blood spurting from it. Sasquatch picked up the gun, then smiled with satisfaction. He took a deep breath as he composed his thoughts and got ready to use his fog and escape. There was no time to set the garage on fire and destroy evidence, but he didn't care any more. He had moved to a whole new level of primal existence where avoiding the needs of the justice system were no longer a priority. In fact, nothing was a priority now except mayhem and vengeance. He felt alive and eager! This was going to be fun!

Chapter 30

Dave jumped at the sudden lightning and immediate crash of thunder. He peered through the bushes. Risso had slipped into the garage a minute ago, so now what? Was that him at the window? There was a shout, then a crash, then a shot, all from within the garage.

"Oh shit," he said, and keyed his radio. "This is Dave. Go, go, go!"

Just then the storm broke, the wind driving rain and even hail before it. The team rushed across the open space, some tripping and swearing on the way, but quickly reached the garage. They hollered over the crash of thunder that they were the police, banged on the doors, then pulled both the front and side entrances open. Dave had been slowed over the uneven ground, but just as he reached the now open garage door he felt something brush by him.

He turned but saw nothing. Maybe there was a shadow, then it was gone. He shone his light around, but there was just what seemed to be an empty yard. It had been a vague feeling, familiar but unpleasant, sending a chill down his back. He looked up as the rain stopped and the wind dropped, the storm over as quickly as it had started, the dark clouds dissipating.

Dave walked back into the garage light. Risso's body lay on its back on the floor, in a massive pool of blood, arms outstretched. There was a gun clutched in one hand, and a bloodied shovel lay beside him. The neck was still pulsing out blood and it took Dave a few moments to realize the head was not attached. He looked around the garage. Where was it? And where was the killer? It was not a very big place, with nowhere to hide. He was pretty sure now that the resident of this cabin was still Sasquatch, but where was he? Was there anybody else living here as well? He made a few hand gestures to the police team, directing them to search around the garage and in the cabin for the unknown assailant. It was then that he noticed Risso's head under the workbench covered with filth and drying blood. Okay, found the head, but not the killer, yet.

The team quickly returned, reporting there were no other people in the cabin or around the garage. They stared at each other in puzzlement.

"Looks like it was quite a swing, whoever did it," said Reese.

"So where is this shovel-killer?" asked Dave. "Are you sure he didn't slip past us?"

"How could he?" said Norris. "We came in both doors at the same time. The lights were already on in here, and all we saw was each other at the doors and this poor sucker on the floor. We checked up in the rafters too—nothing. Sorry boss, it's a real mess."

Dave sighed. "No, it's not your fault, you planned this raid by the book. Somebody else was here, but they seem to have disappeared into thin air. Let's focus on the next steps." He looked at his constable expectantly. "Norris?"

"Right," she said. "Okay, let's not walk around too much here. Dave, could you call the dog handler and see if he's available? Although I suspect he won't be too happy getting his dog to track when we don't know where or how the murderer left the building. Reese, give me a hand securing the scene with tape. You other two better check the other cottages to make sure they really are empty."

Reese pointed to the floor, just inside the door. "Here, what's this? Looks like more blood."

Dave walked carefully over. "I heard a gun go off, so maybe Risso got a lucky shot in. Maybe the dog will find something. Mark it." He sighed. "And now, I guess I'd better update Staff. I'm not looking forward to that. He really prefers this to be a very quiet town."

He looked around the garage one last time. He could not figure out how somebody, other than him, could disappear into thin air. Was that it? Was there somebody else who had his disappearing skills? Could it be Sasquatch? Dave had observed him for quite a while in Toronto and as far as he knew he'd never faded before. It was a puzzle. He looked around the room again.

Other than the body and blood on the floor it looked like a normal garage—in fact it was cleaner than his was. A few tools and implements hung on hooks on a wall, but most of them looked to have fallen in a jumble on the floor, likely during the struggle. A workbench ran across one end of the garage, its square legs on casters. There was no trace of drugs or even drug paraphernalia like scales or packing material. Staff Scully was not going to be happy at all.

He looked closer and noticed some scratches on the floor in front of the workbench.

"Give me a hand here," he said. They tugged on one end, until the bench swung forward, revealing a square opening between the studs, filled with baggies of white powder, some pill containers, and larger bags of brown leaves.

"Bingo!" Dave was relieved. His upcoming discussion with Staff Scully was going to be a little easier. He watched thoughtfully as Norris started video-taping the crime scene. If, as he suspected, the mysterious murderer was Sasquatch then he was going to have to figure out how to track him down. Maybe his own power could help somehow. "Okay you guys, now you've got everything secure you can glove up and search the cabin for drugs. I'll join you once I make a few calls."

Norris nodded at the cabin next door. "It sure would be nice to have a search of that place too, except I don't have it on my warrant. That's where Risso's friends live but they're not home now. I heard from Sam that they were at the bar since late afternoon, quietly nursing a few beers. They were crammed in a corner, back to the wall, and looked, as she said, 'spooked'."

"Keep your eyes open for them," said Dave. "Their car is still there." He assumed Sasquatch was long gone—maybe to warn his friends.

They all froze as they heard rustling sounds coming from behind the cabin. One of the constables stealthily slipped out the side and around the back of the house as Norris slipped into the door frame with weapon drawn and pointing at the noise.

"Come out with your hands over your head" she ordered in a firm voice.

There was a pause and then a familiar voice called out "Norris my dear, don't shoot me or I'll nay cook you another steak."

Everybody breathed a sigh of relief as Angus, in jeans and his police jacket, walked around the corner with his hands up, smiling. "Good evening to you, boss. Glad to see you back in town. If you're wondering, I could be persuaded to work a wee bit of overtime tonight if you needed an extra hand."

Dave smiled. "Thanks, Angus. This case just got a bit bigger than we anticipated. We have a murder, but no murderer. We could use the help."

Angus nodded. "Looks like this turned into quite a mess. Too bad, but as we say, the best laid plans of mice and men—"

"Gang aft agley," said Reese.

Angus laughed and slapped him on the back. "Aye, so you know Robbie Burns, do you? There's hope for our education system yet. Okay boss, I'll get right on it. Just let me put a band-aid on this wee scratch. I seem to have been attacked by a tree branch on the way in. I do have a bit of a confession to make, though. Since I live just down the lake, when I heard a shot fired I came over to see what was going on. And being new to the area I got all turned around and managed to go into the wrong cottage." Angus nodded at the cottage used by Louie and Bonnie. "You know how they all look alike in the evening."

Dave smiled. "Anything interesting while you were accidentally there?"

"I may have unofficially seen some drug things around—like scales and empty baggies. Right there in plain view. No product though. And maybe there was a gun under the couch cushion."

"Thanks," said Dave. "We'll get a warrant and see what we can stir up. Meanwhile, I'll send someone down to the bar to keep an eye on our friends. Now, let's get this place done."

What he had seen—or not seen—bothered Dave. He knew that if Sasquatch was still in town after all, they hadn't really solved their drug problem. If anything, it would probably get worse. He closed his eyes for a moment, trying to use his senses to feel for anything evil close to him. Nothing, although he didn't really know what range this was supposed to have. At any rate, it was probably safe to talk now. He motioned his staff to come closer.

"Guys, I want to try something. I'm convinced Sasquatch is somehow involved in all this, and that he's key to the whole operation. Let's leave Risso's friends, and their place, alone for now. We'll get a phone tap on these two places and see what this can stir up. We'll process the crime scene, then back away. Let them think we're happy we've solved the drug problem. I'll spread the word around town, leaving poor Risso out of it. In the meantime, I think these guys may have brought some sophisticated eavesdropping equipment with them, so no chatter on what we're planning. Not while you're out in the field, either face to face or over the radio. Back at the office is okay. We'll seal up the crime scene until we get the coroner here."

With all of Dave's team, plus the backup, the cleanup went quickly. By midnight the coroner had come and gone, and they'd found several more stashes in the cottage, as well as some firearms. It was probably enough to send Sasquatch back into prison with enough time to complete several university degrees if he wanted to, especially if they found his prints on the shovel. But, in spite of patrols and roadblocks, the biker seemed to have vanished like a ghost.

Chapter 31

Sasquatch's arm stung from where Risso's shot had clipped him, but it was still easy for him to slip back into his fog and disappear. He braced himself as the doors opened. Both ends of the garage filled with cops, staring at each other. As they pushed in, he rushed out, almost running into one of them, and kept on going down the road.

He was pumped. His senses were filled with the smells of the bush, the sounds of small animals in the grass, the play of colours in the stormy evening sky. It had been years since he had felt this good. He slowed to a walk, and peered ahead, looking for something to kill. As he crept toward the road, his blood lust gradually subsided and his breath slowed. He noticed that old cop walking toward him. Sasquatch considered him thoughtfully. It would be so easy to break his neck and perhaps twist his head off. His hands twitched with anticipation as he tensed for the jump. But no, maybe later. He had things to do in town. He satisfied himself with a quick razor sharp scratch to the cheek as he walked right past him, barely breaking the surface but making the old guy start. His arm still hurt, and was oozing blood, so he ripped a strip from the bottom of his t-shirt and wrapped it around his bicep. He sped up again, loping along the road toward town at a steady pace, soundless on the soft dirt. Things had changed, but he wasn't really worried. First he needed to find out where Louie and Bonnie were.

As expected, his two confederates were in the Roost, huddled in a corner, beer in hand. At least they'd have an alibi. He stayed invisible and sat down next to Louie.

"Louie. Don't look, it's me, Sas."

Louie and Bonnie both turned toward the empty chair. Louie gasped and Bonnie went white as a ghost and gave a sharp little cry.

"Quiet!" said Sasquatch. "I'm right here."

Louie looked around. "Stop doing this! It's like you're one of them ventriloquists now."

"Yeah, and you're my dummy," said Sasquatch. He reached out and grabbed both their arms. "See, I'm right here."

"Shit, now I see you," said Louie. "How the hell does that thing work?" Bonnie just gulped, and looked like she was ready to make a dash for the door.

"Stay still and stay quiet," said Sasquatch. "Both of you. I still don't know how this works, just that it started up when I got to town. Maybe it's some sort of native thing I picked up. What's important is that I can stay invisible if I want." He sat back.

Bonnie rubbed her arm. "You're gone again. Jeez, that touch felt like ice."

"Can you teach me how to do that?" said Louie.

Sasquatch was impressed that Louie had moved so quickly from fear right back to cunning. "No. I don't think so. I don't know. Right now we've a problem. We're busted, or I am. Risso led the cops right back to me in the garage, stupid idiot. I just managed to get away."

"What happened to your arm?" said Louie.

"He winged me," said Sasquatch. It hurt a lot less now so he cautiously peeled back the bloody bandage. There was a scratch, but that was all.

"Risso shot you?" said Louie. "Good thing he's got a lousy aim. Did they get him?"

"Don't worry about Risso. I took care of him. Permanently. I should have done it earlier. It felt so nice to do. This whole operation is getting too sloppy, though. You guys are next."

Louie paled and started to get up, but Sasquatch reached out and pulled him back down.

"Sit down, bonehead. I mean you're next for the cops. But if you piss me off like Risso, you're done for. Now, your place is right next door to me, and you've been seen with Risso. If you're carrying anything now, get Bonnie to dump it down the can. Here, take this bandage too, and flush it. And don't think of running off on me. I'll hunt you down like a dog. Or a bitch. Go."

Bonnie just nodded and headed to the bathroom.

"Louie, if you've anything in the cottage get rid of it. Quietly. I'm sure they've found all my stashes in my place. Luckily I had Risso hide some stuff around town, so we'll be fine for a while. They'll be watching you two, so use a couple of those summer kids as runners." Sasquatch rubbed his temples. "Jeez, this hurts. Okay, let me think a bit."

When Bonnie came back, she sat and stared ahead for a moment. "We are so screwed," she said.

"Shut up," said Sasquatch, "or I'll shut you up. I'm going to get this stupid cop. And his town. Thinks he can bust me? No way. And now it's time for you two to give me some reasons to let you live. Talk to some of your contacts in Winnipeg, tell them to spread the word I've just been sighted up there. Then get some of the boys to come down from Winnipeg, but tell them to do it quietly and blend in. Which means not a big flashy car, right? I'm going to stay out of sight—literally—for a while." He hadn't yet tried to use his power for an extended period, but it was getting easier and easier to turn on.

"Sure, we can do that," said Louie. "We can front for you."

"Just remember I'm watching," said Sasquatch. "Right now, just head back to your cottage, act innocent. I'll be in touch." He grabbed Louie's beer, let go of his arm, and disappeared.

Louie heard Sas's chair scrape back, then nothing. He sat quietly for a while, then looked around cautiously..

"Sas ... Sas?" said Louie. "Are you there?" He sat back. "Guess he's gone."

"That smell is gone too," said Bonnie. "Like something had gone off. Maybe he stepped in some dog crap."

"Or maybe stepped in some Risso," said Louie.

"Aw jeez," she said. "Don't say that. Louie, I can't stand this anymore. I want out."

"Nobody gets out," said Louie. "We're in this together."

"Great," she said. "Jeez, he's always had a mean streak, and now he's like a freaking ghost. With the touch of death. I just know we'll be next."

As Sasquatch walked out of the bar, he could still hear Bonnie talking. He smiled. Yes, bitch, you are so right, you two are going to be next. But first he needed to hide out for a bit. There was another empty cottage Risso had said they could use if they wanted to. It was a smaller place, out of the way, back in the woods. Risso had even had the intelligence to have a friend rent it for him and set it up with some supplies. He had the occasional bit of smarts—just not often enough.

Sasquatch rubbed his head. It was feeling worse. Time to shut this thing off for a break. He tried, but it was still there. He concentrated harder—no change. He started to panic, and a rage overcame him. He felt like running back and smashing that smart ass cop right in the face, over and over. He paused and took a couple of deep breaths, trying to focus. After a few minutes the feeling passed, and he continued slowly up the overgrown path to the cottage. The clouds had cleared a bit, and in the moonlight he saw his hideout, hidden behind some trees. It looked ready to fall down, but Risso had assured him it was dry and draft free.

He let himself in, pulled the heavy drapes shut, and switched on the battery lamp on the table. He'd have to see if they could steal some hydro for this place. In the meantime supper would be cold food. He rummaged through the cupboard and found crackers, some tinned meat, chips, and a bottle of red wine. Luckily it was a screw-top, as in his present mood he'd likely have tried to bite the end off. He smiled, at least he had a bit of a sense of humour left.

He had a hard time settling down that night. The wine and a joint helped, but he keep seeing things in the shadows, things that whispered in his ear.

Chapter 32

JB checked her watch—time to quit for the night. She walked over to Ron's table. "Mind if I settle up with you two? I'm heading off shift early."

Ron's buddy looked at his watch. "Midnight is early?"

JB smiled at him. Friendly, and big, Like Ron. Another one of his friends from his earlier motorcycle days, as opposed to his current pedal-bike crowd. "I have a nine o'clock class tomorrow. So—that was just one pitcher, right? That was all?"

Ron handed her a twenty. "Yup. We're heading off too, as soon as we finish this off. Keep the change."

After cashing out she waved goodbye to everyone and headed out the side door. She usually took a cab the few short blocks home, but she needed the walk to clear her head anyway, after a busy night. And Dave's latest call. He had planned on coming down for a couple of days to visit, but had begged off at the last minute. Big problems with drugs, he said, as well as that Sasquatch character, plus a murder. It was never quiet up there it seemed. She could understand that he needed to focus on the town—their town—but she was still disappointed. Their phone calls had cleared up a lot of misunderstandings but they still really needed a face to face. She was so lost in her thoughts she didn't even hear the bike until it rumbled up right behind her. She turned with a smile. "Ron, did you bring your Harley tonight?" Except it wasn't Ron. It was another biker, one she didn't recognize.

"So, looks like I found me a little Indian girl," he said. "Coming out of Danny's, just like they said. Sas has sent me to teach you a little lesson."

She backed up, fumbling for her purse. Stupid girl, forgetting to be street smart—if she could just get her Mace out. The professional version that Dave had given her. There was a roar behind her, of another bike, then her purse was grabbed and thrown aside.

A hand reached out to her. "I think I'll go first," he said.

She was trying to decide whether to scream or bite or scratch when there was a growl and a shape came out of the darkness, pushing one biker right off his bike. And leaving him with a leg trapped under it as it fell on him. "Get it off me, get it off," he yelled. "It's burning me."

The other biker was reaching into his jacket—for a knife or gun she assumed—when someone else rushed him. She got a glint of metal on her saviour's knuckles before he was upon the biker, driving a solid blow to his chin. There was a thunk, the biker's head snapped back, and he sagged. He didn't fall, but he was wobbling.

"Are you okay, JB?" It was Ron, along with his friend from the bar.

She nodded, then picked up her purse. Her knees felt weak, but she took a deep breath and smiled. "My knights in shining armour." She paused. "He said Sas had sent him—whoever that is."

Ron and his friend glanced at each other. "Sounds like Sasquatch, Hell's Angels in Toronto. That's the biker I'd heard was headed up to your little Manitoba town. But these guys are local, I think. Looks like you were tracked down to Ottawa somehow." He led her over to the curb. "Sit for a sec, have a smoke. This will only take a minute." He and his friend walked over to the first bike, lifted it off the biker, then roughly pulled him to his feet. After a few minutes of them talking and him listening they walked over to the second one, and spoke to him. A minute later both of her attackers started up their bikes and rode off.

Ron came back over and reached out a hand. "Are you okay to stand up now?"

She nodded and got to her feet. "What did you say to them?"

"I confirmed that Sasquatch had put them up to this, as a favour for him. Then I pointed out that you were under the personal protection of me and my friends, so maybe this little freebie for Sasquatch was not worth their while. They agreed."

"Thanks," she said. "But won't he just send someone else?"

"No, they'll tell him they are still looking," said Ron's friend. "But they never will end up finding you. You should still tell that cop friend of yours, though."

"Oh, and there's another one they may be looking for too," said JB. After she explained who Crystal was and her connection, Ron told her not to worry, they'd watch out for her too. JB was still shaken, but relieved. She just wasn't sure what to tell Dave. She trusted Ron's assurances, and Dave had more than enough to worry about. He'd just get angry and frustrated and caring. Probably insist that she quit her job, tell her that she doesn't need the money and it's just a distraction.

"Maybe," she said.

"Up to you," said Ron. "But now we're walking you home—both of us."

Chapter 33

Sasquatch ran up the trail, barely able to see in the moonlight, swatting away bushes as they grabbed at him. He risked another look behind, but it was even closer. Damn. The black cloud kept gaining on him, and getting larger as it did so. Already there were tendrils from it probing into his head and back. Sasquatch swore and put on one last burst of speed. He burst into the open, right on a cliff edge, too fast to even consider stopping. He hurtled over, into the air, then crashed to the bottom, feeling both pain and relief.

He awoke as he fell to the cabin floor—sweaty, heart racing, bedclothes twisted around his ankles, echoes of his scream in his ears. He lay there a moment, catching his breath. It was dawn. The dark shadows were gone, and now, in the first light of dawn, it was just a plain little cabin. It was quiet too, except for an annoying squirrel chattering in a nearby tree. He debated getting up to throw something at it out the window, then realized he could probably sneak up on it and swat it right off the branch. He smiled at that image. He'd save that pleasure for later.

He sat up, and tried again to turn off his invisibility. Nothing, he still had the same feeling, like it was still there. No need to panic, yet. Bear, or Dave, seemed to be able to turn his on and off, so maybe this was just a glitch. But this new ability did have its benefits. After a coffee and some breakfast, and another toke, the day seemed a little more bearable.

He stepped outside and looked around. This place was really quite isolated. That damn squirrel, sitting on a low hanging branch, was still jabbering noisily, though. He tiptoed slowly over, stick in hand. It paused, ears and nose twitching, feet shuffling on the branch, but before it could run he swung. He laughed as he knocked it into the bushes, where it exploded into a chatter of rage before racing to the top of a tree.

Sasquatch spent the day drinking the wine and reading some trashy novels he'd found on a bookshelf. It was starting to get dark when he heard a quiet knock at the door. He grabbed his gun.

"Who is it?"

"Sas, it's me, Louie."

"Are you alone?"

"Just me. I brought a pack full of stuff. And I know I was not followed, honest."

Sasquatch opened the door, and gestured. "Come on in, grab a seat."

Louie stood in the doorway. "Where are you? I can't see you at all."

Sasquatch reached out and put his hand on his partner's shoulder.

Louie jumped. "Wow, okay." He tried to pull back. "Don't hit me."

"I'm not going to hit you—not today," he said.

"Sure felt like you were going to when you touched me," said Louie. "Can't you just turn this off? It's pretty scary looking. Or not looking." He laughed nervously.

"I think it's stuck on for a while," said Sasquatch. "Get used to it."

Sasquatch turned toward the table. "Come on and sit, I've been doing some planning."

"Whoa, you're gone again," said Louie. "Sort of. When you talk I can see you as like a dark shadow—weird. It's like my ears don't believe my eyes. At least when you touch me you look pretty solid."

"Too bad pencil dick, I'm not going to hold your hand while we talk. Jeez, sit down will you? And stop trying to find me. Look out the window or something."

Louie put down the pack and sat on the edge of a chair. "I didn't want to walk around with a case of beer in the woods, so I grabbed this old pack I use sometimes. Brought some wine, painkillers, and snacks."

"Thanks, Louie, good thinking for a change." He paused. He did need the creep's help, for a while at least. "First off, what are the cops up to?"

"Well, they got a dog in," said Louie. "But he couldn't find much. They came in searching the Roost, and tried to blame me, but that bartender had to admit Bonnie and me had been sitting right there all night. They had roadblocks up at the highway too, but found nothing."

"Still, I'll stay in here for a bit," said Sasquatch.

"How will you get in touch with us?" said Louie. "Do you want me to leave you my phone?"

"No, too risky," he said. "They'll be putting traces on them. For now, if I need to talk with you, I'll just stay invisible and go over to your place."

"I don't know, Bonnie was pretty freaked out when she couldn't see you in the bar," said Louie. "She spent the night huddled in a corner with a pillow and blanket."

Sasquatch reached out and grabbed him by the throat. "That's too damn bad. I don't need backtalk from either of you. Tell her to wait in her room for me, I'll come in when it's dark. She won't know the difference." He pushed Louie away and sat back down, breathing heavily.

Louie rubbed his throat, "Sorry, no problem. I'll just give her a few hits first, to mellow her out." He looked ready to leap for the door. "Oh, I think the guys were planning to come down from Winnipeg in a couple of days. Is that still on?"

"Of course it is, you idiot. We need to create a distraction. We need to keep pushing these hicks. Tell them to come on down on their bikes and be themselves. But not so much that they get busted or run out of town, just a show of strength. Oh, and make sure nobody has an outstanding warrant."

Louie looked down at his list and crossed a few names off.

"Now, when the boys get down here from Winnipeg, you'll have to be the one to talk to them. Not me. I want to keep this ability a secret for now. Only you and Bonnie know about it. And frankly it might make a few of those guys cut and run. Some are pretty superstitious. Don't come here too often either, we don't want to leave a trail. Head off into the woods first when you leave here too, don't just follow the road straight back. My plan is to have those stupid cops so busy worrying about minor things that we can keep running all the drugs we want. Make sure the guys don't just sit around, I want them staying active around the town. Just keep it relatively legal. Are the cops still watching you two?"

"Not directly, but probably still lurking around," said Louie.

"Well then, your job is to keep them busy. Keep on the move, then wait somewhere, then move on again. Have the guys do the same. Set up some fake deals."

"How about you here?" said Louie. "Got enough stuff? I can drop off a cooler and some ice and more food." He sniffed. "Should have aired this out for you too, smells musty or something."

"That's okay," said Sasquatch. "I'm good for now. I can always come by your place if I want. What you could do is get me a burner phone for local stuff. You guys, too. Now, get your sorry ass out of here. You've work and I need to rest."

After Louie left, Sasquatch finished another glass of wine, a joint, and some painkillers. Hopefully it would be enough to keep him dead to the world for the night.

The mid-morning quiet of Kirk's Landing was broken by a roar, as ten big bikes, saddlebags bulging, pulled into the highway restaurant parking lot. They parked carefully in a row, then the riders, in leathers and denim, filed into the restaurant and ordered lunch. They followed the script Sasquatch had given them, saying that they were just passing through on a road trip. He'd checked the place out, and knew the waitress was chatty and would surely go on about the town. That was their cue to decide to take a side trip into Kirk's Landing.

Sasquatch was downtown when they rolled down Main Street. He was eavesdropping on a young couple complaining to each other about the lack of real excitement. As soon as they saw the bikes they froze, watching the riders file by.

Sasquatch nodded with approval as the bikes rumbled slowly by, two by two, pausing to let people scurry across the street in front of them. They continued down to the lake, where they were supposed to stop in at the bar and meet up with Louie. He liked it—peaceful in action, but menacing in appearance. They wouldn't all stay at the hotel, though. Some would be in a couple of cottages, some up at the highway motel. That would split them up, and divide any watchers. He texted the news of the arrival to Louie, then headed down to the bar himself. Last night's mix of drugs had chased away the nightmares, but his head was starting to throb again. He could do with a cold beer but that might be difficult if there was any crowd in there. There was too big a risk that someone would notice a bottle fading away as he grabbed it. There were a number of people hurrying out the bar door, so he went around to the open patio doors and stood just inside, out of the way.

"It's not like Sas to hide from the cops like this," one of them said.

"They've got some serious heat on him," said Louie. "This makes them waste more time. He's in touch though. I'll text him your questions." He stepped outside to light a cigarette, putting down his beer. When he reached for it, it had disappeared. He looked around, raised a finger, and went back in.

Sasquatch sipped his stolen beer and studied the gang, picking out the leaders and the followers—those likely to have some good ideas, and the hot heads. Louie passed on a few questions the bikers had for Sasquatch. They were all impressed with Sasquatch's fast responses, not knowing he'd already heard them ask the question. He smiled. It just helped to build on the mystique he had. As expected, one of the local cops came in, the young guy.

"Just dropping by," he said. "Everything cool in here?"

"We're okay," said Louie. "I know some of these guys, they're all right. The waitress up at the highway had recommended the town to them so they were just checking it out. They're just on a trip, sometimes they stay a bit in a place, sometimes they don't."

Aside from them scaring out most of the other patrons, there wasn't much the cop could find fault with, not that Sasquatch could see. That would change tomorrow, once they started their program of subtle harassment.

Later that evening, Sasquatch texted Louie to make sure everyone had left for their rooms, then walked down to the cottage and tapped on the door. When Louie opened it he slipped inside, still invisible. He'd finally been able to turn his ability off, but it took a real effort, and hurt even more, so he usually just let it turn itself back on.

"Good work today," he said. "Now leave us alone." He crossed over to the bedroom door, and pushed it open. It was pitch black inside. He felt his way over to the bed and pulled off his sweater.

"Where the hell are you," he said.

"Here, against the wall," said Bonnie.

"You know, you can see me if we're touching," he said.

"That's okay, I still want the light off."

"Don't be so damn scared," he said. "Come over here." He reached for her.

She flinched. "Hey, your hands are like ice." She put her hands on his chest. "Jeez, babe, I can feel your ribs. What's with that? You didn't look any skinnier."

"Just stop talking," he said.

Chapter 34

Norris looked up from Dave's desk as Sheila stuck her head in through the door. "Constable, I've calls on all four lines now. I can't deal with these, they all seem to think everything is my fault. I just want to yell back at them," said Sheila.

Norris sighed. It was just crazy this week. Thankfully Dave's call to the district office had resulted in a couple of detectives assigned to look after the murder investigation. Apparently HQ had never had a decapitation with a Hell's Angels suspect before and Kirk's Landing was quickly becoming the talk of the division. There was no room for them in the office, so they were set up back in Dave's attached house, commandeering his dining room table. Reese had quickly run data and phone lines in for them so that they were up and typing away within hours. Norris shook her head. On TV nobody saw all the work of entering evidence and notes into computer files. Good thing too, since it would make a pretty dull TV show. Norris was supposed to be helping them out, but this rash of complaints had taken priority.

"What's wrong with people this week?" said Norris. She'd hoped to hide in Dave's office to tackle some emails but obviously that wasn't going to happen. She shrugged her shoulders. "Thanks, Sheila, I'll take some of the calls. Give me the ones that sound the most urgent, ask the others for details, say we'll look into it." She picked up the phone. "Constable Norris here, how can I help you?"

"Hey Violet, it's Mike. Nothing urgent, but Sheila said you needed to hear a friendly voice for a minute."

Norris smiled and gave Sheila a thumbs-up. "Yes, we've been getting busier every day. I was supposed to be off about an hour ago, and I still have reports to finish. And the phone is still ringing non-stop. We're still looking for that big biker guy, but are getting reports he may be in Winnipeg now. We're seeing more bikers in town lately, and lots more little crimes are cropping up."

"From those bikers?"

"Well some are from those guys," she said. "But, generally there are just more crimes. We've been trying to keep a close watch on the bikers, in the midst of all our other call-outs. Maybe they are just here to annoy us."

"I agree, the whole town is on edge," said Mike. "You'd think it was a full moon and people were possessed. I was just at a council meeting, where everyone was in a foul mood and looking for an argument. Even I got into a shouting match at one time with some councillors. We've got lots of complaints coming in to my office too. We had thought it was bad when Risso was constantly calling in but this surpasses even him. People are just rubbing each other the wrong way. And of course this nasty rainy weather doesn't help."

"Thankfully most of our calls are minor complaints," said Norris, "but we need to follow up on them all, so it takes time. Thanks for calling, but I gotta run now. All the lines are flashing."

"If you've time later I can buy you a quick meal at Rosie's," said Mike.

"Maybe just a tea or something. I have to get home and see Bobby. I'll call you."

She took a deep breath, and looked up at Sheila. "Thanks. Now, next?"

"Line three is one of councillors, McNeely, down on beach road. He's complaining that a dozen bikers have been riding up and down all morning past his place. And now some are parked on his lawn and won't leave."

"That's just great. Do we have anyone available to check it out?"

Dave had just come in the door. "We're all pretty well busy. Why don't you get out of here and get some action instead of suffering behind that desk. Sheila can tell him you're on your way."

Norris smiled gratefully at Dave and headed out to the SUV.

When she got to the councillor's house she found just one bike, parked on the edge of his lawn, with someone fiddling with the chain.

"What seems to be the problem?" she asked the biker.

"I had some chain problems, so pulled off the road, then this guy started yelling at me."

"Can I see some ID?" she asked. She ran the info through the CPIC system and found that the bike was clean and the rider only had a few minor priors. She handed his papers back and then walked up to the cottage, where the councillor was waiting.

"What took you so long?" he said. "Most of them have left by now. But you can see from here where there were two others on the grass. They left deep ruts when they left."

"Do you want to file a complaint?" she asked.

"What, a form?" he said. "I don't have time for that crap—just deal with this. That's what I pay you for."

Just then the bike started up and slowly, carefully, drove off the lawn and onto the road.

"Stop him, chase him down!" said McNeely.

"I have his information already," she said. "Anything else while I'm here?"

"Yes, I already called about our dog and no one called back. He's been missing all day. And so has Steve's, next door. We tied them out in the morning, then noticed a few hours later we hadn't heard them bark. The leashes are still there, almost like they were unclipped. Wouldn't have happened if you were all out patrolling, like you're supposed to be."

She just smiled, sighed to herself, and took down McNeely's information. Just as she was finishing Sheila called on her radio.

"Got a call from the Highway Restaurant. A couple up there are refusing to pay, say they didn't like the food."

"Anyone we know?"

"Two of our summer folk," she said. "They've been on the lake for years, normally very nice people. Oh, and the cook is threatening to take the husband outside and fight him."

"On my way," said Norris. "Sorry, Councillor McNeely, have to get back on patrol."

Norris managed to defuse the situation at the restaurant fairly easily. The rest of the day went like that, with a whole series of incidents that were all bigger than they should have been, people stressed out, with little patience for each other. She hoped it was just a fluke, that things would calm down in a day or two.

"I'm heading home for a bit, Sheila. I need to see Bobby, get some dinner and tuck him in."

"Good thing you have Andrea living with you," said Sheila.

"Yes, she's a godsend. I'm glad I could give her a place to stay and study. Having her there is a big help."

When Norris got home she was still feeling annoyed with everyone. Andrea sensed her mood, so after Bobby gave Norris a big hug, Andrea called the boy into the kitchen to give her a hand and sent Norris into the living room with a glass of wine.

Norris turned on the TV, took a sip, and promptly fell asleep. When she woke up, Andrea was working on an assignment at the dining room table, and the house was quiet.

"Sorry," she said. "Guess I missed dinner. Is Bobby still up?"

"You were out like a light," said Andrea. "Bobby had a quick bath and went to bed with the new book Constable MacGregor gave him. I saved you a plate in the fridge if you're hungry."

"Thanks Andrea, but I think I'll just head to bed too." Damn, she hated missing time with her son. She sent Mike a quick text goodnight, with some x's and o's, then crashed again.

Chapter 35

Angus woke up to a bird screeching at him through the open bedroom window, a pounding on his front door, and a haze of smoke in the air. He rolled out of bed, coughing, then ran, stooped over, to the front door.

"Angus, open up, fire! Open up!"

It was Reese.

"Angus, get out. There's a fire in your shed, right next to your bedroom. Looks like it might go to the house too. Come on, get out."

"We need to call—"

"Already done, Angus. Volunteers on their way, be here in a flash."

It seemed like forever, waiting in the cold of the dawn for the truck, watching the flames grow, but when the volunteers arrived they worked quickly. Some started pumping from the truck, while others ran a line and pump down to the lake—a forest fire pump from Natural Resources. There was soon a Niagara of water dousing the shed, and within another minute it was out. Meanwhile Reese came back from under the front deck.

"We found what looks like an arson device under there, but it failed to go off. That may be what started the shed fire too—we'll wait to hear what the fire chief says."

The crew had just finished loading the truck back up when their radio squawked with another call. Angus cleaned up the mess of his shed and called his insurance. They didn't need to visit, just needed some photos and a list of anything in the shed. Good thing, as he was due for the afternoon shift, so he hurried to change and check in.

By then Dave had pulled everyone in. Besides a host of minor complaints, there had been a couple of collisions on the main street, and someone had all his meat stolen from his outdoor freezer. And there was another fire, in some brush up at the highway.

It was a day of fires, in fact. Nothing big, just some trash in a can against a garage, or a smudge pot under a house, but still fires, and still taking time. By the end of the day the volunteers were exhausted. This was more activity than they normally saw all summer.

One of Angus's many calls was to stop a big brawl in the Roost over a Foosball game. He didn't understand that one at all, and neither did the participants. They seemed as surprised as he was at how quickly everything had escalated. Within seconds it seemed, punches and chairs had been thrown and there was now a new dent in one wall.

"What the hell happened, laddie?" Angus asked Sid, the bartender. "Do we need to ban Foosball as a violent sport?"

"I don't know. Caught me by surprise. Nothing serious though, no bones broken. It should be easy to clean up."

The fight had ended just as easily as it had started, and all the participants were now sitting down, drinking the jugs of water that Sid had brought them after he had taken away their beer. None could explain what had started the fight or why they had all jumped so quickly into it.

Angus went for one last patrol loop. He checked in at the Highway Restaurant for any problems, out to both ends of the highway limits, then back down into town. He stopped in at the cafe to defuse a couple's argument with Rosie over their cheque, then headed down to the park and beach area. There were yet more issues there, with people upset over the smoke from their neighbour's hibachi, and way too much alcohol being passed around, open and obvious. The mood wasn't helped when he confiscated it all, but at this stage he didn't really care. It took all his patience to not just write them all up and the hell with them. He didn't see any drugs, but from the way some were acting he had his suspicions. He did see some of the bikers hanging around too, but they actually looked like the calm ones of the crowd, just there for a simple picnic. They were even tossing a Frisbee around.

He headed back to the Raven's Roost and parked. No stampede of youth out the back door—a good sign. He checked out back first, by the kitchens, just in case. Nobody there, although there was a distinctive smell of marijuana in the air. Possibly the kitchen staff. When he looked inside it was surprisingly quiet. Sam and Sid were doing their shift change, busy bickering about counts for bottles and draft, but in a good-natured way. He waited a minute until they paused for a breath.

"Quiet day here so far?"

Sam laughed. "Hi Constable. Well, other than the Great Foosball Brawl, not too bad. For a while it was just a lot of grumpy customers and cheap tippers. Dave dropped in mid-afternoon just as things were starting to ramp up yet again, but he calmed them down."

"Were people drinking too much?"

"No way," she said. "We were watching that. No, people just seemed to get angry with each other all of a sudden. I think it's all this shitty weather."

"Those two over there look to be in the bag," said Angus. He pointed to two scruffy looking guys in the corner, beer in front of them, arms waving and voices rising and falling."

"Actually, no," she said. "They're just two old buddies. When they came in, stone-cold sober, they were already arguing with each other. So after a few beers it's really hard to tell the difference. Now if you'll excuse me, I have to do prep for the supper crowd. I'll call if we have another riot."

"Please, don't," said Angus. "Or at least wait, as I'm on for another hour." He sighed as he climbed back into the patrol truck. He'd likely be on longer than that. He prayed that this crime spree wasn't going to continue all summer. Everyone kept saying it wasn't normal, but he really hoped that Dave could figure out what was causing this, what was making everyone act crazy.

Chapter 36

Junior walked into the cafe and slumped onto the stool. He was beat. "I need a drink."

"I'll whip up a double-chocolate shake," said Rosie. "Bad day?"

"Thanks. It's actually more of a bad week. All the kids are arguing in the drop-in, fighting over things like their t-shirt designs, and the video they are doing for the mayor. Malicious is painting dark evil black things with black smoke coming out of their mouths. The other kids started to put together an art show, but their styles all seem to be copying hers. One of the elders, George, dropped by to chat and saw their work, and seemed quite troubled by what he saw in the images. The kids were even bickering over little things, like who's using whose coat hook. Really?" Junior had blown up with them over that, then promptly apologized for his own lack of control. "I've been spending most of my time being a referee." He sighed. "And then there's Kurt's Goth phase."

"Tell me about it," said Rosie. "He's dyed his hair that ghastly black, never brushes it, wears nothing but dark colours, and mopes around like the world is his enemy. Barely even talks to his girlfriend when she calls too. I've heard him—just yes and no and grunts. Maybe the kids in the centre all need a break. Have you tried just kicking them all out?"

"I sort of did yesterday," said Junior. "Even though it wasn't that nice a day, I dragged them all out in the bush for a field trip. We had a great time."

"Where did you go?" asked Rosie.

"Just up that road past the village on the reserve, where I took Dave to set rabbit snares last winter."

"And where you lost him, too, right?"

"He wasn't lost," said Junior. "I mean, I knew where he was. He panicked at first, then paused and listened to himself and calmed down. Once he looked around, he figured out which way to go. It was a good test of character." The elders had wondered if Dave was strong enough to resist the evil spirit in him, so Junior had tried to provoke it while out in the woods. Luckily for Dave, the test showed that it wasn't too late for him to be helped.

"Was that the same time Dave did the sweat lodge?"

"Soon after," said Junior. "We went for another walk, and the beautiful country out there put him in the right zone for it. The sweat lodge followed quickly after that, and that ceremony, along with some counselling from the elders, really helped him to focus."

Junior left out the part about casting out an evil spirit. As far as Rosie and most others knew, the lodge was just a native version of a sauna.

"Sounds like the kids liked the country air too," said Rosie. "So what happened to all those smiles?"

"As soon as we got back into town they all turned back into frowns."

It had been weird watching the change, like moving from clouds to sun and then back again. As they'd walked further from the town, everyone's mood had brightened, and they'd started joking and playing around. After a great day together, as he'd led them back, their steps had slowed, shoulders slumped, and the bickering started.

"And they weren't even that eager to come back in," he said. "Maybe they need to stay out for a sleep-over."

"In this weather?"

"Sure," said Junior. "It's only a bit of rain."

Just then Dave rushed in, shaking water off his hat and raincoat.

"Hey!" said Rosie. "You're like a big dog that just came out of the lake."

"Sorry. It's kinda damp out there. Good for the flowers, I'm sure. What are you making?"

"Double chocolate milkshake, want one?"

"Make it a double hot chocolate," said Dave. "I need to warm up. So, how are you today, Junior? Grumpy and irritable like everyone?"

"Yup, part of the crowd," said Junior. "I think the only cheerful person left is you."

"Yes," said Rosie, "and if you keep it up we're going to run you out of town."

"It is strange how widespread this is," said Junior. "Even the animals are affected. Friendly dogs are either snapping at everyone, or cowering, like they've been spooked. Then there's the squirrels. We normally have a lot down by the beach road, but lately the only ones I have seen are a few dead ones."

"Road kill?" asked Rosie.

"No, just dead," said Junior. "Although some look like their necks have been broken. Maybe we've got some that are missing their jumps and don't know how to tuck and roll."

"They do that?" asked Dave.

Junior just looked at him.

Dave laughed. "Okay, got the city boy again. But the bears have changed too. They're a lot more aggressive. Chasing tourists back to their cars, then scratching the hell out of the paint. We'd been trying for ages to convince people to stop going to the dump to watch the bears. No problem with that now, as word has spread."

Junior glanced over at Rosie, who'd gone back in the kitchen, then lowered his voice, "I've been trying to use my own powers to see what it might be, but I can't pinpoint a specific person. Trouble is that it's weaker for me if it's coming from a non-native person. I get just a feeling of unease, and danger. It's sometimes stronger than other times, but it never goes away completely. My grandfather and some of the other elders feel it too."

They'd told Junior that they didn't like what they had felt either, as it had reminded them of the evil that they had sensed within Dave, before they'd helped him chase it out.

"Lately I've felt something different myself," said Dave. "More often by the park or out on the beach road, I'd say. And then there's this whole Sasquatch issue. He's the suspect in Risso's murder and it was in his garage where the murder happened. We haven't seen him around lately, though. He's just vanished. Maybe there's a connection."

Junior nodded. "I'll bring this up with the elders." Once at the Roost he'd thought he'd seen a shadow of a spirit around Sasquatch's head. Maybe it was the same sort of thing they'd seen with Dave. Maybe it was the same spirit, the Wendigo, back again. If so, they could be in big trouble. Usually it was only out in winter. To still be prowling around at this time of year was definitely not a good sign.

"Here you go," said Rosie. "One double hot chocolate. Just the thing to perk you up. And a side of fresh butter tarts, just made today, by Janie's mom."

"Thanks, I needed that," said Dave. "By the way, Junior, how is your girlfriend, Janie?"

Junior gave him a poke in the shoulder. "Cut it out, man. She's not my girlfriend, I mean, she's a girl, and my friend, but we've known each other since kindergarten, when she stopped some kids from bullying little me."

"You mean you weren't always this tall?" asked Dave.

"I was the same size as the other kids back then, but bullies don't just look at physical size. It's how big you feel about yourself inside. And I had almost zero self-confidence back then."

"And little Janie helped?" asked Rosie.

"She was the one full of confidence back then," said Junior.

"What happened to her?" said Rosie.

"Egbert happened to her," said Junior, "her stepfather. Her dad left when she was in Grade 6, I think. It devastated her mother. A few years later her mom remarried, to a real jerk. Everyone knows what he's like, what he does to them. They need to file a complaint, so he'll get out of her life and she can get back to her old self."

"I agree, but they're not ready yet," said Dave. "And we don't have anything we can use to lay a charge. It's hard for people in these situations. The victim might make excuses, say that it's not the fault of the abuser. And if they do make a complaint, or we do on their behalf, they refuse to testify. Even if we get to court, and get a conviction, in a short while the abuser is out on parole. Often welcomed back again."

"They've had enough," said Junior. "She says they're fed up with him now."

"Good" said Rosie. "Both Janie and her mom deserve more than that. And Egbert doesn't even deserve the air he consumes."

"I worry about Janie," said Junior. "She's been depressed off and on for a long time. She cuts herself too, when the stress gets too much."

"Isn't social services involved?" asked Dave.

"Sort of," said Junior. "There's someone that visits here every few weeks. The reserve has some people that can help in these sort of things, especially the elders. Usually just for our people, but I had her talk to my grandfather a few times. That's helping."

"As is having you as a friend," said Rosie. "Has her stepfather tried anything inappropriate with her?"

"No," said Junior. "He wouldn't dare. She's gotten tougher as she's grown up, defies him more. He swats her occasionally but he backs down easily. And he's seen how she cuts herself. I think it scares him when he sees there's a harder side of her. No, he takes it out on her mother instead, which makes Janie feel guilty, of course."

"You're pretty good at this. Ever thought of social work?"

"Just common sense to me," said Junior. "Janie writes stories too, a weird blend of regular small-town people and situations with fantasy creatures as heroes and villains, lots of dragons and monsters. In her sketches too—she's done some great stuff on our computers. But in the last few weeks she's started looking worn down, and her stories and drawings are taking a darker twist, with lots of big black monsters. She says that's what she sees now. In her imagination, I mean." He figured Dave didn't need to know that Janie was convinced this fantasy world was real, that she considered it was a parallel world.

"Well, like I said, we're trying to look out for her," said Dave. "And trying to find out what's wrong with this town. All these little crimes, everyone's crappy mood, the dreary weather, and an open murder investigation. Lots to do." He wished he could share all this with JB, or even just joke around, but between his long shifts and her mid-terms they never seemed to connect.

"Thanks for the snack and the chat Rosie, Junior. I've got to get back out there."

Chapter 37

Janie flinched as her step-father shook his fist at her. "If you don't come right back here, you'll be sorry."

"Get lost," said Janie, as she slammed the screen door in his face. What a loser.

Her mom called out to her, "He didn't mean it honey, it'll be okay."

"You shut up," said Egbert. There was a crash inside.

Janie was tempted to go back to help her mother but she was too angry. He'd stolen from her, again, and of course lied about it. She'd been making some extra money this summer, nothing big, the usual small stuff, such as life-guarding at the beach, babysitting, and house cleaning for some of the rich cottagers. She'd also sold some articles to a magazine, and got a few hundred dollars—her first as a writer. Not only that, they wanted to see more of her sketches too.

Then Egbert had found the money, and claimed it for 'room and board,' that they were broke and she had to help out. Her mother had two jobs, and he had none, claiming some kind of back disability. Janie knew he got checks for whatever he was pretending was wrong with him, because he was always flashing around cash. But still, he had her mother on a strict budget for food and clothing. Janie was going to give some of the money to her mom, but it was the first big cheque she'd ever received, so she'd wanted to savour it for a couple of days after cashing it. Of course Egbert had taken it all from her, starting up yet another fight in their crowded trailer. He was always angry lately too, more than usual. Janie was quick to snap back at him too, since the dreams kept coming back almost every night to disturb her sleep. Dreams filled with dark shapes, chasing her, clutching at her neck with icy fingers. She'd wake in a sweat, and lie awake for hours, afraid to close her eyes again. Sometimes she'd just get up and draw, which helped for a while.

For now, she just tried to stay away from him as much as possible. At least he didn't hit her as much lately, now that she was bigger. She would just glare at him, fists clenched, tempted to swing back in retaliation. Maybe—being a bully—he could sense that.

Janie had grabbed her bag with sketchbook and pencils in it, pulled on a jacket, and headed out. She thought about going to see Junior but she hated to keep bothering him. She passed Dave in the street, but just kept her head down, long hair hiding her face. She didn't want to talk. As she stalked through the town, she sensed more of that evil around her. She'd felt it lately not just from her step-father, but from some others in town too, people that used to be fairly nice but had turned a little bit mean. She used to enjoy having her own fantasy world around her, even wishing at times she could somehow step over into it. Now, it was filling up with black monsters, so she was just fine where she was. Still, as ugly as these new creatures were, their variety still fascinated her. It was a new challenge to try to capture them accurately in her drawings, and to show their evilness. She must be getting good at it, because the kids down at the centre, even tough little Mal, were scared by them. Mal acted like a tough little kid, but Janie knew that under all that bravado there was really a scared little girl, a lot like she'd been when she was younger. She did wonder what would happen if those creatures—either the good or evil ones—decided to reach out and somehow touch the normal folk.

She headed down to the park, to her favourite thinking-bench, but there were some local kids playing there already.

"Hi Janie," they called.

"Hey guys," she said. "Just passing through. I'm heading into the woods for some quiet."

"We were in before, but it felt too spooky so we left. Be careful."

That was interesting. Maybe more of 'her' creatures were there, maybe some new types to draw. She waved goodbye and continued on the path into the woods, parallel to the beach road. She usually liked to just wander in there, listening to the animals, the distant sounds of people having fun by the lake, maybe even sing a little as she walked. This time though, as she walked in, she could feel that evil sense around her again. It was very quiet today. No birds, no rustling leaves, and the cottage sounds seemed muffled. She came to a little clearing and was thinking about turning around when she paused. She did hear something. Flies. There was a cloud of them swirling above a small pile of something in the middle of the space. She picked up a stick, inched closer, and poked at it. Something rolled off the top. Squirrel. She backed away, and saw that there were ten or so squirrels in the pile, all definitely dead. Who would do something so sick? She skirted the pile, and continued on, clutching her bag. The next clearing had nothing in the middle, but there was something on the tree opposite her. As she got closer she saw what it was—yet another squirrel. This one had been nailed, spread-eagled, through its four paws. It looked so much like a high school dissection project that she peered even closer. There were tear marks where the paws had been nailed, so maybe it had struggled. It had then been slit right down the middle, and the sides peeled back and nailed down. She slowly looked around—there was another one on the tree next to it. She couldn't see any of her fantasy monsters, but the feeling of dread seemed even worse.

"Hello?" she said. "Is anyone there?"

Nothing. She pulled out her cell phone and grabbed a few quick pictures of both animals to show to Dave. There was one sick person out here somewhere. She'd better tell Junior. With one last glance behind, she hurried up the path, to the beach road.

As she reached the road, the bird noises resumed around her. There was a whistle from a black and white one on a branch just above her.

"Hey buddy, want some company?" she said.

It seemed to chirp right back at her, and stayed with her all the way back to town. She wasn't sure if she was keeping it company or vice versa.

As she hurried up the main street, she almost bumped into Junior.

"Whoa, slow down! Who's chasing you?"

"Not sure who, or what," she said. "I was in the woods down by the cottages and found something sick, and scary."

"What, those creatures from your other world?" he said.

"Nope, from this world," she said. She described what she'd found, and showed him the photos on her phone.

"That's gross," said Junior. "We need to show these to Dave right away."

Luckily, Dave was in the detachment office. After she went through the same story, Dave looked carefully at her photos.

"Did you hear anybody else there while you were there?" he asked.

"No, I didn't hear anything at all," she said. "It was unusually quiet, not even any birds. But I did have a weird feeling of being watched. Why?"

Dave pointed to an image. "Look here, behind the tree. It looks like someone, or something, is there in the shadows." He handed the phone back. "Can you blow this up on a computer or something?"

"No need," she said. "I can do it right here. Look now. Definitely something there. Something dark. Not a bear, but more like a person, a big person I think, peering through some leaves. Damn, I can't quite make out the face. But I swear there was nobody there. How could that be?"

She saw Dave and Junior exchange a glance. "Junior, you stay here with Janie," said Dave. "I'll go down and check this out. I'll get Norris to put a sign up by the trail too, asking people to stay out for now. I'll say we're concerned about wild animals coming closer to town lately."

As Dave walked into the woods, the normal sounds started to fade away, just as Janie had described. He used his invisibility, just as a precaution, and noticed that the feeling of evil intensified as he kept on walking. When he found the pile of squirrels, he squatted down next to it and examined each one closer. Many had their heads at a strange angle, likely with snapped necks. What bothered him even more was that some also had their throats torn open, as if something had bit them. Further on, he found the two that were nailed to the tree, spread and empty. Their insides had been scooped out and taken away. He took several photos of the squirrels, both those on the tree and the pile, and added a few of the surrounding forest. Maybe he'd catch a glimpse of that shadow again. He was about to head farther into the woods when his radio crackled.

"Boss, Sheila here. I just got a call from the Highway Restaurant. There's some kids whooping it up and annoying customers. Can you take it?"

Dave eyed a faint trail through the trees. It looked like there might be a cabin in there. "Sure, be right there." Maybe another time.

Chapter 38

Sasquatch groaned and rolled over. Bonnie was gone, of course. As soon as it started to get light she'd take off. She didn't seem to mind him in the dark, but once she could see that she couldn't see him then that was it. He'd taken to staying at her and Louie's place now. The place in the woods was nicely isolated, but it held too many shadows and voices in the night. At least here, with someone next to him, and the sound of the other bikers snoring in other rooms, he felt a little more secure at night. The nightmares were still there, though. He just couldn't seem to get a good sleep anymore.

Bonnie's room had its own outside door, so it was easy to sneak in and out without anyone getting suspicious. He stayed quiet if she was out, and if the others did hear any creaks or noises, they figured it was just an old cottage. Or the ghost of Risso. That was a rumour he'd had Louie start around town, and it had spread quickly, helped by all those random events—the small fires, broken windows, petty theft. All of it fun, but he wanted something more. Maybe like stealing those drugs from the post office.

He reached over for a cigarette. It was quiet outside—not even any dogs barking anymore. Probably too scared. He'd learned that if he walked up to a leashed dog with the wind at his back, it just went crazy, pulling at its collar and snapping at the empty air. And if he came from the other direction, very quietly, he could sneak right up to the dog before it knew he was there. He'd crept up to one down by the cottages like that. When he petted it, it turned, but saw him too late. Before it could do more than give a little yelp he'd grabbed it, undone the leash, and carried the tiny thing into the woods. The dog next door to it was larger, but not brave at all. Once he'd snuck up and grabbed it's leash, it couldn't see who was pulling at it. That one had whined and pulled all the way into the woods. He just meant to tie it up and leave it, but the whining got to him. After that—he didn't remember. Those lapses had been getting more frequent lately. Once he got angry he didn't remember what happened next.

Sasquatch finished his smoke, then yawned and rubbed the back of his neck. He fumbled on the table for some pain-killers, then rolled over and waited for them to kick in. He was so tired.

There was a click as the outside door opened.

"It's only me," said Louie. "Sas, Sas, wake up buddy."

"Yeah, I'm good, just give me a sec here." He shook his head. It seemed to take him longer each day to clear the fogginess out. And he seemed to be having more blackouts in the day, too. He'd suddenly find himself on a bench in the park in the middle of the day with no one near him, as if he had something repelling them. Or walking in the woods, with scratches on his hands, and blood. More blood than there should be from those scratches. And even worse, a coppery taste in his mouth.

"The boys are all out, Sas, headed up to the Highway Restaurant for a big breakfast. Here, I brought you something to eat." He handed him a paper bag.

"Thanks, Louie," said Sasquatch. He dug into the bag. "Any more news from Toronto?"

"More drugs are on their way, this time in an RV. Some people that were heading this way anyways, and there's lots of hiding places in it. I'll meet them at one of the campgrounds tomorrow and pick it up."

"Any trouble getting stuff to our customers?"

"Not really, between the boys wandering the town and your invisible work, there's more than enough to keep the cops busy. That fire at the retired cop's place really shook them up. And then the other ones all around town made everyone a little spooked. I like that Ghost of Risso thing too."

"Well, apparently he was quite a pest when alive," said Sasquatch. "Good to know he can continue to be one even when dead."

"It looks like most of the cops are doing double shifts," said Louie. "They all look tired, especially that broad. I hear she's got a young kid, want us to scare him a bit?"

"No, leave him alone for now," said Sasquatch. "We can save him for something special later."

"How's your undercover work been going," asked Louie.

"I'm learning a lot as I spy," said Sasquatch. He took a bite of the local version of an Egg McMuffin. "They're all baffled, so I'm not worried about them. Well, except that damn cop, Browne. I know I'm invisible but he looks like he's staring right where I am. I just keep my distance. And that big Indian kid gets so jumpy when I go near I can hardly keep from laughing. His grandfather is the same. Maybe they have some kind of Indian voodoo going."

"They're buddy, buddy with the cops," said Louie. "Don't get them too nervous."

Sasquatch grabbed Louie's shirt and pushed him into the wall. "Don't go telling me what to do, dog breath. I'm the only one holding this whole operation together."

He paused. There it was again, this rage that seemed to take him over. It did give a nice feeling of power, but he'd rather get angry on his own terms. "Shit. Never mind, sit down again. Here, want my fries? I'm not hungry anymore."

"Thanks, I'm okay," said Louie. He stayed by the door. "Hey, I was talking to Spider this morning, back in Toronto."

"I meant to call him yesterday. What's he up to? He'd better not be thinking of taking over while I'm gone."

"He's cool," said Louie. "Busier than ever trying to compete with all those young punks and their new gangs, though."

"They're pushing us hard, and will fight as dirty as we do. He sound like he's hanging in there?"

"Oh yeah," said Louie, "but getting burned out I think. He asked if there was a pension plan he could apply for, but he was joking, I think."

"Maybe they're getting too old in their minds down there, won't take risks anymore."

"Well, they were impressed with all the stuff we are doing up here," said Louie.

"Minor tricks," said Sasquatch. "High school stuff."

"I think it's a good strategy you have," said Louie. "It's a small town, so we're pretty visible. Nothing drastic enough to get us all busted, just enough to keep them all running around like chickens with their heads cut off."

"We are keeping them hopping," said Sasquatch with a small smile. "But I've an urge to do something big."

"Just don't come after me with a shovel, please. That definitely entertained the boys in Toronto."

"It was kinda cool," said Sasquatch. "No, I'm thinking of a drug heist."

"From who?" said Louie. "We're the only suppliers in town."

"From the cops. All that stuff they found a few weeks ago in the post office."

"It's still there?"

"Yes, I heard those two young cops talking about it. They've just left it there for the summer, waiting for people to pick it up. No takers, so they are going to seize it eventually. Probably just waiting for the paperwork."

"But wouldn't it be all locked up?"

"You'd think so," said Sasquatch. "But I went and checked, on a quiet day. They're not being smart—typical hick town cops. It's all sitting in the back of the post office, in a small box, in the safe, but with the door left open all day. Just waiting for someone to go in and pick it up."

"But we've lots of stuff coming in, we don't need that stuff. Isn't that a little risky?"

Sasquatch grabbed Louie again. "Listen punk, don't you tell me what's risky and what's not. I want to do this so it's going to happen. It will be so nice to take that right under the nosey noses of those cops. I'll wait until after the long weekend. They'll be off their guard by then." He pushed Louie away again. "Now get out of here so I can change and get busy on today's anarchy."

Chapter 39

"Junior, it's Janie, he's got hold of another gun and he's—" The line went dead.

"Hello? Hello?" Junior looked around the room then beckoned Mal over. "I just got a call from Janie on her cell, her dad's managed to get another gun and I think he's going to use it. I'm heading over to her place. Call Corporal Browne, but don't tell Rosie."

Junior ran the few blocks to Janie's, hoping he'd be in time. Just as he ran up the front path he heard shouting. Then a shot. Then a scream. He banged on the door, but the yelling continued. He tried the doorknob. Locked. He backed up a bit, and hit it with his shoulder. Luckily it was just a trailer door so it just popped out of the frame. He burst inside, to see Janie, her mother, and her dad all struggling together in the front hall. Egbert turned and raised a pistol, but before Junior could react there was a flash and a sudden pain in his head. As he fell, Egbert pushed past him and out the door. There was more yelling, then another shot.

Junior lay on the floor of the trailer, looking up at the ceiling in astonishment. He'd actually been shot in the head! You go through life taking one step after the other, and then suddenly something like this sneaks up and unexpectedly hits you! He wiggled a few fingers, then his toes. Well that was a relief! He was still alive and moving his body parts. A good start.

Norris rushed in the door. "Police! Junior, are you all right?"

He waved a hand at her. "Sort of. My head hurts."

She bent over him. "Just grazed your head, I think." She grabbed a tea towel from Mary. "Here, hold this to it. Geez, you idiot. Couldn't wait for us, could you? Mary, Janie, are you okay?"

"We're fine," said Janie. She knelt down next to Junior. "Damn it. What were you thinking?"

"How's Egbert?" asked Mary.

"Under arrest," said Norris. "He took a shot at Corporal Browne, of course. Luckily his aim is pretty bad, so all he took out was a pine cone. What about you guys? Did he hit you again?"

Mary smiled at her. "Yes, but not too bad this time. But that's it for me, I want him locked up and away from us. He used to be bearable, but lately he doesn't seem himself. Always muttering to himself, always angry with us and the world. He's a very sick person. And I think Janie is ready to testify also, right dear?"

Janie nodded. "Damn straight, I'm fed up too. But we need to keep him away for good."

"Don't worry," said Norris. "He will have two assault with weapon charges, for Junior, and the corporal, and some related weapons charges. We might consider attempted murder for shooting Junior. I'll have to talk to the crown counsel about that. Likely there will be a few more on the list if there are unregistered guns or illegal drugs in the house. Your statements about assaults in the past will help, but the rest will keep him in jail for a while. I'm not sure what the final list will be but you get the idea." She smiled. "He was actually going on about how he wanted to charge Junior for breaking in."

"That ass-hole," said Janie. "Can he do that?"

"Yes, he can," said Norris, "but I don't think it would get very far. We'll need to take a look around now. Any more guns or anything else we should know about?"

"No, it should be okay," said Mary. "I don't know where he got that latest gun from. He has been hanging out a lot with those bikers that have ridden in lately, so maybe there. He's likely seeing them for drugs too, as he always seems to be high or drunk lately. And he's probably selling to others. Let me grab my purse and get out of your way. Oh, I guess you want to check it first."

"Thanks," said Norris. "We need to do that, sorry. Do you want to go somewhere, maybe to a friend's?"

"No, we're okay for now," said Janie. "We just need to sit for a bit and catch our breath."

Mary and Janie helped Junior get outside, where a crowd had already started to gather, including Mal and Rosie.

"Sorry man," said Mal. "I panicked and spilled it all to Rosie. Wow, what happened to your head?"

Junior tousled her hair. "That's all right. I'm good."

He and Janie sat together on a bench in the yard, arms around each other, while Norris and Dave went through the trailer. The police came out twenty minutes later, carrying some boxes. Mary mouthed at Norris, "Drugs?"

She nodded back. "You can go back in now, if you want. You should be okay. I don't think Egbert's friends will be coming by. He's already talking of plea-bargaining in return for info on them and we've barely had a chance to charge him. Don't worry," she continued at their looks of concern, "we won't deal away jail time."

"Damn right," said Janie. "How does Junior look to you? Looks to be a lot of blood."

"He's okay. It's just a scratch to his head. They always look worse than they really are. Still, Junior, you'll need to get to the clinic for a couple of stitches and some painkillers."

"Give me a sec," said Junior. He smiled at Janie. "Sorry about the door. We can go up to the hardware tomorrow and get some things to fix it."

"Don't worry about it," she said. "Right now we need to get you fixed up. Thanks for coming so fast. We didn't know what he was going to do, and I panicked and thought of you first. Not the police. Sorry, Constable."

Norris smiled. "Just don't do anything like that again."

"I'm just glad you called me, Janie," said Junior. "I wouldn't want anything to happen to you." He started to get up. "I gotta get back to work, we have the hip-hop festival this weekend." He closed his eyes, paused, then sat back down. "Whoa. This is really starting to hurt."

"Let the rest of us worry about getting things ready," said Janie. "You need to get looked after."

"I agree," said Norris. "Time to get you to the clinic. I'll drive you there. You look a little wobbly."

"I'm coming with you," said Janie. "If you need stitches, I can hold your hand. Just as long as I don't have to watch."

Chapter 40

Dave winced at the sudden screech. "Sorry folks," said Mal. "Just a bit of mic feedback. Alright, let's go. Once again, helping you celebrate this August long weekend's hip-hop festival—thank you Junior—Kirk's Landing's finest band, Mal and the Maniacs."

There was a crash of drums, a piercing guitar note, and then the band charged into another song. Still as loud as the first set, maybe a bit wilder, but obviously a hit with the crowd. Junior had revived the hip-hop festival that JB had done a few years ago, and so far it was going well. She'd given him a few tips over the phone from Ottawa, but had told him he'd be fine on his own. And so far, she'd been right. Since noon, there'd been an impromptu break-dancing competition-- with some kids leaping and spinning on a makeshift linoleum floor, the band had been persuaded by their fans to play another set, and the nearby wall, and some plywood sheets, were covered in new art.

Dave nudged Charlie. "What do you think? Still want them to headline at this year's pow-wow?"

"What?" said Charlie. "No way! Oh, you're just teasing—good one. No, they will be there but as part of our reaching out to the community."

"And the art?"

"Maybe," said Charlie. "I've looked over some of it. It's nice to see some of our native themes blended in, although some is a little too dark for me, especially the ones by Janie." He looked up at the gathering clouds. "It started off as such a sunny day, but looks like there's a storm brewing again."

"I think the mood is changing with the weather too," said Dave. "Mal's band sounds less polished, and the latest pieces being painted look different."

"It's anger," said Charlie. "I can feel it in the air. Speaking of which, here comes a couple of Risso's old buddies."

Dave pulled his friend to the side, out of the crowd. "Louie and that girl. Bonnie, I think. They haven't noticed me yet. I'll just fade for a bit and see what they are up to."

Dave watched as the two pushed their way through the crowd. They were smiling, but he sensed they weren't that friendly. People seemed to be giving them an unusually wide berth, too.

Charlie put his hand up to his mouth, and muttered to Dave. "Do you see that? They shouldn't really be that intimidating."

"I know," said Dave. "It looks like there's some kind of shadow cast over them. I know it's cloudy out now, but it's some kind of lighting thing."

"Really?" Charlie squinted. "Nope. But whatever it is, it can't be a good thing, not if it's associated with them."

Just then, Louie and his friend reached the front of the stage. Mal was in mid-note when she broke off and screamed, pointing at the two of them.

"It's there, the monster! Just like I see when I paint!"

Her band-mates rushed to her side, and Louie and Bonnie moved back, as if dragged, bumping into the people behind them.

Things went downhill from there. Fists were thrown by Louie and Bonnie, but blows were returned too. Dave and Charlie, along with

Junior, managed to drag the two troublemakers away, after which the crowd seemed to calm down by itself. Mal had disappeared, and it started to drizzle, so Junior wisely decided to quickly thank everyone and shut the festival down. Dave hoped that Norris was having a better time out on the lake with her patrol.

The inboard motor sputtered a few times, then stopped. Norris turned the key but the starter just whined. Nothing. And it had started to rain. Reese usually checked their boat out carefully, but things had been so hectic lately maybe he hadn't had a chance. She lifted the lid of the engine compartment, and smelled gas. A lot of it.

She backed away, right up onto the bow deck, and grabbed her radio. "Brian, I think I've a mayday thing happening here."

Luckily her counterpart Brian Gleason was out there already, patrolling his Park half of the lake. She had a life jacket on of course, but would prefer to not have to abandon ship. Within a few minutes, the other boat pulled alongside, barely giving her time to call her status in to the detachment office.

"Here, jump in," said Brian.

Once she was on board, he grabbed his fire extinguisher, poked it under the rear cowling, and pulled the trigger. "Just in case," he said. "Drives out any fumes." He opened the engine cover. "Whew, sure smells like a leak."

"We've had a lot of suspicious fires in town lately," said Norris. "Along with a lot of other minor crimes, bickering residents, and snapping dogs. I'm wondering about this failure. It's unusual given how well Reese looks after our boat and ski-doo. Can we tow it back to your dock instead of the public one on our side?"

"No problem," said Brian. "We've had some weird things this summer too. Bears, even some smaller animals, all are more aggressive. Skunks, which normally will scurry away if you give them a chance, have been spraying every chance they get. We had to get in cases of tomato juice in the camp stores to clean up people. And bees! You'd think we had those South American killer bees. The campers aren't much better either. I've never seen a surlier, grumpier, more argumentative bunch. Some days we just want to hose them down, give them a refund and close it all up."

"Any pattern at all?" she asked.

"Only thing I could say is it's worse in the southern sites, the ones nearest the town. Maybe what you have is contagious."

By the time they reached the dock, there were several people waiting for them.

"This is one of our mechanics," said Brian. "I asked him to meet us to check it out, to make sure first it wasn't going to catch on fire, and also to try to figure out what happened."

"Thanks," said Norris. "I'll need to watch as you do this. Also, would you mind putting on these evidence gloves? I want to examine this closely after. Don't wipe anything down."

Brian's mechanic was impressed with how well Reese had maintained the engine. He poked around and after a few minutes they found the loosened connections. He tightened them carefully, blotted up the remaining gas, and closed it up.

"Should be okay now. Everything else looks good. Even cleaner than the ones I maintain."

"I'd just as soon not drive it anyway," she said. "I'll ask Reese to bring the trailer over. I'd like to see if I can get any prints in here."

"Sure," said Brian. "While you're here, I could use your help on my latest problem. In fact, I was just getting ready to call your office with a missing person complaint."

"A party-goer sleeping it off somewhere?" she asked.

"I'm not sure," said Brian. "A couple of young guys were staying at one of those southern sites I mentioned, close to the town. Up just to relax, they said. They picked a spot that was a little more isolated, near the edge of the campground. So, anyways, one of them walked over to the showers yesterday while his buddy stayed in the tent for a rest. When he got back twenty minutes later his friend was gone. Not just walked off, as it looked like there had been a disturbance of some sort."

"One of those bears from the dump?" she asked.

"I don't think so. He didn't report him missing at first because he thought he might have just left to go into town. Apparently they'd been disagreeing about something."

Norris nodded. "A lot of that going around this week."

Brian continued. "The tent door was still tied open like when he left for the shower, and the tent looked fine. Only difference in it was that the sleeping mat and bags were dragged out and to the side, toward the woods. Usually bears tear right through the side of a tent."

"But?" she said.

"But no tracks, no bear signs. People on the next site didn't hear anything either."

"Where's the friend?" she said.

"He initially wanted to stay there to wait for him, but got too freaked out when it got dark, so got a room at the motel. He was back this morning, but we had nothing more. He's at the office, and getting pretty impatient. Can't say I blame him. Did you want to talk to him?"

"Let me grab my stuff out of the boat and we'll check the site first," she said.

When they pulled up to the campsite she turned to Brian. "You haven't roped it off or anything?"

"Well, we don't think it's a crime scene or anything. Do you think we should have? Jeez, we've all been stomping around in here, looking around."

"That's okay," she said. "The tent looks pretty tidy from here, though. Did anyone change it after the incident?"

"Yes, the guy's partner did, before he left last night for the motel.

Sorry, I wasn't thinking it was anything serious."

"But you did look for tracks?" she asked.

"Yes, we looked but couldn't find any. There's a few rocky areas around the site, so I suppose the bear might have taken those. If it is a bear we'll have to track it down, hopefully to trap and relocate. But if it's too aggressive, we may need to shoot it." He handed her a raincoat.

"Thanks," she said. "Just wait here for a sec while I take a look."

She walked carefully up to the tent, pulling her hood up against the fine rain that had started. As she scanned the ground ahead of her, she did notice marks where something had been dragged partway to the woods, but other than that the area was covered in boot prints. She called Brian over, then looked where he'd just stepped.

"You all have the same style boots, right?"

"Sure," he said, "standard issue. So?"

"Let's not assume this is a bear."

"I don't think a person would do this, too weird," said Brian. "But okay, let me look again. He said his buddy likely had on sneakers. And he was a little guy." He pointed. "There. Those look like his."

They walked, side by side, scanning the ground.

"Aha!" said Brian. "Look at this one. Very different tread from mine and bigger by a couple of inches anyways. On top of his track, so likely following."

"This doesn't look good," she said. "I'm going to give dispatch a call. They're on as it's the weekend, and I think they need to be in on this anyway. We'll need backup on this in case we do catch up with our mysterious big foot. I would normally call the K-9 team to search but they take at least an hour to arrive." She looked at the sky. "I'd really like to keep going before the rain washes this all away." She glanced at his holster. "You've used that pistol, have you?"

"Yes. At the range. But never at people. I do have pepper spray, though. We carry it mostly for small wild animals, like a fox or someone's dog. I'm pretty good with it. Except for the skunks. They always win."

"Well, keep behind me, but ready."

They followed the trail through the woods, seeing a footprint here and there. As they walked, Brian tagged the occasional tree with a bit of fluorescent tape.

"For your backup to follow," he said. "These tracks look really deep. Maybe it's not just a big guy, maybe he's carrying something, or somebody."

The trail led to a clearing, with a dark shape lying in the middle.

"Wait here," said Norris. "Watch my back, he might still be around."

She walked carefully over to what appeared to be a body.

"It's a person, and," she paused. "Yes, definitely dead. Stay away unless you have a strong stomach."

"I've done my share of hunting, and field dressing," he said. He bent over. "Damn. Something's taken some bites out of him." He bent closer. "Those don't look like the bites you'd get from a wolf or dog, either. Look at this one for example, almost looks like human teeth marks. And looks like some pieces are actually bitten out." He looked around. "I don't see any pieces here though."

Norris pulled her gun. "This is not good. Where's that backup?"

"We should be almost at the boundary road," he said. "It's just the other side of those pines. Tell your guys to take it instead. I'll mark the spot for them with some more tape."

Norris got back on the radio and passed the new directions on for the backup. She also changed the status of the file from missing camper to found dead body, and asked for a camera, a tarp, and some boundary tape.

"You guys are going crazy out there this week!" the dispatcher exclaimed. "Is there something weird in the water?"

"Here Norris," Brian said. He reached into a coat pocket. "For now, we can use one of these space blankets. Poor bugger won't need it for warmth, but at least, it will keep the rain off. How far away is the coroner likely to be?"

"The chief one for Manitoba is in Winnipeg, but there's an assistant one in St. Anne, I think. I'll ask HQ to contact him. He has a cottage just around the lake from Constable MacGregor, so we might get lucky. Once he's done here, I imagine he'll want to do an autopsy. We may need to move the body somewhere temporarily, though."

"We've got a big cooler back at the district office that we use if we seize illegal game. It's empty now, so you're welcome to use it."

She nodded. "We'll need to have his partner identify the body too. We'll cover over these cuts of course, and say we're investigating. Let's keep the details of this as quiet as we can. I don't want to freak everyone out."

Chapter 41

"Maybe it's back," said Junior. The elders just looked back at him. Nobody was nodding.

Charlie cleared his throat. "George, Peter, he may have a point. Let's consider what we know." That helped, since as band chief his word was listened to. Junior had asked them to join him at the band office to discuss the recent troubles in town, and they were speculating on the cause.

George spoke first. "We all saw the spirit leave the police chief, driven out, as we expected, by the sweat house ceremony. With our assistance he found it within himself, wrestled it, and rejected it."

"Yes, we did see that," said Junior. "And then we looked deep into him and found him pure. It's not in him this time, but maybe it's still around and has found someone else to enter."

"It will always be around," said Charlie. "Just stronger sometimes. How about the images your youth were doing for their art show at the festival? All the same style, very dark, like a glimpse into the dark side of the spirit world. And I saw hints of something evil when that fight started. Evil that we've all felt in the last few weeks."

"This spirit can lay a dark cloud over a whole village," said Peter. "But what it really needs is one specific victim to feed from. It still needs a way to sneak into a person. Maybe through an ability already in there, as Dave had when he arrived here."

"Or an evil nature already in someone, that craves more," said George. "But who? There are some in Kirk's Landing that have a bit of evil in their heart. As we know all are not as perfect as the Creator had hoped they would be. But none I would think are evil enough for this."

"But we also have many more people in town now for it to choose from," said Junior. "Cottagers, campers, tourists passing through. Even a biker gang—a first for here."

"Could it be one of them?" asked George.

"It might be," said Junior. "There was that big hairy one that they are sure killed Risso. Apparently he has a long history of violence. Dave had indicated they were suspicious of him, but then he suddenly just disappeared from town."

"Are they sure?" said George.

"Well, supposedly he's back in Winnipeg somewhere," said Junior. "As for the other bikers, while in the movies we see them tearing up a town and running wild, here they are just an annoyance."

"Maybe that is on purpose," said Peter. "The crows can distract a mother robin so that one of them can raid the nest. Maybe they just want to keep all the police busy."

"It's sure working," said George. "Even our two band police are always on the go. But why do you think this is the evil spirit?"

"According to the legends," said Charlie, "the Wendigo—and I think that's what this is—is associated with bad weather, and cold and ice. I know it's the middle of August, but we've had more than our share of sudden storms, some even with hail."

George nodded. "Well it is unusual to see it out this late. But not impossible I suppose. It would depend on how strong the hunger is.

How about the cannibalism though? We've not seen that, have we?"

"Actually, we may have," said the Chief. He described the dead squirrels that had been found in the woods, tortured and partially eaten.

"Definitely the work of a very troubled person," said Peter. "But these are animals."

"Do you remember that missing camper last week?" said Junior.

"Yes," said Peter. "But they said they found him in the woods. That he'd gone for a run, tripped, and broke his neck."

"That's the official story for now," said Junior. "Dave told me, and keep this quiet please, that they found the body with bite marks on it. Human bite marks. And some of the flesh missing."

George grunted. "You've convinced me," he said. Peter nodded too.

"But what do we do about it?" said Junior. "Many people in town are affected. While we know that this spirit will attack and possess only one person at a time, it can also spread its influence to others nearby. Not only the people seem changed in the town, so do some animals—dogs, bears, even the birds. And the stronger it gets the farther will be the range, and the tighter its hold over its host."

"When Dave used the spirit to fade," said Peter, "he claimed it seemed to get easier to use it each time. What would have happened if we had not been able to help him get rid of it?"

"I think every time he used it, the hold on him became stronger," said Charlie. "And I believe eventually he would have been totally under its power, and stayed invisible permanently. By then he would have been unable to stop the spirit from controlling him."

"Would we have been able to help him force it out?" said George.

"I don't know," said Charlie. "The legends don't talk of any specific weapons against it."

"I assume no one has seen this spirit yet?" said George.

"No," said Charlie, "but Junior and I have felt its influence, as an evil feeling. All in the town, too. Nothing out on the reserve, at least not yet. We feel this just like we feel many of the other spirits. We just can't see this one, or feel any specific focus or direction."

"But you could see this spirit in Dave," said Peter.

"Yes," said Charlie, "but I think that was because he has First Nation blood in him."

"What about Dave?" asked Peter. "Is he feeling this evilness too?"

"He tells me he senses something," said Junior. "Easier than we can, I think. Sometimes even in a specific direction. If it's in a non-native person, maybe Dave's mixed blood is helping him to focus on it better than we can."

"Well, at least we'll be able to keep an eye on it," said Charlie. "But it still is going to keep growing and getting more powerful. And so far we have no way to get rid of it."

"Want me to talk to Dave?" said Junior.

"Not quite yet," said Charlie. "Let's talk to the elders on some of the other reserves, see what they know of this creature. We need to have a way to find it, and a way to kill it. Before it takes over the town."

Chapter 42

JB was worried about Dave. They'd both been pretty busy lately, but they still talked enough for her to know he was feeling overwhelmed. There was the increase in minor crimes, way more drugs, an invisible murderer, and an overall evil presence in the town. She checked the time—seven. Maybe he would be home and done for the day. She picked up the phone, dialed, and was pleased to not just get the machine.

"Hi Dave, it's JB. I know you're busy but I thought I'd call anyway."

"Hi. I'm sorry. It has been crazier up here than usual. Your grandfather is here now too, he just dropped by after supper to talk."

"Oh, I can call back later," she said.

"No, now is good. Here, he wants to say hi."

"Hello, little one," said Charlie. "How have you been?"

"Busy, Grandfather, but a good busy. I'm learning more about our culture, of all the People, as well as other subjects like sociology and economics and how to fund a new business. I'm looking forward to when I can come home and use this knowledge to help our people."

"You can certainly share with all the elders," he said. "There are a lot coming here for the pow-wow at the end of the month."

She was looking forward to that, as it was the first time in years they had hosted one. Plus her little brother was one of the main planners. "I miss home, but I think I've made a good choice being here."

"I'm glad you have finally found your path," he said. "We are all very proud of you."

"And Junior?" asked JB. "I hear he's found a path too. When he's not trying to be a hero."

"Very much so," said her grandfather. "He's doing well with the youth centre. He's skilled at leading the youth without telling them what to do. And he's trying to develop an Outdoor Education program too. He has some good ideas, but still needs someone to help him pull it all together. Like a big sister, for instance."

"I know, Grandfather, I know." She missed her little brother too. "Soon. Exams are coming up, and my assignments are almost finished. I worked the long weekend and made a fortune in tips. We had live music all three days and the forecast was perfect for the patio. This was a busy summer trying to fill in a lot of courses I'd missed, plus work. The fall term should be more normal. Tell me, what are you and Dave up to?"

"I came over with some questions on this evil thing that has taken over our town," said Charlie. "And I'm hoping he may have some solutions. But you called him, little bird. Do you want me to put him on?"

"No, I mean yes, but first, I've been thinking too about our problems up there, and may have a solution. But I have some questions too. Ask him to put us on speaker-phone."

"Hi again Dave," she said. "All right, I may have something to add to this whole evil thing problem. Grandfather, is it possible this might be due to Dave's old enemy?"

"What? The Wendigo?" said Dave. "Damn. Has it come back for me? Why didn't you tell me?"

"We didn't want to alarm you until we were sure," said Charlie. "But we think you're okay."

"I hope so," said JB. "This sounds similar to what I've heard from you and the other elders about it. And I've been learning about creatures like this in other cultures too. But what about the cannibalism?"

There was a pause.

"Go ahead, Dave," said Charlie.

He described the mutilated squirrels, and the missing dogs that had been found savaged, by something. "Then, we found our final link. The Park had a camper disappear from his tent, while his buddy was off at the showers. Looked like he was carried off in broad daylight."

"Bear?" said JB.

"Nope. The only tracks were human. Norris followed it up, and they found his body about a mile away. Bitten. By human teeth. Some of it eaten."

"Yup, that's it," said JB. "Sure sounds like a Wendigo."

"But the problem is we can't find it," said Charlie. "We can't see it. Junior and I can only feel it. We can sense a force of evil in the town, that seems to come and go."

"And I've been feeling that too," said Dave. "An evil feeling, but reminds me of something I've felt before. And with direction to it. I mean it will seem to be pointing in a particular direction, but there's nothing there."

"Interesting," said Charlie. "That's more definite than what I feel. How about your dreams?"

"A lot more lately," said Dave. "Like I had before, and with the same animals—the bear, the buffalo, the whisky jack—but they are more mixed up and confusing. And there's always some big dark cold 'thing' that chases me. Sometimes I try to battle it but it seems to always slip through my fingers like smoke. And then I wake up and it's all gone, except for my racing heart."

"You know, the way this comes and goes," said Charlie, "is almost as if it's a real thing moving among us, as if it's near us sometimes, but invisible. Part of a real person. We know that it needs that actual possession to be really effective, so maybe that's what's happened."

"Any ideas who the lucky person might be?" asked JB.

"It's easiest if it finds a streak of evil already there, when it takes over someone," said Charlie. "In spite of the mill clean up, we still have a few possibilities in town, a few with a nasty streak hidden in them. Look at Janie's step-father for example. He has got worse, but he's still around, definitely not invisible. Besides, while a creep, I'm not sure if he'd be evil enough. Maybe it's one of the bikers that have decided to stay here for a while."

"What about that Sasquatch you'd mentioned?" asked JB.

"No, we think he's in Winnipeg now." said Dave. "Or at least we had a report he was. Come to think of it, I never did hear any follow up on that. I'll double-check."

"How nasty was this Sasquatch?" asked JB.

"From what my staff tells me he seemed okay when he showed up, but I think he'd just cleaned up nice. He used to be pretty mean, with a long record, and several jail terms served."

"And now a suspected murder," said Charlie.

"Oh yes," said Dave. "I'm pretty sure it was him. We even got prints from the shovel we think he used. But the problem remains that if we can't see him we can't catch him."

"This invisibility he has sounds like the thing you have Dave," said Charlie. "We need a way to zero in on him with more accuracy."

"Well, I learned that with this power you show up when you touch someone," said Dave. "That can be avoided, but you also show up on a device such as a camera, cell phone, surveillance system."

"So we could catch him like that and find him?" said Charlie.

"Well, yes," said Dave. "But as soon as he slips out of range we've lost him. And we still don't know how to get rid of this thing."

"I was thinking," said JB, "maybe you are the key, Dave."

"Me? I can't see him," said Dave.

"Yes," said JB. "Not yet. Hear me out. Grandfather, you and Junior —and some others—have developed this gift of seeing, and can see these spirits in others of our race, right?"

"Right," said her grandfather.

"And you could also see the spirit in Dave, because of his partial native blood, but you can't see it in any white people, right?"

"Right."

"But Dave has some variation of this ability in him, and both kinds of blood in his veins, right?"

"Ah," said her grandfather. "So maybe he could learn to use this ability, and see the spirits in both our people. Including Sasquatch."

"Exactly," said JB.

"Very good," said her grandfather.

"Yes, it sounds all well and good," said Dave, "but I believe you took years to develop this. We don't have years."

"I agree," said Charlie. "The longer this spirit is in him, the stronger it will get. Right now this Sasquatch still has some control over it. He might even be able to get rid of it, with help."

"And that would be like taking a thorn from the paw of a wolf," said JB. "First you'd have to catch him, then you'd have to persuade him to let you help. But I don't think we can afford any kind of delay. We need to focus on getting Dave ready for this as soon as possible."

"I think the process may go faster for him," said Charlie, "because at one time Dave already did have some of this spirit in himself, along with his own powers. And he did develop a lot of inner strengths to quickly cast the evil portion out. Let me talk with the elders tonight, to see what we can come up with. And now I'll leave, and let you two chatter on. Goodbye, little one."

"Bye, Grandfather, love you."

She paused. "Are we off speaker now?"

"Yes," said Dave. "Thanks. Well, that went well, I think. We just have to wait now. So, what's new with you? Almost done your courses I hear."

"Just about," she said. "It's a lot of work, but I'm doing much better this time around. Crystal is settling in well. She got a good job, in a dress shop, and has sent her portfolio in to a design school."

"Kurt has settling in too," said Dave. "His design work at the youth centre is good for him. Looks like he might have some good business skills too. How's your work? Treating you well?"

"I'm doing okay. I do wish I could come home for a break, but I'm too busy trying to keep up with all this work. Work pays well too, especially with tips on the patio days."

"Especially in those cute shorts of yours."

"Aww, thanks," said JB. "Glad you like them."

"Speaking of tips," said Dave, "those ones you got from your biker friend were a help. And, I was discreet. Do thank him for me."

"I will," she said. "Actually, about him and his buddies . . ."

"More coffee dates?" said Dave.

"No, it's not that, not at all. I wasn't going to say anything but, well, let's be open here." She took a deep breath then explained the attack on her, and how Ron and his friend had saved her. Dave was glad she was okay but sounded ready to hop on a plane and come down. She managed to talk him out of that but he still was upset.

"For God's sake, just quit working there!" he said. "With your grant and savings you don't need the money. If you're as serious as you say about being there, then focus on your grades, do well, and get your cute little self back up here."

"But I do like the work," she said. "Even for just a few shifts a week. I need to socialize with people other than young students. Don't worry. I take cabs all the time now, and Ron's friends are looking out for me. And I've cut some shifts." It was nice to hear his concerns, and be reassured that he missed her. She finally managed to get Dave calmed down, but he assured her he was going to contact some officers he knew in Ottawa, just to keep an eye out for her assailants.

"Thank your friend when you see him," said Dave. "I owe him one."

"Actually, I haven't seen Ron around lately," she said. "He's trying to do a balancing act with his former gang, keep them happy while staying on the legal side of things."

"Sounds like me when I was in undercover." Said Dave. "Trying to be illegal enough to gain acceptance, without going so far as to scare the RCMP."

"But back to you," said JB. "Are you managing to at least take a break once in a while?"

"Not really," said Dave. "It's been way too busy for any social life, especially the last couple of weeks. I went over to Angus's for dinner one night and I occasionally get down to the Roost."

"How is Sid doing?" she asked.

"He's managing, but I'm sure he misses you being there to run it," said Dave. "We all miss you, me especially."

JB smiled. That was nice to hear. "Miss you too, sweetie. Only a few more weeks until I'm back. Gotta run now. I have a shift. Love you."

"Me too," said Dave.

Chapter 43

Dave had spent a restless night, wondering what the elders' plan would be. He'd been really shaken up when he'd had that internal battle with his demon last winter. It was definitely not something he'd expected to have to do when he was transferred up here. Sure, it had ended up okay, but still he wasn't looking forward to going into the spirit world on purpose once again. The elders had explained that only some of the spirits were evil, that most were supportive and helpful. On the other hand, he'd also heard that even those good ones could be capricious and unpredictable at times. He wasn't looking forward to today, but he finally got up, had a shower, and made some breakfast.

Charlie called just as Dave was sitting on his back deck, trying to relax by quietly coaxing a bird to eat from his hand. At the first ring, the bird took off, scolding him for scaring it. The Chief said that it was time to talk, but wouldn't give him any details over the phone.

"Just meet me at the lodge out on the reserve," said Charlie. "And bring four coffees from Rosie's."

When Dave arrived he found Charlie sitting out on the front step, along with three others. Two were from his sweat lodge ceremony, George and Peter, and the third, he was surprised to see, was Junior.

"Hi, Junior," he said. "I didn't think I'd find you here with these venerable minds."

"Hopefully that term doesn't mean old and frail," said Charlie.

"No, it's respectful, sir," said Dave. "I do respect the knowledge all of you have, even or maybe especially, Junior."

"He shows a lot of promise for someone so young," said Peter. "He's here today because we want him to learn even more about our ways."

"We think Junior will be able to take his place as one of the elders some day," said Charlie. "He has a genuine interest in his culture, and a good way with people. Plus he has a strong connection to the world around us, and shares the vision of the spirit world that some of us do. Which is why you're here, Dave."

"We think we can teach you how to see these spirits, as we all had to," said Peter. "And do it quickly."

Dave looked at them in astonishment. "Come on now, it's not as if it's a thing any of you did overnight, is it?" he said. "Remember, I'm just a rookie here."

"True," said Charlie. "But I pointed out to the others your unique background, and links to the spirit world. They think it's worth a try."

"And if it doesn't work, what's your Plan B?" asked Dave.

"We don't have a Plan B," said Junior. "If it doesn't work, we're screwed. Sorry, Grandfather."

"Great," said Dave, "so what's Plan A?"

"A vision quest," said Charlie, "where you will focus on what you are searching for, and wait for a vision that shows you the way."

"So do I just sit and think hard about this?" asked Dave. "Is that how it works?"

"Not quite," said Junior. "When I did it, I had to go away by myself, alone. I had to fast and meditate, until a vision came to me, an answer to my question.

"And what am I looking for?" asked Dave.

"In your case," said Charlie. "I think what we are hoping is for you to develop a closer connection to the spirit world that is all around us."

"This is the world you all can see into already, right?" asked Dave.

"Yes," said George. "We see it as it really is, and we also still see the world that others see. Both are separate, both are one."

Dave looked confused.

"Think of it as layers," said Junior. "A doubling, an overlay onto the normal world most people see. We can see spirits and connections as if they've been drawn over top of the world everyone else perceives."

"I'll go with that," said Dave. "And where can I do this retreat? On my back deck?"

Peter looked shocked. "No, no, it must be a holy place. And one you are connected with in some way."

"How about the place from his dream last winter?" said Junior. "When he saw the bear?"

"His totem?" asked Peter.

"Yes," said Junior. "He dreamed he was on that tall cliff at Loon Lake, and the bear showed him where to look for Charlie's son."

"Yes, then, that would definitely be a good place to wait," said George.

"And how long do I wait?" asked Dave.

"Until it happens," said Charlie. "But don't worry, it's hardly weeks. More likely days."

"I never know if you're serious," said Dave. "It's just that if I assume we're talking only a day or two, it will make it easier for me to trust all you guys and go into this."

"We know what you have to go through," said Charlie, "but we also know what you are capable of."

"But I'm thinking this is somewhat new ground for you," said Dave. "Doing it with a non-native person. I assume you think it's possible?"

The elders all looked at each other.

"It's not impossible," said Peter.

"Okay, whatever," said Dave. "I trusted you all before, might as well again. I need something to help me battle this evil. When do I do this?"

"As soon as possible," said Charlie. "The best timing is to be at the location the evening before. Then we can do the preparation ceremony overnight and leave you on your own in the morning."

"How about tomorrow night?" said George.

"Tomorrow?" said Dave. "Hell. Yesterday I didn't even know this was an option." He paused. "Fine. I'll need to let my staff know I'll be off for a bit and shuffle some schedules. But you're right, this has to be soon. Let's plan for tomorrow."

"Will you tell your people what we think the problem really is?" asked Junior.

"No, for now I'll just try to explain everything in non-supernatural terms. They are all good people, perhaps open to some different explanations, but right now I need them to focus on things they know, like the normal crimes in a normal town, and bad guys that are just good at hiding from us. Nothing more. Not an influence of an evil spirit that expands over a whole town, and invisible villains that are possessed like someone from the Exorcist."

"What?" said Junior.

"An old movie, grandson," said Charlie. "Never mind."

"You're probably wondering why I called you all here today," said Dave.

His team were all in the office: Norris, Angus, Reese, and Sheila. Luckily the two detectives were back at headquarters for the day, so he wouldn't have to explain his latest out-of-the-box scheme to them.

"Okay," he said. "I have an idea that may help us deal with this recent crime wave. An unusual idea, but think it will work. First some background—mostly for you, Angus, but it will help me to go over it with you all again.

"Last winter I'd come from a stressful undercover life down south to the relative quiet of Kirk's Landing. And no sooner had I arrived than it seemed things started to go bad for me, I started having headaches, blackouts, nightmares. And I understand I became somewhat miserable to work with."

"Somewhat," said Norris. "Go on."

"Back in Toronto," said Dave, "I would have been out on sick leave and stuck on some shrink's couch, watching him digging into my childhood and hangups until I was certified sane. Up here, I ended up in a very intense purification ceremony with some of the local elders. And it seemed to work, I'm feeling a lot better now. Now interestingly enough, the elders had told me before my session with them, almost before I started feeling bad, that they could sense already there was something wrong with me, something didn't appear right to them when they looked at me."

"What, like your aura or something?" said Angus.

"I don't know what it was, an aura or some subtle behavioural quirk that they saw, but after our session they said I 'looked' better to them. I wasn't sure at the time what that meant, but I know that they have a long history of myths and symbolism, and a strong belief in the spirit world, so I try to keep an open mind with them."

"He did seem to change drastically," said Norris. "Almost a black and white change, with a better focus."

"And a joy to work with," said Dave.

"How about not quite as miserable anymore," said Reese. "But we did a good job cleaning up the town and solving a murder. So whatever it was that they saw and did, whether they got rid of something in Dave or just changed his attitude, it worked."

Sheila and Norris nodded, but not Angus. He still looked unconvinced. Dave nodded at him. "I'm not asking you to believe all this, just support me."

"Aye, I can do that, laddie," said Angus, "but I must say that I never thought my final posting would be such a peculiar one. Carry on, MacDuff."

"Thanks," said Dave. "All I'm saying is that the elders, and Junior too by the way, can spot these changes in people. Maybe they really can see some kind of spirit or aura we can't see, or maybe it's no more than an ability to be really good at reading body language."

"It would be great at security checkpoints," said Angus.

"That it would," said Dave. "But I don't think it's anything they want to hire out, as it's part of what some elders do as part of their whole belief system and culture."

"I can see that," said Angus. "But how does this tie in now?"

"We've seen a lot of unusual things happening here," said Dave, "negative things that are not normal behaviour for the townspeople. Kirk's Landing has changed over the last few months. Norris and Sheila can attest to that."

Both women nodded.

"And the elders have been sensing a new, more intense negative vibe throughout the town," said Dave, "especially over the past few weeks. There's a pattern to it now too, that suggests to them that while there is a general effect over the whole place, there's a central focus too. Something that moves about as if it were a person. But unfortunately they can't pin it down to anyone in particular."

"Then it's really not much help to us, this sense they have," said Angus, "other than saying there is something wrong somewhere."

"Yes, but they think they can build on that focus," said Dave. "Since my session, I've been able to sense some of these things that they can—not nearly as well as any of them but their chief thinks there's some kind of ability there. So he wants to try sort of a combination workshop and retreat with me, to see if he can increase this ability. I'll admit I'm getting desperate for ways to solve our current problems, we all are. So if there's a chance this can give me an added edge I need to try it."

Dave scratched at his tattoo, then noticed Reese smiling at him.

"But you're worried that there is some risk in this?" said Reese.

Dave smiled back. "Yes, it's not risk-free. I'm hoping the only problem is that it doesn't work and just turns out to be time wasted. The elders did a lot of frowning and muttering to each other as they explained it to me, but in the end I think they decided to be optimistic. I know that they are making a recommendation about this that's based on a heritage of thousands of years of culture, of ancient teachings. I mean, what could go wrong?"

"Don't even say that," said Sheila. "Let's say you go ahead and do this. We'll all be filling in during this, and poor Norris here will once again be trying to juggle schedules so we know who's on first. Do you know how long this will be and when?"

"Likely two days, and starting tomorrow afternoon," said Dave.

There was a collective gasp.

"Cheer up," said Dave. "I have to be fasting as part of this too, starting tomorrow. We have two extra staff to help, remember. While you're putting in extra hours, think of me starving somewhere, cut off from our coffee and Rosie's excellent desserts."

"Does your supervisor know about this plan?" asked Angus. "Just wondering what our story is, that's all, in case he calls."

"No," said Dave. "I think it would be difficult to explain, and perhaps more detail than he needs to know. Let's think of this as a field operations decision, that doesn't need to go up the chain. I'm sure you are aware of the concept from your experiences in the Force?"

"Oh yes," said Angus. "I may have instigated some of them myself."

"You know, Corporal, you do look a little worn out," said Sheila. "I think you're coming down with the flu. I predict you'll be sick as a dog for a few days, unable to even come to the phone, then magically right as rain."

Norris smiled. "Get well soon."

Chapter 44

It was late afternoon by the time Dave and the elders drove down the mill road to the Loon Lake trail, unloaded the ATV's, and were ready to set off. There were only three vehicles, since Dave would be riding on the back of Junior's. He'd managed to catch JB the night before, and she'd done her best to reassure him, but he was still nervous.

"Calm down," said Junior. "It's an easy ride on the same trail as you took last winter with JB. It pretty well follows the side of the stream, maybe two or three hours. The weather also looks good for your quest. Cool nights but clear days. Did you have anything to eat at Rosie's?"

"Of course," said Dave. "I went in today to talk to him to get some courage."

"Did he help?" asked Junior.

"Not really," said Dave. "He let me ramble on, and said I already knew I had to do it. Not much help in talking me into or out of it. But I figured the fasting hasn't started yet, so I had a big brunch of bacon, eggs, toast, home fries, and pancakes. And several good cups of coffee. That should carry me through."

"That's too bad," said Junior. "Hope you enjoyed it."

"I did," said Dave. "I guess I sort of know what I'm trying to do here, but I still don't understand how I'll know I've succeeded, once I'm done. What if it doesn't work? What if I can't do it?"

"Don't worry," said Junior. "The elders would not have set you this task if they didn't think you had the potential in you to succeed. They believe it is possible for you, even if it is definitely not easy. But they are at least confident that it's not impossible. Come on, let's get going."

Once they started on the trail the roar of the ATV's blocked any more conversation. They stopped a couple of times for tea, and trips into the bushes, but everyone was pretty quiet. When Dave tried to talk, Junior just told him to be quiet, think why he was here, and enjoy the world around him. To Dave's surprise they made pretty good time. The elders, while seemingly slow when walking, drove their ATV's with the reckless abandon of young kids. And of course all had refused to even consider wearing helmets. Dave was relieved when they finally got to the lake, just before sunset.

"We'll park here," said Junior, "and walk the last few hundred yards. Here, you can help carry some stuff. George especially has enough to do just getting himself up the hill to the cliff top. But please don't tell him I said that, it bothers him, especially since he was such a dancer in his younger days."

Dave looked at George. "He doesn't look like a dancer. He's a little short and, well, too chunky for it."

"I know," said Junior. "But he won many competitions as a youth. His name fits too—Dancing Turtle."

Dave snorted, then bent over to pick up a pack. He and Junior walked together to the top of the cliff. By the time they got to the top the tall pines were casting dark shadows over the clearing. A breeze sighed through the skinny trees, bringing a chill to the air.

Junior handed him a thermos. "Here, drink this, it's part of the first stage. I'll gather some wood for tonight while we wait for you to finish."

"Finish what?" said Dave.

"Never mind," said Junior, "trust us, it's all part of the process."

It tasted like some sort of bitter herbal mixture, but Dave drank it down obediently, then wandered around the clearing while the elders sat and talked together in low voices, sharing a cigarette between them. It was a small open area at the cliff edge, with some tall pines in the back, small aspens on each side, and lichen and moss on the rocks. He spotted some wild blueberries growing here and there, so he went to grab a few to kill his hunger. He felt queasy as he bent over, so straightened, burped, and apologized. The elders just watched him and smiled. Suddenly Dave's eyes widened. He rushed over into the shrubs, and was violently sick, several times. He hadn't realized he'd had such a big breakfast. As he held his stomach, a small black and white bird watched him, chirping, head to one side. He stood, then grasped his stomach again, fumbled with his belt, and ran behind some bushes.

Finally he was ready to step back into the clearing, only to find Junior grinning at him.

"Sorry," said Junior. "You needed to be cleansed in and out—guess we just did part of that. Here, have some warm spruce tea. Trust me. It will settle things."

Dave cautiously sipped the tea, it did feel soothing to his gut, but he still glared at Junior.

"I did mention fasting," said Junior. "Okay, now strip, right down. Don't worry, you'll get some of your clothes back. Now you need to be cleansed in the lake."

"I don't have to jump in from here, do I?" asked Dave. He peered over the edge.

"Not unless you want to," said Junior. "No bonus points, though. We can just take the trail down."

They walked to the base of the cliff, and, with a bit of prodding, Dave jumped in, then under, then quickly right back out.

"My God, that's cold!!" When his yell stopped echoing around the lake, he could still hear the elders laughing above him.

He hurried, shivering, back up the path. At the top, Junior handed him a small towel, then his t-shirt and jockey shorts.

"That's it?"

"We went easy on you because you're a white man," said George. "We all had to stay naked."

Dave tried to not think of all the elders as naked.

"Now what?" he asked.

"Now you stop asking questions and being impatient," said Charlie. "We will tell you how to prepare for what is next. Then, you wait, until what you find inside talks to you."

Junior spread a multicoloured blanket out on the rock, then folded it in four.

"This will protect your skinny butt from the rock," he said. "Stand in the middle for now."

Peter lit a bundle in his hand, then blew out the flame, leaving it smouldering.

"This is a smudge," he said. "We'll use the smoke to cleanse you." He chanted as he walked around Dave, using his hand to gently waft the smoke over Dave's skin, from head to toe.

Junior had cleared off a space on the rock, carefully re-positioning the moss to another spot. He piled some wood in the middle, and started a small fire.

"Okay, sit now," he said.

Dave sat down, and fingered the edge. "Nice-looking blanket."

"Yes, it's mine. I used it for my vision quest too. I got it from another native when I was on the streets in Winnipeg. He had two, and I had none. How are you feeling now, comfortable?"

Dave was surprised. "Yes, in spite of the bumpy ride, the lost breakfast, the icy bath, sitting in my underwear with smudge in my hair, and not knowing what's next. Sure, I feel okay."

"You could have just said 'I feel okay'," said Charlie. "Try not to ramble, as it annoys the spirits. And Peter. Now, why are you here?"

Dave paused. "I want to learn how to get rid of the evil in our town and make it safe again."

"Good, but think more generally," said Charlie.

"Okay," said Dave. "I guess I want to be able to see the evil spirit and track it down."

"More generally."

"I suppose I want to be able to see all the spirits, good or bad, like you do," said Dave.

"You suppose you do?" asked Charlie.

"No, I do want to be able to. I need to learn how to do this, no matter what," said Dave.

The other two elders grunted.

"Now we can start," said Charlie.

As dusk settled over the lake, Dave started to shiver in the evening breeze. Junior added more wood until the flames leaped high, then sat just behind Dave. Charlie sat across from him, on the other side of the fire, in the east, George and Peter were to the right and left. Junior had a small drum with him, that he started gently tapping.

"I want you to think of your goal, your quest," said Charlie. "And think of the evil power you once felt inside of you, and the good power you feel now. Think of how the world feels around you, the birds, the animals, people, the wind, the sun. It's all tied together, you just have to see the connections. Keep trying, it will happen. When it does it will hit like a thunderclap, like a new intense world. You'll wonder how you could have missed it for all these years. Now, sit comfortably, be quiet. Let your mind focus on the quest, and at the same time wander through the possibilities."

Dave nodded, then just stared into the fire. Junior kept up the quiet heartbeat of the drum, while the elders chanted rhythmically, over and over. Dave thought back to the feeling his secret ability had created in him as a child, and how it had changed over the years, strengthening, but not really in a supportive way. How in Kirk's Landing it seemed to gain power over him, giving a bigger rush every time he used it, but how it was harder to stop every time too. He could see now how it would have turned him into a person as evil as the spirit was, and would have likely been impossible to get rid of.

In his mind he relived his time in the sweat lodge, the vision of the bison leading the herd, of the swirling black crowd of crows, his choice, the sudden noise and confusion as he wrestled with someone, or something, in the lodge rolling through the hot stones in an explosion of sparks. He remembered the feeling of relief as the spirit left him, and the feeling of another spirit within him, similar, but different.

He thought of the little birds on his feeder, some hopping to his fingers, of the eagle soaring over head, of the wolf, one winter's day, that had crossed right in front of his truck, and just looked calmly at Dave. Of the wild bears in the park, and the tamer ones at the dump—the same animal but feeling different somehow. He thought of the northern lights on a cold winter's night, the crunch of the snow underfoot, the spring rains outside his window, the fireflies by the edge of the forest, the sun on a hot summer day, the cool of an evening on the porch of the Raven's Roost, the hum of mosquitoes and the mutter of voices from inside. He thought of his family, his friends down south, his staff at the detachment, his friends in town, of JB. He realized they were all somehow connected—that everything was. He just didn't know how. He couldn't work it out.

As he sat quietly, the fire died, the drumming and chanting faded into the distance, and his thoughts started circling around the same ideas of nature, of his friends, of life. As it got colder, he pulled the blanket over his shoulders, and thought more about his search for something to give meaning to everything, to show him a new path. Gradually the sun came up in front of him, warming his chilled body. He looked around—he was alone. The others had slipped away in the night, unnoticed. He might have heard a distant sound of ATV's. He might have imagined it.

All day Dave sat there, occasionally sipping from the bottle of weak spruce tea Junior had tucked in next to him. He sat and watched, as the sun rose overhead, then fell behind him, into the trees, casting a dark shadow over him again. He watched the wind play across the lake, the birds fly overhead. One of them swooped down to land on his knee for a moment, then an inquisitive mouse paused in front of him, cleaned its whiskers, then scampered away. He heard the wind in the tree, the cries of the birds, the bark of a nearby fox, the gentle beating of his heart.

As the day drew to a close, he started to feel a little lightheaded. His thoughts of what had been, the sights and sounds of the world around him, his imaginings of how it might look, all linked by some sort of thread—all started to blend together. Again, as it cooled, he wrapped Junior's blanket around him. It was surprisingly warm. He sat there all night, dreaming, singing to himself, dozing off for a minute then jerking awake. He was starting to forget why he was there, but he knew it was important, and that something would happen. At the false dawn, the birds started singing, clearer than he had ever heard them. He imagined that he was whistling and chirping to them, and they were replying. He felt like he was floating above himself, and he could see his body sitting there, but it seemed to be made up of several layers of images—some dark, some light. He stretched his hands out in front, and saw that they were brown, covered in hair, with claws. He grunted in surprise, and his voice sounded deeper, rougher than it should. Just then the sun came above the horizon, full in his face, and his eyes widened in astonishment. There were multicoloured lines streaming from the sun, from the lake, from the trees, from the same brown mouse, from his hands—he had hands again. The little bird landed on his knee again, chirped twice, then took off. As it flew away, its wing gently brushed Dave's cheek. He smiled, closed his eyes, and fell over.

Chapter 45

He was trying to rest, but that annoying little bird was back, calling, trying to wake him up.

"Dave, Dave, wake up, Dave."

He opened his eyes.

"JB, what are you doing here?"

"It's over and time to bring you back to town."

"No, I mean you're not in Ottawa," he said.

"Grandfather told me you were doing this, so I grabbed a standby flight. I've a couple of days off anyway, as the term's winding down."

He sat and stared at her face, fascinated by the subtle colours and shadings, her smile, her bright eyes. "You look beautiful."

"Thank you."

"Everything is beautiful—the sky, the sun, the birds, the lake, the trees, the moss, the bugs, even you."

"Okay, well, thanks anyways. You're sounding a little spacey right now," she said. "Drink some of this sweetened tea."

Dave leaned against JB and sipped some tea, while admiring the world around him.

"How do you handle it?" he asked. "Don't you find it all a little overwhelming?"

"Well, I don't think I can see everything quite as intensely as you do," she said. "I have some ability to see things, but not what you and some of the elders have. And Junior. Give it a bit of time, and it will fade to what will be a normal level. If anyone could call this experience normal."

"So I'll lose some of this?" he asked.

"You'll never see the same rush of going from nothing to full awareness," she said. "But you can basically dial this up or down as you want to. It just takes some time to focus on it and practise. But it will always stay at a low level in your perception, a background of awareness and connectivity with the world and everything and everyone in it."

"Wow," said Dave. "This is awesome, you guys are so lucky. I wish more people could learn to see this."

"We're working on it," said JB. "I did a presentation on it for one of my classes on aboriginal studies. It had a mixed reception. For the other First Nations kids, it was like preaching to the choir. For the whites, it was more of a struggle. Some had read the Carlos Castaneda books about peyote experiences, others had read about dropping acid, so they related it to tripping out on drugs."

"Yeah, I can see why they might think that," said Dave. "It is quite a rush when it happens."

"Yes, but the difference is the alternate perception, the new reality you see, doesn't go away as the drug fades. It stays as a new way of perceiving the world. It's like you've been viewing everything through dirty glasses, when you clean them it's all changed."

"Until they get dirty again," said Dave.

"So not a perfect analogy," said JB, "but you know what I mean. Feeling a little better now?"

"Yes, I'm starting to perk up a bit," said Dave. "And I'm hungry now, too."

"I brought some things for you to snack on, some fruit, some juices, some crackers. Keep it light, and keep it gradual is the plan. If you feel up to it we can go back down to the cabin.

When Dave woke up he looked at his watch, it was almost noon and JB was sweeping the floor.

"Hello again," she said. "You started nodding off so I just let you be. Feel better?"

"Yes," said Dave, "the rest helped."

"How's the light show?" said JB.

"It was a lot to wake up to. Nice, but glad I was able to tone it down. Nice to see you in it, too. You look even better. I'm glad you came to get me. I missed you."

"I missed you too, Dave," she said, sitting on the bed next to him. "Here, have some juice and something to eat. And we can talk. I've some things to say."

"Me too." said Dave. "You first."

"Okay, here goes." She paused and took a breath. "I love you, Dave. I like spending time with you, as a friend and a lover. And I would like to get to know you better, and share things with you. But I also need to follow my plan now—to be down south at University and learn so that I can come back and help my people. It doesn't mean I care any less for you, its just what I have to do now. I'll be back in a few weeks to visit and catch the pow-wow, then it's the fall term. Should be an easier work load, so I'll be able to come back more." She smiled. "Now it's your turn."

Dave paused, then reached out and took JB's hand. "I think I get it. It took me a while. Ditto on all those friend and lover and sharing things. I guess I had assumed a lot before, and was surprised when everything didn't work out exactly how I had planned. I would like to see you more often than school breaks though, maybe we could alternate trips. I could come down to Ottawa and get a tour."

"Or we could meet in Montreal," said JB, squeezing his hand. "For a bit of a romantic rendezvous."

"That would work," said Dave. "When do we have to leave to get back?" asked Dave.

"Not for a little while, why?"

Dave reached over and pulled JB to him. "We could have a romantic rendezvous here, too."

She ran her hand over his chest. "Okay, and I think you'll find these new senses can make some things . . . interesting."

Chapter 46

Norris looked up as Dave walked into the office. "Good morning boss. Did you see the light? Are you going to be weird now?"

"Not any weirder than usual," said Dave. "It went well for me though, I think it worked." He paused. He needed a way to explain the changes without sounding too peculiar. "Like the elders had predicted, it's just an even better awareness of what's around me. Especially, a better sense of people now. It helps me focus in a way that I can read them even better."

"We'll have to be careful around you now," said Reese. "You'll be analyzing us and discovering our every secret. Not that I have any of course."

Dave laughed. "Don't worry, I won't be using this on you. Besides, I know you guys already. What I see is what I get. No, it's some of our new criminals in town that I'll be focusing on."

"Well, I hope it works," said Reese. "We need all the help we can get in tracking down whatever is loose in our town."

"I think it will help," said Dave. "And I have some ideas on how to flush out our quarry and put us on the offensive. We've been going on the assumption that this Sasquatch was back in Winnipeg. I've used another contact to double-check that, and they tell me that he's likely not there, but still right here in town. I think someone deliberately fed the Winnipeg office false information. The clerk we suspect is still there, so I'll feed her some misinformation about here. About those drugs still sitting in the post office. As expected, nobody came to pick up their packages."

"I thought we were planning to seize it all soon and send it in to Winnipeg," said Norris.

"That's still on," said Dave. "Next Wednesday, or so we'll tell Winnipeg. What's really going to happen is that the box of drugs in the post office safe will just have in it a few bags of icing sugar from Darlene's store next door. And the real drugs will be safely locked up here."

"How will we manage to pull that off?" asked Reese.

"Norris is going to go to Darlene's store Monday morning on her way in to work. Darlene will let her into the post office before it opens, through her interconnecting door. She'll swap the drugs, and bring them here in regular plastic bags from the store, just as if she was bringing us groceries for lunches and stuff. Once our friends take the bait, we follow them and arrest them with the goods."

"Sounds like a plan," said Norris "So we'll need to set up surveillance overnight?"

"Yes, I'll set up a rotation for that." said Dave. "Just one of us should be enough, as there are cameras inside the post office. We'll put the alarm on silent too. As for today, keep an eye on the place while you're on shift, but don't make it too obvious."

"Can do," said Reese, "but I doubt they're going to be stupid enough to try anything in broad daylight."

"You never know," said Dave. "When people get arrogant they like to take big risks. I'll be back in a bit—I need to talk to Junior, over at Rosie's."

Rosie beamed at Dave as he walked into the cafe.

"Hey, buddy," said Rosie. "Grab a stool. Unofficial word is that things went well on your quest."

That was fast. "Yes, they did, thanks."

"And are going well with you and JB?" asked Rosie. "I heard she was in town."

"Yes, extremely well." said Dave. "Other than that, no comment."

"Smart move, buddy. So, what are you here for? Coffee? Lunch?"

"No, I was looking for Junior. Is he here?"

"Yes," said Rosie, "he's in back, go ahead."

Junior was talking with five or six other teens, but he looked up and waved as Dave came in. "Give me just a sec, Corporal, we were planning another hike, and I'm needed to fill everyone in."

Dave nodded to the group and sat in an overstuffed armchair to watch. He 'turned up' his new ability, like a mental volume control, and looked at the crowd with his new eyes. He could see threads between some of them—very faintly. He'd talked to Charlie after he returned from Loon Lake, and apparently this threads thing was a rare addition. He could see an overlay on each person too, nothing definite except for Junior, who somehow reminded him of a wolf. Some of the kids 'looked' lighter, and felt okay in some way, others were darker tones, and felt like a bad vibe sort of thing. Interesting. It varied too, with some looking more defined than others. Malicious? Well, she was a complicated mass of swirling colours. She looked over and waved.

"Hey, copper." She bounced over and perched on the chair arm. "Guess what? Me and my boys are playing at the pow-wow this summer."

"They're all right after what happened at the festival?"

"What, you mean when I freaked out? That was pretty weird. Not sure what I saw, but it disappeared pretty fast. Must have been all those Red Bulls. Yeah, the guys are fine. All keen to do more stuff, with me as lead singer of course. Junior set the gig up, since he's one of the pow-wow organizers. He says they need to get some variety for the young kids, so that's us. Guess we need to think up some more songs now. See ya." And with that she was off, back chattering to her friends.

Junior finished talking, and let the kids out the back door.

"Nice kids?" asked Dave.

"Most are," said Junior. "That Mal is really something, isn't she? A pretty good artist, and a musician too. Mind you, her band's songs all sound the same to me but some of the younger kids like them." He laughed. "Jeez, listen to me going on, you'd think I was as old as you."

"Thanks," said Dave. "I was watching your group. I'm guessing one you'll need to work on is the one in the blue hoodie, right?"

Junior looked at him with a smile. "Yes, he has a lot of issues bottled up inside. Your new vision is working just fine."

"I can see how that ability would be a help to you here," said Dave. "And will be a big help to me. It would be really amazing in undercover work down south."

Junior looked at him. "Thinking of leaving after all?"

"No," said Dave. "Just an observation. This now means I'll be able to observe people around here, if I need to, without having to be invisible. And up here is where I want to stay. I've discovered that I prefer the people and the atmosphere in a small place like this, present company included."

"Don't you miss the excitement of the big city, though?"

"Well, yes, there definitely is a rush in working undercover," said Dave, "hanging out with gangs, flashing money around. That's why some of us do it, I think. But in a way you also have to become the person you're emulating, to make the fiction more believable. And sometimes you start to believe it yourself."

"Maybe that's how the spirit in you started to turn dark, leaving you vulnerable when you came up here."

"I never thought of it that way," said Dave. "I'd assumed there was this dark side that had always been in me, since I was a kid, something that had always been wrong in me."

"Maybe not," said Junior.

"Hmm," said Dave. "You're pretty perceptive for someone so young. I can see why the elders are interested in you."

"Thanks," said Junior. "Sometimes I bring friends along to talk with the elders too, but I'm not sure if the elders find my youthful views and those of my friends always easy to take. But they have said they want the youth to be more involved, so here we are. Some of our youth want to scrap it all, the whole system of band governance, of Federal control, of government handouts. I try to show them ways to work within the system, to take advantage of the loopholes in it to use the system against itself to help create change."

"Ha, are you running for band council next?" asked Dave. "Or maybe local MP?"

Junior laughed. "I'm still pretty young for all that. Maybe someday. I do get fired up at times, so I sometimes need to tone it down, both for my friends and the elders. But I'm learning to choose my battles."

"Speaking of battles," said Dave, "I think we have one brewing here." He filled Junior in on his suspicions about Sasquatch, and the plan to lure him into the post office. "I don't think he's that aware of the drawbacks of his abilities, such as being visible on cameras. I'm hoping to catch him in the act to add to the evidence we have against him.

"I feel sorry for him in a way," said Dave. "I know how it felt even for me, when it would try to take over. It was like I was in there, somehow still aware of myself, but powerless. Do you think when we catch him we can somehow get this out of him?"

"I've talked to the elders about it, and they've talked to other bands about the Wendigo. All seem to feel the only ending is to kill it. And the person it has taken over."

"Well, we'll certainly try to take him alive," said Dave. "But if we're forced to shoot to kill, then that's what we'll have to do."

"Not sure if shooting will be enough," said Junior. "There have been tales of the Wendigo in our legends where people tried wooden stakes, silver bullets, drowning, but it's not clear if any of those were more than temporary."

"Really?" said Dave. "Is there nothing else they suggest might work?"

"We have been talking it over," said Junior. "We know he has a heart of ice, so one of the elders thinks that if perhaps we find a way to melt that, he would die."

"Perhaps?" said Dave. "No, that's okay, I did ask for anything at all. Fine then, any ideas how we do that? We're not going to be able to get him into a sauna, and even if we had a flamethrower we need to catch it first. Not a very subtle thing for me to carry through town either."

"I know," said Junior. "We'll just have to keep thinking about it and trust that one of us has a flash of insight when the time comes."

Chapter 47

Dave had spent all morning checking out the town through his new eyes. He'd learned how to control the strength of his new power, so that the images and colours didn't overwhelm him, but were just an overlay on the world. He'd started his testing up at the Highway Restaurant, then visited the gas station, down Main Street to the various stores, through the crowds on the sidewalks, and eventually to the hotel bar, where he found JB's grandfather sharing a beer with another elder, George. He got a ginger ale from Sam at the bar and walked over.

"Mind if I join you?"

Charlie Bourbeau smiled, "What, no pitcher of beer for us all?" He turned to George. "Remember, that was his gift when we first met?"

"I prefer it to tobacco," said George, "as I'm trying to quit smoking. Which means I never have my own cigarettes."

"Sorry, no," said Dave. "On duty. I've spent the morning cruising the town, looking at everyone again with my new vision."

"I hope we both look okay to you," said George.

"Of course," said Dave. "Both of you have extremely strong and well defined images. But if I dim my vision somehow—don't know how I do it—then it's like sunglasses or something." He looked around the room, squinting a bit.

"So what do your new eyes show you about people?" asked Charlie.

"It's almost like the old westerns," said Dave, "where the good guys had white hats and the bad guys had black ones. I can see a lightness or a darkness in people's image, in their aura, as I call it."

"What you're seeing," said George, "is somehow related to the inner person—how much evil or good is mixed in and how it relates to the rest of the world."

Dave sipped his drink. "I guess that's what it is. Maybe evil is too strong a word too, because I know most of these people—they are basically good folk. So what I'm seeing is a reflection somehow of their inner thoughts and feelings, their tendencies. And it's not as if I see little signs above them with a list of pluses and minuses. Someone could be cheating on his taxes or bullying his friends or running drugs, but all I see is a relative intensity. And to be honest, we can't expect everyone to be perfect, no extremes really. Well, except you two, you're pretty white looking. Sorry, you know what I mean. Most are varying shades of grey. I think the blackest one I'm going to find around here will be this Sasquatch guy. Who I haven't seen yet."

"If you do, keep your distance for now," said Charlie, "until we know how to defeat him. We believe that he's almost permanently locked in the spirit world now. We don't think this Sasquatch person —who calls their child that?—has the strength to break loose permanently. Even if he wanted to learn how to control it, he couldn't now. It's too strong. Now this spirit image is the only part that can be seen, so when we do track him down the battle is going to be between just you and him."

"And our only solution still is to somehow melt him?" said Dave. "That's it?"

"We're working on it," said Charlie. "We will be shown the way when the time comes."

"Fine," said Dave, "In the meantime, I'm getting some insight into which people in town I should focus on more. I was able to spot those bikers easily in a crowd. They're all pretty dark looking. Although, that woman, Bonnie, seemed more frightened than anything. Speaking of which, I just saw her poke her head in here and leave. She must have spotted me and gone to warn people that I'm back after my few days off. She may lead me to Sasquatch. Gotta run. Later, guys."

Dave spotted Bonnie, walking toward the beach road. He needed to shake her up a bit, to make her feel unsafe, and see what happened. He checked to see if anyone was watching, and then faded. Bonnie glanced behind herself a few times to see if she was being followed, then slowed her walk. She walked as if she really didn't want to go to wherever she was headed. He carefully caught up to her, then unfaded. The next time she glanced back she yelled in surprise.

"Oh! Shit, where did you come from? You bastard, are you following me?"

"No, just on patrol. But you look really stressed. Are you okay?"

"Yes, I am," she said. "What do you care?"

"I have a feeling you've been caught up in some things that have got out of hand, maybe I can give you some alternatives."

"I'm not going to rat out my friends for you."

"No pressure to do so. But we are going to start cracking down. I just wanted to let you know, in case you wanted to catch a bus out. Preferably not to Winnipeg, but if you want to try a fresh start, just let me know. I'm more concerned with the next steps for you than past history."

"We're just visiting here, not doing anything wrong," she said.

"Come on now, we know about the drug dealing, especially by Louie. And we know Sasquatch isn't really in Winnipeg."

At the mention of his name, Bonnie paled. "Don't even mention his name, please. He'll kill me." She peered back down the road. "He might even be near us now." She paused. "He's . . . he's got this trick he does."

"Let me guess, he moves like a ghost, right?"

She nodded, then swallowed. "He mostly comes to me now after dark." She looked around. "It's like he's made of ice or something, he's always so cold. Freaks me out."

Dave sensed something approaching down the road, something evil. He bent toward Bonnie.

"Remember, I can help if you want. Now trust me, we need to put on a show. I think he may be approaching."

He shoved Bonnie into the side of the road, then yelled at her "Get out of here, you scuzzy little tramp. If you won't talk I'll find one of your friends that will."

He walked past her up the road, and could feel the presence pulling back ahead of him, then moving off to one side. He used his new power, and could now see something, like a dark malevolent cloud, vaguely human in shape but taller, gangly looking, and blurred around the edges. He could feel it watching him, could sense the evil emanating from it, but he kept his eyes forward and walked past. Now that he'd come close to it, he was confident he could pin-point its unique presence again anywhere in town. He just hoped they would be able to stop it in time.

Chapter 48

Dave smiled as he walked into Rosie's. "Good morning. Nice tie. Congrats on being the maitre d' now in addition to the chef. Is Junior here?"

"Yes, smart alec. He's in back with Sharon."

"Sharon?" said Dave.

"Sorry, I mean Miss Goodall. She's that outdoor-ed teacher he was developing a business quote for."

That would explain the tie. Dave grinned at his friend. "I think you're developing something for her too."

"Quiet, you," said Rosie. "He said they'd be done by 3, want to wait?"

"No, I'll just stroll down to the lake and back," said Dave. "Maybe I'll spot Louie and his friends."

As Dave walked down the main street he experimented some more with his new way of seeing, looking at the overlays everyone had now. They still were varying degrees of grey, and if he looked harder he also could see the network of threads again, multi-coloured, interconnecting people and things like a web. As he followed the threads, he had the feeling he was being watched, and it didn't seem to be from something nice. He paused and casually looked around, searching for the unusual. Across the street was a form that was almost pitch black. Behind it, part of it, was the shape of someone, a very tall someone. It felt like the same evil he had come across near Bonnie. He looked more carefully—without staring he hoped—and realized it was in fact Sasquatch, the biker. He looked next for some threads. There were a number of them leading from the person, creature, whatever it was, some black, some an angry red. He was able to follow one thread across the street, right to Louie, one of the other bikers in town. Another thread headed off down the street, so he decided to see where it led him. It was a challenge to walk, stay aware of his surroundings, smile a hello to people, and follow the thread in the midst of the others. It helped that each one seemed to have a sort of flavour to its colour, so was slightly distinctive.

"Hey, Corporal!"

It was Mike, across the street. "Oh, hi there," he called. When he looked back for the thread he'd lost it. He waved to Mike then checked his watch. Junior should be done now. He'd check out more threads later.

Rosie, Sharon, and Junior were all laughing at the counter when Dave re-entered the cafe.

"Sounds like things went well," he said.

"Yes, indeed," said Sharon. She extended her hand. "Hi, I'm Sharon Goodall. You must be the boss around here."

"Corporal Browne," he said. "In here, Rosie's the boss, and a great cook. How was the meeting?"

"Junior did a good business case for his proposed outdoor program," she said. "I think my school will go ahead with it this year, on a small scale, and expand as we go."

"And Sharon will be liaison for it," said Rosie with a smile.

"Rosie said you were looking for me earlier," said Junior.

"Yes," said Dave. "Just for a moment. Can you pop out front with me?"

Once outside, Dave explained the plan they had set up to catch Sasquatch.

"I still think he may surprise you with his new powers," said Junior.

"He might try," said Dave, "but I think we've got this covered. Actually, could you help me keep an eye on him?"

"I'm not sure if I can spot him," said Junior. "My powers don't seem as discerning as yours."

Dave looked around—yes, that same dark shape was watching him from across the street.

"Okay," he said. "Don't stare but he's right across the street, standing behind that bench."

Junior turned slightly. "Just a sec. Okay, I see it now. It's a different kind of image. It has a distinctive sense of evil coming from it, like its own signature. Now that you've pointed him out, I'll recognize him again."

"Do you see all those threads too?" asked Dave.

"Barely," said Junior. "Not all of us can see them, you know."

"Do the elders know what they are for?"

"Not really," said Junior. "They talked to some elders in other bands, and as best as they can tell they may have several functions. They show links between people and things first off, so you can follow them like a network. And the colours and strength relates to the type of relationship somehow. One of the elders also thinks they can be used to actually move things, but he doesn't know if that would be mental or physical things. Like that hand thing you did before, but different. Sorry, wish I was more help. You're breaking new ground here."

"Well, it's better than nothing," said Dave. "Thanks."

"Would you like some of the elders to help watch for Sasquatch too?" asked Junior. "I'm sure I can pass on the same trick you showed me."

"If they'd like to, that would be a help," said Dave, "but please make sure they stay well back. Don't let them go all vigilante and start stalking this guy. He's dangerous. He was evil even before he was possessed by this spirit."

"Will do," said Junior. "What's next?"

"Now we do the setup for a trap," said Dave. He explained the drug sting they'd set up for that night. Norris had already done her switch that morning, now all they needed to do was dangle the bait a bit more. Once he took it, they'd follow and capture him.

"And how do we do that?" said Junior.

"Strength in numbers," said Dave. "Once we have all of us there, I think we'll have no problem subduing him."

"Maybe," said Junior.

"Sure," said Dave. "I'll give Reese a call. He's just over in the office. Then the three of us will put on a show. I'm betting if our evil friend sees the three of us out here, heads together, he'll want to eavesdrop."

"What can I do?" asked Junior.

"Just play along," said Dave. "And try to keep a poker face when he comes over in spite of any evil vibes you feel. Remember, Reese can't see anything."

"No problem," said Junior. He winked. "I can do inscrutable."

Dave called Reese over, and the three of them huddled next to the cafe. Sure enough, Sasquatch came over, close enough to hear Dave explain the plan to move the drugs out in two days. Once he had finished, they split up, Reese down the street, Junior around back to the youth centre, Dave across the street to the detachment office, behind a group of tourists. He used the cover to use his own fade, then walked back across the street. As he'd suspected, Sasquatch gave no indication that he could see Dave. Whatever his powers were they seemed restricted to just keeping him invisible. Maybe that was because he was just letting it use him, rather than learning how to use it. Dave watched as Sasquatch slowly walked down the sidewalk, heading for his buddy Louie.

Sasquatch smiled as he listened in on the plans to move the drugs out. The cops would all be watching carefully tonight, but it would be too late. He didn't need to wait for dark, he could slip in whenever he wanted to. He saw Louie across the street, so he walked over and tapped him on the shoulder.

Louie jumped, "Jeez man, don't do that! You'll give me a heart attack."

"Calm down," said Sasquatch. "I got some news from my contact up in Winnipeg. The cops are planning on getting the drugs out of the post office first thing tomorrow morning. I just heard them talking about it too, so it's definitely on. I want to get them out before then."

"Won't they be watching closely tonight?" asked Louie.

Sasquatch smiled. "We're not waiting until tonight. I'm going in this afternoon, right under their noses. I've been watching, if it's quiet the woman that runs it often looks after her store next door, too."

"Geez, man, I heard there were only a few packages left," said Louie. "Don't get me wrong, I'm not saying what to do, but is it worth the risk?"

Sasquatch felt a surge of anger flow though him. His hands grabbed Louie by the neck, lifted him, and squeezed. He watched Louie's eyes bulge, felt his friend's feet kicking his shins, his fingers pull at his shirt.

"Don't tell me what to do, you little worm! I'm not doing it for the drugs, I'm doing it because I can steal it from right under the nose of that ass-hole of a Toronto cop and make him look like a fool. You just wait behind the store with your car an hour from now." He threw Louie back against the wall and stomped off.

Louie coughed and gasped, "Sorry man, sorry."

Sasquatch felt the red rage gradually subside as he walked away— he'd been close to choking Louie right there, and the scary part was how it felt. Once again he was inside himself, powerless, as he watched his hands squeeze Louie's neck.

He walked down the main street toward the lake, invisible as usual, slowing, watching a few tourists as they wandered about, laughing and joking like a bunch of idiots. Little did they know he was right there in their midst, and at any moment could trip someone, or hit them, or push them into traffic. He saw a couple of his old friends, even some locals he recognized, but they were out of touch for him now. Louie was the only one that knew his secret, the only one he talked to. Well, Bonnie knew too, but he wouldn't waste his time trying to explain anything to her. He still forced her to be there for him at night, but as soon as they were finished she'd leave.

He needed a beer before hitting the post office. He dropped in to the local bar, and just stole one from behind the bar, rather than bothering to unfog to order it. Lately, turning his ability off brought more pain than just giving in to whatever was in him.

As he walked through to the bar's porch, he thought he saw that Indian kid, the chief's grandson, looking at him. He paused, but the kid's gaze just slid past him to a table of young girls. Sasquatch leered at them. Time was he could have the pick of a group like that. Now he needed to focus on his drug business, and getting back at that damn cop.

He walked out onto the empty porch and sipped his beer as he looked over the lake. It felt good to calm down a bit and relax, as it seemed he spent all his days now feeling jumpy, getting angry with everything. As he stood there, quiet for a moment, someone bumped into him, some young kid with too much beer in him.

"Hey, where'd you come from?" said the kid. "Watch out where you stand, buddy."

"I'm nobody's buddy," growled Sasquatch. He grabbed the kid and slammed him into the log wall of the hotel, then dropped him to the floor, unconscious. "Quiet time's done," he said, "time now to have some fun." He emptied the rest of his beer over the front of the kid's pants, then headed up the street to the post office.

It was fairly quiet in there, just that old cop, the one whose cottage they'd set fire to. Sasquatch resisted the urge to pluck his gun right out of the holster. He smiled, that would give the old guy a heart attack probably. Instead, he waited until the cop left the counter and was checking his mail, off to one side. No one else was in there, so Sasquatch waited until the woman left the counter, then carefully walked around the end. He checked the back room. Empty, and the safe was open. So easy. He picked up the box with the evidence tape on it, and walked back into the lobby. Just as he got there the old cop raised his eyes, looked back toward the counter, and called out.

"Thanks Darlene, see you later."

The cop then headed out the door, with Sasquatch right behind him. The biker hurried behind the store and stuck the box in the trunk of Louie's car.

"Here," said Sasquatch, "head back to your place, take out the drugs, then ditch the box somewhere. Make sure to wipe it down first. I'll be down in a few minutes, after I watch these hick cops run around in circles."

Louie slammed the lid down, jumped in his car, and took off in a spray of gravel.

Chapter 49

Dave had finished some reports and was eyeing his in-basket when Darlene called.

"Corporal, it's gone!" she said.

"What's gone?"

"The box of drugs you left here. Well, not drugs anymore, but you know what I mean."

That was fast, he hadn't expected Sasquatch to be so bold. "Do you know when?" asked Dave.

"Maybe in the last hour. I'm not sure. I've stopped checking on it all the time, but it was there around two I think, then there was a few people in after that. Constable MacGregor, a few tourists, some parcels, some regular mail, no rush really so I was back and forth a few times into the store. I just noticed now it was gone. Oh, we've the new surveillance system. Want me to check it?"

"No, just leave it alone for now," said Dave. "Close up the post office for now and—."

"Already did," she said.

"Great, we'll be down in a minute."

Angus and Reese were both off, but he called them and asked them to meet him there. Darlene was waiting to open the front door. Dave looked around with his senses. He thought he could "see" Sasquatch watching from just down the street. He didn't want to spook him—yet—so he continued in with his team.

"Where's Norris?" asked Angus as they filed in.

"I had her doing some surveillance," said Dave, "First, let's check in here."

He did a quick check to verify that yes, in fact, the box was missing, then turned to Darlene.

"Could you wait in the store for a bit while we check out the video? Thanks."

Reese was already at the PC. "I've set this up with a password and encrypted drives," he said, "so it should be secure as well as legal. I can put the cameras on split screen too. Lets start at two o'clock, and skim through quickly to just after Darlene called you. Let me know if you need me to slow down."

The three of them watched the few images of customers in the post office—two views from the lobby, one for the back room. As Darlene had said, it had been quiet, with only the occasional customer.

Dave pointed, "There, stop there. I think that's our guy." He pointed to the image—it showed a very big man carrying a cardboard box toward the doorway. "Could you jump back a minute or two?"

Reese tapped some keys. "Here," he said. "I'll slow to real time, with all three views on screen so we can track things."

They watched silently. After a few minutes, the door opened.

"Aye, that's myself coming in," said Angus.

"And now our big mystery person," said Dave.

They watched this second person wait as Angus got his mail, talked with Darlene, then turned to look through his mail. Another view showed Darlene leaving the counter, then the mystery man walking around the end of it.

"Stop," said Dave. Can you enlarge the face? Ha, as I thought, looks like our friend Sasquatch, still in town after all."

"Ach, is he crazy?" said Angus. "Or am I just sloppy? I was right there, I know I was checking some bills, but it looks like I don't even see him."

"Just wait," said Dave. "It's not your fault, there's more going on here than meets the eye."

They kept watching, as Sasquatch picked up the box, came back around the corner, and headed back out. Right behind Angus.

"I can't believe it," said Angus. "Not only did I not see him, it almost looks like I held the door for him. I might as well have carried out the box! What is he, a magician?"

"More than that," said Dave. "I've talked to the elders, I know this may sound far-fetched, but you have just seen the video. They believe, and I agree, that this Sasquatch has been possessed by some kind of spirit, that gives him the ability to cloud the minds of others some way so they don't see him. Unfortunately for him, it also clouds his own judgment and ideas and drives him into rages, rages strong enough to kill others."

Angus shook his head. "Part of me doesn't believe what you're saying, but I also know what I just saw now and what I didn't see before. I'll need to think later on about this wee bit of weirdness here, but for now, how do we catch this guy if we can't see him?"

"Well," said Dave, "remember what I talked about at the meeting yesterday morning? Since that vision quest I've been on, I can sense some additional things in people. It's like a combination of reading body signals, more empathy, and intuition, but it seems to work. And it breaks through whatever this Sasquatch is using too. So I think I'll be able to track this guy down, in spite of his efforts to hide."

"But where did he go?" said Reese.

"Norris was on, and called while I was on my way," Dave said. "She saw Louie, that biker guy, hanging around behind the store mid-afternoon, car trunk open. Then he suddenly slammed it shut, and took off down toward the beach. It seemed suspicious to her, so she's following at a distance. I'm guessing we'll find him, and the drugs, and Sasquatch, all down at Louie's cottage. I'd like to catch him right away, but he can be quite dangerous, so I'll see if I can get some backup, maybe from Sainte-Anne, before we move in. Too bad the two extra detectives just left."

Dave made his calls, then led his team outside. He checked around just in case—no Sasquatch. He was debating whether to head back up to the detachment office when his radio squawked.

"Norris here, I'm down the beach road near Louie's cabin, 10-30, shots fired."

"10-4," said Dave. "We're on our way. Hold back until we get there. Sasquatch may be right where you are."

They all piled into the SUV and headed down to the beach road.

As they approached the cottage turnoff, Dave saw a car in the ditch, with Louie and Bonnie fighting next to it, rolling in the dirt, yelling and swearing at each other. Norris was trying to separate them, unsuccessfully, so Dave and Angus each grabbed a combatant, yanked them back, and handcuffed them.

"Shit, let me go," said Bonnie. "I was winning."

"Yes, I think you were," said Dave, "but we need to settle more than this. First, are either of you two armed? Anything sharp we need to be aware of?"

"No, not now," said Bonnie. "Louie had a gun but left it in there after Sasquatch beat him up."

"Sasquatch?" said Dave. "Okay, start at the beginning but make it fast. Reese, keep an eye on Louie. Norris and MacGregor, keep an eye on the cottage. There's some cover behind that woodpile."

He turned and noticed one of the elders standing by the side of the road. "George, what are you doing here?"

"I was following the evil person for you," said George. "His spirit is very strong now, blazing like a fire. Junior showed me your trick of looking for it—a very good trick. I look forward to passing it on to some of the other elders that already have some of the vision."

"Well, thanks very much for the help," said Dave. "It's good to confirm he's in there. Now wait back by those bushes please. I need to talk to Bonnie to get a few more details."

He turned to Bonnie. "Now, what happened?"

"Well, I was actually packing to leave. I'd had enough of these jerks. Then Louie like comes rushing in with this big box, says it's full of drugs, and we have to hide it all. It wasn't mine, like I didn't know what he had, okay?"

"Don't worry," said Dave, "I'll keep your cooperation in mind. So, the box of drugs?"

"Okay, so in a bit Sasquatch showed up and we opened the box. It was like full of these clear bags of white stuff. I thought it was all coke—major score—then we saw that each bag had a little smiley face sticker on it. So Louie, he's like starting to look worried and we open one of the bags to check it."

Dave smiled. "And was it coke?"

"No, it was icing sugar." She stared at Dave. "But you knew that already, didn't you? And I bet you put on those smiley faces." She smiled. "Damn you. Anyways, when Sas saw those he went crazy. He started like yelling and throwing furniture around and then throwing us around. Shit, he's way stronger than ever." She lowered her voice. "And he was doing that trick of his, you know, that thing? And he kept fading in and out, like one of those fluorescent lights." Dave just nodded, so she continued. "So then he grabbed me, and shook me like I was nothing. He looked sort of like a black cloud. I can't describe it, it was scary. So, he's shaking me, with those long bony fingers of his, and Louie knows he's next, right? Well Louie, he reaches under the mattress and pulls out this gun and like shoots where me and Sasquatch are. The bastard could have hit me, for Christ's sake."

"Did he hit Sasquatch?" asked Dave.

"I think so, cause he gave a yell and let go of me and fell to the floor. So we were out of there."

"And the car?" said Dave.

"Yeah, so then Louie jumps in the car, and I barely make it in, then he's like trying to drive and push me out at the same time, says we need to split up, because Sas can't come after both of us at once. Meaning he's hoping Sas is coming after me. So I got pissed off and pulled the keys out. Then we like hit the ditch."

"Okay," said Dave. "I'll talk to Louie after. Right now you two are going in the back of the police cars, separate cars."

Dave and Norris moved closer to the cottage, where Angus and Reese waited, behind their SUV.

"I'm pretty sure Sasquatch is in there," said Dave, "and he's likely wounded. And even angrier, if that's possible." He moved over behind the woodpile. "I've called dispatch in case we have a standoff, but we need to let him know we're here and hope for the best. Spread out, stay behind cover, and get ready." He realized that George was somehow right behind him. "Damn. Just stay down, okay?"

Dave called out. "Sasquatch, this is the RCMP, we have you surrounded, Louie and Bonnie are already in custody, come out quietly, we can look after your injury. No one else needs to get hurt."

Silence. Then a series of shots from the cottage.

"Stay down!" Dave yelled. "Everyone okay?"

"Good here," said Angus. "Some holes in the SUV though. More paperwork. Now I'm really annoyed."

Dave was about to call for return fire when, with a roar, some-one or something burst out the front door in a swirling black cloud.

"Screw you and your smiley faces!"

There was a shot, and Angus grabbed his arm in pain. Before Dave could raise his own gun the monster was almost upon them. Dave raised his hand reflexively in front of him, then felt something flow through him, and a heat in his palm. The thing—Sasquatch—flew back ten feet, as if pushed. Ha! His 'power of the hand' thing was back, but it felt different now, and even stronger.

"Whoa," said Reese. "What the hell is that thing? And what did you just do to it?" Reese and Norris both fired several shots. Dave could see them hit, and the monster paused for a moment.

"Angus, the shot gun!" said Dave. Besides buckshot, they also had some slugs for the 12 gauge. Good for a bear, maybe for a Sasquatch. "Norris, fall back."

"I dinna ken what kind of beast this is," cried Angus, "but I'll get it." There was a boom from beside the SUV. Dave saw the shot hit, but Sasquatch kept right on coming, still roaring. Now he was too close to them for anyone to shoot, so Dave raised his hand again. Once more Sasquatch flew back, but this time with no sensation in Dave's palm.

There was a sigh next to Dave, and someone grabbed his sleeve. Damn, it was George, struggling to hold himself up "You needed to recharge so it was my turn. Nice trick, but it drains us a lot." He leaned closer to Dave as his voice grew fainter. "Keep going, and remember, burn his heart out with fire." He coughed, then fell to the ground.

Dave turned as the creature came at him once again, grasping, growling like a wild animal, burning with fury but ice cold to the touch. Dave felt his rush of strength start to decline as he grappled with the monster. He kept punching it in the face, but with little effect, as its cold hands squeezed his throat.

"Fire, fire," he gasped.

Norris pointed her gun, and paused. "I can't get a shot, hold still."

Reese's face lit up. "No, he means we need fire." He grabbed at his jacket and pulled out a flare gun. "I was taking this down to the boat. Here, Dave."

Dave grabbed the gun and pushed it against the monster's chest. For a second the cloud faded, and he saw his old enemy Sasquatch, face inches from his, pleading, "Please. Stop it!"

Dave pulled the trigger, and pushed himself away from the white hot explosion. The black cloud expanded, even as a white fire burnt in its middle. An inhuman scream came from it, rising in pitch and volume as the blackness dissipated, until there was nothing left but a body. Dave staggered to his feet, ready to battle again, but Sasquatch was very definitely dead, with a black hole in his chest. Dave looked at the rest of his team, gave a thumbs up, then realized he felt very weak. And his chest felt like it was on fire, too.

"Just give me a minute here," he said, as he passed out.

Chapter 50

Dave was very cold, and very tired, but there was that sound again, pestering him, pecking at his sleep, trying to wake him up.

"Dave, Dave, wake up Dave."

He opened his eyes, and smiled.

"JB, you again—good. You keep appearing, like an angel. But where am I? And why is it so cold? Give me a blanket!"

"You're in our town's clinic, and you have a blanket," she said. "Several in fact. You were almost in hypothermia when they brought you in, not something they see very often in the summer. You've been out for a couple of days, but the doctor said you just needed to rest." She gave him a hug. "We were all so worried, though. Norris told me about your big battle with the Wendigo, and Reese's quick thinking. A flare gun! Who'd of thought?"

"Sasquatch is dead, though, right?" asked Dave.

"Oh yes, very dead," said JB. "And the Wendigo is gone too."

"For good?" asked Dave.

"Sorry, not for good," said JB. "I mean it's definitely gone from Sasquatch, he's not going to start walking around like a zombie. Oh, and Junior passed on some interesting news. You know Janie's new creatures, the dark ones she'd been seeing? Gone. And probably related to it all, or maybe just from the beautiful weather now, people seem to be in a better mood too. Even Janie's dad."

"So only slightly an ass-hole?"

"You got it," she said.

"That's great," said Dave. "So we're in the clear."

"Well yes, for now," said JB. "However, the Wendigo is one of our people's major spirits. It's been around forever and will always be, as a reminder to us of the danger of choosing the wrong Path. At least we know more about it now, how to detect it and one way to get rid of it. It's not necessarily an easy way to get it out, but it's a start. You'll definitely be top of the list of stories from the elders. Don't worry, nothing specific, we use spirit names in the stories. But you'll be added to the legends, the stories that the elders tell on winter nights. And that 'talk to the hand' thing? So cool."

"I only had enough for one of those though," said Dave. "Luckily, George was there next to me with a zap of his own. How is he? Good, I hope?"

JB paused for a moment. "George didn't make it, that last battle was too much for his old heart. He was always a warrior, always ready for a fight. And it was a good way to go, too, to move on. We will all sing his praises at the pow-wow."

"That's too bad," said Dave. "I will miss him. He was a quiet little guy, until you got to know him."

She leaned closer and lowered her voice. "Well, Dancing Turtle has not completely left. Some of our people stay around as their spirits." She nodded at the corner. "Look, with your new vision."

Dave saw a large turtle, standing on its hind feet, that did a little jig back and forth, winked at him, then disappeared.

JB laughed. "Cool eh? I think you may see him again, if you need some advice, some guidance, some laughter." She fluffed up his pillow. "It's good to see your powers are coming back okay. You used the last bit up trying to protect yourself from the flare."

Dave felt the bandage on his chest. "I wasn't completely successful, I guess."

"Not too bad," said JB. "The doctor said the hair will mostly grow back, but you will have a faint scar. He said it sort of looks like a face. Your friends can hardly wait to see."

"Great," said Dave. "Now I can be a tourist attraction for the town. Wait, how's Angus?"

A voice boomed from the other end of the room. "I'm fine, but I dinna ken this is much of a quiet retirement place. Fires, monsters, invisible men, bullet wounds. I'd have been better to pick the slums of Winnipeg. I'd come over to visit you but they've got several wee tubes in me, one of which is too embarrassing to even contemplate."

Dave laughed, and called back. "Well, I was glad to have you there with me, but I would totally understand if you wanted to retire again from the easy part time job I promised."

"Hell no," said Angus, "I'm having a great time. Just as long as I keep enough spare time for the cottage and my grandson."

"Oh yeah," said Dave. "How is that going?"

"Much better," said Angus. "I've been talking a lot more with him, and with his dad. They are actually coming for the day next Saturday. They'll see the town, have a nice BBQ lunch, maybe some fishing. My arm should be a lot better by then."

"Good for you," said Dave. "Guess I'm caught up. Oh wait! What about Louie and Bonnie?"

"Norris was in earlier to visit," said JB. "She said Bonnie wants to take you up on her offer of relocation in return for information on Louie and his pals back in Winnipeg. And Staff said that he wants to talk to you as soon as you're awake. He's here now, in Kirk's Landing, just to help sort things out. Three murders here this summer is three too many for him, but he is happy they're all solved."

"That's good," said Dave. He closed his eyes. "Shit, sorry, I'm very tired."

JB bent over, tucked in his blanket, and gave him a kiss. "Take care hon, I'll be back later."

"I'm looking forward to you warming me up later on," said Dave.

Angus's voice boomed again from the corner, "Ach, would you two get a room?"

Chapter 51

Dave smiled as he watched the crowd in his living room. Another crisis averted, and another party at his place. It was getting to be a habit. He was just moving closer to the fireplace when Charlie slapped him on the shoulder.

"Corporal, are you trying to burn the place down?"

Dave laughed. "No, Charlie, I just like a big fire in my fireplace lately, even if it only is the beginning of September. I guess I'm still trying to warm up."

"Well, it has only been a few days, so you can be excused for being in recovery. I hear it was quite a battle, with fireworks and everything?"

"Not really fireworks," said Dave, "but I guess the story will grow as time goes on. My hand thing came back too, but different."

"I heard about that," said Charlie. "One more thing for the elders to consider. I'm looking forward to re-telling your story to my people, starting with the pow-wow next week. All names changed to protect the innocent, of course."

"I hear you're expecting a pretty big crowd," said Dave.

"Well, we promoted it big," said Charlie. "Not just word of mouth. We used emails, Junior set up a web site, and we even have a special Facebook page." He smiled at Dave's reaction. "We're very with it." He laughed and waved his hand around the room "This is good too. It's nice for you to be hosting a party so soon."

"It's not that hard," said Dave. "Most of the food and beer is compliments of Rosie, paying off a bet from the baseball tournament. And Reese and Norris pretty well have everything under control."

"They do work well together, don't they?" said Charlie.

"They do," said Dave. "Which reminds me, Norris wants to talk to me about something. Would you excuse me while I see what it is?"

Dave grabbed a couple of cold beers and walked over to his constable. "So, buy you a beer?"

She smiled. "Thought you'd be only drinking hot coffee, to warm up."

"Always a balance," said Dave. "You'd said you wanted to talk?"

"Yes. I was thinking I'd like to try my Corporal's exam-, and would like to have my Detachment Commander's blessing."

"Sounds like giving away the bride," said Dave. "Are you trying to tell me something about you and Mike?"

"No, no!" Norris laughed. "I just thought I should start thinking of moving on. It will be a while before I'm actually ready to write the exam, and then I'll have to wait for an opening, but I want to start preparing."

"A great idea," said Dave. "You know, when I first came here, I wasn't sure if you even wanted to stay in the Force. But you've learned and developed a lot in the past year. I'm very impressed. I'd be proud to recommend you."

"Thanks Dave," said Norris. She paused, then gave him a quick hug.

"Any idea where you want to move to?"

"Not yet," said Norris. "I do like it here a lot."

"What about Mike?" he said. "Things going well?"

"Going very well," she said. "We're just seeing where it goes. Mike likes being Mayor, but he likes his work at the mill too. He's thinking of getting some training, eventually moving to a better job. His IT skills are pretty marketable, so he could go anywhere. Nothing definite." Norris paused. "Oh yeah, before I forget. Reese finished the court paperwork on Janie's stepfather Egbert and ran it by the Crown Attorney. Feedback is that he likely won't qualify for bail before the trial. And then a substantial prison sentence after that. Mary has decided to move out west to her sister's—I know, no more of those great pies—but Janie is going to stay here in town, finish up school. And maybe do some baking for Rosie in her spare time."

"Is she still keen on writing?"

"Yes," said Norris. "She was telling me she already got some short stories published. Just some on-line sites, but it's a start."

"I'd like to help her get on to the next step," said Dave. "You remember Amanda, the business reporter that covered the big mill bust? She has some publishing contacts I'll try to hook Janie up with. Just don't tell her until I have something arranged—she might be too shy to accept the help."

"Thanks Dave," said Norris. "Sometimes you can be such a nice guy. Now, if you'll excuse me, I'll see if Mike needs any help."

Dave had just selected a couple of cigars and was heading out to the deck when Rosie grabbed his arm.

"I wanted to tell you again how glad everyone is to see you are part of the world still, and to see that Sasquatch guy is not part of it anymore. You're quite the local hero now."

"I keep hearing that," said Dave.

"Maybe I'll name a dish on the menu after you," said Rosie. "But tell me more about this big battle."

Dave repeated the story once again, an edited version. He wasn't ready to share the spirit part with most people, as he was still getting used to it himself.

"Enough about me, how's your new lady friend, the teacher," said Dave.

"That's going well," said Rosie. "It's nice to chat with her when she comes out to check on the program. I'm not sure how much more I'm ready for right now."

"Well, good luck," said Dave. "How's Kurt doing?"

"Okay," said Rosie. "He even wore some colour today, as opposed to all that depressing black." He clicked his bottle against Dave's. "Here's to teenage angst. Speaking of which, I see Junior over there, with Janie and my nephew. I need to check with them on what's happening with the program. You go ahead outside for your cigar."

Dave stood in the twilight, enjoying the sounds of the surrounding forest, the closeness of his friends inside, a cool beer and a smooth cigar. He heard the patio door slide open, then closed, behind him.

"I think even without any special powers, one could see you are a man at peace with himself."

Dave turned. "Oh, hello Charlie. Yes, I do feel surprisingly peaceful, but I do have a few questions for a respected elder."

"Be glad to help, my son. But is it not customary to first offer a gift of tobacco?"

Dave smiled. "I had a feeling I might need another of these." He handed Charlie a cigar, then held a match for him.

They stood for a few minutes, together, watching the smoke drift into the woods.

"JB tells me the Wendigo is gone for now," said Dave, "but is never really gone. Is that true?"

"That's what our stories tell us. They talk about the Wendigo being driven from people in various ways, usually along with the death of the person possessed, unfortunately. If it's a mild possession, and the person is still strong, a sweat lodge ceremony can drive it out. But in most of the cases the cure has been something drastic like drowning, or burying alive, or throwing in a fire. Now it seems that we can add marine flares to the legend."

"Not much of a cure," said Dave. "We still lost the patient."

Charlie smiled. "Your battle is interesting though. We think it's the first time someone attacked the Wendigo so quickly, so directly, right to his icy core. I talked to Dancing Turtle after, and he was surprised by the ferocity with which Wendigo tried to fight back, and by the violence of its leaving. We think you may have really hurt it."

"So it will stay away now?" asked Dave.

"It may look for easier targets now, but it has been around a long time. We fear it will want to get its revenge on you somehow, sometime. Or maybe those close to you."

Dave turned suddenly. "What, like JB? Or you? If what you say is true, then the first thing for me is to get away from here, and the sooner the better. And get back to being Dave the Loner. And no more use of my powers either, so it can't find me."

Charlie reached out and laid a hand on Dave's arm. "Actually, my son, those are the three things you should not do." He paused for a moment, then drew slowly on his cigar. He gestured back through the patio doors. "Look at your friends in there, smiling, carefree. Listen to their voices, your friends and neighbours, as they laugh and talk, some quietly, like Mike and Norris, some loudly, like Junior and Janie, some serious, like Rosie and Reese." He paused again.

"I know," said Dave, "that's why I have to go, and change back to the person I used to be. To protect them."

"No," said Charlie. "That's why you have to stay here and be the new person you have found, and hopefully grow even more. Sit down here, I'll get you another beer and explain."

"I need to get back to my guests too," said Dave, "they'll wonder where I've gone."

"Not to worry," said Charlie. "I've taken care of that. Each one is relaxing and enjoying your party, appreciates the chat you had with them, and—with a little nudge from me—thinks you're somewhere on the other side of the room chatting with someone else. So sit, think, I'll get those beers. Here, hold my cigar for me."

Dave looked at the elder, smiled, and shook his head. "You never cease to amaze me. Go."

Once the chief returned, they settled on a bench by the rail. Charlie had also grabbed a couple of small blankets from somewhere for their shoulders, as the September night was turning cold.

"Okay," said Charlie. "Firstly, the Wendigo is a spirit that moves from place to place, from person to person, but like many of our spirits, it is also everywhere at once. So it is aware of all of us, watching, waiting for a chance. And now these people, your friends, have come under an extra bit of attention. So if the Wendigo decides to be vindictive, it will be so even with you gone. Secondly, the change from Dave the Loner to Dave the Friend was part of what changed your focus inside you, made you a better person, made you strong enough to get rid of your demons, made you strong enough to develop your skills and powers to be a better person and a better policeman. And made you strong enough to defeat the Wendigo—no small feat in itself. No, you need to keep what you have become and build on it as a base to become even stronger for future battles. And so thirdly, you can't just turn off your power and not use it, it's become part of you. The Wendigo would find you anyway. You've been marked by it in your battle, as you have marked it. You two are linked now. No, if anything, you have to use your power more, study it, explore the possibilities, push the boundaries of each new discovery."

"Like my new 'talk to the hand' thing?" asked Dave.

"Exactly," said Charlie. "That's something some of our elders have been able to do once in a while. We're not sure how or when it happens though. You may discover more powers like the ability to light a cigar with a finger tip."

"Really?" asked Dave.

"No, that would be silly," said JB.

They both turned. "How did you know we were here?" asked Dave. "Didn't your grandfather do some sort of voodoo thing so everyone would leave us alone?"

"Yes, he did," she said. "But I recognize his touch. And I've discovered I have a nice link of my own I can follow to you." She gave him a hug, and a quick kiss on the cheek, then hugged her grandfather too. "Come on, I think you guys are done for now. I heard enough to say I agree completely with my respected grandfather, for a change. Now put out those stinky cigars and come back in."

Chapter 52

Dave and JB settled into the cafe booth across from each other. "So, here we are again at Rosie's," said JB. "More surprises?"

"Not this time," said Dave. "I think last spring we both had good intentions, but also some assumptions, some pride, even some fear of risks. A lot of things I suppose."

JB smiled. "I agree, but it's nice to hear it first from the mouth of a strong silent male."

"Well, I guess I'm changing from the guy you met last January," said Dave. "Hopefully you like this new guy."

"Yes I do," said JB, as she reached out and took his hand. "Very much."

"Me too," said Dave. "I mean I like the new me, but I like being with you, snuggling with you, talking with you, and I want to keep on doing that somehow."

"Ditto," said JB. "So how do we do this?"

"Well, we talked about this after my vision. I feel the same, that we need to work at this. I know you need to follow your studies in Ottawa, and there's more work for me to do up here still. We've this drug problem to finish cleaning up, for starters."

"We've Skype and email to connect us," said JB, "and I'll be up here for a break whenever I can. I've a lighter load this term."

"Very nice," said Dave. "As for me, I've had a talk with people in the RCMP gangs groups down south, in both Ottawa and Toronto. They want to talk more about what went down here, about the infiltration and intimidation. I'm thinking about it, just haven't decided how to explain it without bringing in demonic possession."

"Actually, don't hide all that quite yet," said JB. "Grandfather tells me he was talking to an elder in Ottawa about you."

"Does everyone know about this now?"

"No, calm down, it's only between a few select elders that can help with this. Not all know the same legends, not all believe in the old ones, and very few realize we can also start new ones."

"What, I'm a legend already?"

"Not quite," she said. "Don't get a swelled head. But like I'd said, what you did, and how, will become massaged and generalized a bit to become a part of our oral history, to be passed down to others, so they can learn and maybe even explore this more. Remember, those stories are how we learned about your opponent's fear of fire. So, this elder's son is a researcher at Ottawa U, doing some sort of neurological studies. He's indicated he'd like to look at your unique brain waves sometime."

"Is that what attracted you to me, my unique brain waves?"

"No," she said, "I think I love you more for your nice butt." She grinned, then looked serious.

Dave gazed at her. "Me too. I mean I was going to say ditto but that's a cop-out. I love you too."

Rosie called over from the counter. "Would you two stop with the googly eyes? This is a family restaurant."

The End

Acknowledgements

I owe my thanks to the many people—and places—that helped me develop this sequel from just an idea to a published work of fiction.

Ian Shaw of Deux Voiliers Publishing convinced me that there was still more story to be told about Dave and his new home in the North.

The National Novel Writing Month—the concept, the website, and local members—gave me the encouragement in 2011 to crank out a draft in 30 days.

My many Beta Readers had the patience and skill to work with me over the years to both add and destroy characters and plot. Thanks to Joyce Juzwik, Millie Norry, Lynne McGuigan, Patty Archer, and especially Angeline Woon, for valuable encouragement, perspective and suggestions.

Two other talented members of the Deux Voiliers team, Geri Newell Gillen and Norman Hall were kind enough to spend many hours copy-editing and proof reading. And finally my publisher Ian Shaw was kind enough to review my story, often, and suggest many excellent improvements.

To help me describe the North, police work, and First Nations, I relied on my early years in the small town of Kirkland Lake, various police and First Nations friends, and of course the Internet. For the aboriginal content in particular, my intent is to present it with both accuracy and respect. I hope I have achieved that.

As for writerly places, there were many in addition to the office in my home in Ottawa. My local Bridgehead café, O'Connell's pub, and the Carleton Tavern all offered a relaxing atmosphere in which to create and craft, whether inside with a beverage or out on a sunny patio.

I hope that you enjoy Return to Kirk's Landing. Online reviews are welcome, and please send me your comments to ravensview@gmail.com. My first book, Kirk's Landing, is available online as a paperback or ebook, from Amazon, iBooks, and other sources.

Mike Young
www.ravensview.ca/mikeyoung/

About the Author

MIKE YOUNG was born and raised in Kirkland Lake, a small northern mining town with a nearby First Nations reserve.

He grew up with a love of the north, winter or summer, exploring the surrounding woods with his friends, and his grandfather. He moved down south in his 20's to follow a career in quality management, but his real pleasure was still heading outside the city, with canoe and tent. While in Toronto he also developed an interest in back-alley murals, in artistic graffiti, and worked with some police there that saw its potential as a community building exercise.

He'd always been a voracious reader, so several years into retirement he decided to try writing, and hasn't stopped since. This is his second book, following the publication of Kirk's Landing. He has several more drafts of novels waiting in the wings for his red editing pen.

About Deux Voiliers Publishing

Organized as a writers-plus collective, Deux Voiliers Publishing is a new generation publisher. We focus on emerging Canadian writers. The art of creating new fiction is our driving force.

Other Works of Fiction from Deux Voiliers Publishing

Soldier, Lily, Peace and Pearls by Con Cú (Literary Fiction 2012)
Last of the Ninth by Stephen L. Bennett (Historical Fiction 2012)
Marching to Byzantium by Brendan Ray (Historical Fiction 2012)
Tales of Other Worlds by Chris Turner (Fantasy/Sci-Fiction 2012)
Bidong by Paul Duong (Literary Fiction 2012)
Zaidie and Ferdele by Carol Katz (Children's Fiction 2012)
Sumer Lovin' by Nicole Chardenet (Humour/Fantasy 2013)
Kirk's Landing by Mike Young (Crime/Adventure 2014)
Romulus by Fernand Hibbert and translated by Matthew Robertshaw (Historical Fiction/English Translation 2014)
Palawan Story by Caroline Vu (Literary Fiction 2014)
Cycling to Asylum by Su J. Sokol (Speculative Fiction 2014)
Stage Business by Gerry Fostaty (Crime 2014)
Stark Nakid by Sean McGinnis (Crime/Humour 2014)
Twisted Reasons by Geza Tatrallyay (Crime Thriller 2014)
Four Stones by Norman Hall (Canadian Spy Thriller 2015)
Nothing to Hide by Nick Simon (Dystopian Fiction 2015)
Frack Off by Jason Lawson (Humour/Political Satire 2015)
Wall of Dust by Timothy Niedermann (Literary Fiction 2015)
The Goal by Andrew Caddell (Non-Fiction Short Stories 2015)
Quite Perfectly Dead by Geri Newell Gillen (Crime Fiction 2016)

Please visit our website for ordering information
www.deuxvoilierspublishing.com

www.ingramcontent.com/pod-product-compliance
Lightning Source LLC
LaVergne TN
LVHW011928070526
838202LV00054B/4546